AFRAID TO GO HOME

By

Baden Hill

ISBN:1-884730-25-6/978-1-884730-25-2

JB & ME Publishing, an imprint of InterLinguacom, Inc.
PO Box 3879, Manhattan Beach, CA 90277
eMail: afraid.to.go.home@gmail.com

This is a work of fiction. Names, characters, places and incidents either are the product of the author's imagination or are used fictitiously, and any resemblance to actual persons, living or dead, businesses, companies, events, or locals, is entirely coincidental. Further, neither the publisher nor the author have any control over any third party websites that reference this book, and assumes no responsibility for their content.

Dedication

To all those who have suffered at the hands of others

Chapter 1

"Do you really have to leave right now and go home to your wife," she moaned from the bed. "I'm not finished yet."

No, he didn't have to go, but he was getting bored with her and wanted to get out of her house as quickly as possible. "I have to go. She has a light case load these days and is getting home earlier."

He desperately wanted to take a shower and wash the smell of sex off before he put his clothes on, but she would want to shower with him and indulge in their usual soapy massage, and that would lead to sex in the over-sized bathtub, and that's exactly what he didn't want. Besides, if he had the time for a shower, it would cast doubt on his story of having to rush home.

"Rushing home to your loving wife has never been a concern before." She saw it all ending between them. "It's not the way it used to be. We used to lie in bed for hours and you would hold me in your arms till we both fell asleep." She pulled the pillow against her face to suffocate the pain.

He hated to hear a woman cry, especially one he just had sex with. What was it about a woman's tears that made a man commit to things he didn't want to? "You're not being fair."

Realizing that he sounded more like an attorney arguing a case than a wounded lover, he dropped his voice to a soft, compassionate whisper, as if leaving was difficult for him, too. "Just because your husband travels a lot on business, and your kids stay late at soccer practice, it doesn't mean we can spend hours in bed every time we're together. I work in an office where people see me coming and going." That sounded sincere, he thought, smiling at himself in the wall of mirrors that lined her bedroom . Pulling up his pants, he tucked his shirt in his pants, zippered his fly and tightened his belt.

"You used to have the time." Desperately wanting that last orgasm he was denying her, she pleaded, "Please come back to bed. Your wife's a workaholic, she'd never come home early." It was useless. His love was already gone, and soon his body would be, too.

Six months ago, maybe even three months ago, he would have dropped his pants, slid under the sheets, and had another go at it. But now, all he wanted to do was get out of there, go to the club, take a shower, go home and have dinner. Besides, he wasn't... inspired... enough to satisfy her any more today.

Afraid she would call his house just to see if his wife did indeed come home early, he sat on the bed to comfort her. Tugging the pillow from her face, gently wiping a tear away with his finger, he pulled her up, and stretching his face forward, he kissed her again and again; on her forehead, on her nose, on her neck, on her lips. He wanted her to feel all his love, but he also didn't want to get the sticky gumbo of warm sweat, semen, mango-scented oil, and pubic hairs that coated her body on his white shirt. Thrusting his tongue into her mouth, he wanted her to feel his passion. But she still wanted more than his tongue inside her. She wanted a total joining. She wanted every part of her body touching every part of his, so she let the sheet separating them drop, and lassoing him with her arms, she pulled him to her with all the strength in her thin arms.

Fighting back against her attempt to be prone again, he arched his back, but it was useless. The warm wet of their love-making traveled through the cotton of his shirt to his skin. There was no doubt now, he had to go back to the office to pick up the extra shirt he always kept there, then head to the club and dive into the spa, so he would smell more like chlorine than sex when he got home. Why don't I just keep a shirt in the car, he chastised himself. This always happens.

It was useless. There was no hope for arousing his passion again, so she dropped back to the bed in disgust. "You even used to tell me you love me."

In the split second of delay before he could say, "I do love you," she began to cry again.

Rolling towards the wall and pulling the sheet over her head, she whimpered, "Just go. Go back to Santa Monica. Go home to your wife. Leave me alone." She so hated being a victim of his whims. How she swore she wouldn't let it happen again, not with him, not again.

It had been over between them for some time and they both knew it. But it was still good sex - not great sex anymore - but good sex, and neither wanted to give that up just yet, so a couple of times each week they still played the "There's Something Special Between Us" game.

Opening the bedroom door, he looked back at her slender, curving shape under the wrinkled king-sized sheets. She looked so small; even smaller than the pile of pillows. It reminded him of an assignment he had in art class many, many years ago, vanishing shape with no hard edges.

She was still crying, something that seemed to be happening more and more these days. *We used to spend a lot of time laughing. When did it all change?* He thought. What he said was, "I really do have to run. I love you. I'll call you tomorrow."

As he exited her Hancock Park house, he swore, yet again, never to return. In an odd way, he thought, he's going to miss her house more than he'll miss her. He just loved the feel of the old English architecture, with its intricate stonework, carved figurines, and long hallways that were filled with nooks and crannies to display art. Every time he came to visit

Susan, it made him feel as if he was walking into the country estate of British royalty.

For someone who, at one time, thought of becoming an architect, this was a wonderful neighborhood to visit, with all its sophisticated and beautifully designed homes, and their well groomed lawns. He especially loved the older homes, built 50, 60, even 100 years ago. They had such craftsmanship, history and permanence, and were not just something modern and disposable, like most of L.A.

Driving back to his Century City office, thinking about what had just passed between them, he was very concerned. It wasn't as easy to find a woman to have an affair with as it used to be. And without something happening on the side, he was stuck having sex with his wife. *I guess it's not bad sex, it's just… the same sex.*

What was it, he wondered, *that made having sex with someone else's wife so much more interesting than having sex with your own?* After 20 years of marriage, was it the sameness? The intrigue and mystery vs. the repetitive routine? The desire to perform and impress vs. the need to just do it before going to work or calling the plumber?

Turning off her street, he started to review. There was no gap between the first and second affair. Quite the opposite, there was that "interesting" overlap. Grinning with salacious delight, he dropped one hand between his legs to massage his penis as he re-lived the heroic day when he provided erotic pleasure to both girlfriends and his wife all within a ten-hour period. *Phew, that was some day. I couldn't that again.*

But the time between affairs, the TBA, had been steadily increasing, and that worried him terribly. The time between the last one and this one was almost two years. It wasn't easy to find a woman who was attractive, that you can trust not to ruin your marriage and career, that was geographically desirable, available at the right times, not interested in getting married someday, and most important of all, willing to sleep with a married man.

That biological clock thing changes women a lot, he thought.

Younger women know how to leave a relationship when it's over... they're not so clingy. They always assume they have time to meet someone else. But these older women (which he hated to admit were the only ones he could attract now) were a lot more desperate. Once they hit menopause, all they wanted to do was find someone to live happily with for the rest of their lives.

Thinking about the first time he made love to someone outside his marriage, he remembered how surprised he was that he even cheated on his wife; how upset and saddened he was; how panicked he was that Melanie would find out about it; how he told Anna that they couldn't do it again; how he wanted to bring the excitement of their early love making back into his marriage; how they were successful at it... for a while. Then, things pretty much fell back onto a schedule and into a routine.

After six weeks of separation he called Anna, pleading with her to come back to him ("I can't imagine a life without you."), and their affair began again with all its passion and energy. Though he never said the words to anyone, he fully expected to divorce Melanie and marry Anna. Someday. In the future.

As he turned onto Wilshire Boulevard, he had to wonder, *if I had gotten a divorce and married Anna, would I still be coming from Susan's house tonight? Would marrying Anna have been just exchanging one routine for another? Maybe I'm better off just not being married at all.*

"If only she hadn't gone around telling everyone that we were getting married. We would have had time to figure it out," he explained to a billboard with a picture of a happy couple boarding a plane to Athens. After a year of stolen afternoons, business trips to romantic inns, quickies in offices, public rest rooms, and homes for sale, Anna started telling her friends and family that he was leaving his wife and they would be getting married, soon. Even worse, she began a daily interrogation, demanding to know when he was going to divorce Melanie, when he was going to be moving out, when she should start looking for a place for them to live together. The extra-marital affair was becoming more burdensome than his marriage, and he knew he had to get out.

And then, just at the moment that he wasn't sure what to do, Marjorie, literally, walked through his door, selling advertising for a radio station. He was instantly smitten and ready to walk away from the heavy baggage of both his marriage and his affair. She was in a marriage adrift in a sea of indifference, and desperately needed him to be her life raft.

But she brought her own baggage to the relationship – a beautiful three-year-old child, named Nina.

He smiled as he remembered playing with Nina on the living room floor, and going with Marjorie and Nina for walks along the beach. She was so incredibly smart for a three-year-old. She could read. She could talk in whole sentences. She could write her name and his. "Hi, Chris," she would call to him as he came to visit. Oh, how he had liked the picture of them as a family. She'll be graduating elementary school this year, he mused, proud like a father. I'll bet she's at the top of her class.

But it just couldn't work out between them. Nina's real father loved her, too, and there would have been a hideous and painful custody battle if Marjorie tried to leave him. After months of stolen passion, Chris just drifted out of her life.

He recalled how sad he was when he couldn't be with Marjorie and Nina any longer. How he would actually sit in his office staring out the window, crying occasionally. How he must have picked up the phone a thousand times to call her, and how he always put it back down before dialing.

He was sad, and everyone at the office noticed. He would say things like, "We're having some difficulty at home," or, "After all these years, we're still newlyweds and having some adjustment problems." Because everybody liked him, at least the women did, everyone thought of him as a wonderful, faithful husband who would never cheat on his wife. Melanie rarely attended company functions, but when she did, they were cute together. A perfect match. He the attentive husband, she the gracious corporate wife.

Was it only six months after Marjorie and I broke up… maybe it was more like nine… that I met Diana.

At a meeting to prepare for a new business presentation, he could see one of the agency's new account executives staring at him from across the conference table. She was gorgeous. Blonde, buxom, thin. Probably was a cheerleader in college. But her eyes were so sad. As he looked back at her, they both knew they were kindred spirits. Both suffering in their hearts. Both needing the other to help survive the day.

Just saying her name, or at least what he called her, Lady Di, brought back such incredible memories of sexual encounters that he got an erection, and again, dropped one hand between his legs and massaged his penis.

He remembered "the foreplay" as he called it: how she went from being virtually invisible to him at the agency, to suddenly appearing everywhere. He'd see her in the corridors and they would stand and chat for long periods. She was often in the coffee room when he was there. They seemed to be riding in the same elevators more often. And, then, the touching began. Nothing erotic. A hand on an elbow, being pressed against each other in a crowded elevator, his hand on her chair in a restaurant, playing footsies at staff meetings.

Then, one night, on the floor of his office, the titillation game ended and the serious activity began.

He remembered his fascination when she introduced oils and scents to their love-making, and every now and then she would introduce a new toy that she had picked up at A Hole in One or Up The Flagpole or one of the other sex stores in West Hollywood. She was the first partner he ever had who would do absolutely anything and everything to please him. It was a true awakening. For the first time, he knew the full pleasure of two bodies coming together as one.

Eventually, inevitably, they got caught. One of the account supervisors, returning from a business trip, stopped by the office late one evening to pick up her mail and there they were, naked, in the conference room.

Humiliated, she never returned to the agency, and he never heard from her again. He was able to convince Melanie that this was the first time he cheated on her, "A mid-life crisis. It's over now," he had said, and like the enraged divorce lawyer she was, she swore, "If you ever have an affair again, I'll throw you out and crush you financially," which she was quite capable of doing.

To his credit, he suggested that they go to marriage counseling, but she wouldn't hear it, and he remembered how she commanded, "Get your head, and your penis, straight."

While the other people at the ad agency were shocked, they accepted that it was his first fling, and were quick to blame Diana; after all, she wore very suggestive clothing that emphasized her large, round breasts. Now that she was gone, he put on his Boy Scout uniform again, and while a few of the female employees wondered why they weren't the objects of his affections, for the most part, everyone believed him when he let it slip that he and Melanie were having some trouble and going to a marriage counselor.

Turning his head to see who else was on the road, he had to admit, the whole process, from the explosion of euphoria at the beginning to the tear-laden explosion at the end, was getting too wearying on him, not too mention that it was becoming too much of a routine in itself. His story of a marriage gone cold, was losing credibility as he too swiftly and too easily progressed from first meeting his "new love" to getting into bed with her. He could no longer even fake doubts and regrets about cheating on his wife.

Turning down the busy street to his office building's garage, he joined the line of cars whose progress was halted by a stop sign. Inching forward, waiting for his turn to cross the intersection, he caught a glimpse of the reflective stripe on the helmet of a young girl, maybe 10 or 11 years old, standing on the curb, next to her pink bicycle, with pink and white streamers hanging from the handle bars. Frightened to enter the crosswalk with so many cars barely slowing down at the blinking red light, her face was distorted with fear. "She probably went to that computer games store in the mall," he mumbled, looking at the 6:23 P.M. digital readout on the car's clock. "And she probably stayed way too long."

She eased the pink front wheel into the crosswalk, but jumped back as a black Ford Excursion rolled through the signal only a foot or two in front of her. Waiting a few moments, she tried again, easing her front tire off the curb, but again she quickly pulled back as a gray Chevy Tahoe pretended to stop at the sign but then accelerated.

She started yet another reckless attempt to enter the crosswalk, but a white Nissan Armada didn't stop long enough to sneeze, and the little girl almost fell backwards as jumped out of its path. Rubbing the tears from her eyes, she knew she would never get home now.

Watching this drama unfold, Chris was disgusted by his fellow office workers for their cruelty, but did concede that those being disgorged by the office buildings weren't used to seeing pedestrians, especially a small child, on this dimly lit service road outside the garage. Besides, after a day of office stress, they had only one thing on there minds: get as far away from work, and back home, as fast as possible. With that attitude in mind, they neither had time to follow the rules of safety on the road, nor be terribly considerate of anything or anyone that inhibited their movement.

When he reached the front of the rolling line of cars, he stopped and gently tapped on his horn to attract her attention. By now, she had given up all hope. Her whole body collapsed on that pink bicycle as she imagined the punishments she would receive.... if she could ever get home. With an inviting wave of his hand, he indicated that she could safely cross in front of him. Her sad face turned happy, and wiping her tears away with her pink sweatshirt sleeve, she mouthed, "Thank you," and pushed her bicycle into the crosswalk.

She was truly adorable; blond hair, beautiful smile. *Your parents shouldn't let you out alone at night*, Chris thought. *If I were a pedophile, you're exactly the kind of child I would want to grab.* The left side of his mouth curled up in a slanted smile. "I may be pretty immoral, but at least that's not one of my perversities."

The smile fell away as he wondered if Melanie and he would have had a child as adorable as the little girl framed in his headlights. His aunts used to say, "You two are such beautiful people, yours will be a gorgeous baby. Don't wait too long."

As the little girl passed in front of his car, he thought, *You're going to be a heart breaker someday. Whoever you date, stay away from someone like me.*

The sport utility vehicle behind him didn't see the little girl, and honked at him to follow protocol and pass quickly through the intersection. Chris started to stick the middle finger of his right hand in the air, but concerned that the little girl would see it, he quickly morphed his fingers into a gesture pointing towards the little girl. In his rear view mirror he could see the driver, recognizing his mistake, throw his hands in the air apologetically, and resign himself to being a Good Samaritan.

The little girl froze in front of Chris' car, perplexed at how to proceed, since the cars in the lane to his left weren't stopping long enough to allow her to pass. Turning to Chris, with a plea for help with her eyes, he unbuckled his seatbelt and put his hand on the door handle in order to get out of the car and walk her across the street. As he opened the door about an inch, he hesitated, fearing the havoc it would create with the cars stacked behind him (who were already honking at the slow progress), so he stayed in his car, but resolved not to move an inch until the little girl reached safety. Raising his hand to her as if to say, "Wait a second," he turned to see who was in the left lane.

A silver Lexus pulled up beside him and the driver, a young woman on her cell phone, was fluffing her hair in the mirror and beginning to roll through the crosswalk without looking. Chris honked to catch her attention, which it did, and disgusted that someone would dare interrupt her call and her progress, she turned towards him with hate in her eyes. Seeing the little girl, she acknowledged her responsibilities, and with a look of resignation, waved at her to proceed.

The Lincoln Navigator behind Chris looked down at him in his Toyota Prius and honked, as if to say, "The kid's not in front of your car anymore so get moving because I have some place to go even if you don't," but Chris wasn't going to abandon the little girl in the middle of the street, and he stayed long enough to see that the opposing traffic caught sight of her and obeyed the law, letting her cross to the safety of the sidewalk. Once there, she got on her pink bike with the pink and white streamers, waved at her guardian angel, and raced around the corner, disappearing into the night.

Thinking about all the pretty children he'd seen over the years at casting calls for commercials, he mentally shouted after her, *And don't let your parents force you to grow up too quickly by sending you on auditions. Enjoy being young.*

Finally, it was time to move forward, much to the relief of the ever-increasing, horn-honking cars stacked up behind him.

Pulling into the garage of his office building, it occurred to him that it would be better to go to the health club first since people could still be working and it was pretty obvious he had lied and hadn't gone to see his client. So, even though it meant throwing himself back into traffic, he turned the car around and headed to his health club to sit in the hot tub until the smell of sex was expunged from his body.

Chapter 2

When he first joined the club, at thirty-two, he was just about the average age of its members. Fifteen years later, he was now one of the old guys, and, while it certainly had all the athletic equipment anyone could want, this club seemed more geared to those who wanted to show off their bodies rather then build them. Without a doubt, the most popular activity, if you could call it that, was sitting around the edge of the oversized hot tub in revealing bathing suits and chatting with members of the opposite sex. Anyone who didn't understand the dynamic of the club would have assumed that the people of this city were suffering under an epidemic of corns and bunions, since significantly more people dangled their feet in the hot tub, than actually went into it.

Until a couple of years ago, Chris was one of the danglers, trying to sniff out his next extra-marital affair. But about two years ago, as he was working one of the young lovelies with his most amusing, and well rehearsed, advertising war stories, she blurted out between laughs, "You're hysterical. You'd be perfect for my mother."

Every bubble and gurgle of the spa seemed to stop just at that moment. Every grunt and groan from the nearby weight-lifters seemed to silence just at the moment. The whine of the ventilation system, the background music, the laughter of the staff. Everything. Everything seemed to end just at that moment. And, every eye of every member, every employee, and every guest seemed to focus just on him.

Covering her mouth in genuine embarrassment, she apologized profusely, as if finally understanding what his real intentions were. But no words could repair the damage that was done, and from that moment on, he became one of the soakers and hid himself in the hot bubbling waters.

What he did find was that the steaming, cloudy, churning water was a good blanket. It allowed him to masturbate undetected, though it took him a while to get used to doing it with his eyes open. Wearing a lose fitting bathing suit, common to the older men at the club, he would focus on one of the beautiful danglers, slip his hand through the loose leg, and fantasize about having depraved sex with her. At the point of climax, he always splashed hot water on his face so it would hide any sudden change in his demeanor, and demonstrate to everyone that his hands hadn't been touching his private parts.

The more time he spent in the hot tub, the more he realized he wasn't alone in his auto-erotic behavior; lots of the other soakers seemed to be similarly engaged in self stimulations. It so intrigued him that he went on the internet to find out if a woman could get pregnant from all the sperm floating around in the hot tub. *I wonder if that's how the Virgin Mary got pregnant?*

Since it wasn't a topic generally covered on the medical websites, a brief trip to some pornography websites relieved him of the worry that he was going to remotely impregnate someone whom he never actually had the pleasure of meeting. However, his research led him to a new line of investigation, and he began to seriously worry about catching a disease, like herpes or aids, from one of the hunks or babes that decided to enjoy a plunge with the old guys and gals.

For a month or two, he returned to the ring of danglers and refused to go any deeper into the hot cauldron of bubbling sperm and disease than his ankles. But eventually he so missed his masturbation ritual that he re-joined the self-satisfying soakers. He did, however, change his schedule so he could slither into the hot tub as soon as possible after the spa's daily cleaning.

After twenty minutes in the hot tub, he felt that he had sufficiently replaced the mango/sperm cologne he had been wearing with the hygienic scent of bromide, so he left his fellow undesirables-to-the-opposite-sex and headed for the shower.

An hour later, opening the door to his office, he congratulated himself for making the right decision. Everyone was gone, except the crew from the janitorial service that took note of nothing except the piles of paper in the waste baskets.

Knowing that his wife wouldn't be home yet, he busied himself sending e-mails and putting a few papers on peoples' desks, so it would appear as if he had rushed back to the office after his meeting. Checking his voice-mail, there was a message from Susan, "I'm sorry about this afternoon. I hope you'll still come over on Friday. Call me. I love you."

Maybe it was the desperation in her voice; maybe it was that he was burdened with providing the little happiness that she had and he didn't want to bear the load any longer; maybe it was that he was thinking more about who would be number eight, even before it "officially" ended with number seven; but, whatever it was, he didn't like himself, or his life, very much at that moment.

Is this it? he heaved a sigh. *Is this all there is?* Looking around his cramped, paper-laden office with disgust, he asked himself, yet again, *After all these years, does it all end here?*

The scuffed walls, stained chair and scratched desk were vivid reiterations that he worked for an employer who cared little for the mental or physical health of his employees. When he was shown to his office ten years ago, the same unsightly and uncomfortable furniture inhabited the space as did now, and if he was still with this company ten years from now, he believed he'd still be sitting in the same chair and working from the same desk.

It wasn't the physical environment that saddened him the most; it was that after all this time, all this energy, all this commitment, he had to admit, no one cared about what he did. Management didn't care if it was he or someone else creating budgets for the clients, only that the budgets were as big as they could be. The clients enjoyed his expertise and creativity, but they weren't upset when his predecessor left, and they wouldn't pine for him either. And even though he was relatively popular with his co-workers, they were just so used to seeing people come and go, his leaving would hardly be noticed.

Recruiters weren't calling; job offers weren't rolling in; magazine writers weren't calling for quotes; and no one asked him to speak at conferences or seminars.

After 25 years in the business, he had to concede, it didn't matter that he had just spent 25 years in the business.

Scanning the ever growing piles of research reports, unread magazines, sales figures, computer printouts, and consumer data that littered his floor like the collapsed columns of the Roman Coliseum, he could only see a career that didn't progress in many years.

Changing jobs, he thought, *wouldn't make it any better; it would probably be worse. Instead of reporting to the president of the company, I'd probably have to report to some Gen-Xer fifteen or twenty years younger than me. If I stay here, I die of frustration,* he exhaled in defeat. *If I change jobs, I die of humiliation.*

Standing at the window, looking out at the horizon, he wondered, *How did I get to this point? It was such a promising career at one time... wasn't it?*

Images of his life flooded his thoughts like movie trailers: the first day of his first job; the first time he was allowed to present to a client; meetings with senior executives who became his career models; being anointed one of the industry's "Young Turks" by the leading trade magazine; calls from headhunters who had a choice of jobs for him to take.

Those days were gone.

When did being old... well, middle-aged... and experienced become a negative? Why is everyone only interested in young and aggressive? What happened to the idea that wisdom comes with age and experience?

When did being experienced come to mean being too expensive?

Often, as he walked the corridors of the office, he would have an urge to grab by his or her throat one of the smug, highly-valued, aggressive, new "Young Turks" and say, "Don't be such a smart ass... someday you'll be older, too, and no one will want you, either."

Within the context of the company, Chris was actually one of the lucky ones. His office had a magnificent view of the Pacific Ocean - a view equal to, though much smaller than, the Corner Office - while most of the rest of the staff had views of parking lots or other office buildings. Without exaggeration, he spent hours every week staring at the sun's reflection on the ocean, wondering how he could break the downward spiral he inconceivably found himself in. He also spent hours wondering how many hours he spent staring out the window.

For the ten thousandth time, he repeated what had become an all too familiar litany. *Since at my age, it will be hard to change jobs at this salary, the best thing I could do is improve my situation here. But how can I change things here?*

Trying to distract himself, so he wouldn't have to admit the truth about his reality at this company, he found the traffic congestion up the street unusually interesting. But, as the light turned green and all the cars disappeared, he had to look his life in the eye. *I can't stay here, and I can't go,* he concluded one more time.

After a moment watching a Plymouth Voyager pulling out of the garage across the street, he asked his reflection, "I just want to be a happy person again. Is that asking so much?"

Sitting at his desk, staring at the computer screen, wondering which file to open and what to do, *he confided to his reflection, "Susan used to make me happy.*

Susan.

What do I do about Susan? Opening the digital picture of her that he had buried deep in a computer folder marked Competitive Product Ads, he got hard again, thinking about all the wonderful times they had together in bed; how all she wanted to do was please him. She was beautiful with an arresting smile, and incredibly intelligent. They actually had - or used to have, he reminded himself – animated conversations about literature, art, politics. Everything between them wasn't sex. They genuinely enjoyed being alone and being together.

Just remembering how he first saw her at some charity function at a museum, and how he knew he had to meet her, made him smile and think about returning to her tonight. He remembered thinking that she truly was a work of art, and when she spoke, it was more music than words. He remembered how from the moment their hands touched in greeting, they both knew they would be lovers. A suspicious observer from across the room would have said that they held each other's hands a bit too long, but fortunately, there were no suspicious observers so that touch went unnoticed.

Soon after that first meeting, they were getting together two or three times a week, usually at her house, before the kids came home, whenever her husband was traveling. "I feel so alone," she whispered, laying in his arms, when they were in bed for the first time.

"What about all those people gathered around you when we met?"

"They all want something from me. They all want me to be someone I'm not."

She was a divine woman, in every conceivable way. How he had wished he was free to marry her and spend everyday in absolute ecstasy with her for the rest of their lives.

But now, months later, she was becoming a burden, so he had to end it.

"So, is this it?" He asked her picture on the computer screen. *Is this it?* He asked himself. His eyes moved away from the computer screen to scan his desk and the walls of his office, searching for some solution in the piles of paper and rickety shelves that represented his career... his life... and, sadly, his future. *This is it*, he sighed.

Chapter 3

"Can I please have my cell phone?" Cathy begged, her voice quivering, as she slid behind his black leather La-Z-Boy chair, as if looking for some place to hide. Her wounded puppy dog whimper was little more than a whisper. She wanted to cry so badly that her eyelids hurt, but she wouldn't give him that pleasure. He had seen, and enjoyed, her crying far too often.

"What do you need it for?" Fred demanded, with the bravado of a World Heavyweight Champion who knew that no man could best him in the ring.

Afraid that he would wake up her two daughters and the housekeeper with his loud, belligerent voice, she summoned what little courage she could and said, "I told you. I have a 7:00am flight to New York tomorrow morning, which means I have to leave the house by 4:30am. Unless you're going to take me to the airport, which I doubt, I'd like my phone, now." Angry that she had to explain herself, she added, "You know, if the girls need to call me or if there's an emergency, it's important that they can reach me."

Annoyed that her convincing argument was stronger than his iron will, he pulled a dull brass key from his left pants pocket, unlocked the top desk drawer of his wooden desk, and removed her cell phone. Powering it up and scrolling to the recent activity menu, he wrote down the phone numbers of the calls she had made and received, and shoved the paper into the same pocket.

Defending her use of the phone, in a voice that sounded like a frightened child challenging her father, she argued, "You know the company pays for the phone so I can stay in touch with the office when I'm traveling."

As the words escaped her mouth, she regretted each one, but at the same time, celebrated her boldness, because she knew that each word was an attack on his manhood, and a violent reaction was certain to follow. "The Office" was his Achilles heel. "The Office." The mere mention of those words was a Trojan's arrow penetrating his soft flesh. "The Office," was where she triumphed and he faltered; where she danced up the corporate ladder to a Vice President of Human Resources position, and he was relegated to being a Territory Manager in some insignificant corner of the corporation's worldwide empire.

He may be the World's Heavyweight Champion, but they both knew he was only the World's Heavyweight Champion inside this house, inside these walls, and he hated to be reminded of that. Outside, beyond the walls, in "The Office," he was just one of those faceless lackeys that popped up in the corner at the end of every round, sliding the spit bucket in front of the real Champions.

His anger, and response, were instantaneous. Like the Champ letting the Challenger know who owned this ring, he threw the cell phone at her with a sudden, quick jerk of his right arm, so she could suffer the full force of his power.

Having learned from experience that when he couldn't think of some smart retort, he responded by sending a projectile through the air, she instinctively shrank her body inward, dropping her head to her shoulder and twisting sideways to make herself a smaller target.

Her automatic defenses made his attack more a softball than a spear, and the phone hit a fleshy spot on her arm, stinging for a few moments, but doing no real damage. She rose, with a smirk on her face, out of her crouched position knowing that she had absorbed the best punch he had and was still erect. Her smile of satisfaction with her maneuver quickly disappeared as once more she was disgusted with herself for letting episodes like this become the routine of her daily life.

Bending to pick up the phone, she missed the second sharp jerk of his arm, which meant she didn't see the battery charger flying at her in the second volley. Smashing into her forehead two inches above her left eye, the metal prongs pierced her skin and drew blood, sending the Challenger to the canvas. The Champ gloated in yet another win. It was a dirty trick. It was a punch after the bell had rung. It was a victory conceived in deceit and guile.

"I'm sorry," he said, "I thought you wanted the charger, too."

Stunned by the sharp pain just inches from her eye, and dizzy from the scent of her own blood, she dropped down to the brown, leather couch. Raising her hand to her forehead, touching the warm blood, she was catatonic, as outside of herself, watching a scene on TV, so repulsive she couldn't look away.

Too shocked to even attempt to stop the bleeding, she could only bemoan her fate. *This isn't really happening... not to me. This has to be a horrible nightmare. I'm going to wake up soon. This can't be real... this can't be happening... not to me.*

Seeing that she wasn't doing anything to make the situation better, he pulled a handful of tissues from a nearby box and thrust them against her wound. Taking hold of her wrist, he forced her hand against the tissues to hold them in place, sending another arrow of pain to the back of her head.

She sat very still.

This can't be happening to me. I'm White. I'm middle-class. I'm educated. I'm a vice president at a large company. I'm not even married to this person. This has to be a nightmare that's going to end soon.

"You shouldn't have moved," the Fred bellowed, clearly taking delight in knocking his opponent out for the count. "If you didn't move, you wouldn't have been hit in the head." Pulling her hand from her face, and letting the bloody tissues drop to the floor, he examined the cut over her eye with all the care of an attendant at a self-service gas station. With the authority of an applauded brain surgeon, he diagnosed, "It's nothing. Don't make a big deal out of it."

"It hurts," Cathy cried, wiping her drippy nose on her blood-streaked sleeve. "You could have hit me in the eye."

"You shouldn't have bent over. Go put some ice on it."

Too stunned, too weak, too defiant, she remained in the same spot; crying more in despair than in pain; confused at how she got here; frightened that she'd never be able to get to a safe corner; that she would die here, on the canvas of this boxing ring.

"I can't stand this," he spit in disgust, wiping her blood off his hands and throwing the tissues on the floor. Turning his back to her, he was finally able to unleash the sinister smile he fought to hide, and once again, he savored the delight of his total destruction of the challenger to his title. "I hate when you play the victim."

Opening the drawer of her desk, and grabbing the keys to her car, a BMW provided by the company, he announced, "I'm going to the club." With that, he climbed out of the ring and headed for another victory celebration with the other real men at The Club.

She heard the garage door open and close, the car accelerate up the street with a grinding burst of energy, and she wished he had taken his own car. It wasn't that she objected to him driving her car, but his car was an old Pontiac Grand Am that didn't have airbags, and he never wore seatbelts. So, if he got into an accident, chances were better that he would die if he was driving his own car.

How repulsed she was by her own hateful thoughts the first time she admitted having them. It wasn't what a white, educated, professional woman was supposed to think of the man she lived with, especially, not one she thought she was going to marry one day. But then again, he wasn't a man. He was the lowest form of scum born in the test tubes of toxic waste.

Like the addict that needed stronger and stronger drugs to get a high, each time she imagined his death, she relished thoughts of greater and greater pain. Smashing his head through the windshield and crashing into a tree. Flying off of a bridge and watching the water rising over his trapped body. Smelling his flesh burn after a collision with a gasoline truck.

But, as with all drug induced highs, when they wore off, there was only sadness; a bleakness that came from knowing that no matter how much alcohol he drank, no matter how many speed limits he exceeded, no matter how many red lights he sped through, that no matter how many bridges he traveled across, he never seemed to get into an accident, or even stopped by the police.

For the sake of other drivers on the road, she knew it was better he didn't get into an accident with another car. But wasn't there a cliff he could drive off, a sharp turn he could swerve off, or a tree he could crash into? Once again, her mind traced every road and turn on the route he would take to and from The Club, and her grief only deepened. No sharp turns, no narrow bridges, no icy inclines. No hope. He would be back, stinking, and vulgar, and cruel.

As her blood stopped flowing and she admitted that this nightmare was real, she lifted herself from the overstuffed couch and shuffled towards the bathroom.

Several months ago, the first time he bloodied her, she was horrified and confused; trying hard to believe that it was just an accident; not able to comprehend what had happened and how he could have hurt her. After all, this was the man she said, "I love you" to. This was the man she wanted to share her bed with; this was the man she wanted to grow old with; this is the man she thought would care for her daughters as his own.

But, now, standing in front of the mirror, once again appalled by the red stain down the side of her face, she decided not to cleanse herself of him until she did what she had to do.

Sliding onto the chair behind her desk, she turned on the computer. With her hands stained reddish-brown, she reached into a small, inner pocket of her attaché case and removed a plastic case containing a memory stick whose label read, School Information.

Waiting for the computer to boot up, she focused on the small mountain of bloody tissues that served as a monument to the battle she had just lost. How she would love to leave them there for the housekeeper to see, so if she ever killed him, and there was a trial, Esmerelda could serve as a witness. But she feared that the girls would see them first, so she committed to flush them away and toss out yet another silk blouse.

As she typed, flakes of dried blood dropped between the keys, joining the remnants of other battles fought... last week... last month. She reminded herself to bring home from the office one of those little keyboard vacuum cleaners, and then she double-clicked on the memory stick's icon. Typing in the password, she opened a window with seven folders, and slid the mouse to the folder titled JamieErin's Classwork. That folder contained eight sub-folders, and she double-clicked on JamieErin's Math Class. Another series of six sub-folders opened and she double-clicked on JamieErin's Geometry Materials. Finally, a long list of documents appeared. Moving the mouse to JamieErin's Test Scores, she double-clicked on it.

A Microsoft Word document opened with the bold header: A Record of Physical and Mental Abuse Performed against Catianna Isabel Circe at the Hands of Frederick Mardred.

Heaving a sigh, she glanced over the first few entries, trying to understand how she ended up in the middle of this nightmare. She had started keeping this record of abuse after listening to Dr. Nimue, one of Minneapolis's most popular radio talk show hosts, advise a young girl to do so, not only for legal reasons, but more importantly, to track the aggression to see if it was increasing to a dangerous - even life-threatening - level.

Dec. 2 - Since the week before Thanksgiving, something strange has been happening with Fred. He has started pushing me into things... nothing terrible... but the pushing has become more aggressive and is occurring on a more frequent basis. What's been more annoying than the actual pushing is his devilish laughter afterwards, telling me that it was my fault, that I must have tripped on something or that I'm just clumsy. He always apologizes, but it's always insincere and accompanied by that annoying laughter. What made things worse today is that he gave me a "gentle push" when I was on top of the staircase. Luckily, I caught the handrail so I didn't go sliding down, but I wrenched my shoulder and it hurts. I don't know what's going on with him and I thought I should start keeping this record.

Dec. 15 - Fred came home from his office party really drunk. He's been drinking a lot more lately. I don't know why. He's a terrible drunk. I had some ladies over for a small holiday celebration, and as soon as he saw the women, he began screaming at the top of his lungs, "Get the fuck out of my house!" Naturally, they all ran out as fast as they could. He went into the den and passed out on the couch. It was the first good night's sleep I've had in weeks. He started keeping the bedroom lights on and the music turned up loud to all hours of the morning. I'm not getting as much sleep as I should. I hope the girls are able to sleep.

Dec. 25 - Christmas was spent in the emergency room. Fred was drinking heavily at his parents' and a few remarks by his brother about his lack of athletic prowess seemed to upset him so much that he punched his hand through the kitchen window. Fortunately, they were able to get him to the emergency room before he lost too much blood, and the doctors were able to take him immediately. One of the nurses told me that this happens quite a bit around the holidays.

Jan. 2 - I wasn't in the mood for sex tonight since he still smelled of alcohol and sweat, but he wouldn't be put off, so he forced himself onto, and into, me. It was the worst experience I've had since being raped 25 years ago. I told him I didn't like it, but he says he's entitled since I'm sleeping in his bed and we're going to get married one of these days. I don't know about marriage anymore, but I do know that the bed was mine before we moved in together. A few bruises and a lot of vaginal pain. I took a hot bath and felt better.

Jan. 13 - I don't know if Fred had anything to do with this or not, or if he could have prevented it or not, but I slipped on the ice and have a huge black and blue mark on my butt. I don't think I'll be able to go to the health club for a week. The reason I think Fred may have had something to do with it is that he was walking closely behind me and I felt a thud against my left heel before I went down. With all the snow and ice piled up on the sidewalks it probably wasn't his fault, but he laughed that devilish laugh when I went flying.

Jan. 21 - Got kicked out of bed, literally, when I resisted having sex. I banged my head on the end table and now have quite a bruise. I told the girls I walked into the door while going to the bathroom in the middle of the night. I didn't sleep much since I had to spend the night sitting on the chair in the bedroom. I didn't want the girls to find me sleeping on the couch in the living room or den.

Feb. 3 - We've been arguing a lot about money lately. He doesn't like the idea that I make so much more than him, and he doesn't like not knowing where I spend the money. I told him it cost a lot to raise two girls, but he didn't believe me. He made me sign up for an automatic deposit program so my paycheck goes straight to the bank and he announced that he will be giving me an allowance. After lots of screaming and cursing, I agreed. I probably shouldn't have done that, but it seemed like the best way to avoid violence. I feel so stupid. I make three times as much as he does and he's giving me an allowance and telling me how I can spend it.

She stopped reading. It was too painful. Not wanting to be reminded of the humiliations she suffered over the past six months, she scrolled to the bottom of page ten, and began typing.

April 1 –

"How ironic," she forced a half laugh, "April Fool's Day. Can there be any greater fool on this planet than me?"

After checking one more time to see if the bleeding had stopped, she placed her stained hands on the keyboard and described yet another incident of violence.

As she finished describing this latest incident, she added the following:

When did he go from being my Knight in Shining Armor to the warden of my prison? We were talking about getting married and spending our lives together, now it feels like I'm sentenced to life in jail with no hope of parole. When did it change from making love to being raped?

With the camera in her cell phone, she snapped five pictures of her wounded and bloody face, and transferred the photos into the same file on the memory stick. Deleting the photos from the camera's memory, she removed the memory stick from the computer, placed it in its plastic case, and slid it back into the hidden, inner pocket of her attaché case.

As she zippered the compartment closed, a thought occurred to her. Maybe if she drove nails into the tires of his car he'd swerve off the highway and into a ditch.

Chapter 4

Alone in the house. Far away from a world she used to know. Desperate to put the evening's incident out of her mind, she decided to do some work. There was great comfort in work. At the office, she was respected and sought after for advice. At the office, she had authority and was praised for her efforts throughout the company. At the office, people acted on her instructions and held her up as a role model.

With her blouse and hands still crusted with blood, she logged on to the corporate e-mail system to check her e-mail; hopefully, she prayed, some business crisis had occurred that would take her mind off the horrible mess her life had become.

Opening the in-box, she was confronted by a list of over 300 e-mails, which was typical for someone in human resources. Since her promotion to vice president, a day didn't go by that she wasn't inundated with e-mail - usually resumes or follow-up messages from candidates applying for jobs. In addition to these, there was the endless stream of meetings being scheduled; requests from Senior Management for reports, analyses and opinions; bad jokes being passed around the internet; and, the never ending stream of spam advertising from mortgage re-finance companies and pharmaceutical mail-order houses.

It usually took the better part of an hour just to decide which e-mails had to be addressed immediately, which had to be forwarded to her staff, which could be deleted un-read, and which could wait until there was nothing better to do.

But today, something different, something unexpected, something never seen before appeared in the long list of headlines. The subject line read: Kennedy HS Class List.

"Kennedy High School," she read aloud, smiling. "That's a name I haven't heard for a long time." Just seeing the name in print evoked a flood of wonderful memories - friends, boyfriends, parties, football games, class shows, teachers, graduation.

Maybe because high school was 30 years ago and far away from the horror of her daily life, maybe because high school was truly the last happy time she could remember, she decided to ignore the requests from Senior Management. She double-clicked on the e-mail, quickly downloading the spreadsheet attachment. There in front of her were almost 200 of her high school classmates - not just 200 names and e-mail addresses, but the classmates themselves. She had only to look at a name and she could see the chubby face of a girlfriend she once knew, or the paint stained hands of the boy who sat next to her in art class, or the pink dress of the girl who ran against her for class president. Memories of each popped into her head, as clearly as if it were yesterday, as if they were standing right in front of her.

After quickly rushing to the bathroom to wash her hands and face, she raced back to the computer and scrolled down the list.

Eric Walsh. *God! He and I used to get into so much trouble in Mrs. Finegold's class. That skinny runt hated math. Look at that. He's an investment banker now. That's funny.*

Judy DeVine. *She was always so clingy. I hated when she used to sit with me in the cafeteria. Nice girl but she scared away all the good-looking guys.*

Oh my God, Marvin is a doctor now. I hope he's a psychiatrist. He was always dropping things. Bad hands. I think he was the first boy I let touch my breasts. I remember thinking he was a little weird. Maybe psychiatry isn't the best thing for him either. I wonder what kind of doctor he is?

Gary Goldstein. *How did a Jewish boy from Brooklyn end up in a small town in Mississippi? There has to be a woman attached to that story.*

Jessica Caliburn. *That's funny. We were in the Mystery Book Club together and now she's an FBI agent.*

Steven Roth. *Wow! That was a party to remember. Boy, did we get into a lot of trouble for that one.*

There was nothing on the spreadsheet that required such intense scrutiny - just names, locations, and a few personal comments - but she could have stared at it for hours. Had anyone seen her, they would have assumed she was having some kind of catatonic seizure; she barely moved, except for the facial expressions that alternated between laughter, curiosity, delight and surprise. Moving from one name to the next was like turning the page of a good novel, or sipping a fine wine; it was done slowly, to enjoy all the pleasures of the memory.

Finally, her eyes rested on the name Christopher O'Dess... Chris... the man she swore to love her entire life. There he was, right in front of her. The only boy - man - she had thought about, even if it was just for a moment, everyday for the past 30 years. Back then, she was convinced - they were convinced - they would spend their lives together.

I wonder if it would have worked out between us. A smile came to her lips, a tear to her eye.

It wasn't that going to different colleges in different states separated them. He went to Ithaca College in upstate New York, and she went to Stanford University in California. They managed to stay lovers throughout those four years. In fact, their love only increased as it grew from a teenage flirtation to a more passionate adult love.

They had been talking about marriage, children, and having a future together. She remembered how they would toss stones into the lake in Central Park, and as the ripples from their stones crossed, they would turn to each other, intertwine their fingers, and he would say, "Like the ripples in the water that blend into one, so will our two lives become one."

Why did the rape have to change everything?

As hard as she tried, she couldn't remember exactly the words, or exactly the moment, but at some point, they both knew there would be no future for them together. Almost as if they had agreed to it, their conversations were no longer about their hopes and dreams or how they saw the next few years unfolding or when they would see each other again. Where once there wasn't enough time during the day to talk about everything that happened, suddenly, thinking of things to say once a week seemed painful.

And then it just ended.

She remembered that Sunday afternoon. Her phone was ringing and she knew it was him – the first time in her life she never answered his call - but she just didn't want to talk to him that day, or any day afterwards. How empty she felt when the phone stopped ringing, because she had to admit what she already knew. She no longer had a fiancée. She no longer had a best friend.

Staring at Chris' name on the screen, she could hear him saying the words he had recited so often, "At some moment, I don't know when, I don't know how, I don't know where, but part of you became part of me, part of me became part of you. We truly are one." It must have been true, because once they were no more, she felt her heart being ripped from her body.

Do I write? Do I call? What's the appropriate etiquette for contacting an ex-fiancée?

Every year, Kennedy had an Open House, where they welcomed alumni, local employers, colleges that still have space available for graduates, and people from the community to come to the school to talk with the faculty, administration and members of the senior class, tour the new equipment in the science labs, enjoy a presentation from the theatre department, and to listen to a concert from the school orchestra and chorus.

Sammy, the creator of this e-mail list, suggested that they have an impromptu class reunion. It would be Saturday, June 10th. They could all meet at the school and then walk over to Kings Avenue, where Kennedy students hung out, and descend on one of their favorite restaurants from years ago.

A reunion. She hadn't attended any of Kennedy's Open Houses since she graduated and she had no plans to be in New York on June 10th, but seeing some old friends - maybe seeing Chris - made the thought of going much more palatable.

Do you think he'll attend? She wondered. *He had lots of class spirit.*

She glanced at the calendar on her computer and smiled, "I won't have to put up with Fred for two whole days."

Chapter 5

At the center of the Kingsley & Quincy Advertising Agency, known in the industry as K&Q, was a vast space filled with 200 workstations for the secretaries, clericals, and junior executives of the Creative, Media, Production and Client Services Departments. The five-foot high cubicles, clad in shades of beige, tan, and brown, appeared to have no real pattern or logic to their layout. But in reality, because this was an ad agency, and the need to be unique and unconventional was ever-present, the workstations were carefully arranged to appear random. Once a year or so, just to keep things interesting, management would change the layout of the cubicles and the staff had to scramble to find their desks and file cabinets. The arrangement of the cubicles was so complex, people who didn't work in them frequently got lost and had to be guided out.

The staff called the area The Maze, and at times, when the intense pressure of the profession became too much for them, they would play Maze Games, like Maze Races where climbing over walls was permitted, or Maze Basketball, where wads of paper created from bad advertising ideas were tossed into the cubicles of the creators of the bad advertising ideas.

Soon after The Maze was constructed, the "Rats," as the occupants called themselves, found ways to give their spaces individual identity - and also to help "Outsiders" find their way to their destinations.

It began when a British junior account executive hoisted England's flag on a miniature pole. An Australian paste-up artist, who always hated being confused with the British, hung her nation's flag from the ceiling above her desk. A secretary of French ancestry demonstrated real class. After hoisting the French flag, she attached a fan to the pole, so the flag was always fluttering. A very conservative Republican balanced a stuffed elephant on the ledge of his workspace, and an ardent Elvis Presley fan inflated a rubber replica of The King. Soon signs started appearing, *Californians married 24 years and still going strong, I'm over here, Melanie*, and *Please think of me for the next copywriter's job, Frank*.

The management of K&Q found it amusing, and made certain all new clients and prospects saw The Maze, supposedly demonstrating that creativity existed in every aspect of the agency.

Chris hated the Maze. He always got lost and had to ask for directions. Remembering the route to his secretary wouldn't be so bad, he frequently remarked, had the Rats and all their paraphernalia remained intact. But people came and went, so the teddy bears, signs, model cars and what have you, kept appearing and disappearing, the result was confusing. Once, Chris advocated street signs at a management meeting, but everyone else just laughed at his ineptitude and suggested that he buy a GPS for his Blackberry.

Because his secretary had been with the company a long time, she had moved up, or "moved in" as the Rats referred to it, to a bigger space near the center of The Maze, which meant that every time we wanted to put something on her desk, it was a considerable journey from Management Row on the other side of the floor.

Distracted by thoughts of Susan instead of his path, he made a wrong turn and found himself in the Creative Department's territory. A Client Services person in the Creative Department was like a man in the lady's room: it just wasn't done. Junior art directors and junior copywriters stopped working to toss visual knives at the unwelcome intruder. Some graphic designers actually bent over their drawing boards or covered their computer screens so the alien invader couldn't see any work in progress.

Feeling foolish for having gotten lost once again, he raised himself on his toes and rotated around, looking for the *30 pounds less by New Year's* sign that hung over his secretary's work station. Seeing it, he managed to make his way via a very circuitous route to her desk with only one or two more wrong turns.

He dropped several handwritten sheets into her "in" tray, and picked up several printed spreadsheets from the "out" tray.

"I'm printing the last page now," she said. "I told you we'd have everything done in time for your meeting." Candy was an interesting contrast to Susan. Every feature that made Susan attractive - her face, her shape, her poise, her hair - made Candy unattractive.

"With those fingers of yours flying over the keyboard I was never worried. Now we have to hope there's no problem with what's on the pages." Chris caught his reflection on her computer monitor and pushed a few hairs down that were sticking up on the back of his head.

"Your numbers for the third and fourth quarters are way up. Why should you be worried?" Her real name was Elaine Shallot, but she had been called Candy most of her life. Just about everyone she met had to wonder if she acquired the nickname because of her kind disposition or because of her uncontrollable sweet tooth. She was at least 100 pounds overweight, and was always popping something caloric into her mouth. Her hair, reminiscent of used steel wool, was completely unmanageable; so no matter how tightly she pulled it back in the morning, during the course of the day, one strand after another would free itself from the clip or band and reach outward. By the end of the day she looked like a cartoon drawing of someone who had put her finger in an electric socket.

"Because this is the second quarter and I don't know if Mack will wait that long. According to him, we're losing money every day on this client."

"According to your numbers we're profitable." She handed him the last page with the projected income and expenses for the remainder of the year.

Unusually plain, she had a very kind and generous personality, which made her thoroughly pleasant to be around. But more important, she was extremely efficient. She could type 120 words per minute with no errors; took clear and accurate messages; never had one of those three-foot high "to be filed" piles on her desk; and Chris could turn many of his smaller tasks over to her and not worry if they would get done on time. In fact, Chris had been known to say that if she ever changed jobs, he'd follow her.

"It's called Hollywood accounting. Nothing ever makes money."

The secret to Chris' longevity at K&Q was that he always maintained a skeleton staff. He could easily have justified hiring another account executive and assistant, but by keeping the staff small - and doing some of the work himself - he was able to show a profit on even the smallest budgets. He hesitated for a moment. Candy could see there was something he wanted to say but was having trouble getting the words out.

"Yes," she whispered. It was obviously something he didn't want overheard.

His mouth started to move, but no words came out. Finally, he bent very close to her ear and in a hushed tone asked, "Do people around here think..." He hesitated for a moment, as if he feared saying the words would make them come true. "I'm gay?" He moved his ear closer to her mouth.

She pretended a shocked tone. "You? Gay? No! Not at all!" She tried to keep her voice low, but wanted her response to be emphatic, even if it meant that those in adjoining cubicles heard some of comments. "Why would they think that," she asked.

"You know... a guy... working on a tampon account..."

"It's quite the opposite," she reassured him, putting her hand on his. "Most of the women around here wonder if you play around on the side. I'm constantly being asked about you and your marriage."

"Really?" He always assumed that every woman he ever met wanted to have sex with him, but he pretended surprise, just to go along with the tone of the moment.

She nodded several times.

Continuing the thread, he asked the expected question, "Maybe you can give me some names?"

She shook her head, "Not a chance. I hope someday I can be married as long as you two have." He and she both smiled.

Turning to leave, he stood motionless at the entrance to her cubicle, surveying the path ahead as if he were plotting a path through the jungle. From behind him he heard, "Make a left at the French flag, and a right at the stuffed walrus, and you'll be okay."

Following her directions, he exited The Maze at the coffee room. Since it was going to be a long, boring meeting, he stopped in for a re-fill. Unfortunately, Gary, one of his least favorite people at the agency, was there, lecturing to a new junior account executive who had just started working for him.

"Women know from the time they reach puberty - I don't know how they know it, but they know it. It's in the DNA or something - that they only get 1,000 orgasms during their life spans." Gary, the account supervisor for the agency's sporting goods client, was the agency's youngest "Good Ol' Boy." Every company had one - a young man in a time warp that hadn't noticed the changing attitudes toward women and minorities in the work place. Like most young Good Ol' Boy's, Gary was vulgar and offensive, didn't realize it and didn't care. When criticized, he always fell back on the defense, "It was just a joke. Why is everyone getting so sensitive lately?"

Chris moved past him without acknowledging his presence.

"Jewish women prefer to bank their orgasms and collect interest on them," Gary continued. "In fact, Jewish women never really spend any of their orgasms. They save them because they believe 'you never know when you'll need one.' They only spend the interest, that's why they only have sex once or twice a year.

"Catholic women, on the other hand, think they should use them as fast as they can because chances are their husbands are going to turn into fat slobs and they won't be able - or maybe it'll be too nauseating - to have sex with them after a few years of marriage."

Pausing for a moment to let his wisdom sink in, Gary sipped his coffee. The junior account executive shifted from one foot to the other uncomfortably, wishing he could walk out, but afraid to offend his new supervisor.

"Most black women I've met just can't count, so they don't know when they run out. It just comes as a big surprise one day. That's why there are so many big black women. Once they realize they can't have orgasms any more, they just start eating.

"And Hispanic women... "

Chris turned to leave and unavoidably caught Gary's eye.

"Hey, Chrisie. Getting any lately?"

"Shut up, Gary. You're a pig." Naturally, Gary was the chosen protégé of management. He played golf, drank scotch, talked incessantly about women's body parts, and always, always, bragged about how much work he was doing and how the clients thought he was the best thing that ever happened to their business. "You're going to get this agency into a lawsuit someday. Half the secretaries in this place can hear your filth. I promise I'll testify against you."

"All those women out there are just pissed because I know their little secrets," Gary shouted as Chris walked out of the coffee room. Turning back to the junior staffers, "Where was I," he asked after another sip. "Oh, yes, Hispanic women..."

Chapter 6

Monday morning, Cathy's e-mail in-box was clogged with correspondence from old classmates.

Hi y'all,

WOW!!!!!!! This e-mail list is great!!!!! can you imagine, we graduated HS something like 25 years ago… where has time gone????? Married, two GREAT kids (one's about to make me a grandmother, oy vey), living in Florida and selling real estate…

Let's hear what everyone is doing…

Judy (formerly) Saulstein

Brooklyn College

Kennedy High School

Christopher Columbus Junior High

PS 10

***

this is mind blowing… like, awesome… I used to say that a lot, remember? I cant believe it… we're older than our parents were when we were in hs. is that possible? still in Bklyn... though don't live in the same building anymore (ha, ha)... teaching at a new elementary school in Coney island... I'll be at the reunion... who's going? does anybody know where Susan Fulwright is? I've been trying to get in touch with her for years.

Susan (still) Briseis

***

Thank you Thank you Thank you, Sammy, for compiling this list. Maybe I'm just toooo sentimental but I have to admit, seeing everyone's name brought tears to my eyes. My mind's blown away at how spread out everyone is, and even more at the professions everyone has gone into. Shit, I didn't realize we were that smart. Gosh, we've done good!!! and considering we were the anti-Establishment generation, it's great to see that we all sold out together. As for me, I'm in Texas. Won't make it to the reunion. Now divorced from my fourth wife (still looking for Ms. Right, girls). CEO at a defense contractor. (boy, did I really sell out.) One spoiled daughter, 3 spoiled Australian Sheepdogs. Still love Calypso dancing but can't quite get under the pole anymore. Anyone in the Austin area?

Bruce Warner

Hunter College

Kennedy High School

P.S. 189

***

Hi everyone, this is Sharon (Gold) Silverman from San Diego. I'm a travel agent now. Anyone coming to California, pleeeeeze call me. I would love to have a reunion with anyone from Kennedy.

***

When I think about how many years I've tried to bury my Brooklyn past (starting with the accent), it's shocking how delighted I am to see so many of my old friends & classmates. A lot has happened in the past two decades - two rotten marriages (my fault, I admit it), bunch of messed up kids who don't talk to me now, one bad business partner, some drugs, and now a struggling yoga salon. It's been rough. I'm in DC and I'm going to try to make the reunion. It'd be great to drive up with someone from the area.

It'll be nice to be in touch with people from a simpler time.

Alice Somerset

***

Hi,

Anyone remember me?? I was reeeaalll shy in Kennedy. I don't think I ever got invited to any parties (embarrassing to admit) but   I'm a more interesting (and very rich) person now, so I'd like to finally ask the following 20 girls if they'd go out on a date with me.... on second thought, maybe I'll send them private e-mails. I'll be at the reunion. Wouldn't miss for my first million.

Does anyone know if Mr. Hyde is still teaching or if he's retired? (Or, if he's till alive)

Brian Boyd

Harvard Medical School

Harvard University

Kennedy High School

Christopher Columbus Junior High School

P.S. 10

For the most part, the e-mails were directed at the whole class, and everyone was incredibly delighted to be in touch with each other again. It seemed important for some to let everyone know that they were successes - like the Italian football player that wanted the whole class to know that he was now a vice president at a major entertainment company, and the homeliest girl in the class wanted make certain that everyone knew that she'd been happily married for 20 years. Some e-mails did come to Cathy directly.

Cathy,

It's wonderful to touch base with an old friend… every now and then I still think about that party we went to together and laugh… that was some night… let me know what's happening with you.

Steve

***

Dear Cat,

How have you been???? Hard to believe it's been this long… I think the last time you and I talked was at least 10 years ago… you were either heading to or just leaving Denver… I can't remember which. I see you're in Minneapolis now. Great city. Had some real good times there, once. Funny how we're all so convinced we'll never lose touch with each other and then one day we realize we haven't talked or written in a decade. Sad to loose good friends, there are so few of them in life. Carl and I finally separated after 22 years of not communicating with each other… I always wondered if you and Chris detected problems when we were double dating back in school. I decided to get out of the state and took an assignment as Chief Medical Officer at a small hospital in Arkansas. I think more people lived on my block in Brooklyn than in the whole town here. The people are real glad to have a full time doctor in the town - even if it's a Jewish one - but they still think it's odd for a woman to be a doctor and many of the men are too shy to take their clothes off when I need to examine them. It's been kind of lonely, but fortunately, it's a beautiful part of the country and I've been doing a lot of photography. I'll send you some pictures. I'm thinking about going to the reunion. How about you? It would be great to see you, again.

Let me know how things are going with you. Let's try to
stay in touch this time around.

Maxine

Opening her e-mails the first thing in the morning and taking one
last look before she shut down at night, she impatiently waited for an e-
mail from Chris. There was always a slew of messages from other
Kennedyites, but no word from Chris. His name came up in a few e-
mails, and since there was no response from him, she began to wonder if
he just wasn't internet-friendly, or maybe, something worse had happened
to him, like an illness or accident.

Friday morning she stared at her in-box like a kid looking at their
wrapped Christmas presents, just waiting for the right second to open
them. Resumes piled up; messages from management were ignored;
phone calls weren't returned. But there was no mail from Chris. A million
things ran through her mind, from a domineering wife that forbade him
to write (*He was kind of easy to control*) to lingering hostility for what
happened decades ago (*Can he still be angry with me?*).

What to do? What to do?

As morning drifted into afternoon and as the sun sank lower and
lower in the sky, all she could think about was Chris. She hovered around
her computer waiting for the e-mail she prayed would come. Pretending
to look at resumes and New Hire Request forms, she barely left her desk,
and turned her head to see every new e-mail that came into her mailbox.

Now, with Fred at home, she wouldn't be able to check her e-mail
till Monday. Besides, weekends were supposed to be spent with the girls.
She couldn't let them suffer because she hoped an old boyfriend was going
to write to her.

Knowing that she couldn't survive the next forty-eight hours
thinking about an e-mail that might never come, she finally decided to
take the first step in opening the lines of communication between them.

If he still held some sort of grudge, at least she would know she tried and she wouldn't have to spend hours staring at a computer screen. She closed the office door and began to type.

Subject: Hello from an old girlfriend

Chris,

I can't tell you how excited I was to see your name on the class list. I've wondered a lot about you over the years. Glad to see you made it to Los Angeles... you always wanted to live there.

As for me, I'm back in Minneapolis. Can you believe I've been with The Home Computer Company for over 20 years? No one stays at a job that long anymore. They've been really great to me, but I've had to move around a lot. I think we lost contact when THCC transferred me from Minneapolis to Houston... God, that was a long time ago. They moved me around five or six times since then, but I'm home now.

Married, divorced twice, two kids (not in that sequence), and am now living with someone.

Please let me know if you are going to the reunion. If you are, I can find some reason to visit our NY office.

Please write back. I would really really love to hear from you.

Cathy

Reading over her e-mail before sending it, she asked herself, *Should I use the word "love" in the last sentence? "Love" carries too many memories. We used to say it to each other all the time. Maybe I should re-phrase the line,* "We lost contact when THCC transferred me...." *We didn't lose contact. We broke up. Do I really want to tell him about my "insignificant other?" It nauseates me to think of Fred and me as having a relationship, but I can't take a chance that Chris will call the house one day and hear a man's voice.*

She changed the word "love" to "be delighted," but that sounded too indifferent. She called Fred her roommate, but that made it seem like she had a girlfriend living with her. She couldn't think of any way to change the phrase, "lost contact." So, after an hour of cutting, and pasting, re-writing, she sent the e-mail exactly as she originally wrote it... and then waited.

There were a couple of hours before the end of her day. Not a minute of that time passed that she didn't wonder if she would hear from him. *Does he still harbor ill feelings after all these years? Maybe he isn't an e-mail junkie and didn't see the list even after a week. Is he in good health? Did something prevent him from writing? Maybe he was bothered by the phrase "I think we lost contact when THCC transferred me from Minneapolis to Houston..." It was a lot more than losing touch; it was the end of their dreams of being together.*

In the world of the internet, where instant communication any time of the day or night is possible, it was extraordinarily frustrating when people weren't as instant as you wanted them to be.

Cathy's office was fairly small, especially for a vice president, but she paced back and forth anyway, stepping over piles of papers that littered the floor. Lifting one pile of computer print-outs onto another, she made bigger piles so it would easier for her to pace, and when that didn't work, she stuffed the piles onto her already crowded shelves. She sat down. She stood up. She stood up; she sat down. But the one thing she wouldn't do... leave her office if she didn't have to.

Going to the bathroom had all the qualities of an Olympic 100-meter race, and at meetings she hid behind her laptop, pretending to take notes, but really watching the e-mail that entered her system. Rushing through interviews, she passed people along as quickly as she could, under the guise that it was good training for her assistant.

"Beep," the computer in her office chimed, signaling an e-mail had just been dropped into her in-box. Her hopes rose. Finally, he's written. She lunged at the computer as if she was finally being allowed to open that Christmas present. *Is it from Chris?* No. It was from someone named

Chad who had attached his resume. She forwarded it to her assistant.

This is ridiculous, she admonished herself. *I can't sit around waiting for him to respond. I have things to do.* She picked up some papers from a pile on her desk and moved them to the far corner.

"Beep," the computer chimed again. She turned to it with hopes of re-connecting with her lost love. But this was from Leonard, in accounting, who needed additional information before processing an invoice. She forwarded it to her assistant.

"Beep, beep." Two more e-mails, two more messages to forward to her assistant.

Starting to write an e-mail to her staff about vacation schedules, she couldn't think of the first word to use in the first sentence. Visiting websites, she couldn't remember what she was looking for. Opening mail from the Labor Department, she didn't even bother taking the contents out of the envelopes. Staring at the little mailbox icon was all she could focus on. Like the ancient Japanese expression, she was watching a rock grow.

"Beep." Another resume. She opened and closed it with scant attention.

"Beep." A policy change regarding dental insurance. Filed away in a folder.

"Beep, beep, beep."

The low volume alerts from the computer were hardly noticeable before. But, today, they were church bells ringing at midnight. No matter what corner of the office she stood in, as soon as the "beep" sounded she charged back to the computer, even smashing her leg against an open file drawer. *That's one black-and-blue mark I can't blame on Fred.*

Examining her torn pantyhose, she berated herself for the ridiculous waste of time. She turned off the sound on her computer and began reading a budget report. But once beepless, she found herself lowering the report every ten seconds to see whose e-mail had arrived. Pity the person who sent a resume on this day, for his or her chances of seriously being considered for a position lay between nil and none. The last time she stared at a monitor so intensely, she was lying in the maternity ward and was watching a taping of her first daughter being born.

The in-box icon blinked again. She quickly double-clicked it. Another resume. Another disappointment. She gathered some files and headed to the cafeteria for a cup of coffee.

Walking to the door, she turned toward the computer and said, "I'm leaving now. Do you have anything else you want to say to me?"

It blinked again. Despite knowing that it wouldn't be what she was waiting for, she gracefully maneuvered around the piles on the floor, and doubled-clicked on the icon.

Oh, my God, it's from him!!!

Dropping what she was carrying onto her desk, she threw herself into the chair and moved her eyes closer to the screen.

Catianna Isabel Camlanski!!!!!!

How are you?!?!?!?

I can't believe it's you!!! How wonderful to hear from you!!!!

I was just about to write but you beat me to it. Just like the old days (did I say that?), I'm still searching for the perfect words to say to you. :)

I don't know about the reunion but let's plan on talking very very very soon. I'll have to think of some excuse to get there so the company pays for it. I would love to hear your voice.

It's so great to hear from you!!!!

I made it to California. (You'd be proud of me. I only got lost twice getting here.) As you can also see, I didn't make it in acting... some community theatre every now and then... but not much anymore. I'm in advertising now... a

Management Supervisor at some sleazy local agency. (Way toooooo looooong a story to explain here.) Not exactly what I had planned in life but, hey, who gets everything they want?

There's a lot of catching up I'd like to do with you now, but I don't have time this minute. I have to go into a management meeting... :(

Anyway, very quickly, married 17 years, no kids. Still have my hair (though it's a lot grayer)

Have you been reading those emails all week? What is it about high school that has made this list so important to everyone? Maybe it's because high school was the last time we all truly had a clarity of vision and unbridled hope about the future. Hey, I'm getting a bit deep here.

Your life sounds quite interesting. Please fill in some of the details for me. Really got to run.

Let's talk... soon... please.

Chris

Chapter 7

Chris' career could hardly have been called successful. In fact, looking at his resume, one might say he climbed down the ladder of success, rather than up it. It wasn't a matter of competency; he was actually rather good at what he did. It was just that he made a number of really bad career decisions in the early years and had been haunted by them ever since.

He spent most of his 20's, first trying to be an actor, and then after realizing that it was a hopeless pursuit, searching for the right career. So, on both the East and West Coasts he ended up in a number of jobs that never went anywhere: working in a bookstore, selling men's clothing, teaching, and so on. By the time he found advertising and realized this was the field he wanted to pursue, not only was he older than the other junior executives at his level, but his supervisors were all younger than he was. Anxious to make up for lost time, he quickly changed jobs, moving to whatever agency would offer him the most money and the best title. In the first decade of his career in advertising, he worked at six ad agencies. While he quickly caught up to his peers in title and compensation, the price turned out to be quite high, and he was branded a "job-hopper," so no respectable agencies would hire him. Eventually, he could only find a good paying job with a good title at the "bottom-feeder" of local ad agencies - Kingsley & Quincy. But neither the Vice President's title nor the better salary could prevent him from being embarrassed when he told people where he worked, and who his clients were.

At this point in his career, he no longer thought about "his career" and took whatever satisfaction he could from the work he did for clients.

Chris hated to admit it, but he had to give the two partners who founded the agency credit because they knew how to make money in a difficult industry. They turned their very small, one-client advertising agency into one of the - if not the - most profitable independent ad agencies in Los Angeles.

Everything about K&Q was about making money, even the agency's name. When the two partners decided to start the agency, they realized they couldn't follow the industry trend of using their real surnames. "After all," the owners joked, "how much business would we get with an agency called Chiavelli & Mjczoleskicz," so the more waspish-sounding Kingsley & Quincy Advertising Agency was born.

At one point K&Q even had some decent clients on its roster. But the partners soon found that the big name clients were the stingiest with compensation, and so they only pursued those clients that were shunned by the respectable ad agencies (like the penal implant company and several gentlemen's clubs). Ironically, as its reputation sunk (it was called a Haven for Hucksters in one trade magazine), K&Q just continued to become more and more profitable, which was good since they had to pay employees a premium to work there. It was truly a case of the owners laughing all the way to the bank. As they got richer, many of the top competitors disappeared either from poor financial management or creative styles that just got "old."

Everyday at K&Q was an opportunity to squeeze more money from someone, and once a month the owners called a meeting of the management to find out just how successful they had been at squeezing the clients.

On the first Thursday of every month, the agency's five VPs/Management Supervisors were required to present an overview of his (there had never been a "her") clients' planned advertising and projected billings.

Then... open fire.

Anyone in the room - partners, vice presidents, department heads - could shoot questions, criticisms, or comments at the presenter. What should have been an open, mature discussion between professionals, always degenerated into personal attacks, accusations, and invectives. Mack (how Maurice Chiavelli, one of the two owners, preferred to be called) made the meetings detestable, but he wasn't alone. Whoever presented had to expect malicious attacks from every quarter.

Chris' first supervisor at K&Q had been an ex-Army officer, so his perspective on everything related to advertising was framed in military terminology. He had a small squad of buddies around him, and everyone else was the enemy. His instructions were filled with phrases like, "Let's not go over the top on this one," or "It's time to retreat and re-group." Before each of the management meetings (which he referred to as "Trench Warfare") he would tell Chris, "Take the high ground," and "Watch your flanks."

For the two years that they worked together, Chris never really understood how military strategy could apply to the advertising profession. However, once he left and Chris became the presenter, he quickly understood. The management of the agency, as well as the managers of the other departments, looked for every opportunity to bring him down, so any inconsistency, any hint of a problem, any drop in activity, was an exposed flank that could be probed. In preparation for the meetings, Chris spent hours shoring up his defenses - trying to find his fallibilities, as well as planning his counter-attack strategies.

It was a lot of wasted time and a lot of wasted energy, He made it clear to the other department managers, in both subtle and not so subtle ways, that he had the ammunition to take them down. If they chose to attack him, they would get it back, too. He always walked into the room with an accordion folder of exhibits that he claimed contained the ammunition he needed to prove that the other departments lost money, failed to satisfy their clients' needs, or slowed up the billing process. While his military approach to the meetings made him hated by the other department managers, it also made him feared, so Chris usually survived these management meetings with only minor injuries.

In some ways, K&Q was no different from any other ad agency. A continuing, illogical, and exhausting battle raged between the Creative and Client Services departments over who got credit for the successes, and blame for the failures.

The copywriters and art directors of the Creative Department generally viewed themselves as artists using their talents for commercial purposes. Since they created the words and pictures consumers saw, they wanted the credit for the successes. If the campaign failed, then it was the fault of the Client Services personnel who didn't provide the right information on which to base the creative.

At the same time, the account executives, account supervisors and management supervisors of the Client Services Department took the credit for the successes on the grounds that all creative work sprouted from their brilliant marketing strategies. Failures always rested with the dilettantes in the Creative Department who couldn't execute those strategies.

At some agencies, the Creative Departments even established strict rules about when Client Services people could see the rough concepts for commercials and print ads, and at other agencies, the Client Services Department forbade Creative personnel from ever speaking to clients.

Whether the Creative or Client Services Department scored any victories in their never-ending, seesawing battle, was completely irrelevant to those in the Media and Production Departments. They worked in the shadows of the agency, and they toiled with a sense of being overlooked, abused, and used. These two departments enjoyed little glamour or prestige, and rarely received the recognition they deserved for all the work they did.

So, everyone came to the meeting with a hidden agenda, looking to build themselves up by tearing someone else down, or at minimum, to settle old scores in the most humiliating way possible.

Chris didn't expect too many problems at today's meeting, and in fact, he really didn't spend too much time preparing. Not only was his client's spending in the first half of the year on track, but, more importantly, he was scheduled to be the last to present. So not only was there little to attack him for, but much of the hostility in the room would already have been vented and everyone would be ready to go home.

His thoughts had wandered to Cathy and away from whether some adult entertainment client was going to spend as much as originally projected. He had read in the newspaper how a couple from high school had re-connected after decades via the internet, and then got married. He wondered if he and she could be another instance of, "let's start the clock over again." If not, he wondered if they would have an affair, though he hadn't seen her and he generally preferred his lovers to be five or more years younger than he.

But Cathy wasn't just any woman. This was the woman he wanted to marry and have children with. This was the woman who broke his heart and sent him into the arms of someone else. This is the woman who loomed so large in his heart that once they broke up he couldn't bare to walk the same streets they used to walk, eat at the same restaurants they used to eat at, talk to the same friends they used to talk to.

He had moved from New York to Los Angeles just to get away from the memories. But memories have no borders and they followed him for all the years they've been apart. Sitting in the conference room, pretending to care about something he cared little about, he remembered how great their love was, and sadly, he remembered how he violated it by not going to her side when she needed him. He remembered...

What?

Like a car alarm waking someone from a sound sleep, his sub-conscious snapped him back into reality. A strange announcement was being made by Mack Chiavelli.

"At this time, Barry Balin is being relieved of his Management Supervisor's responsibility, and Gary Accolon will be taking his place. During this transition period, I would appreciate it if everyone would assist Gary as much as possible. We are not sending out press releases regarding Gary's promotion. It has to be a quiet transition. I will be calling Barry's clients personally to advise them of the change. Since Gary is obviously not in a position to present today, at this time, you're up, Chris."

Looking around the room, wondering if everyone else was as surprised as he was, Chris suddenly realized that Barry Balin, one of the Management Supervisors, was hidden in a dark corner, staring at a blank sheet of paper, empty of all life, emotion and tears. The usually fastidious and fashionable executive hadn't been out of his clothes in two or three days, and the shadow on his face meant he hadn't shaved either.

What happened to Barry? He looked around the room hoping for an answer, but no one would make eye contact with him. Everyone except Gary, who had a wide grin on his face, as if some well-conceived plot to overthrow his boss had succeeded as planned.

"Chris, let's get going," he heard Mack's voice boom at the back of his head.

"Just a minute," he said. He tried to collect his thoughts, and his overheads. He couldn't stop looking at Barry. *What happened to him? How come I didn't know there was a problem? Barry and I went out to lunch together every week and talked about all sorts of things? Why didn't he confide in me that there was a problem with Mack or with his accounts? I could have helped him. I wonder what happened with the client. Jesus, I could have gotten that account. In fact, it was supposed to be my account. It has the biggest budget in the agency and I'm the most senior Management Supervisor. If I hadn't been on vacation when the client came to "see who his team would be" I would have been on that account.*

Then the thought occurred, *Hey, why aren't they moving me up?*

Chris slowly shifted his eyes from Barry to the agency's management at the front of the room. There was an unusual look on Mack's face. His cold eyes were focused, like a hunter targeting his prey down the barrel of a rifle.

What's going on here? Why wasn't I brought in on this? If anybody, I should have been moved onto Barry's account. They're the biggest and most respectable client in the agency and I have the most marketing experience of anyone here. Gary's much too junior, and too stupid, to take on this responsibility. Something's happening here.

"Wake up, Chris. We need you in the front of the room... now," Mack called out.

Is it because Gary's such a pig that they don't want to give him the tampon account and instead gave him the one decent client in the agency? He's got twelve years less experience than me. He can't handle this account.

"Now, Chris. We all want to go home soon."

Chris could feel his body rising and gathering the papers in front of him. In a matter of seconds, his whole universe had shifted. His closest ally at the agency was in complete ruin. He had clearly been overlooked for a promotion - and everybody knew it. Something was out of sync. Looking around the room, no one was as shocked as he about Barry's situation and Gary's promotion. They all seemed to be smirking, as if they were all in on a secret. Maybe he was imagining it, but he had the incredible sense that everyone had a look of "getting even" on their faces; as if they had waited months for this moment and now they were finally getting satisfaction.

Purposely bumping into one of the chairs and dropping all his papers, he used the seconds he bought himself to try to think this through.

The General, as Chris used to call his former supervisor, frequently cautioned him to watch for Mission Critical Moments - or MCM's as they were called in military jargon. MCM's were hints, clues, events... anything that could effect the outcome of the mission. It was too quiet; it was too noisy; a path suddenly appeared in the jungle where there was none before; a trail suddenly ended; something didn't smell right; something was out of sequence; whatever it was, it was different. "One time in the jungle," the General illustrated, "I turned and looked at the face of a prisoner we had picked up in a nearby village. We had to beat him up quite a bit to subdue him, so he was in pain. But once we get to a particular spot, he started smiling. A big wide smile. He had a rope tight around his neck and his hands were tied behind his back. He shouldn't have been smiling. I screamed to everyone, 'Hit the dirt!' Just then Charlie opened up on us with everything they had. We all came out of that one okay because they dispersed as soon as we returned fire... everyone, that is, except the prisoner. I guess he didn't speak English."

As Chris edged around the chairs of the conference table, inching his way to the front of the room, he shifted his eyes from person to person. No one, except Mack and Gary, would look back at him. Gary's smile only got wider, and Mack's focus never changed.

It was unusually quiet. The room had never been this quiet. There was always background chatter as the combatants licked their wounds or trumpeted their victories. And Mack was always on the phone. That's what's wrong with this picture. Mack was a rude S.O.B. and he never hesitated to make calls during presentations and between them. But he was sitting there patiently... waiting... staring. He wasn't on the phone. He wasn't scribbling notes about the numbers from the previous presenter. He wasn't calling anyone stupid. He was just sitting there, crouched forward, like a lion in tall grass, waiting for his prey.

Every nerve in Chris' body said that if he went to the front of the conference room and gave the presentation he was expected to give, something would happen that would have major ramifications. "I don't like it. This was a Mission Critical Moment if I ever saw one," the General's voice boomed in his ear.

Meetings, events, loose phrases, smirks and smiles of the last few days rolled around in his head. Was there a pattern? Was there something unusual? Have Gary and Mack been spending more time together? Have they been interviewing new job applicants? Has Mack been spending more time going over budgets? Have there been more closed-door meetings? Have there been more off-site meetings? Come to think of it, he hadn't seen Barry around. The memo itemizing today's agenda requested more financial information than usual. The meeting was scheduled an hour later than usual. Do these add up to something or am I imagining things? Is this a Mission Critical Moment or am I getting carried away by the General's war stories?

General, he conferred in the War Room of his mind, *My flanks are covered. My numbers are on track. The client's happy. With Barry Balin gone, now I'm the most experienced marketing person at the agency...*

A hand grenade dropped right into his foxhole. *You're the highest paid marketing executive at the agency! Hit the dirt! Hit the dirt!*

His pace slowed ever so slightly. "They're not coming around your flanks, you idiot," The General screamed in his ear. "Are you blind. It's a frontal assault and there's a lot more of them then us!"

With a sudden clarity he realized, *I'm about to lose my job.*

This was a set up. Once all the latest client information was transferred at this meeting, he was going to be fired. He and Barry were the two highest paid members of management - excluding the owners - and replacing them with more junior people could save the agency $500,000 a year or more.

Chris had always thought of himself as indispensable because of his strong marketing skills, and he was often brought in on new business presentations to write the marketing strategy portion of the proposal. But with Gary's ascension, it was obvious the agency's management didn't really care about those kinds of skills. Penal implant clients rarely cared about marketing plans. It was all about money.

Confused. Panicked. He wished he had the General there with him now. *If I lose my job, can we afford both cars? What about the condo? What am I going to do? I'll never find another job in advertising? Not at this salary! Who's going to hire someone at my age, especially someone that spent the last ten years in this cesspool? Where do I go from here? Back to selling books or lady's shoes? I can't believe they're doing this to me. God, I'd love to wipe that smirk off Gary's face and shove it up his ass. Melanie never liked advertising. She'll finally be able to say 'I told you so.' What a pathetic ending to a rotten career.*

Mack crossed his arms and leaned back in his chair. Gary did the same. Sandy and Debra leaned forward. They wanted to savor every moment as their shrewd adversary finally got roasted and eaten alive.

Turning on the projector, he knew he had to say something dramatic... something that would elevate his status again... something that would guarantee he wouldn't lose his job... something that would give him time to think.

"One time, when the enemy was about to overrun our position," the General recollected, "I had the men dig in deep and had the air force carpet bomb the whole area. We were surrounded. We were out of ammo. We were dead meat if we didn't do something dramatic. This way, we at least had a chance to survive. And here I am, so you know how it worked out."

As all the eyes in the room targeted him, as his mouth began to open, as he saw his career - whatever there was of it - coming to an end, he looked Mack directly in the eye and declared, "There's no point in presenting the information I prepared for this meeting."

Mack's stare didn't waiver for a second, his target was still in his sights.

He paused for a moment to formulate what he had to say - and to gather up the strength to say the words critical to his survival. "I just got off the phone with my client and I have some good news." He desperately wanted to close his eyes, but he knew no one would believe him if he did, so he continued. "The good news is that the client has expressed an interest in going on television."

Mack's eyes opened wide. Gary's overblown chest sank. A buzz broke out in the room because that wasn't the scuttlebutt that had been floating around. Everyone anticipated Chris being chopped up into little pieces at this meeting. How could this be? Envira's budget was too small for TV advertising. They were a woman's magazine advertiser.

"The enemy's massing on your right flank," the General whispered in his ear. "They think you're out of ammo. They don't think you can hold this position against another attack. You'd better put up some show of strength."

I'm committed now, Chris figured, so why not? "I'm delighted to say that the President of Envira Tampons has agreed with my suggestion to test the concept of television, and if it works, to broaden it to their top ten major markets."

This was big news for an agency whose existence depended mostly on small newspaper ads for penile implants, bowling alleys, discount tires, and used factory equipment.

Television. You could almost hear the word reverberating throughout the room. Television. This wasn't just another ad campaign. This was redemption. This was an 8.0 earthquake. They hadn't done a TV commercial in years. Scaring away the big, stingy clients, as they had done, meant they didn't get to do big projects anymore. Sandy, the Creative Director, drooled over the thought of doing a TV commercial because this would finally demonstrate his enormous creative talents. It would be his ticket out to a real ad agency. Debra, the Media Director, saw a commercial as her way back into working with the networks and big media companies. Spending money, gaining respect. Mack saw the billings, and maybe a chance to have something new to sell to other clients.

Television. Every other agency in the city seemed to be doing television. If it was a good commercial, people could be proud to work here again. They wouldn't have to go to industry parties and lie about where they're working.

Television. Everyone wanted this to happen... even more than seeing Chris eaten alive.

"You did it," the General cheered, "you got them on the run. Now cut them down so they can't attack again!"

The mood in the room had shifted. People were sitting straighter, and the level of chatter in the room had increased dramatically. Someone must have turned the dimmer light switch because the room just seemed to get brighter. But Chris could feel he wasn't off the hook yet. More details were needed to convince them.

In one of those "Negotiation Tips" classes he once took, the instructor had said, "Always throw in some small negative. It convinces people that you're willing to reveal the downside, and therefore, you must be honest."

So in a voice slightly above the noise he added, "Please don't get carried away. We're not going network with this. I have to remind everyone that this is just a test, and even if it works, we're just going into selected markets. They're very conservative fiscally and we haven't even discussed budgets yet." Then, he decided to throw all his reserves into the battle, "But, as you all know, I have a good relationship with the client, and I know they would be open to discussion of a budget increase after they see some good commercial concepts."

Chris impressed himself. He knew the General would be, too. Mack still had his doubts, but at least he took the bull's eye off Chris' forehead. Gary was practically in tears as his arch-enemy averted the ambush and was now growing too strong to attack again.

As the reality of what he had just done, settled on him like dust in a sandstorm, he knew what he had to do now... set someone else up to take the fall for when Envira Tampons eventually decided not to go with television.

As he scanned the room, it was obvious - the perfect fall choice - Sandy, the Creative Director. That hack - another of Chris' least favorite people - hasn't had an original idea in twenty years and certainly couldn't come up with one now. Feeling pretty good about this ad hoc plan to save his career, Chris wanted some insurance. What if Sandy, through some small miracle, accidentally came up with a good idea? Or, more likely, what if he steals one and no one knows where it came from? He had to do something to guarantee Sandy's complete failure.

"Let me just say this about the test. I know this client. They're very comfortable with me. We only get one shot to impress them. I know it's a commitment on our part, and it puts Sandy and his people into a bit of a spot, but..." He paused for emphasis, just enough time for everyone to switch their eyes to Sandy's apprehensive face then back to the front of the room, "...but we have to show them a whole campaign. Multiple commercials, direct mail, PR, the whole enchilada."

Chris looked over the battlefield, and he felt the victory in his bones. His enemies were on the run, dropping their weapons as they raced off the field. Debra was scribbling notes about which television reps she would call. Mack was entering information into a spreadsheet, estimating how much budget he was willing to spend to get this campaign done. Sandy was... well, the initial euphoria was already fading, and he began to feel uncomfortable with the immense pressure that was being placed on him.

"Now!" the General screamed, "Bring in the B-52's. Wipe them out! Destroy them! Don't let them come back tomorrow!"

This was an enormous project, which would take three or four months to be done properly. So, in front of everyone, he tossed his glove right at Sandy's feet.

"We have a little bit of a problem." The room went silent again. All eyes turned towards him. His quickly formed plan was, simply, that he wouldn't give Sandy enough time to develop a good campaign. Trying to repress a smile, he couldn't help but enjoy his own brilliance. "The client goes out of town for a six month cruise right after his anniversary. He's celebrating his 50th wedding anniversary on June 10th. I've been invited to his anniversary party, so that's the day I have to present to them." Chris patted himself on the back for the good detail, and thought, *hopefully, this'll give me enough time to get a new job.* For the fun of it, he looked directly at Mack and said, "Unless you all want to wait till he gets back."

Mack snarled at him and Chris took a small step backwards. The older people in the room pulled out Filofax's and Day Runner calendars.

The younger people checked the date on their cell phones and Blackberry's. Those in the middle scanned the date books on their Palms. There was chatter in every corner of the room about doing a TV commercial. Chris mulled over how he was going to convince the client to at least look at the storyboards for a television campaign.

Finally buckling under the strain, Sandy shouted, "That's not enough time! Tell you client we need more time."

Debra joined her ally, though she wasn't quite as loud. "I don't have enough time, either. You don't even know what markets we're supposed to be planning for."

Others joined in. Cries rose from every corner.

"Impossible!" Brent and Harry, two of the sub-creatives (as Chris referred to them), called across the conference table to Sandy, waving a white piece of paper that looked more like a flag of surrender than an convincing argument for not doing the commercial.

"Stupid." Gary grumbled, wanting everyone to know that he was on their side against Chris.

"Can't you control your clients?" Doris, the number two in the Media Department, criticized Chris, and not for the first time today.

"I have a vacation planned," Beverly, from the Production Department, whimpered as she saw her Alaskan cruise float away in front of her eyes.

"The bowling alley ads are due next week," Sandy, unconvincingly argued.

Something like this would interrupt the entire agency, and everybody's work would be affected.

Chris just looked at Mack and said with his eyes, "That's the date. Take it or leave it. It's up to you." This was the moment. Victory or defeat? Was the battle won or lost? Will the enemy surrender? Mack had to commit. Did he believe the story or not?

Mack stood up, and there was a deadly silence in the room.

Whatever his next words were going to be, it would determine their fates, and their schedules, for the next two months. If he said, "Go," it would mean long days, late nights, and no weekends until this project was completed. Sandy secretly hoped that Mack would tell them it couldn't be done in time. Gary sulked because all of his limelight had faded. Debra wanted to go forward regardless of the cost to the agency since there were a lot of free lunches with reps waiting for her.

Turning to Chris, Mack said, "Tell your client we'll be ready to present before he leaves for vacation."

Chapter 8

As he left the meeting room, with a few pats on his back for getting the agency back into television, he realized he had completely forgotten about Barry. He changed direction and rushed into the Maze to talk to Candy. "What happened to Barry? It looks like he slept in his suit."

In a hushed tone, Candy confided, "His wife walked out on him a couple of days ago. She was having an affair with some actor who just got a part in a Broadway show, so she's going to New York with him."

Dumbfounded, Chris leaned against the cubicle wall for support. Only two weeks ago, he and Melanie went out with Barry and Jane. There didn't seem to be any problems between them. Quite the opposite. They always seemed to be kissing and hugging each other. They were so lovey-dovey, it got uncomfortable after a while. They chatted constantly with each other, as if other people didn't exist, and there were lots of private, little jokes and expressions. They even looked alike.

"Did he know about it?" Chris asked.

"Not a clue. According to Lillian, his secretary, it was a complete surprise. It was just like a movie. He came home and saw that her closets were empty. He thought they had been robbed. When he went to the phone to call the police, he found a note from her. Rumor has it, she cleaned out their bank accounts, too. Poor guy, he's walking around like a zombie."

Shaking his head in disbelief, Chris kept saying to himself that there must have been signs. A marriage of seventeen years just doesn't end that suddenly. "He always talked so lovingly about her."

Was she acting all this time? If she was, she fooled everyone... especially Barry. Could she have been planning to get out of the marriage and just waiting until the time was right? Did this actor come into her life and just sweep her off her feet? Had she been harboring doubts about her marriage for a long time? Could she have been...

"Maybe you should talk to him," Candy suggested, interrupting his silent questioning.

His mouth dropped and his eyes opened wide, as if to ask, *Me? Why me? Yes, we worked together. We drank together. We even occasionally socialized, but we're not close.*

"I think he needs a friend," Candy insisted softly.

We're co-workers, not friends. We never shared intimacies or thoughts. We shared war stories at the bar after work, that's all. We're not friends. There has to be someone else he could talk to. I don't know anything about him.

But he couldn't think of anyone at the agency who would have called Barry a friend.

"You know how people avoid anyone who has just gotten bad news," Candy said. "Everyone is walking around to the other side of the floor to avoid passing his office. He's all alone now. Maybe he would like to talk to someone." She was genuinely a kind person, always considerate of others, always the one to remember someone's birthday or ask about someone's health.

She was right. Someone should say something to him. He just hated the thought that that someone should be him. But if he didn't do it, who would? Inching his way out of the Maze, he slowly trekked down the long hall to Barry's office. What do you say to someone who's lost every hope and dream he's ever had? The one sure thing he knew—whatever he said, it would be irrelevant.

Barry sat behind his desk, as if someone had lifted him like a statue from the conference room and placed him there. His body was a deflated balloon... the whole of his insides had been sucked out and only a shrunken, formless shell remained. He bent over his desk, staring at nothing. He was beyond pain. Everything was gone - all feeling, all recognition, all senses - only labored breathing seemed to remain.

Chris mumbled a few words, not even certain what he had said. It didn't really matter, Barry didn't hear them anyway. Not knowing what to do, and feeling very awkward, Chris quietly lowered himself into one of the guest chairs. He sat in silence for a few moments, hardly moving, and thought about how sad he was when Marjorie left him and returned to her husband. His eyes even watered a bit, though not enough to shed a true tear. He tried to imagine how he would feel if Melanie walked out, leaving a note next to the phone. *I talk a big game,* he thought. *I'd really miss Melanie if she wasn't there.*

Eventually, Barry managed to eke out, "Everyone's avoiding me like I have a virus. If they get too close, they'll catch it, and their marriages will end in disaster." Barely audible, he couldn't summon the strength to say more, so he lapsed back into the world of the semi-living.

"People just don't know what to say," Chris offered as a pathetic excuse.

A few minutes passed in silence. Chris shifted his position in the chair several times, and wondered what the appropriate length of a visit to someone who lost absolutely everything in the world should be before he could make some excuse to leave. "Can I help you with any of your clients?" *Good question*, Chris congratulated himself. Not that he really wanted to take on any more work, but it demonstrated a willingness to help on his part.

"Don't need anything," Barry said, nearly too low to be heard. "Gary is taking over my account."

Looking around Barry's office, he was impressed by how neat it was in comparison to his. It was much bigger, so there was more room for shelves and cabinets, but it didn't have a view of the ocean. Unlike Chris', Barry's shelves weren't cluttered with sales reports and magazines, there were personal items, like his wife's picture - actually many pictures of his wife - on their honeymoon, at a ski resort, in Hawaii.

Chris' eyes focused on a high school football trophy. It was a small bronze statue of a quarterback, showing no concern for his personal safety, soaring upward like an ascending eagle, searching for a receiver. The eyes of the quarterback spoke one word, "Winning." It was a rather unusual statue, not one you'd typically pick up in a sporting goods store, so Chris had to wonder if this actually depicted something that occurred in Barry's life.

For all the years they've worked together, Barry never mentioned football, nor the events leading up to this trophy, which was further evidence to Chris that they weren't friends, just brothers in the battle to survive at K&Q. After what felt like hours, but was really less then ten minutes, Chris stood up to leave, "I've got an angry client to call." He moved toward the door, but Barry's tears stopped him. "How about spending a day or two at my place?" Chris asked, knowing Melanie would be absolutely livid that he offered.

In a voice that seemed to come not from a human soul but from the air itself, Barry exhaled, "No. I think I just want to be alone."

Frightened that this fallen warrior might do harm to himself, he offered again, "Maybe you shouldn't be alone. How about just for tonight?"

Defeated, devastated, without the strength to speak, he said no, but with his eyes, not his words.

Wanting to say, "I know it seems tough now, but you will survive. Tomorrow will be better than today. I promise you," Chris decided not to, and just eased out of the office, adding, "If you need anything..." Closing the door as he exited, he was torn between happiness that it wasn't him experiencing that pain, and envy that Barry had loved someone so much to be in such pain.

Chapter 9

"Does Grandma and Grandpa have sex?" Erika asked her mother in more than a whisper as they wandered down the corridors of the Minneapolis Institute of Arts.

Frozen in time in front of the Edvard Munch exhibit, Cathy could not move, breath, swallow, feel her heart beat, hear the tick of a clock, or see anything beyond the day her youngest daughter was born. She was indeed fortunate that the air currents blowing through the museum's ventilation system were so perfectly balanced, because, for certain, even the slightest uneven flow would have thrown her in one direction or the other as if it was a tropical hurricane.

At that moment, she committed herself to going down to the school yard, find which pre-pubescent imp defiled her virgin daughter by telling her about sex, and insure that he (for surely it was a he) went to prison for the remainder of his years where he would become the love bunny of a 350 pound inmate named Zeus.

Turning her head towards the voice that asked the seminal question, she could only see the face of a smiling, gray-haired nurse slipping her new born baby into her arms, and how she pledged to her crying infant,

"Don't worry, I'll always be here to protect you."

Patiently waiting for her mother to respond, Erika looked up at her mother as if she were a puppy waiting for dinner.

There were several ways to respond to the question, Cathy decided.

First, there was the grammatical approach. Since Grandma and Grandpa are plural the correct wording for the question should be, "Do Grandma and Grandpa have sex?" He does. She does. They do. While proper sentence structure was important for every child to learn, it really didn't answer the child's question, nor get Cathy out of her obligation to do so.

The second way to respond, the politician's approach, was to completely avoid the question and offer a meaningless response. For instance, Cathy could say, "Older couples enjoy an intimacy just like younger couples, but in a different way."

Again, it didn't get Cathy off the hook, and worse, it taught a bad lesson about intellectual inquiry. The problem, she decided, with taking your children to museums to help them develop inquiring minds, is that they often inquire into the wrong subjects. This trip to the Art Institute was to help them expand their definition of art, to appreciate that one doesn't have to understand art but, can instead, feel the art.

Staring at the painting called *Madonna* that hung opposite them, she couldn't understand what about it could have provoked thoughts of geriatric fornication. But it did. Closing her eyes for a prolonged moment, then opening them again, revealed that for the first time in many years, her daughter's attention span lasted more than 10-seconds. She remained on the same spot, with the same baby brown eyes staring straight up at her, waiting for an answer to her simple question.

Sixty seconds (though it felt like sixty hours) more passed and her daughter still hadn't been distracted by another painting, the cute boy who entered the room, or the sudden desire to eat a Rice Krispie Square, so she said, "I don't know, and I don't think it's appropriate for us to ask Grandma and Grandpa." Clearly an unsatisfying remark, so she offered some consolation. "If you still want to know, when I get as old as Grandma, you can ask me and I promise I'll tell you."

Disgusted that she was being treated like an immature little child who wasn't allowed to know the facts of life, she snapped back, "That's dumb."

Offended, but trying to sound like a mature, conciliatory parent, Cathy answered, "Why do you say that?"

Proving that she wasn't too young to understand "adult things" Erika flatly stated. "Of course you're not having sex, mom. You're not married."

Chapter 10

Cathy opened Chris' e-mail as if it was a present from Tiffany's, and the ribbon and bow had to be appreciated for their sheer beauty.

Subject: My Life in a Nutshell

Dear Cathy,

How does one begin to describe the last 25 years of one's life... I can't say it's been the life I wanted or expected... to be honest, I'm not sure what I think of it, since I rarely give it much thought

As you know, I did some acting in New York... did I ever tell you I got a good review - well, one sentence - in the NY Times when I played a gay Trojan warrior in an off-off-off Broadway musical spoof of Homer's Iliad (Thank the Gods, no one will ever see that one again)

At some point I realized... and I know you knew but (thank you) never had the heart to tell me... that I wasn't a very good actor... so I decided my future was in television and I moved to L.A.

Besides... after you and I... broke up... I couldn't stay in NY... too many memories... I couldn't walk by Central Park without thinking about how we threw stones in the water, and... well, one day I just got in the car and started driving west. You'd be proud of me... I only got lost twice. Remember the old Cougar... I kept worrying that I would break down in Iowa or Kansas and meet some farmer's daughter and end up spending the rest of my life there. Wasn't that the plot of some show we saw???

I made it to L.A... and I really didn't have the stomach any more for the life of a starving actor... so I started looking around for something else to do. Did a bunch of silly stuff. Remember my Uncle Geoffrey... he was in advertising and seemed pretty happy... had that nice house on Long Island... so I went into advertising thinking I would be writing TV commercials. Well, it doesn't work that way and I ended up as an Account Executive - a "suit" as it's affectionately called in the business. My job is to make the clients happy... which usually puts me at odds with everyone else at the agency. So most of the time I'm caught in the middle. It's awful... I walk around angry and stressed all the time.

The first agency I worked for sent me to UCLA to take some business classes... while in a finance class I met Melanie, who was a lawyer just starting out. Long story short, we got married and have been together for just over 15 years. No kids... we never seemed to want them or have the time for them...

I changed jobs quite a bit and now I'm at a pretty sleazy ad agency... for ten years now... working on... are you ready for this... (drum beat, please)... a tampon account.

You heard me right, a tampon account.

Don't say anything, pleeeeease. I've heard every joke there is about working on a tampon account. I've stopped going to industry parties because I'm tired of being called The Tampon Guy.

I don't know if they assigned it to me to get me to quit or they just wanted to humiliate me, but obviously, I'm still there and more than a bit embarrassed about it... They're actually a pretty decent client, nice people, and in this business that's the best you can hope for... it's actually an interesting product form a marketing point of view.

That's all I'm going to say on the subject... you're NOT permitted to say anything to me - or to any of our high school classmates - about it. :-)

That's my life in a nutshell. When we talk I can give you the long version, but the ending is the same. Do you still like mystery books?? I'm reading the Da Vinci Code now and it's great.

I'm probably going to make it to the reunion... looks like I'm going to have a presentation to my client that same day so I should be in NY... Let me know if you're going.

Wow... a Vice President at THCC... I'm real real impressed. You always talked about having a career with a big corporation... I guess you got what you wanted. Is your name in the annual report???

Now it's your turn...

With very very fond memories of you...

Chris

Reading the e-mail, Cathy instantly knew how unhappy he was. Unhappy at home. Unhappy at work.

He used to be so enthusiastic. Always talking about the future. Always saying you can't let the past bog you down. Always arguing that he was the captain of his own ship; that his fate was in his own hands. He always had a plan to make things better. Always wanted children; lots of them. When he was happy, everyone in the room felt it.

All that was absent from this e-mail. He was happy to be back in touch with her, but little else spoke of happiness. The spirit had gone out of him.

As someone who read resumes every day for the past two decades, she knew that people gave the most real estate to those parts of the past that excited them: being captain of a soccer team in college; volunteer work at a museum; lifeguard during the summers. Resumes that gave scant attention to the current employer, but elaborated on the past, were clear indications of problems at work.

Chris wrote a great deal more about tampons than his wife, and he had nothing but disparaging remarks about his current employer, while admitting that he had been there for ten years. Not the ingredients of a happy life.

The Chris I knew, she recalled, *wouldn't stay in a 90-minute movie that he hated. He certainly never would have stayed at a job he hated for ten years.* She so wanted to wrap her arms around him, like she used to after he got a bad review of his acting in the school newspaper. Touching the keyboard as if she was touching him, she began typing.

Subject: My Turn

Hmmmm, what details about my life should I tell you? For all the success in business, it's been a rather ordinary life.

First let me say, don't be so impressed by the VP title. There are a lot of us here. It looks good for the stockholders. Besides, the truth is they were being audited by the EEOC and they needed to have more women and minorities in management to make their numbers look good, so on a "Special Recognition Day" they promoted ten women to vice presidents, and I was one of them.

What's funny, besides the fact that there's never been a Special Recognition Day before or after, is that they didn't want to make this seem like they were doing this because of the EEOC investigation, so they promoted nine men, too. What a joke. Anyway, the EEOC seemed pleased with the progress the company was making, so now I'm a VP.

Now, onto the less successful portion of my life... my marriages.

Well, the first marriage... Boy, was that a mistake!

After the rape, I didn't feel safe in Minneapolis any longer and I asked for a transfer to any other city. THCC was really great about everything and found a position for me in our Houston office. It sounds so stupid now, but I was alone, and scared, and I guess at the moment I was looking for someone to protect me. In Texas, men are men and a lot of them still carry guns, just like the old West. I was in the right place to meet a "real man" and that's exactly what happened. He lassoed me, literally, at some corporate barbecue. We got married within a year, and managed to enjoy ourselves for a while. No kids. I don't think we lasted until our third anniversary.

It was a horrible marriage. He was a real man alright, and wanted a woman to be a real woman. My career was an irritant to him. The fact that I wouldn't stay around the house in black lace underwear waiting for him to come home was the source of many arguments. One day he just left.

The second marriage was doomed before I finished saying "I do." I wasn't looking to get married again, but THCC transferred me to Denver, and once again I was in a strange city and alone. I thought I could make it work, but there was no real love there. We weren't married that long, but we managed to produce two of the most beautiful children in the world. (You can tell I'm a proud mother.) I met him when we hooked up via one of those matchmaker websites on the internet. He's a forensic accountant working for the IRS. I can't tell you how boring that can be. He even thought that we'd save money if we gave the girls the same initials. Don't ask, I didn't understand it either, but I went along with it. I guess I was reacting to my first marriage and wanted someone who was more brains than brawn.

We rarely speak or e-mail, but he stays in touch with the girls and is actually a better father to them now than he was after they were born... maybe it's because he only has to be a father a couple of weeks over the summer and during some holidays.

I thought about you a lot in those days. I was even thinking of contacting you. I realized what I really wanted was a sensitive man, someone who would support me (emotionally, not financially), understand me, love our children... all the things that I remembered you to be, and imagined you would be.

Remember how you used to cry at movies like Casablanca and An Affair to Remember? I found myself renting them and watching them over and over... Just for the memories.

I didn't trust my own taste anymore, so I didn't go looking for a relationship again. A few dates with a few men. Nothing much. I focused on the girls and my career.

A couple years ago, I was working out of the San Jose office. THCC asked me to move back to Minneapolis. I was frightened - too many horrible memories - but I didn't want to stay in California any longer and the Minneapolis job meant that I would be on track for a VP title. Soon after I arrived, I ran into Fred in the lunchroom. Years ago, he and I were in the training program at THCC together and he was the only person I still knew here. He had just gotten divorced and was ready to start dating again, and I guess I was finally ready too. He does modem sales at the South St. Paul office.

I know you don't follow sports so you don't recognize his last name, Mardred, but his is a "Sports Dynasty" family. Father was a football player, now a well-known coach. Three brothers, all connected with sports somehow in very visible positions. Fred is the black sheep of the family. He's pretty uncoordinated so he never went very far in sports. He seems to be okay at golf, but he's still the butt of a lot of jokes when the family gets together. As the oldest son he was supposed to be the one to carry on the family tradition, and the best he can do is score under par on an 18-hole golf course. It drives him crazy. The one family tradition he still carries on is the drinking. He's a frequent visitor to the 19th hole at the club.

Anyway, we moved in together about a year ago. We were beginning to get very serious, and we thought if we combined our money we could buy into a much better community with better schools for the girls. In retrospect, it was a mistake. We're definitely not on the marriage path anymore, and things are getting a bit difficult between us.

The girls are home till the end of June, then they spend the Summer with their father in Denver. They have been my happiness and salvation.

Yes, I still enjoy a good mystery book, though I don't have much time to read books anymore. I'm up to my eyebrows in reports, memos, industry magazines, and so on. I'll try to pick up the Da Vinci Code and we can talk about it together... just like we used to.

Let's talk soon. I can't talk from home (Fred is the jealous sort - I don't think he realizes we're breaking up yet), and calling from work is hard because everyone can hear everyone, so let's find a time when we can talk comfortably. I'll let you know a good time for me as soon as I work out my travel schedule.

Take care. It's so wonderful hearing from you... you can't imagine how much this means to me, and how happy this makes me.

Sounds like you'll be at the reunion, so I'll try to schedule something so I can be there, too.

Cathy

Re-reading her e-mail, a smile spread across her face and tears welled up in her eyes. She couldn't say if it was because she had just spent a few minutes with her alternate, happier, life, or if she realized the loneliness she had been feeling and how difficult it had been to find someone to share her feelings with.

For all their years apart, he had always been a presence in her thoughts, and in her heart. Despite the miles and seasons that separated them, the photos of him in her mental album could still light a small ember inside. He was always with her. Once again, she asked herself, *Why couldn't we get passed the rape?* And, once again, she wondered, *Why did he have more trouble dealing with the rape than I did?*

"There are lots of rocks on the road of life," she once told her children. "Some are pebbles you can step over, and some are boulders you can't get around.... and, the odd thing is, it's harder than you think to tell the difference." *There's been a lot of detours around a lot of boulders,* Cathy reflected on the years gone by. She began to wonder, *what if...*

Cathy's computer screen went dark.

Grabbing her by the arm and lifting her out of the chair, Fred barked, "You spend too much time reading those stupid e-mails from your idiotic high school friends." In his other hand was the power cord from the. "Get up. I need the computer," he commanded.

Cathy, stood up and meekly obeyed. *How can this be happening to me?* she cried. Wiping the tears from her eyes, she went into the family room and sat down between her daughters. Hugging them closely, they all watched a popular new reality TV show about families (most overweight) joining marine recruits on Parris Island as they go through boot camp together. *Chris, how could you have let this happen to me?*

Chapter 11

Afraid to open Chris' e-mail again at home, she re-read it as soon as she got into the office; two, three, four times. Each time, she sensed his suffering more intensely. He needed her, right now. She knew she needed him. Though there were budgets to prepare, research to study, and memos to write, all she could think of was writing to Chris and asking him, "Are you happy?"

What would life have been like if we had gotten married back then? Would it have worked out? How would our lives have been different? He was so obsessed with being an actor that we would have had to live in New York or Los Angeles, which means I couldn't have taken the job with THCC, and I wouldn't have moved to Minneapolis, and I wouldn't have been.... She stopped thinking about what could have been, because it always brought her back to her reality - a rape, two failed marriages, a horrible home life. A great career instead of a great love. Long hours of work instead of long hours of passion. Exhausting business travel instead of fun family vacations. Doing anything to avoid going home at the end of the day. Dreading weekends instead of looking forward to them.

She probably could have stared at the seventeen inch wide crystal ball on her desk for hours and imagined what her life would have been like, but her 9:00a.m.employee relations problem knocked on her door.

An employee had resigned, and by company policy, every departing employee was required to meet with a member of the Human Resources department before receiving a last check. It was usually quite perfunctory - an exchange of corporate ID and parking pass for the last pay check - and generally was assigned to lower level staff. Occasionally, an ex-employee would vent a bit, usually about not getting a promotion or a bad performance review, and then they would leave. At her level, Cathy rarely conducted Exit Interviews; however, an employee specifically requested meeting with her, so she had agreed. While she was reluctant to do so, her curiosity got the best of her. This employee was located in the New York office, had never worked in Minneapolis, nor had ever worked in any of the Midwestern offices for which she was responsible.

"Hello, Alexander. I'm sorry to hear that you're leaving the company. Please sit down." That this ex-employee paid his own travel expenses to come to Minneapolis to see her, caused her to be concerned that something ugly was lurking in the corridors of the company. Her ego insisted that it was a compliment to her and her reputation throughout the corporation, but part of her brain forewarned that a bomb was about to explode.

"Please call me Alex." He looked around the crowded office for someplace to sit, and soon realized that every chair was piled high with files, reports, boxes, and magazines. "Gee, the HR people in New York have bigger offices."

Embarrassed, Cathy offered, "I'm sorry. Let me make some room for you. I've ordered more file cabinets, but I'm told that non-essential office supplies are on hold until business improves."

He helped her move a couple of heavy storage boxes from the chair onto other storage boxes. "This is highly unusual. I've never had a New York employee request an Exit Interview in Minneapolis... and pay for his own airfare. Can I ask why you wanted to meet with me here?"

Had Alex not decided to go into business, he probably could have had a very successful career as a model for Abercrombie or Calvin Klein or the Gap. A handsome Euro-American, with an Ivy League education, and the broad-shouldered physique of a football quarterback. His posture was that of a marine sergeant and every step declared him a winner. Every single woman in the corridors - the 21 year olds, and the 60 year olds - stopped tapping on her computer keyboard as Alex strode by. He owned the room he walked into, and Cathy suddenly felt smaller.

As she settled back at her desk, she could see the anger in his eyes - he could control it, but it was there, waiting to lunge. "First, let me say, thank you for taking the time to meet with me." He stood up, closed the door, and returned to his seat. "Let me be blunt and say that the reason I came to you for this interview is that the HR people in New York can't be trusted. They've been corrupted." Cathy turned her head to the clock on her desk and thought, *9:03 am. This is going to be a long, rotten day.*

Cathy did what Cathy always did when she couldn't think of anything cogent to say in a meeting - she gestured with her hand, as if to say, "Go on."

Alex didn't immediately seize the opportunity to speak, clearly determining in his mind if she was someone that could be trusted. In that pause, Cathy did the same. Dropping her eyes from him to his personnel file, it was obvious that this was someone who had to be taken seriously. Yale undergraduate. Wharton MBA. Experience at Goldman Sachs and Morgan Stanley.

She wondered if she should ask the company labor lawyer to join the discussion, but she feared Alex wouldn't be forthcoming with his information under those circumstances.

"That article in that business magazine about you was quite complimentary. It said you're on the side of the employee." In the best business school tradition, he was laying the groundwork for what was about to come, probing to see if everything he heard about her was true. "You have an excellent reputation as an honest and concerned person." He paused for a moment. Having committed to divulge the information he so desperately wanted to share, he added, "You have no idea how bad it is in New York."

Her smile and nod of the head expressed her appreciation for his concerns, and then again, she gestured with her hand for him to continue.

"She's a bitch! The Home Computer Company is lucky I'm leaving quietly and going back to Wall Street. I could probably sue for harassment, or stress, or something. The next person in the job might not be so understanding. The reason I'm here today is for the people I'm leaving behind," Alex offered, again in true Business School tradition, seizing the moral authority.

She didn't really know him or his contribution to the company, nor his level of concern for others, but she could neither ignore his criticisms of management, nor accept them as the singular truth. "Let's be honest here," she couldn't allow him to be unchallenged on the mountain of motive. "From your reviews, it looks as if you were just not a good fit for the Business Affairs Department." Quickly scanning his employee file, she searched for the usual clues - denied promotion, denied raises, denied transfers - that usually motivate such comments.

He was being challenged. He didn't expect to be challenged. He thought the decent and good Cathy would welcome his warnings in the spirit that he intended them, for the benefit of those still forced to work in that department for that woman. Holding back his anger, he didn't know if he should just leave and write off all those stories about how employee-oriented she was, or blurt out what he came to say and let the chips fall where they may.

"Before coming here, I was on Wall Street, and I never saw anything as dirty as what goes on here. They're choir boys compared to that shit hole of a department. Excuse my French." His command of the room slid downward into a mud-wrestling match as he struggled with the tiger inside.

"That's a rather strong comment," was all that she could think of to say, feeling that she had to say something.

Months ago she attended a seminar on the new Whistleblower Laws and what her legal obligations were should she become the recipient of an employee's confidence. Unfortunately, she didn't really pay attention, since the seminar coincided with the first abusive behavior from Fred so her thoughts were pre-occupied with what was happening at home. But this clearly fell under that category. In a moment of silence, she quickly glanced at the piles of papers in her office, wondering where the handouts from that seminar were.

"First, let me say that everything you say to me is in confidence. I won't repeat anything to anyone without your permission. So, please tell me."

He nodded, but he knew that before he walked through the door. His shoulders seemed to slump a bit. His eyes drifted downward and focused on a stain in the beige carpet. He clearly was losing his sense of commitment to the truth.

They sat in silence for a few minutes, but it wasn't awkward. Over the years, she had become used to sitting opposite employees, and ex-employees, who were having difficulty coming to terms with what they had just heard about their performance, their futures with the company, the comments of others about them and so on. Once she sat opposite someone for almost an hour with barely a word being spoken.

Her eyes focused on the black Prada briefcase that rested on Alex's lap.

How come I can't afford that briefcase, she thought. *It's beautiful.* I've always wanted one just like that. *How many times have I picked one up, rubbed the leather between my fingers, and almost convinced myself that I deserve something like that. That briefcase must be over a thousand dollars.* She reminded herself that even if Fred hadn't taken control of her money, if she had a thousand dollars to spend, she'd use it to buy the girls new clothes for the Summer or stash it away in their college savings plans.

Since Alex didn't get up and walk out the door, she knew he would eventually tell her what he came to say, it was just a matter of time until he settled his internal struggle. Again, Cathy wondered exactly what to do next. Take notes. Call the corporate labor lawyer. Record the conversation.

Finally, wanting to move the meeting along, in a most understanding tone, she said, "As a human resource person, what I find so strange about what you said is that even though I'm in the Minneapolis office, if there were serious problems with someone at Samantha's level, I would have heard about it... and I never have. You're the first indication I've ever had that there's a problem in the Business Affairs Department."

Raising his eyes to meet hers, for what seemed like the first time in hours, he said, "That's why I came here. The HR people in New York are covering up for her." Committed to getting the truth out, proving that he wasn't just venting or trying to get even with a demanding supervisor, and restoring his self-esteem, he opened the silver latch on his black Prada attaché case, reached inside and began to extract a manila folder.

When it was halfway out of his briefcase he stopped.

He knew he had the proof he needed to get even for all the insults he had endured for three years. He knew he had the information that could force the company to terminate her. He knew the information in his hands would be fodder for the newspapers and business magazines for weeks. Humiliating his former boss would be so delicious. But, for the first time since he collected the information and decided to fly to Minneapolis, he thought about the consequences of revealing such explosive materials. Suddenly saying the words, and handing over the papers, was surprisingly difficult. As he sat in the chair opposite her, his hands grasping the manila folder, perspiration began to form on his forehead.

"Alex, you're making incredible accusations about someone in a very high position. I can't ignore them, but unless you give me some proof, I'm just going to have to write this up as an angry employee venting." He still didn't say anything. Like the bomb squad staring at a suspicious package, she wished she had x-ray vision and could see the papers in the folder.

While her curiosity about one of the most senior people in the company was intense, if she was honest with herself, she would rather he left without saying anything substantial or giving her any evidence of misdeeds. If he left now, he was just an angry employee who could be forgotten. If he went forward from here, she could be in the middle of corporate crisis, and right now, she didn't need another crisis in her life.

Dropping the folder back into his attaché case and closing the silver latch, he broke the silence with voice of defeat, "I came here prepared to tell you everything, but I realize that every situation involves someone who is still in the department. If she even gets an inkling that someone working for her talked to HR, there'll be a witch hunt. Heads will roll. The only reason anyone stays in that place is because the economy is so bad, and finding another job is difficult."

His face wore both the pain having to internalize his hatred for his former manager, and disappointment in himself that he wasn't strong enough to say what he came to say. "People have kids, they have mortgages. I can't do this to them. If it was a better economy, no one would stay there longer than a week. As much as I hate her, I don't want anyone getting fired because of me. They're good people in a very bad situation. You have to help them." He removed his hand from the lock on his attaché case, apologized for taking her time, and stood up to leave. Still good-looking, still able to make the women in the corridors swoon, but he no longer had the posture of a marine sergeant.

Lassoing him with her words she said, "How can I help them if you won't help me." More silence. "You're leaving the company. What about something that happened to you?" The little she had heard thus far had unnerved her. She really didn't want to know more, but she had a need to know, a conflict caused by two decades in HR.

"I can't believe I'm saying this, but I'm frightened that she can get to me outside the company." Distressed by his own lack of commitment and strength, by his loss of principle, that winning smile sank into a sorrowful frown. "This truly is confidential. I'm going to trust you. I'm going back to Goldman Sachs. No one knows that but you. I told everyone I was going to work for a small investment bank in Boston.

Samantha used to work at Goldman, and still has lots of friends there. I'm just hoping one of them doesn't mention me to her."

He surrendered to the futility of this venture. "This was a stupid thing to do. I'm sorry I wasted your time." He put his hands on the doorknob and began to turn it, but stopped. He just couldn't let Samantha beat him, yet again. After three year of harangues, he just couldn't let her escape unscathed. After all, he was an ivy league graduate. He had worked at the premiere investment banks in the world. He had made deals involving billions of dollars.

Standing just a little bit straighter, he half turned back to Cathy, not really looking her in the eye and in the low, clandestine voice that an informer would use when sharing information with a foreign agent, he said, "Follow the money."

"What?"

Pondering his own words for a second, he smiled. As silly as it sounded, he was giving her an excellent clue. More confidently, he repeated, "Follow the money."

"You have to give me more than that. What money? She's involved in dozens of deals a year and is responsible for billions of dollars of revenue. What money? Is she taking bribes? Paying out bribes? Give me something."

Relieved that he didn't reveal any secrets that could be traced back to him or any of his former co-workers, but delighted that he cast some doubts about his former supervisor, he was once again the poster boy of a confident American youth. "I can't say more than that. If you just follow the money, you'll find what you're looking for." Opening the door to leave, he extended his hand to her.

Under her breath, she mumbled, "Great, I have my own Deep Throat."

"Who?"

Shaking his hand, she added, "Never mind. It was before your time.

Thank you for coming in. I don't know what I can do with this information, but everything you said will be held in confidence. Can I call you if I have any questions?"

Stepping through the doorway, and into the lusting gaze of all the women on the tenth floor, he said, "No, I just want to be gone." He turned, looked her in the eye, and added, "By the way, my reviews weren't always bad. Records can be altered. They're just electronic dots in a computer memory filled with trillions of other electronic dots." With that he strode down the corridor, still a winner, still with a bright future.

"Follow the money," she repeated to herself. No inspiration struck her. Considering the amount of money that passed through the Business Affairs Department that was like saying look for a teardrop in Niagara Falls. *What could she do with that piece of advice? Besides, she didn't have access to any financial information from that department other than compensation, recruiting fees, severance packages, and other personnel related expenses.*

Was Samantha getting kickbacks from sub-contactors? She made well over a million dollars a year in salary and bonuses. Would she really risk that for an extra fifty or hundred thousand? No, that doesn't make sense.

Was she filling the payroll with friends and relatives? Doubtful. Her department had a great deal of responsibility. She couldn't risk performance problems by hiring incompetent friends and relatives?

Was she sidestepping the official bidding procedures and awarding contracts to friends and relatives? Gee, that would be unique in this company. Let's start the investigation with the President's brother-in-law.

Besides, Alex was talking about the department being a living nightmare. Things like awarding contracts to relatives or taking kickbacks don't affect anybody in the department. No, this has to be something involving the personnel in the department. Where does money and performance intersect in the Business Affairs Department?

Is this an employee venting? Is he a whistleblower? His performance reviews weren't very good, so maybe he was just getting back at her. He said his reviews have been altered. I doubt that. That truly would be against company policy and would involve access to quite a bit of information that lots of other people see. I'm sure Samantha has access, and truth be told, if anyone could do it, she could. I have to admit, his poor performance reviews are surprising considering his credentials and references. Goldman Sachs is taking him back. They wouldn't do that if he wasn't a top quality performer. What should I do? Bring someone from legal into this discussion? But then I would have to identify Alex and I swore not to.

If Samantha is so odious, why is this the first time I'm hearing about this?

In the twenty five years she had been with The Home Computer Company she had heard several thousand complaints by employees about hundreds of bosses. But this was the first accusation she had ever heard against someone so high up in the organization that the very mention of legal problems could send the stock plummeting.

Entering her password (recently changed to Kennedy), she began searching the employment records of the Business Affairs Department since Alex was hired. As 507 names and employee numbers popped onto the screen she mumbled, "It's only 9:30 am. Is it time to go home yet?"

Chapter 12

The "follow the money" advice mummified as she dealt with the daily flood of problems: this employee showed up drunk today, that employee is wearing a revealing tank top in the office, where are the resumes for the audit supervisor's position, can you call that candidate and tell her that $55,000 is the final offer, and so on, and so on, and so on.

An hour didn't pass before she received a call from the Senior Vice President of Human Resources in New York. Minneapolis didn't report to New York, but since he was a level higher than her, and since on the corporate organization chart he had a dotted line (as opposed to a solid line) responsibility to her department, she had to treat him as if he was an immediate supervisor.

"Good morning, Bob." She thought that Bob was a good name for him. Both in physical stature and personality he was reminiscent of one of those figurines that that sat on the dashboard of a car and bobbed up and down with every bump in the road.

"How did your meeting go with Alex?" Fourth of July fireworks exploding in her office couldn't have set off more alarms than the mere fact that he asked about her meeting. Not only were Exit Interviews with employees so routine that Bob wouldn't even know about an employee having one, but what really put her on alert was that Bob never really cared about the employees at all. The only reason he got into Human Resources – and, unfortunately, he was proved right - was that he thought a man in a typically woman's field would rise up the corporate ladder more quickly. He also like the fact that HR was not taken as seriously by the corporation – after all, it wasn't sales or manufacturing – and the chances of being fired for lack of performance were minimal.

"Okay. Pretty typical." Until she determined what was going on, she decided to be cautious with the information. "Just a lot of venting."

"Even so, I'd be interested in knowing exactly what he said. It's highly unusual for an employee to pay his own way from New York to Minneapolis just to vent. He could have done that here." Bob's reputation in the company was as Management's Lackey and he rarely knew the name of anyone below the vice president's level.

"Actually, it's not so strange. He has family here, so it was just an excuse to make the trip. He thought by doing it this way it was tax deductible."

"It still doesn't make sense." His voice was insistent, but he knew he couldn't push too hard without being obvious.

Manufacturing a tone of extreme irritation, she burst out, "To be honest, Bob," which she wasn't about to be, "he used quite a number of expletives which I was pretty offended by. I'm not a prude, but I have no intention of repeating them. I was quite surprised that someone with his education would talk that way, especially to a woman, but he had a lot of anger he wanted to get out. I'll be putting my comments in his employee file." This would also give her an excuse to review his employee file to see if any data had been altered.

Realizing he wasn't going to get any more information from her, he changed the subject. "I'd like you to come to New York next week so we can talk about some hiring issues." He could hear the surprise in her silence. She was trying to find some polite way of saying, I don't work for you, and was groping for just the right words when he added, "It's okay, I've cleared it with George. Let's do it over lunch, so you can fly in and out the same day."

Immediately she responded, "Monday is my only clear day," which wasn't true. Within a nano-second she plotted out the weekend to arrange a respite from her dilemma. *I'll tell Fred it's an 8:00am breakfast meeting so I have to stay over Sunday night. I'll catch a three o'clock flight, which means I leave for the airport around noon by the time I shower and pack. Thank God, Sunday is taken care of. I'll tell the girls to go visit friends for the weekend. Glad that the two-day weekend was cut down to one, she turned her head back to the computer screen.*

"Why don't you come to my office around 11:00 so we can talk a bit, then we'll go to lunch." Before she could confirm, he hung up.

Pondering the morning's events, her eyes turned back to the open database on the computer and the employee roster of the Business Affairs Department. "Five hundred and seven employees. I didn't think the department was that large."

Pulling up the company's census report, she scrolled down to Business Affairs. Under the "Approved Positions" column, it read 116. Under the "Current Openings" column, it read 17. "My God, a three hundred percent turnover in three years! That's absurd. And in this economy, to have a 15% vacancy rate. Resumes are pouring in by the truckload. We can't open them fast enough. Alex is right. Something is terribly wrong. But where's the money?"

Without a doubt, she would have to review each employee's file. But what seemed like a tedious task, actually gave her reason to smile. This was going to take days, if not weeks, to accomplish, and she really didn't have the time to dedicate to it with all her other responsibilities.

"Oh, well," she said with a happy voice to her reflection on the computer screen, "I guess I'm going to have to work very late, every night, and probably be very exhausted when I get home."

Chapter 13

Scanning the internet for new job openings, Chris studied Monsterboard.com, Hotjobs.com, AdvertisingJobs.com, and MarketingPeople.com. Despite the nuances and cleverly written job descriptions, it was clear that everyone wanted to hire someone who was young and aggressive. No one wanted anyone with lots of experience or with proven credentials. Young, aggressive, and cheap, that's all anyone wants these days.

Maybe I bought myself a month with the Big Lie, he guessed, *but that wasn't much time to find a position that would pay the same salary. And, with K&Q on my resume it's virtually impossible to find a position at another ad agency.* Scrolling from job listing to job listing, he kept thinking, *there must be some company out there that never heard of K&Q and is looking for a Director of Marketing*. But, after hours of searching, even he was beginning to believe that was impossible.

The phone range and he absent-mindedly he picked it up. It was Cassandra (Casey, as she recently decided to call herself), a sales rep from a local television station. He had met her years ago when he was handling the advertising for a bank, but it had been a long time since he ran commercials on her station.

He always snickered a bit when he saw her at an industry function. "Cassandra" should be the name of someone who was exotic and attractive. This Cassandra was quite overweight and not very attractive. The once a year that they chatted for five minutes at an industry Christmas party was just about all the time they needed to catch up with each other.

So, when he realized it was her, he could only imagine that she heard about a job and she wanted to share it with him. With a bursting delight that he never used when seeing her at a holiday party, he belted out, almost as if in song, "Casey, it's so good to hear from you."

Caught by surprise, she was equally effusive with her delight in speaking with him, which made him doubt she was calling to do him a favor.

After the usual pleasantries, Casey got down to business, and his hopes of fleeing K&Q were shot down like a pheasant in hunting season. With manufactured Southern charm (she was from New York) she used with clients, she asked, "How come you didn't tell me you were planning to go on television this year," she chastised jokingly. "I guess we never really got around to talking about business at the Christmas Party."

His eyes popped wide open. Caught off-guard, he could only mumble, "I was just hoping to get a free lunch from you. Er... how'd you find out about my client using television?" Perspiration erupted from every pore of his body like water from a fire hydrant, and suddenly he had trouble breathing and needed to loosen his shirt and tie.

"I have my sources. I told you I was good at what I do."

"You certainly are. Seriously, how did you hear about it?"

Proud of her own investigative capabilities, she bragged, "Your media people contacted my office requesting demographic information for our stations with emphasis on women, 18 to 49. It didn't take a genius to figure out it wasn't for your bowling alley client."

Fuck! This thing is escalating out of control.

Excited to finally have a television client, the media department was calling reps all over the country to let them know they still existed - and to get as many free lunches as they could.

Shit! I can't tell her. Her boss knows about it by now and he'll be expecting a sales report. Fuck! This isn't what I had in mind. Actually, I didn't have anything in mind, except saving my ass, and giving me time to get out of here.

As Casey started rattling off demographics and advertising rates, Chris' mind returned to the impending nuclear explosion he had set in motion. Speaking of time, he wondered, how much time - and money - the agency was spending on this presentation. If those creative jerks got carried away with themselves, the investment could be $50,000 or more in time and materials. Mack will be out for blood when the client rejects the commercial. Looking skyward, he prayed, "Sandy, I'm counting on you and that bunch of hacks you call a Creative Department to screw up here. Don't let me down and suddenly come up with a good idea."

Casey interrupted his musings, "So are you going to tell me how big the budget is?"

What do I say? It's confidential. I really wish I could throw a number at you, but I can't. The silence on the other end of the line was laden with disappointment, as if Rhett just offended Scarlett's honor by saying a bad word.

Afraid that being overly secretive would cast doubt on the story he hastily added, "The client is unsophisticated about advertising and it'll be the first time they go on air, so they're nervous about exactly how much to commit right now. We're doing a bottom-up analysis right now and we'll give them a number in a couple of weeks and hope they buy it."

Bothered that he wouldn't share with her, and wanting to prove that she was well connected and couldn't be toyed with, Casey cut him off with, "Well, your media department told me you're going into the top ten markets, so we know you're dealing with at least $10 million here."

Oh my God! Oh my God! Is that what people think? I've got to put a stop to this now! As calmly as he could, he offered, "I hope you're right, Casey. It may grow to that, but right now, it's just a test... in one or two markets. If it works we'll roll it out over time.

The flood poring out from under each of his arms was beginning to meet in the center of his chest, and he grabbed yet another tissue to wipe his face. *"Ruined" was the only word that came to mind. Cars, condo, job... all gone. He could see the video of himself on Youtube, walking up and down Wilshire Boulevard, wearing a frayed blue suit, carrying a sign saying, "Please help me. Ex-ad exec who lost his client!"*

"But if it works, and I'm certain your creative people can do a good job..."

He stopped his angst-laden self-pity long enough to laugh and say to himself, *You don't know our creative people.*

"...then it can grow to that size budget." Casey continued. "Besides, you really should consider my station for your test. We can do a lot of tie-ins with local magazines to help guarantee a successful launch. I think it's a good idea to lay the groundwork for the future now."

Yeah, groundwork, like six-feet under. This thing has taken on a life of its own, and I can't stop it. I'd better make sure Sandy gets the blame.

While plotting Sandy's ultimate failure, Casey was saying things like, Cornwall Media would do everything they could to aid the success of Envira Tampons; they were confident they could deliver the right audience for the product; they were willing to work with K&Q to develop the most effective advertising; and so on, and so on.

Finally, to his relief, the other phone in his office, his client phone (which was a Mickey Mouse phone) began to ring. "I've got take this. It's the client. Good talking to you, Casey. I'll call you when I know something about the budget."

She was saying something about going to lunch, but he just dropped the phone in the cradle. He was wondering how he was going to break the news to his client that that they were going to spend $10 million on advertising.

Shifting his eyes to the caller ID on the phone, he realized it wasn't his client, it was Susan.

Chapter 14

"Am I going to see you, tomorrow?" she asked.

Susan. What to do about Susan?

Of the seven extra-marital relationships Chris had, five were woman who had never had an affair with a married man other than he. One of the reasons for the lengthy TBA was the long seduction process he had to live through in order for his lovers to overcome the morality dilemmas they were encountering for the first time in their lives. Susan clearly was experienced in extra-marital relationships, and while he and she both declared that this was the first time, it was pretty obvious by the speed with which the affair progressed that neither was new to cheating on a spouse.

In absolute fear of being alone, Susan was desperate not to lose Chris. Without him, all she had was a mentally and physically absent husband, and two selfish kids who sucked the energy out of her like a vacuum cleaner. Without Chris, there was no one to make her feel like a woman, there was no one to make her feel loved and needed, there was no one who cared about her happiness. She couldn't lose him. Not now.

As many times as Chris said he wouldn't go back to Susan, he always did. Her willingness to do absolutely anything to please him was addictive, and despite all the tears and arguments, he didn't want to live without that. But today, for some reason, it didn't seem right. He knew that Cathy would be so disappointed in him if she knew about his affair, and he didn't want to do anything that would upset his renewed relationship with her.

He couldn't let himself believe that they would be lovers again, yet all his emotions from long ago rose to the surface, like a chest of hidden treasures that finally escaped the hold of a sunken Spanish galleon. Inside this treasure chest was everything he once was, everything he once hoped his life would be, everything he once thought was important. It was who he once was, not who he is now. As he opened the Treasure Chest with a key named Cathy, inside was love, and kindness, and laughter, and ideals, and dreams, and good intentions. *Would they ever share vows of spiritual commitment again, or ever speak of their two bodies, their two souls, being one again?* It was out of his hands, but he knew, it was with Cathy that he wanted to be.

Susan was crying. He hated the crying when the affairs ended, but there was always crying, lots of it. In the iPod of his mind, he could hear the words of Paul Simon's song, *50 Ways to Leave Your Lover*:

You just slip out the back, Jack

Make a new plan, Stan

You don't need to be coy, Roy

Just get yourself free

Hop on the bus, Gus ... (Hey, Paul, this is L.A. No one takes the bus here.)

It really didn't matter what he said now. Affairs always ended the same way. When he ended his first affair, he used some of those stupid television lines like, "It's not you, it's me. You're a beautiful woman. I'm not good enough for you." But it made no difference, just saying "It's over," seemed to have the same effect.

Begging him to come over one more time, Susan said it was too abrupt, too cold, but genuinely feeling her pain, he whispered, "I can't."

As she ran out of tears, the only thing Susan said was that she wished he had told her this on Monday instead of today, since it would have given her a few days to compose herself before her husband got home, now she has only a few hours. Then she added, in complete resignation to the reality of her life, "I'll just tell him that I just found out that someone from my aerobics class is dying of cancer."

Just like that, it was over. There was no Susan any more.

Not really harboring any hope of an affair with Cathy, he only could see his life with Melanie in front of him, and he wondered how long he could endure an existence without the hope of being touched and of feeling loved.

Chapter 15

Cathy didn't get home till almost 10:00 p.m. She slowly climbed the stairs. Having mapped the land mines that would explode with creaks or groans, she moved upward. Sometimes stepping to the left, sometimes stepping to the right. The television in the living room was still on, and Fred was asleep on the couch. As she neared the top of the staircase, she heard his slurring, raspy voice, with his dreaded pronouncement. "I've been waiting for you to get home. I'll be upstairs in a minute."

Oh, God, no! Please not tonight! She began to cry. *Not tonight. Not again.* Gripping the handrail, she wondered if she could pretend to slip down the staircase and fake being in pain. *Would she actually hurt herself?* And then she sighed, *Would my being in pain even discourage him from having sex? Probably not.*

Climbing the last few steps, she moved less cautiously, but slower, because now she was burdened with a ton of tears. *Not tonight, please. Maybe some other night. But not tonight, please.*

She shrunk three inches as she imagined the yells, the slaps, the accusations, if she didn't let his coarse hands touch her breasts... his alcohol-soaked lips press against hers... his penis push into her body. If she didn't pretend to enjoy, it would be far worse.

How did my life come to this, she begged herself for an answer. The girls were safe, and as long as he didn't touch or threaten them, she could live with what he wanted to do to her.

Dutifully getting undressed, she slid naked under the sheets of their bed, and waited.

There was a loud thud. He was on the first step. Then, another thud. He had been drinking a lot tonight. It sounded like he was struggling with the steps more than usual. Thud.

Please slip on the stairs and kill yourself, she prayed. It was an evil prayer to wish someone dead, so it never came to pass.

Thud.

I should just go out there, she plotted, *and push him down the stairs. Just as he reaches the top step I could probably kick him in the chest and send him flying down the stairs.*

Thud.

What if he didn't die from the fall? What if he grabbed my leg and took me with him? What if he caught the handrail and didn't slide down the stairs, but attacked me instead? What if he decided to take his vengeance out on the girls?

Another loud thud vibrated through the room. He was on the eighth step.

Night after night, more often drunk than not, he climbed the staircase to their bedroom and made her nights sleepless with terror. Even the nights he wasn't drunk or didn't want sex were filled with their own terror. If something was bothering him, if she rolled over and crowded him, if he wanted to touch her and she pretended to be asleep, he would find her with his feet, shove her out of their bed, and she would have to sleep on the floor.

Fortunately, he spent many nights passed out on the couch, and those were the only nights she slept comfortably. But this wasn't going to be one of those nights. As drunk as he was, he wanted his pleasures.

She shifted her body to be a little closer to the edge. *Maybe he would slip off the mattress as he climbed on top of her, and maybe, he would bang his head on the night table.*

Sliding her head off the pillow to the very edge of the mattress, she hoped he wouldn't try to kiss her on the lips, just push inside her, cum, and then get out.

Thud.

He's on the top step now. If I'm going to do it, I have to do it right now. Just kick my leg out, hard and fast. No one would know that I did it. Everyone would think he just slipped because he was drunk.

I have to do it. Right now. Right now, get out of bed before he reaches the top step and kick him dead center in his chest. I'm going to do it. Right now.

But it was too late.

On the landing now, he shuffled along the wooden floor to the bedroom… far too drunk to even lift his feet up. Leaning against the wall for support, he left picture after picture askew to be straightened in the morning. Something fell to the floor, but there was no sound of glass breaking. *Too bad*, she thought, *he could have cut himself on the broken glass and bleed to death.*

If only I could just lie here and let him do what he wanted to do, it wouldn't be so terrible, she cried. But she couldn't do that. If she didn't "fully participate" and pretend to be enjoying it, he would get violent. She touched her head where he struck her months ago, teaching her that lesson.

Opening the door, he staggered towards the bed, dropping his clothes onto the floor for her to pickup in the morning. As he fell into bed and pressed against her, she touched his penis to make it hard, just as he said he wanted her to do, and he put his greasy French-fry-and-ketchup-stained fingers inside her. No matter how much she tried, she just couldn't get wet for him anymore, which caused much shouting, many tears and excruciating pain in the past as he shoved his way in anyway.

Now, before he climbed into bed, she rubbed lubricants in her vagina so it didn't hurt as much when he pushed his way into her.

As he shoved his whiskey-laden tongue into her mouth, it was hard for her to believe that she once looked forward to pressing her naked body against his. Now, each thrust of his penis was no different than the rape and beating of many years ago.

Touching her thumb to the ring she wore on the finger where a wedding band would be, she felt the letters that spelled out Kennedy High School. Soon after the e-mails began, she looked for and found her high school graduation ring in a box in the cellar. Sliding the ring onto her finger (and delighted that it still fit), she wore it to bed, twisted around so he wouldn't notice. It helped her focus on a happier time, so her mind could be in the past, while her body was being violated in the here and now. She groaned often so he would think she was enjoying what he did, but since he was so obsessed with his own pleasure he never appreciated that they were groans of torture.

Disgusted with having to kiss him, and let his tongue into her mouth, she gently put her hands on the sides of his head and moved his mouth to her breasts. She moaned the loudest when he did that, hoping he would think it gave her the most pleasure. In a different way it did, since it meant she didn't have to look at or smell him.

More than being inside her vagina, he enjoyed oral sex, so for fear of not satisfying him and invoking his rage, she did what disgusted her most, and put his penis in her mouth, massaging it with her tongue. As much as he wanted her to, she would never swallow his cum, and she spit into tissues she kept on her side of the bed. Once he held his hand over her mouth, all the while laughing, trying to force her to swallow his semen, but she spit it into his hand and he was so disgusted, he never did that again. Since he wrote it off as a "girl thing," he never got violent about it; besides, he got what he wanted.

What's fair is fair, he always said after she sucked on him, so he would slide down her body and put his tongue in her vagina. Without a doubt, this satisfied her the most, since he was down there and not making her kiss him. While he licked her thighs and put his tongue inside her, she usually stared up at the ceiling and tried to calculate how much cyanide she would have to put in her vagina to poison him, and if that would leave traces of her DNA so the police could trace it back to her.

If there was any saving grace, it was that he was quick to cum, even when he was drunk, so the whole experience - including foreplay and oral sex - never lasted more than ten minutes. He was always a bit embarrassed at how quickly his penis would shrink after ejaculating, so he didn't want to prolong the sex too long afterwards for fear that she would want another orgasm and he would be humiliated at not being able to satisfy her.

As soon as he was done, she jumped out of bed and headed to the bathroom. He never enjoyed "snuggling" afterwards, so it didn't bother him that the first thing she would do after sex was brush her teeth, and then take a bath. He mumbled something like, "I love you," then rolled over and went to sleep.

Sitting on the edge of the bathtub, the tears in her eyes flowed freely again, one more time she asked herself, *What terrible thing did I do to be punished like this?*

Chapter 16

"I feel so badly for all those women," Melanie said quietly before she inserted the fork into her mouth. "Tomorrow I'll send a donation to the shelter."

Tonight, just like every other weeknight, she and Chris ate their dinner in front of the television, jumping from one cable news show to another. At some point, years ago, when there didn't seem to be anything left to say to each other, the TV morphed from being the evening's entertainment into a garrulous dinner guest that filled the air with vivid stories of destruction, debauchery, and despair.

"Typical politician," he shouted out. "I can't believe he said that." It sounded as if they were talking to each other, but anyone listening would quickly realize that most of their words were directed towards the electronic guest in the corner.

As they finished dinner, rather than just sitting back and watching a discussion about the President's appointment of some judge or a bill in front of Congress, Melanie reached forward and, picking up the remote control, turned the TV off.

Worried that Susan called her office, he tried to look more surprised and less anxious.

"Can we talk about something?" she asked. *This is a good sign*, he thought, *She's not just launching into an attack. Maybe this isn't about Susan.* But, as always, he was a bit wary. All too often, she brought the office home, and he never knew if the role he was supposed play that evening was that of the loving husband or the opposing counsel.

She seemed to have trouble speaking, which was quite unusual for her, and there actually was some pain in her voice, which was also unusual. As a defense lawyer (in the courtroom, and all too often at home), she was always aggressive and always on the attack. She was expert in ferreting out human vulnerabilities and undermining the credibility of the victims who had already suffered humiliation, financial ruin, or mental/physical torment. She searched for holes in stories, inconsistencies, opportunities to obfuscate the truth, and she didn't have the luxury of being soft, tender, and human… unless it would be a useful tactic.

"I don't like what's happening to me, anymore. I don't like what's happening to us." She was sincere, but her training as a courtroom litigator taught her to pause long enough after a critical statement to allow the effect to settle in. His training as an actor taught him to recognize when she was in her "courtroom role."

"What do you mean?" After he said it, he thought his tone was a bit too casual in response to her sincerity, so he leaned forward and reached for her hand.

"This." She pointed to a never-shrinking pile of folders and documents that she looked through, even as they watched television. "I'm always working. We're never together anymore… in any sense of the word. We're leading completely separate lives. We don't communicate anymore."

We don't communicate anymore. We don't communicate anymore. That was the one phrase that ninety percent of her clients used to explain why they wanted a divorce. We don't communicate anymore. She'd repeated it to him a thousand times about a thousand cases. We don't communicate anymore. We don't communicate anymore.

But then it occurred to him, *Does she want a divorce because we're not communicating?*

After all these years of marriage, for all the women he professed to love and swore he would marry if he was free, for all the claims that he would not marry Melanie again if he could do it all over again, he wasn't sure how he felt. He wasn't sure if he really wanted to be "free" to date lots of women, to come home to an empty house, to marry someone else and start getting used to living with a new person.

"Are you telling me you want a divorce?"

He wasn't thinking how his voice should sound, but it must have been appropriate since Melanie, realizing the message she was sending, and delighted to see his concerned reaction, bent over and kissed him with the comforting words, "No. No, of course I don't want a divorce. I can't imagine being married to anyone but you." Her eyes filled with tears, and he kissed her several times on her lips, cheeks and forehead.

"I think what's really disturbing me most, is the absolutely negative environment I work in. My clients are not like us. Everyone hates the person they're married to. They steal from each other. They cheat on each other. They beat or torment each other. They're always giving me instructions to squeeze every drop of blood out of their spouse or make sure they don't get a penny of my money." She covered her eyes with her hands, as if she wanted to hide the memories of all her clients from her view. Tears rolled down her face, slipping out from beneath her hands and dripping onto her blouse.

He moved to sit next to her, and wrapping his arm around her, he realized how little they touched anymore.

"I think I'm bringing too much of that home, and I don't mean just the work. I mean the anger and the hostility, too." She bent over to rest her head on his shoulder. It was actually a rather awkward and uncomfortable position, but the gesture was sincere and he didn't want to budge. *Maybe we should go into the bedroom and have sex*, he thought.

"Maybe you need to expand your practice to include other types of law." He thought it was appropriate that he say something positive. "You once talked about getting into adoption law, helping to bring loving families and needy babies together."

Obviously it was the wrong thing to say. Clearly she was looking for one type of response and she didn't get it.

Separating from him slightly so there bodies weren't touching so tightly, she said in frustration, "It's not that easy. After all these years, you can't just jump into another field the same way you jump from one advertising client to another. The law is complex and it takes years to learn the nuances of each field. No. I was thinking of taking some time off, and just sitting on the beach with that stack of novels on my night table. I haven't done that in years. Or, maybe taking a job at a Legal Aid Society. It would mean a lot less money, but at least I would be helping people who really need it."

Whether it was the worry of how a smaller income would affect their lifestyle, or how his extra-marital affairs would be affected by the decreased freedom, or how having her around more often would affect the simple things he did like lingering over coffee in the morning, he didn't like the idea of her reducing her working hours.

"Well, that might not be a good idea just yet," he squeaked, squishing his face because he knew he was about to destroy her dream of changing her circumstances.

Years ago she had stopped listening to his redundant complaints about K&Q, and about the advertising profession in general, he stopped confiding in her. In fact, he was working on the Envira Tampons account for over six months before he happened to mention it to her, and if asked right now, it was doubtful that she would be able to name his client.

He proceeded to detail recent events: Barry Balin ("They were such a nice couple."), the Mission Critical Moment ("I don't know why you listened to him so much. I never thought he was that smart."), the Big Lie ("I never realized that television was so important to ad agencies."), and most importantly, Mack's reaction to the Big Lie and the investment the agency was making into the development of a speculative advertising campaign ("I can't believe you did something so stupid.").

"I suspect I'll be out of a job by the end of the month," he meekly confessed. "So reducing your income may not be the best thing to do right now. I'm sorry that the timing's so bad, but everything seems so out of control right now."

As if he was responsible for everything that has gone wrong in the world, she blamed him for thwarting her plans to get relief from the daily venom that spews between her clients and their former loved ones. Disappointed that he was forcing her back into the cauldron of bubbling hatred, she turned her back to him without saying another word, opened a client's folder, and began to read.

Hurt that she couldn't empathize with his plight, the same way she expected him to empathize with hers, he whispered to himself, "Well, I guess that resolves the issue of whether or not we're going to have sex tonight."

Chapter 17

"Wake up, Mom. Wake up," JamieErin pleaded at 5:30 a.m.

A small, but firm, hand shook Cathy like an earthquake from her sleep. Since Fred came in late last night and passed out on the couch, she was enjoying her slumber and really didn't want to surrender it so easily.

Seeing she was getting some results, the fourteen-year-old flute player, wearing a red and blue uniform reminded her mother, "You promised to take me to band practice."

Yes, she did. She did promise. Not that she wouldn't have taken her daughter to marching band practice at 5:30 a.m. anyway, but when she agreed, she assumed it gave her an excuse to get out of bed, and away from Fred, very early. She hadn't expected to be sound asleep and having wonderful dreams about people she called friends thirty years ago.

Throwing a coat over her pajamas, and without make-up, she and her oldest daughter set forth in the chilly, pre-dawn darkness and headed for the high school's football field. Cathy's first thought was, thank God no one is going to see me looking like this.

Then it occurred to her... *Oh my God! I have to stay so I can drive her home. People are going to see me looking like this.* The only comfort was that none of the other mothers attending the pre-school marching band practice had time to make themselves more presentable to the outside world. Well, most mothers didn't have time to prep before coming to band practice. *That little drummer boy's mother must wake up 4 a.m. to put on all that make-up.*

The Lewis & Clark High School Marching Band was actually quite good and the reason for the pre-dawn practice was upcoming state championships. They already won the Northern Suburbs round, and if they beat the other 10 schools in the statewide championship, they would go to the nationals, which were being held at Disneyland.

With her coat tightly wrapped around her pajamas, she climbed the stands to watch the rehearsal. Noticing Pete Cruzatte, the marching band's leader, she sat down next to him on the cold metal benches. Since Cathy was somewhat generous with her donations to the band (even Fred didn't mind donating to them since it got the kids out of the house), she had frequent occasion to talk to him at donor's dinners or cocktail receptions.

Just as Cathy sat down, the band shouted out, "This is dedicated to Lucy Lu."

A very odd tradition began among the Explorers, as LCHS's marching band and football team were called, ever since Pete began leading the band. Every performance was dedicated to "Lucy Lu." There had never been a Lucy Lu among the faculty or administration of LCHS, nor was there ever a Lucy Lu among the alumni who donated to the school. And, there had never been a heroine of history named Lucy Lu at the city, state, or national levels.

"Who is Lucy Lu and why is every performance dedicated to her?" Cathy asked.

From the first day he started the tradition, he had been asked that question by the faculty, school administration, and parents, and he always gave a quick, practiced, fabricated response, "She was the person who recognized my talent when I was very young and taught me music, never charging me a penny because she knew my parents couldn't afford it. She died of a rare disease at a very early age, and on the last day of her life I promised her to dedicate my music to her."

The story played well and everyone accepted it, so he re-told it every year as new students joined his band and their parents quizzed him on the tradition.

But he liked Cathy since she never asked for (or demanded, as most parents do) any special favors for her daughter, so he told her the true story. "About ten years ago, I was a member of a band called the Ajeans - it was named after the leader, Andrew Jeans. I never liked the name, but we were a fairly successful, though unimaginative band. We were big on the Bar Mitzvah and wedding circuit.

"Let's face it, how many times can you play *Memories* and still care if it comes out sounding alright. So, just to stay sane, I asked Andy if I could write some music for the band, just to liven things up. I never wrote any music before, but we were all dying a slow death from boredom. Andy he always responded, 'Let's not tinker with the toys. We have a good thing going here.'

"Meanwhile my wife, Pamela, you met her at the Christmas party..."

"Sure, doesn't she teach classical literature here," Cathy interjected, delighted that she could remember a detail like that.

"Good memory," Pete acknowledged, and continued his story. "As much as she likes LCHS, she wasn't very happy here. After all, let's be honest, how many high school kids want to read *The Iliad* and *The Odyssey?* It's an intelligent student body, but reading books, as they say, written by a bunch of old, dead white guys is not high on their list. But, as you know, by law, every student is required to take some literature courses and because of scheduling some have no choice but to take Pam's classical literature course.

"Well, one night over dinner I'm complaining about not being given the chance to write music for band, and she's complaining about her students not being interested in what she's teaching. So, I open my big mouth and say, 'Of course, they don't care about the fall of Troy or the Peloponnesian Wars. These are high school kids. They care about music and dancing. You should use music and movement to teach them about the Greeks and the Trojans.'

"To which Pam, replied 'Okay, Big Shot, here's your chance to show us what you got. Write some music that will teach my students about the Trojan War."

Cathy smiled as her daughter's complaints about the "old book" reading list echoed in her ears.

"The next day, I was going to just bring home some flowers and eat a lot of crow, when a tune started running through my head. All day long I'm humming and tinkering on the keyboard. So I start to write it down. It's sort of a combination of Latin jazz and hip-hop. So, while I'm waiting for Pam one day, I'm playing the music on one of the school pianos and, Debbie, one of the dance teachers really got into it and asked me if she could choreograph the piece using two classes of advanced students who were aching to do something original and modern. Suddenly and surprisingly, the music became much larger than just telling some kids about the fall of Troy, it became a school event where they sold tickets and we played several times to capacity crowds in the school auditorium."

"That's a big space," Cathy noted.

"Tell me about it. The school's making money, Pam's stature rises, and student population is happier. I don't see a dime, which was okay, but over the next couple of years, I write four more pieces. It was a good distraction from playing Hava Nagila at Bar Mitzvahs. Well, about the same time, Joe Palamedes, the current band leader..."

"Is he related to Dr. Palamedes, the school's President?"

"His brother. And because of that he was under a great deal of pressure. Under his guidance the marching band had dwindled to just 29 members, and they weren't very good. Anyone who could play an instrument and not miss too many notes got into the band. Forget style, forget energy, forget technique. Play passably, and you got into the band.

"LCHS's marching band became a real joke among state schools. It became known as the smallest marching band in the state, and at football games, they couldn't even spell out the letters LCHS. At this point, the best they could do was an "L" with a tuba or two leftover. Most schools would have abandoned the program at this point, but now Dr. Palamedes is on the hot seat with the state education department for hiring his brother. He figures he has to make the band work, just to prove that it's a real academic activity. Joe clearly couldn't do it, so he started looking around and, poof, there I am filling auditoriums."

"So who's Lucy Lu?" Cathy asked, a bit frustrated that this story was taking so long. "Where does she fit in?"

"We're getting there. It's a bit convoluted, but stay with me. Anyway, once Dr. Palamedes saw how popular my music was with the students, he insisted that Joe adapt it for the marching band, which proved to be a stroke of genius. Not only did the band get bigger - it increased to 40 members - but it got better, much better. The kids were really into it, and by the second year of playing my music, almost 100 students tried out for the band and Joe was actually able to choose a group based more on skill and less on availability. On the field, the band was big enough to spell out "LC" with a few drums leftover, and people actually sat through the half time show.

"All was going well. Pam was happy. The school was happy. I'm really enjoying writing music. Then about seven years ago, Lucy Lu, a beautiful Asian singer with very, very long smooth black hair, and an incredible voice, who fronted the Ajeans announced that she was pregnant and had to leave the band."

Cathy shook her head as if to way, "What does this have to do with the school band?" Pete held up his hand and continued.

"This really wasn't a surprise to anyone. Once Lucy married Louis, everyone assumed they would start a family immediately. They both had lots of brothers and sisters. In preparation for this, Andy, wisely, kept close tabs on the local talent, and as soon as Lucy announced she would be leaving, he recruited Leena Kashmir, a gorgeous, exotic looking young woman who was the offspring of Arabic and Norwegian parents. Beautiful." He gestured with his hands indicating big breasts.

"Where Lucy had an incredible voice and could hold a note longer than most people could hold their breaths, Leena could hold a room in her hand. Her voice wasn't as good, but she was like Billie Holiday, she could stop a room from breathing. Suddenly the Ajeans are getting more dates than ever before. We even started doing clubs and corporate functions, and we were beginning to talk to a record label.

"Unfortunately, as if right out of a B-movie, the story starts getting ugly just when everything seems to be going right. The drummer and the sax player both fell madly in love with Leena, but she only loved the drummer. This created a great deal of animosity, and eventually resulted in a fist-fight between the two at the Berman's Bar-Mitzvah at the Newport Beach Yacht Club.

"Needless to say, Andy fired the two musicians on the spot and refunded the deposit that the Berman's paid. Totally unexpected, though, was that Leena left to be with the man she loved, so now the band was decimated. Andy claimed he needed a few weeks to re-build the band and canceled all dates for the coming month, but the other musicians said they couldn't wait that long and took jobs with other bands. Finally, Andy called it quits and canceled all our gigs. The Ajeans were no more."

Once more Cathy was about to ask what the former singer of a dissolved Bar Mitzvah band had to do with the marching band at Lewis & Clark High School, but before she could utter a word Pete raised his finger to his lips to quiet her.

"Dr. Palamedes heard about this from Pam at a faculty meeting. The next day, he fired his brother and hired me to be the new band leader, which, between you and me, was at substantially more money than I was making as a member of the Ajeans.

"Since then we've grown pretty quickly and now there are 99

members in the band, and more importantly, they're the top 99 from almost 500 students who auditioned. We're even getting students from other high schools auditioning to be in the band. Last year, we lost the statewide championship by one point. This year, we're going to win and go to the nationals. I promise you that. We've even been invited to be in the Rose Parade next year."

Pete picked up his clipboard, whistle and bullhorn and started to go down to the field, but was pulled back by Cathy who grabbed his coat sleeve. Feeling a little stupid because she still didn't understand the connection between the Asian singer who fronted the Ajeans, and LCHS's marching band, she asked one more time, "So I still don't get the dedication to Lucy Lu at every performance."

Like a teacher explaining the obvious solution to a math problem, Pete said, "If Lucy Lu hadn't gotten pregnant, none of this would have happened. Leena Kashmir would never have been hired. The musicians wouldn't have had a fight on-stage. The Ajeans would still be together. I'd still be playing boring music to food-obsessed guests at weddings and Bar Mitzvahs. The school wouldn't have a marching band worth listening to, and you and I wouldn't be sitting here on this bench talking about Lucy Lu."

"Wow," was all Cathy could say, but she wasn't sure if it was because the story was so interesting or because the chain of events seemed to make so much sense. Pulling on Pete's sleeve one more time, she asked, "By the way. What happened to Lucy Lu?"

"Funny you should ask. I just bumped into her at Starbucks a couple of weeks ago. Since she left the band, she's gained 50 pounds and has had three kids. She never sang professionally again, and she said she comes to as many half-time shows as she can, and is very appreciative of the dedication. I guess, if nothing else, it's a reminder of a time when people would hang on every note she sang and applauded the mere mention of her name."

Chapter 18

Staring into the bathroom mirror, Chris pulled a gray hair from his head. *Ouch!*

Damn! Two more, he complained to the reflection. He pulled those out, too.

Another one found and eliminated.

This is getting ridiculous.

A clump of gray hairs looked too plentiful, and painful, to pull, so he buried them beneath the darker hairs. Pulling gray hairs wasn't working any longer.

Stepping back from the mirror, he examined his head. Yesterday it was flecks of gray, now it's salt and pepper. Tomorrow everyone will be calling me dignified. *Soon I'll be "The Silver Fox." I'd rather look young than dignified,* he grumbled, bemoaning his inevitable fate.

Maybe if I start coloring my hair now, before I'm gray, no one will notice. At least my hair has held out this long. Melanie's had turned years ago, he sadistically chuckled at his wife's plight. I wonder if people think she looks older than me. *Maybe I should have made a point of marrying someone ten years younger than me, so we would age gracefully together. But I would have had to marry someone 14 years old. That's a good way to go to jail. Probably, I should have just waited. I didn't have to get married at 24. It was much too early.*

Ending the conversation with himself he recalled how Melanie was talking about their getting married long before he wanted to, as if getting that part of her life taken care of as quickly as possible was important so she could concentrate on her career. Dating for a couple of years would have been too much of a distraction.

I wonder what my life would have been like if I hadn't married Melanie? Visions of bachelorhood, random sex, and parties danced through his mind.

I guess I would have met somebody sooner or later. Maybe Cathy and I could have made up. Maybe people need different relationships at different times in their lives. Maybe...

A bang on the door indicated that breakfast was ready. Still angry that his failures in business were forcing her to continue working in a toxic environment, she wasn't talking to him.

Brushing his hair a few more times to get the last wild strands to yield their independence and conform with the rest of his head, he walked out of the bathroom, rubbing his face to make sure he didn't miss any stubble.

Dressing, as always, in front of a full-length mirror, he checked his appearance with each item he added to cover his body. A food stain on the tie he wanted to wear was particularly annoying since there wasn't a good second choice. The tie went onto the 'dry cleaner pile and he pulled three potential alternatives from his closet. Holding each up to his neck and laying it over the fabric of the suit, he couldn't decide which to choose. None were right for that suit, but eventually, he settled on one and tied it around his neck.

In the kitchen, the coffee and toast were on the table, as was usual for a weekday morning, and Melanie was reviewing some legal papers, also, as usual for a weekday morning. On most mornings he would read the *Wall Street Journal*, and they would sit in silence until she had to leave. But this morning, he was determined to end the silent treatment.

"Good morning," he said, pouring himself a cup of coffee.

She knew what he was doing and really didn't want to engage him in conversation, but certainly didn't want the problems they were having to appear to be her fault, so she deigned to respond, "Good morning. I have to finish reading these papers. I have a nine o'clock meeting with my client and I haven't read his deposition yet."

Sarcastically, he responded, "I promise not to make loud noises when I chew." He picked up the newspaper and started to scan the first page.

Melanie turned up the volume on the 5-inch color TV that sat on the kitchen counter when Willard Scott appeared. "And here's something special, I always like to talk about," Willard announced.

"Sandra and Sanford - Sandy and Sandy - Sandra and Sanford Simmons, married 75 years ago today.

"Isn't that something? A beautiful couple. They met in the first grade of a one-room schoolhouse in Iowa and have been together ever since. Though I suspect they waited a few years to get married," Willard joked, and went on to a centenarian birthday. Melanie lowered the volume.

"I'm always amazed," Chris said, dropping the corner of his newspaper slightly. "A divorce lawyer with a fascination for long marriages."

"I see couples falling apart everyday," Melanie dogmatically reminded him. "It's nice to know that some couples stay together." She started packing her attaché case.

Not really caring much about her clients, but wanting to keep the conversation rolling, he asked, "Which client is this?"

She knew he really didn't care about her clients since in the past he implored her not to share with him the many ways couples abuse each other. He once called their nightly dinner discussions of her work, "A daily dose of depravity, destruction and destitution." Another time, when he made a real issue of not wanting to hear any more about her clients, she accused him of not caring about her work (which she reminded him paid most of the bills), and flew into a tirade of how she has politely listened to his anecdotes about hot dogs, airlines, and tampons for years, so he could, at least, pretend to listen to her.

Recognizing, and responding to, his attempts at reconciliation, she told him. "A man has, shall we say, certain sexual proclivities," Melanie antiseptically explained as if she were detailing instructions on changing a tire. "He meets a woman who comes to enjoy the same proclivities and eventually they get married. Everything is fine until they have a baby. For some reason, the birth of the child changes her attitudes toward their sexual relationship and she no longer wants to participate in the same activities. The question is, is this a breach of contract? Can he sue for divorce, and not pay her alimony, on the grounds that she violated their unwritten, but definitely enacted upon, agreement?"

"No one goes into a marriage expecting the sex to stay the same forever," Chris offered, pretending to be interested, not certain if this was a smart thing to say since their sex life had really deteriorated.

"Why shouldn't he?" Melanie demanded to know. "It's not written that sex has to fall off, just because there's a child in the house."

Oh, God, Chris thought, *I fell for it again. I forgot to ask who her client was. Now I have to get into an argument so it looks like I have an opinion on this. I hate when she traps me like this. She does this every time and I keep falling for it. God, she's a good lawyer.*

Melanie's eyes stared down at him, as if he was an opposition witness, waiting for his retort, ready to pounce on anything he said. Destroying her opponent's argument, whether at home or in court, was a passion of hers.

He knew he had to say something, though he had no idea what. His first intuition was to joke his way out of these confrontations, but that rarely worked anymore. Changing the topic didn't work either. She focused on her prey like a leopard in the jungle.

Rocking slightly back and forth in the chair, he struggled for an answer. Her eyes stayed on him. He lifted the cup and sipped his coffee. Her eyes stayed on him. He bit the end of the toast and chewed. Her eyes stayed on him.

Finally, as if he was about to speak the wisdom of Solomon, he said, "It's 8:32."

"Oh, my God, I'm going to be late." She grabbed her briefcase, kissed him, and ran out the door.

Amused by his own ingenuity, he sat down, sipped his coffee and continued to read the newspaper.

On page four of the second section, a snippet in the Advertising column caught his eye.

EX-K&Q ACCOUNT EXEC HELPING AFRICANS START BUSINESSES

(Entebbe, Uganda) Martha Anne, formerly an account executive with K&Q advertising in Los Angeles, has started a foundation to help Ugandan women become entrepreneurs. Using micro-loans as little as $5 she helps woman start and run their own businesses, such as textile manufacturing, basket weaving, and furniture repair.

"The women are earning $4 and $5 a day from their efforts," reports Martha, "and that's the difference between barely scratching out an existence and being in the middle class. They don't want our charity. They just need a little help to get started and then they're off and running."

Melanie says that she's had a 99% repayment rate for her loans. Anyone wishing to contribute to her foundation can send their donations to the address at the bottom of the page.

"Martha Anne," Chris called out with delight and surprise. "I remember her. She was great. Real smart. Real good looking. I really liked her. I thought she was going to be president of some big agency someday. That's wonderful what she's doing. Who would have thought that she would be helping women in Uganda? Maybe advertising isn't such a useless profession after all."

Chapter 19

9:16 a.m.

Sliding the termination letter across the desk to Harry, the short, thin, balding accounts receivable clerk that sat opposite her, Cathy sympathized, "This is a rotten way for both of us to start the day."

The clerk glanced at the letter, signed it as if he were using a knife to carve his name into her desk, and pushed it back to her. She would have liked to say, this is all your fault, how could you be so stupid, but instead she said, with a genuine tone of bewilderment, "I can't believe I have to terminate your employment because you were playing computer games at work."

Angrily, even defiantly, Harry responded, "Do you know how many people go to pornography web sites or watch their stock portfolios during the day? I don't know why I'm being singled out as an example."

Surprised that he wasn't the least bit contrite, she transferred all her anger to her clasped hands so she wouldn't yell at him. "You're not being singled out. You violated company policy, and you know it." Pulling a document out of his employee folder, she practically pushed it in his face. "Last year you signed the same statement that all employees had to sign acknowledging that you were aware of company policy regarding personal use of computers and conducting personal activities on company time."

Harry didn't look at it since he thought it irrelevant. "I'm not the only one. Why don't you go after the others? You know as well as I do, if I was a vice president or a woman or a minority you'd be afraid to touch me. But here I am a little, chubby, white guy who's just a clerk so you're not afraid to fire me."

"We're here to talk about you. Why were you playing a computer game on company time? You were advised that we would be monitoring computer activity." In order to curb the misuse of company property, the company installed software that recorded the activity on each computer, but for some reason, scores of employees ignored the warnings and continued to use their office computers as if they were at home. After repeated warnings from the Chief Technology Officer, he demanded that HR start firing people as examples. Harry was one of a dozen terminations around the country that Senior Management ordered HR to perform.

"Friends of ours who don't have any children," he explained as if she just didn't get it, "Gave my son this series of computer games as a birthday gift. They're called the *Help Find Series: Help Captain Kirk Find Earth; Help the Greeks Find Their Way Home; Help Lewis and Clark Find the Pacific Ocean; Help Columbus Find America.* They're supposed to teach kids about history and geography in a game format. I was just checking them out to make sure they're appropriate for his age."

Astounded, she exclaimed, "For something as silly as that you're losing your job!"

"I think it's important to protect my son from some of the material that publishers are putting in their games." In his mind, he was doing his duty as a parent and shouldn't be punished for it.

"I agree, but why are you doing it at work. The company is paying you to work during the hours you're here, not check out computer games for your son. You could have gone to an internet café on your lunch hour and played the games there." Harry completely missed the point, which was incredibly frustrating to her.

"I leave here at six and it takes me over an hour to get home," he explained slowly so she would understand. "By the time we finish dinner, Danny has to go to bed, and my wife and I like to watch television before we go to sleep. I don't have any time to do it at home."

Losing all sympathy for him since he refused to understand why he was being terminated, she handed Harry an envelope with his last paycheck. "Well, now you have lots of time to check out all the games you want."

Annoyed that she didn't appreciate how critical it was to protect children from viewing inappropriate materials, and feeling that he was being singled out for punishment, he snatched the envelope from her hand, said something about talking to a lawyer and stomped out of her office.

"Damn, now I have to find a new Accounts Receivable Clerk. As if I have time for that," she groaned.

10:32 a.m.

Completing the termination paperwork, she looked at one of the twenty-seven folders on her computer screen. It read, HR Articles To Read Someday. That's a good title to discourage anyone from opening the folder, she thought when she created it. What it actually contained was the contact information for the former employees of the Business Affairs Department.

She had that meeting to go to in New York on Monday and she wanted to find out if there really was a problem in that department, or with Samantha. Her first approach was to contact the employees still with the company who had transferred out of the department. What she expected was some "bitching and moaning" about the management, what she got was vivid fear.

"I'm not going to say a word, I need this job," Derek responded before he politely hung up.

11:04 a.m.

"Do you know how many of my friends are still unemployed after six months. I can't take the chance," replied Oscar before he hung up, not so politely.

12:20 p.m.

"I just want to forget about being in that department, don't ask me anymore questions," Rachel offered, "What a terrible experience that was."

1:44 p.m.

"Investigating Samantha? That's a laugh. As soon as she gets wind of it, and she will, she'll be investigating you," was Kitty's contribution.

2:16 p.m.

While talking to Jenny, Cathy assured her that her name would be held in confidence. Jenny's skeptical response was, "Oh yeah, I believe that. HR taking the employee's side against management, I should live so long." Then she added, "When it becomes your job versus mine on the line, I doubt you'll be my hero."

2:52 p.m.

She was about to tell Susan that Alex put this whole thing in motion, thinking that she would take comfort in knowing that a co-worker had been involved, but then that would be proof that information couldn't be shared in confidence.

3:23 p.m.

When she explained to Rob that this was a routine investigation into the high turnover rates in that department, she was greeted with, "Another useless report from HR. Not exactly something I'm willing to fall on my sword for."

4:01 p.m.

Looking over her notes, twenty-two phone calls later, she knew there was a very serious problem. Six people asked if their stints in Business Affairs could be expunged from their employee files, and seven asked what kind of comments Samantha put in their files about them.

But the most common comment she received was, "Why are you calling me? Did she say something about me? Am I in trouble?"

Now she really began to worry. The fact that she hadn't heard about it, meant that someone, maybe everyone, in Senior Management, was keeping a tight lid on the situation. And, she knew that the comments of the former employees of the department couldn't be taken lightly. If she persisted in her investigation any longer, it would get back to Samantha; and while she had never feared for her job in the past, she came to appreciate Samantha's power within the organization. Samantha could make things happen with one phone call that others couldn't accomplish with years of filing forms and making up-the-channel requests.

The investigation was becoming doubly painful. Not only was there the issue of Samantha, but apparently the reputation of the Human Resources Department was horrible. Not one of the twenty-two people she spoke with had a kind thing to say about HR, nor did they think it could be effective in resolving the problems that existed in the company. Not wanting to leave a hardcopy of her evidence, she typed her notes into a document she titled, Compensation Factors, saved it to the HR Articles To Read folder on her desktop, then buried that folder, four levels deep. Shredding the notes from her yellow pad, she stirred up the scraps then put them in two separate envelopes, which she crushed and placed into two separate waste baskets.

5:07 p.m.

As if divined by fate, a message from Chris dropped into her mailbox. Delighted that, finally, there was something to smile about, she mouthed the words, "Thank you, Chris, thank you, thank you."

Cat,

I just wanted to say how much being in touch with you has meant to me... there are a lot of problems at work... and, I hate to admit, at home... I don't feel as if there's been anything "good" in my life for a long, long time... until now... I know I shouldn't be confessing this all to you, but

I just wanted to say that you brought a smile back to my face, and you gave me something to look forward to when I wake up in the morning... there have been a lot of wonderful memories playing in the screening room behind my eyes... sort of like a Busby Berkeley film festival... and I'm relishing every minute.

Let's make sure we stay in touch... I can't bear the thought of losing you from my life again.

C

6:01 p.m.

The weekend. It was here already. The five days of the week seemed to move so quickly, but the weekend crawled at a glacier's pace. The weekend. *At least this would be a short one*, Cathy reminded herself. She would leave for New York on Sunday.

But it won't change things. He'll still want his Saturday Night Fuck. He'll still demand to be served his meals. He'll still lash out if the least little thing disturbs him. The weekend. Why does it have to be so long?

Looking at the clock on her computer, she knew she had to leave here any moment and return to her home... her prison.

6:05 p.m.

Barbara, Cathy's secretary, knocked on the door and took one step into her office. With her coat buttoned, purse slung over her arm, and her hands filled with the mail that had to be dropped off downstairs, she asked, "Is there anything you need me to do before I leave?"

"No, have a good weekend."

"And what's the Mother-Of-The-Year doing this weekend?" The "mom's" in the office gave Cathy a tiny Mother-Of-The-Year trophy because every weekend, regardless of the weather, she took her kids to museums, movies, art fairs, festivals and so on. "My kids are always complaining that we never do anything," Barbara added. "I give you a lot of credit for getting the kids out. Have a good weekend," she called as she raced for the elevator.

Cathy whispered, "You're lucky you don't have the motivation to get out of the house like I do."

6:07 p.m.

"Shit," Cathy said a bit too loudly for the office. "I have to get home before he does, and I haven't figured out what to do this weekend yet."

6:09 p.m.

Visiting www.weather.com, tears of joy welled up in her eyes. "Thank God. It's going to be a nice weekend. He'll be out playing golf. Maybe he'll fall into one of those water traps and drown."

6:12 p.m.

"Come on, come on," she commanded the slow opening web page, her heart beating faster than the digital clock on the corner of the screen.

Her fingers moved the mouse from event to event faster than a race car at the Indy 500. Not having any tickets or reservations meant she and the girls were vulnerable, if he came home angry at losing a game, or too drunk just to restrict his brutality to her. She had to get them out of the house. Visiting website after website she frantically searched for something to do with the girls.

Click. "No that's no good."

Click. "No, that movie ends too early."

Click. "We've been there already."

6:17 p.m.

"No. There's got to be something happening in this stupid city."

Looking at the clock again, she typed in another website's address.

6:19 p.m.

Not finding anything, she decided to tell Fred that she was taking them to the outlet mall shopping for summer clothes. Of course, he'll say they don't need any more clothes, but they'll say they do and he won't want to get into an argument with them at the dinner table. The outlet mall's halfway to Wisconsin, which was good. Maybe I can pretend I left my keys in the car and get stuck there till late Saturday night, she thought.

6:20 p.m.

No, that won't work. I've used that too often. Maybe I should drive a nail into my tire so it breaks down while we're out there. No, it might be too dangerous.

6:22 p.m.

Cathy turned off her computer without letting it shut down properly and raced out of her office so she could get home before he did. The corridors that were already dim thanks to the energy-saving protocol of the building.

There was just enough time to get home before Fred.

Please, please, no traffic, she prayed. Thoughts of some teenager pretending to be a NASCAR driver and getting into an accident that spreads over three lanes, raced through her mind. There was just enough time to get home.

Quick walking through the outer offices of the human resources department, she noticed a light in one of the cubicles. It truly was a bright island in a dim sea of empty workstations. She made a mental note of the name on the cubicle – Sari - and hoped she could remember on Monday to stop by and thank her for staying late on a Friday night.

But as she reached the doorway, she stopped with an ill chill. There had been some assaults on woman late night in the garage and now she wasn't comfortable with the idea of one of her staff going into a dangerous place alone. Even though it would cost her minutes, she had to make certain that whoever was in the cubicle wouldn't be going into the garage alone.

But as she got closer she could hear sniffling and muffled crying, so she stopped.

A young girl, working late on a Friday night... crying.

This wasn't a dedicated employee... this was a kindred spirit... this was someone who didn't want to go home.

Instinctively, she was about to loudly clear her throat to announce her arrival, step into the cubicle, and ask the young girl if there was a problem or if she could help her in any way.

But she pulled back as she hit a wall of self preservation.

What if the girl wanted to cry on her shoulder, just as she had searched many times for a shoulder to cry on.

What if the young girl wanted to talk, just as she had wanted to. She didn't have the time to give to her, not now.

Who is this Sari? She couldn't form a mental picture of the girl's face. Since she interviewed everyone who worked in her department, so she knew she had met her, but still she couldn't put a face to the name.

Raising herself on her toes, she caught sight of her shiny, black hair.

Oh, she remembered her now. *Sari is that very attractive young girl, 24 or 25, married just a few years. From Iran or Saudi Arabia or somewhere in that part of the world. Very polite. Always says, good morning.*

A slide show of Sari played behind her eyes, and she realized that the young girl always seemed to be looking downward... didn't smile often... and wore cosmetics very thick on her face. *I should have caught that,* Cathy criticized herself. *I should have known.*

She looked around, to determine what part of her little empire this area was and realized it was the benefits section.

That's right, Cathy reminded to herself, *she is responsible for tracking vacation requests, leaves of absence, sick days... nothing that should warrant anyone staying late. Half the company takes vacations and then sends in the requests after they get back,* Cathy groused at the lax adherence to policy.

Stepping an inch closer to Sari, she so wanted to help her, but she couldn't, not tonight. She knew that just wrapping her arms around her, just letting her know that she's not alone, just letting her know that people care about her, would make such a difference. It would help her survive the weekend.

But she couldn't do any of that now... she should have been on her way home by now... she couldn't let Fred be in the house alone with the girls.

How many woman are in my department? she wondered. *Seventy-five? A hundred? How many are afraid to go home every night? It can't just be the two of us.*

How many work in this company? Thirty-five thousand? Forty thousand? How many have to hide the bruises on their bodies and lie about slipping on ice or walking into a door?

It was too much to think about right now. Next week. But not right now.

Raising her hand, she touched the textured fabric of the cubicle wall with the tips of her fingers. Closing her eyes, she reached out to Sari, and wished that she could drain the poison from Sari's body. *No matter how bad it is for me, I'm stronger than you are, Sari. Let me have your pain.*

She stood for a few moments, hoping that somehow she was a comfort to the young girl, but suddenly a phone rang and Cathy jumped back into the shadow of a support beam, afraid it was her cell phone, and that her presence would be discovered. But then she heard Sari speaking to her caller. It was a beautiful voice, but sad.

"I know it's late. But my boss said I have to finish my work before I can come home.... I know, I know.... It's terrible.... She's a very mean person.... Go out and have dinner with your friends... I'll be home in a couple of hours. Yes, yes, I love you, too." And then the crying began again, a bit louder.

Inching back, and through the doorway to the elevators, she rode down to the lobby and asked security to send someone up to her offices to accompany the young girl who was still working to her car.

Practically, running across the first floor of the garage, Cathy jumped into her car and drove, much faster than the speed limit, away from the building. She cried a little bit, too. She pledged to herself to help the girl... to help all the women at the company who are suffering. But, first, she had to find a way to help herself.

6:45 p.m.

Trying to read phone numbers from her laptop that was open on the driver's seat, and dialing friends of her daughter's while driving on the highway back to Olympic Estates, she frantically tried to make arrangements for them to be out of the house while she was in New York.

7:47 p.m.

She walked through the front door of the house and hugged her two daughters.

7:48 p.m.

Fred walked through the front door of the house and demanded to know, "Is dinner ready?"

Chapter 20

Stopping at the newsstand as he entered the office building, Chris dropped seven pennies and a $5 bill into the collection jar for the Children's Starlight Foundation.

"How come you're always dropping money into that jar and never buying any magazines or newspapers from me?" the old man with remnants of his Middle Eastern upbringing still thick in his voice.

"I'm in advertising. I get all the magazines and newspapers I want for free," Chris smiled, digging through his pocket to see if any pennies were left.

"I think everyone in this building must be in advertising," the old man, never lifting his head from the arm that propped it up, complained.

Just to be friendly, Chris bought a roll of Winter Mint Lifesavers and threw the change into the Starlight Foundation jar.

In his office, watching his computer boot up, he hoped for an e-mail from Cathy. Convinced that she was the one that could have made him happy for a lifetime, he wondered if they could go back... or maybe forward. But he didn't have time to ponder too long, because Candy, seeing that he had arrived, rushed down to his office.

"Do you have a minute, Chris?"

"Always, for you. Is there something wrong?" After all the years of working together in such a despicable place, they were more than a boss and secretary; they were soldiers, sharing a foxhole during a horrific battle.

"Chris, I don't know if you know. I've been dating someone for the past six months." It was cute. She was blushing a bit.

"No, I didn't. We never really talk about those kinds of things." He tried to stifle any surprise. What is it about someone who's 100 pounds overweight that you assume that they have no life other than eating.

"Most people don't talk about dating and things in front of me because they think I'll be hurt. Everyone assumes I'd never be able to attract a boyfriend with this face and body." Even after all these years, she was still grateful to Chris that he hired her. Recognizing her superior skills, the human resources manager sent her to interview for several openings, but none of the other male executives would hire her. Chris, who was engaged with extra-marital affair Number 4 at the time, instantly snapped her up and made her feel welcome and wanted. In those days, he was a rising star, so she got to share this prestige, and was treated just a little bit better than the other newly hired secretaries. Debra, the Media Director, and some of his other detractors in the office, assumed he hired her just to combat the rumors about him and his affairs; others thought that he just didn't want to be tempted. The truth was, he liked the fact that she could type 120 words per minute with no errors, took accurate messages, and had a friendly voice on the phone.

"Don't be silly...." He started a hollow protest, but Candy cut him off.

Raising both hands to stop his protest, she announced, "It's okay, Chris, I know I'm not a prize, but it doesn't matter. I'm getting married," she blurted out.

"That's wonderful," he exclaimed, obviously surprised, but it didn't bother her. "Congratulations." He walked around the desk, wrapping (or trying to) his arms around her, he gave her a warm kiss on the cheek. "That's really wonderful. I'm embarrassed I didn't even notice. I should have known. You're always so good about noticing things about other people."

"Don't feel bad, I kept it a secret from all of the girls in the office, too. I was afraid to jinx it. If it didn't work out, I didn't want the Rats in the Maze talking about it. It can get vicious in there." She rolled her eyes thinking about what would have been said about her.

"I look forward to meeting him. He sounds like a special person." He didn't intend the meaning of that phrase to be, "because he's overlooking your physical features and just seeing what a wonderful person you are," but that was the subtext and they both knew it.

"You'll meet him at the wedding... if you can come." She handed him an invitation in an oversized envelope. "I hope you can come. The wedding's in about five weeks."

"That's very fast." He opened the envelope and looked at the card she had just created on the laser printer to check the dates. He prayed that there would be no conflict with his trip to New York where he was presenting a TV campaign to clients that hated the idea of spending money on advertising.

"I don't want to take a chance he'll change his mind," she giggled, but was deadly serious.

Chris entered the date in his calendar, and also put a yellow sticky on his phone to remind himself to tell Melanie.

"You're going to like him. The minute I saw him, I knew he was the one for me. We met at a Weight Watchers' meeting," Candy volunteered, knowing people would be very curious. "As soon as we met, we went out and shared an ice cream sundae. It'll be a marriage built on Rocky Road," she giggled nervously.

"Trust me," Chris bent forward and whispered, "that's better than sex. Let's face it, sex will get cold, but Rocky Road will never get hot." She giggled.

"Let me ask," he posed with a serious tone, "would I look cheap if I gave you a lifetime supply of tampons for your wedding present."

"Oh, you don't have to give me anything. You've been wonderful to work with all these years. Every secretary in the place wants to work for you - especially Gary's." Though Chris' star in the agency had long faded, he still was the most considerate boss anyone could have, and other secretaries envied Candy for that.

"Seriously, I want to get you something you want. Promise to tell me what you want. It'll make it much easier for me, too."

As she said, "I will," she stood up to leave, and handed him a message from Mack. "He wants you to call him in his car in ten minutes."

"Candy, I'm truly happy for you. I wish you both all the best." He hugged and kissed her one more time, but this time his expression of joy was much more perfunctory, the message from Mack brought him back to reality and the Big Lie. Since the management meeting, Chris hid in his office with the door closed as much as possible. Not only did he want to search for a new job without anyone knowing, but he wanted to stay out of the tumult that was building over the possibility of doing a television commercial. Hundreds of man-hours, which meant tens of thousands of dollars, were being spent by the various departments of the agency on this project, and he knew there would be hell to pay when it all came tumbling down.

Teams of copywriters and art directors were working in every free space of the agency, and the media planners had called every major station in every major market to get an update on rates and viewership. If all this wasn't bad enough, Chris really began to worry when he saw that Sandy was bringing in freelance creative people to work on the project. He was always certain that the agency's "lack-of-creative department," as he called it, could never come up with a good idea, but who knew about this army of freelancers that suddenly populated the corridors of the agency. These were unknowns, and there was the possibility that one of them could come up with a good idea, which would mean that his plan would backfire.

Everywhere Chris went in the agency, he tried to be the voice of reason: "This is just a test. The client hasn't committed to anything."

"We're starting small. If it works we'll roll it out to other markets... one at a time."

"The client is a conservative old man from Eastern Europe, he'll never buy into a Las Vegas show type of commercial. Keep it small."

But his voice wasn't being heard anymore. For the rest of the agency, this was going to be a Broadway musical that wowed audiences and critics alike. Concerns about budgets and marketing strategies and client preferences were all just mere inhibitors to the full expression of their talents, so the copywriters and art directors of the agency completely ignored those restraints.

Even the advertising trade press picked up on the frenzy and every week the progress of the campaign appeared in an industry trade magazine. K&Q was coming back to the mainstream of advertising, and everyone, including Mack, liked that.

So Chris hid in his office, searching the internet for a job at a company that, hopefully, never heard of K&Q.

The client phone range, and so he immediately snatched it from Mickey's hand. It was Mack calling from his car, demanding to know. "What's the status of those television commercials?"

Despite all his concerns about having fabricated this story, he liked feeling he had something Mack dearly wanted. It was as if he held in his hand the power to make the agency a legitimate member of advertising community again.

But the status of the agency was a distant second to his desire to keep his job, so he plotted to turn the heat up on Sandy, make him panic. "It's not going well. We may have to postpone the meeting."

"Don't postpone it!" Mack commanded.

"We won't be ready. The Creative Department hasn't come up with anything I think the client will buy."

"I'll make sure we'll be ready!" There was silence on the phone.

Chris could hear Mack thinking about the money, so he went in for the kill. "I think I could get the budget doubled if we come up with a good campaign." Chris was good at making irrelevant statements sound meaningful. Since there was no budget, doubling it was multiplying zero by two.

Cursing a driver that merged into his lane, Mack ordered, "Let's talk tomorrow morning."

"I think Sandy should be in the meeting, too." Chris suggested. He really didn't care about Sandy's input, but enjoyed watching him squirm in Mack's presence.

Mack dictated, "9:00 a.m. in my office tomorrow morning. Tell Sandy, and tell him to bring whatever creative he's got," and hung up.

"It's going to be an interesting week," he mumbled as he headed to the coffee room with his World's Greatest Boss cup in hand.

Once there, he, unfortunately, found Gary entertaining a small circle of young men. Because of his quick ascension to Management Supervisor (from a plot, he bragged, that he hatched) he had become a hero among the newest generation of male junior executives. From the laughter, it was clear that the subject was women and sex. It was always about women and sex. "What's the difference between a Jewish woman and an Italian woman?" He paused for a moment. "Italian women tell their husbands to buy Viagra, Jewish women tell their husbands to buy Pfizer." More laughter.

Chris wanted no part of the group and turned to leave. But Gary was on a roll and his audience, like the ancient Romans, wanted more and more entertainment.

"Now there's a man we should all admire," Gary loudly proclaimed, raising his surrealistic-phallic-shaped coffee mug to his mouth for emphasis. "Why don't you come over here a second, Chris."

"Go change your diapers."

In a booming voice, Gary announced, "Half the women in the agency want to work for this guy because he's so sweet, and the other half want to sleep with him, and he chooses the only secretary in the agency who needs to put a bag over her face before she has sex." There was lots of laughter from his audience.

Unfortunately, just at that moment, Candy, walked past the coffee room doorway.

"You're a fuckin' asshole," Chris called across the coffee room to Gary, who only laughed at the assault.

Racing after Candy, hoping she didn't hear Gary's slur, he slammed on his brakes because Barry Balin was approaching from the other direction. If it could be possible, Bob looked worse. He looked more like a homeless old man who slept on the street than an executive at an advertising agency. Walking right past Chris, he seemingly had no recognition of him.

Entering the Maze and winding his way to Candy's cubicle, Chris declared, "Bob looks terrible."

"The whole thing gets worse and worse. Poor guy. According to Lillian, it turns out his wife never left Los Angeles. She only said so in her note so he would think she was out of town. On Monday he goes home to find the whole house empty, except for his clothes. His underwear and shirts, thrown in a pile on the floor. She took absolutely everything. The chairs, the lamps, the telephones. She even took the food in the refrigerator and the extra toilet paper in the closet. He's sleeping on the floor. She's cleaned out their savings and checking accounts, sold off all their stocks and took the cash, wrote checks to herself from their charge cards. She's wiped him out."

"All for the love of this actor?" Chris always thought that if he ever left Melanie, he would do it with dignity... if that's possible.

Waving her hands near her head, she blurted out, "There is no actor. She didn't leave him for anybody. She just hated him so much, she wanted to be rid of him."

"You walk out the door if you want to be rid of someone. She sounds like she wanted to destroy him. I can't imagine one spouse hating the other so much." As he said the words, he thought about all the clients Melanie talked about over the years, and suddenly Barry's plight didn't seem so different.

"Mr. Mjczoleskicz ordered Bob to take a couple weeks off and come back when he feels better. They don't want clients to see him. But he says he wants to keep coming in since he has no place to go. The buzz among the Rats is that unless he takes a couple of weeks off and straightens himself out, they're going to fire him. Maybe you should talk to him and convince him to stay home."

Chris could only imagine what must be going on in his head. One day you have a wife, a house, a career and the next day you lose it all because your spouse hates you so intensely - and you didn't even know. There must be more to this than she just wanting out of the marriage. Maybe Bob was cheating on his wife.

Candy changed the decorations of her workstation to pictures of wedding gowns, which made Chris realize he should change the subject from failed marriages to something happier - though it was hard to think of one at the moment.

"Which one do you think will make me look thinner?" Candy asked pointing to the wedding gowns pinned to the walls of her work station.

None, he thought, but said, "This one is attractive," indicating the center picture.

"I don't think they come in my size. I don't think any dress comes in my size."

Chris leaned forwarded and whispered in her ear, "The question isn't which dress you wear, but whether it will be white or off-white."

She giggled, and slightly embarrassed, whispered back, "I'm going to wear white, but actually I shouldn't. We did it, already."

Puckering up his face, as if to say, "You little vixen," he turned to leave, but Candy's voice grabbed him, "Did you hear the latest rumor?"

"No one ever tells me anything. What?" He turned back.

In a loud whisper that would guarantee she was overheard, she revealed, "Don't say anything to anyone, but I hear that Gary is gay. He's a raving homosexual and likes leather and whips. All the dirty jokes and talk about women is just an attempt to cover it up."

Chris fell backwards astonished. This was the most incredible thing he's ever heard... not counting Barry Balin's wife leaving him. But when he saw Candy smile and drop her head, he knew what she was doing and in a very, very low voice asked, "Is this something you've heard, or is this something you... would like to have heard?"

"I don't know how rumors begin," she whispered back. "That's why they call them rumors."

Chapter 21

Are you happy? Cathy asked on Saturday in a brief e-mail to Chris.

   Taking advantage of Fred's propensity to stay at the club drinking till they shut down for the night (or until the bartender refused to serve him anymore drinks), Cathy turned on her computer to reach out to the one person with whom she could share the truth about her life. While she wasn't ready to tell him everything, yet, she knew she couldn't keep the misery of her life to herself any longer.

Are you happy?

It's been bothering me since your very first e-mail... considering the distance between us, I know I have no right to ask... but you sound so lonely in your e-mails... you don't sound happy. Are you? Please forgive me for asking... you've always been important to me...

Her hands rested, poised on the keyboard as she thought of what else to say in this e-mail. After an opening like that it was hard to now say... by the way, I took the girls to the zoo and we saw the Chinese pandas. What she wanted to write was: Where were you? Why didn't you come to Minneapolis after the rape? Don't you know how much I needed you? You ruined us. You ruined our lives. But she didn't say that. She decided to just sent the e-mail as it was.

Chris happened to be on the computer when the e-mail arrived, and opened it immediately.

Frightened that it was so obvious that he wasn't happy, that he felt so alone, he wanted to write back immediately… but, what do you say. Admit to unhappiness? Deny it? Tell all about the seven extra-marital affairs?

C,

It's amazing the effect our reconnecting has had on me… it's as if 20-something years haven't past at all. I could never hide anything from you.

Am I happy? Sometimes… maybe… I guess.

I feel like my life is a giant chess match… at work… at home… I'm constantly maneuvering my pieces to avoid being taken. I'm so surprised and delight that I still feel I can be completely honest with you… maybe its because we're 2,000 miles apart… maybe it's because we knew each other when we were still innocent… maybe, and this is my preference… because there is a special bond between us that never went away.

Remember how you used to say that when I played a character, I became that character… remember how you said, when I played Willy Loman in Death of a Salesman, I walked around looking defeated… and when I played Stanley Kowalski in A Streetcar Named Desire, I wore torn t-shirts all the time… even in winter.

I haven't been in a play in almost 20 years… but… I can't believe I am about to say this, but…I wonder if when I married Melanie, I was just acting out another character in a different type of play… right now, I feel as if I am playin the role of a happily married husband and business

executive... God, forgive me for what I am about to say...
I'm getting real tired of this part and I'm wondering when
this tour is going to end so I can move onto the next role.

What scares me now... and what I have never been able to
say to anybody... is that I wonder if I lost my sense of
reality... I'm afraid I don't know who I am anymore... and
where my life ends and this character begins. I often lay
awake thinking about my life... I don't know if its the life I
was meant to live or its just another script

Forgive me for dumping all this on you.... it scares me how
well you still know me and how much I want to share with
you... I know I could never tell any of this to Melanie... if I
said anything to her, it would destroy the real fiction we're
living in.

Well, you asked for it. You got it. If you never write back,
I'll understand.

Always and always,

Chris

What he also wanted to write was: Why couldn't you forgive me? I
was wrong. I apologized a thousand times for not coming to Minneapolis
after the rape. I was an absolute jerk. But look at what happened to us.
Our lives have been ruined. We've lost decades of happiness together.
Why couldn't you forgive me?

But, of course, he didn't include that in his e-mail.

Chapter 22

Sunday evening, when Cathy checked into the Iliad Hotel in New York, she was still crying. She thought she had escaped this week's Saturday Night Fuck since Fred didn't get home from the club till well after midnight, and once he got home he collapsed on the bed still wearing his clothes. But this morning, before she was even fully awake, he was on top of her, shoving himself inside her.

Ironically, because he had been gone, she was having a wonderful night's sleep, which unfortunately, also meant that she wasn't attuned to his early morning wants. Once he got on top of her, to help her wake up, he playfully slapped her face, as if she was a bongo drum. She could hear him laughing and singing, "Good morning, good morning, the sun is bright and I'm in your hole, good morning, good morning, to you."

The pain was intense since she didn't have time to lubricate, and she couldn't hold back her tears. She was being raped, yet again. But that seemed to turn him on. Watching the tears stream down her face, he kept calling out. "I never realized that you liked it rough. We'll have to do it this way more often."

Again and again he pushed himself into her, and she pleaded, silently, for this to end. Her only hope was that he would cum and get out, so she reached down and massaged his penis. Anything to get this over with. Finally, there was that rush of warm fluid inside her that meant it was over... at least for now.

When she settled into her hotel room, she quickly set up her laptop computer, removed the computer disk from her attaché case and added an entry to her journal.

> May 14 - It almost seems ridiculous to enter aggressive sex in this log since it happens so often. I have the sense that it is not just a matter of a voracious sexual appetite, but rather forcing me to have sex when he knows I really don't want to is his way of proving his power over me. The sex is getting rougher. I think he purposely rushes so I won't have time to lubricate and I'll be in more pain. Fortunately, I guess, other than that and a few shouts, there have been no major incidents this week. I guess I should consider myself lucky.

Removing the computer disk, she hid it again in her attaché case. For some time she'd wanted to research domestic violence on the internet, but didn't want to do it from work, and couldn't do it from home. Finally, she had the opportunity to do it now.

Entering the words "domestic, violence" into Google, revealed hundreds of thousands of websites devoted to the subject. Many were from police departments, and governmental agencies, but even more were from women who wanted to tell their stories. It was frightening to see so much written about violence against women, but in an odd way, it was comforting... at least she wasn't alone.

Clicking on the link for National Clearinghouse for the Defense of Battered Women, she began to read about how widespread and horrendous the disease was.

How many women are battered each year?

The American Medical Association estimates that over 4 million women are victims of severe assaults by boyfriends and husbands each year. About 1 in 4 women are likely to be abused by a partner. Forty-seven percent (47%) of the husbands who batter their wives do so three or more times each year.

Based on domestic crime data kept by 17 states, experts estimate that 1.37 million domestic violence offenses were reported to the police in 1991. This figure, however, substantially understates the problem since battering is usually not reported until it is life-threatening. In fact, some research estimates that one of every two women will be battered at some time in their life.

According to the Uniform Crime Report of the Federal Bureau of Investigation, 30% of women killed in the United States die at the hands of a husband or boyfriend.

What A Battered Woman Faces When She Leaves

Many people assume that once a battered woman takes the first step outside of her home or relationship, the hardship and abuse will end. Battered women face many difficulties when they leave, including fear of injury or death, economic hardship, fear of losing their children, and a poor criminal justice response.

The highest risk for serious injury or death to a battered woman is when she is leaving or when she has left her violent partner. According to the FBI, up to 40% of female homicides in any given year occur when the woman decides to leave the abusive relationship

What Economic Hardship Can A Battered Woman Expect?

Seventy-four percent of employed battered women experience harassment at work by their abusive partner, either in person or on the telephone. This harassment often results in their being late to work, missing work altogether and possibly losing their jobs.

What About The Children of Battered Women

In a national survey of more than 2,000 American families, approximately 50 percent of the men who frequently assaulted their wives also frequently abused their children.

It was painful to continue reading, but Cathy couldn't stop. Other women like her were enmeshed in a horrible crisis, and they, too, were at a loss of how to end it. She was not the only educated, intelligent, professional woman suffering beatings and intimidations from someone she once loved. And, she was not the only woman who felt like she was being raped every time the man she slept with lay on top of her.

Finally, visiting many websites, she began to read the stories of victims:

> I had had a particularly rotten day at the office (I'm a Public Defender in an urban environment) and all I wanted to do was take a hot bath and soak my aggravations away. I was standing over the tub, watching the water fill up and Charley came in and screamed... Did you pick up your birth control pills? I said no, I forgot, besides I wasn't in the mood anyway... not that I'm in the mood any night with that pig. Next thing I know he pushes my head into the wall and I slip and hit my head against the rim of the bathtub. He charges out the door. I'm bleeding in two places and I slip under the water in the tub. I was really groggy, but I have to admit it's peaceful there and I'm thinking of staying. Let him explain to the police what happened when they find my body. But then I think about the kids... we have three... two from former marriages and one of our own... and I push myself up and out of the tub. I grab the kids and head to the hospital wearing a terry cloth robe and they patch me up. I told them I slipped getting into the bathtub. Can you believe...when I get home that asshole didn't even apologize. Instead he, literally, shoves a birth control pill down my throat and shoves his dick into me... all the time chanting... "This should make you feel better."

> (Signed) Defenseless Defender

> ***

> It was his parents' anniversary and we were having dinner at their house. We were supposed to be there at 5 p.m. and it was already 6:00. I knew he was at some bar getting drunk

so I decided to take the kids and go without him. I stopped at a florist to pick up some flowers, and as I'm getting out of the car, from out of nowhere he descends on me screaming, "How could you go without me? How will it look? What will the family think?" and holds me against the car with one hand and slams the car door into me with his other hand. It hurt. I can still feel the pain and it's a week later. Well a police car pulls up at that moment and I think, thank God, I'm saved. We live in a small town and it turns out Jimmy and the cop played on the high school football team together. They're laughing and talking about old times for 10 minutes and finally the cop comes over to me. He saw what happened. He asks how I am and then says, "Do you want to do anything? It will take a quite a few hours till we can get someone to come in to take your story." The kids are hungry and want to know when we'll get to Grandma's so I say "I'm okay. Forget about it." I can still hear Jimmy and that cop laughing as I drove away.

(Signed) Hoping for a knight in shining armor

Cathy could only shake her head and wipe away her tears. She didn't know if it was that the stories of the victims were so sad, or the fact that she was living them was so painful. Tonight seemed worse than usual, more painful, emotionally, spiritually. Could it be because she and Chris were back in contact and she knew how disappointed he would be? Could it be that just one e-mail from Chris reminded her that there was a difference between making love and having sex? Could it be that she realized that she hadn't made love with a man since before the rape, since the last time she and Chris were together. She continued reading.

I guess I'm lucky compared to lots of women telling their stories on this website. I've never been beaten physically, but when Tim explodes and is yelling at the top of his lungs one inch from my face, I'm scared for my life. I feel like a prisoner. He checks my cell phone to see who called me and he checks the phone bills to see who I called... I have to explain every call. I can't go out without him even to the drugstore. I can only watch the TV shows he approves of and I never see any of my friends anymore - he scared them all away. I used to be very athletic. After we got married he threw away my ice skates and my mountain bike (which cost $750). He said since he doesn't like to do those things there was no need for that junk to be clogging up the garage. He drives a delivery truck and whenever he's in the area he just stops by my office to see if I'm talking to anyone and if I am I have to explain why. I had to let a juicy promotion pass me by since it involved travel and he said - "I won't allow it." When we were dating I thought his constant attention was cute. Now that we're married, I'm suffocating. I'm afraid if I say I want to end the marriage, his verbal abuse will turn physical. Help.

(Signed) Need a breathe of fresh air

After reading half a dozen stories of abused women, Cathy decided to add her own:

I was terribly lonely. I was transferred to a major city by my company, and I moved to a wealthy suburb because of the schools. The problem was in the suburbs, married couples don't like to socialize with single women, and because I had my children late in life, I was older than most of the other mothers in the community. Even though I interact with a lot of people in my job, there were a lot of lonely hours every week. I met Marc at work. He recently was divorced, and said, "he lost his friends in the process," so he was lonely, too. I guess that's as good a place as any to start a relationship. Anyway, we started going out. For a while I thought he was my Knight in Shining Armor. We laughed a lot and spent a lot of time together, and it looked like we were heading towards a future together. Since we seemed to be heading towards marriage, as well as for financial reasons, we bought a house together. I remember we laughed and said, "If it doesn't work out we can always sell and make a profit." From the moment we moved in together, it's been a living hell. I make a lot more money than he does and I'm higher up in the company and that seems to have become a major source of conflict. All of a sudden, if I ask him to stop at the store on his way home, he barks back, "Is that an order from management?" I put more money into the down payment, but he now walks around calling it, "My house," as if I moved in on him. I'm a professional woman, and for many years I managed my own finances very well. Now, I've lost all control of my personal finances and I can't even write a check or use a charge card without Marc's permission.

One of the worst incidents between us was a few months ago when we were in Aspen, Colorado attending a corporate meeting. I was an attendee and he came along as my guest. Boy, did he hate that. He thought people were snickering at him behind his back. One night, after a company dinner, I went to bed, and he stayed downstairs to play poker with some of the hotel staff. Just after midnight he came up to the room, obviously drunk, and began tearing things apart. He's looking for my credit cards so he can get cash from the ATM machine, so he can continue gambling. When he can't find them, he accuses me of hiding them from him because I don't trust him, and pulls me out of bed by my hair. I don't know what's going on and I'm screaming, "What are you doing?" He screams, "You piece of shit, get out of my room!" and he drags me down the hallway all the way to the elevators by my hair. Then he goes inside and locks the door. I had carpet burns from my butt up to my neck. It's freezing cold. Could you imagine what would have happened if someone from my company came by. Thank goodness I was wearing nice pajamas. I just sat in front of the door, crying, asking myself over and over, "How did this happen to me?" About an hour later a security guard came by and I convinced him that I had been getting some ice and accidentally locked myself out. He let me back in, but I was too afraid to get into bed so I slept on, this is funny, a loveseat that was in the corner of the room.

"How did this happen to me?"

(Signed) One of the Sabine Women

Wet from the tears that streamed down her face, she turned off the computer and lay down on the bed. It frightened her that it was the fear of others finding out about her situation that kept her trapped in the horrible nightmare. She was a Vice President in Human Resources. *My God, I'm the person everyone comes to for advice. What would people think if they found out my life was a disaster? Who would listen to me then? And, all the smug glances and laughter behind my back. How would I be able to do my job effectively?*

For a long time she did nothing. She didn't read. She didn't watch television. She didn't listen to the radio. She did nothing. She stared out the window at the starry sky and wondered about the universe, and her place in it.

She needed some time to think. She needed a vacation from Fred. Too much was going on at home and at work. She would call Fred and tell him she had to stay in New York a couple of extra days... assuming she could keep the girls out of the house. There was no doubt he would accept the story since his favorite topic of conversation was the unreasonable demands the company made... on him.

Sitting up on the bed, she noticed a small tent card on the side table that listed the amenities of staying at The Iliad. Free continental breakfast in the lobby. Twenty-four hour room service. On premise dry cleaning facilities. Twenty-four hour health club.

Twenty-four hour health club.

Even though it was very late, she decided to go to the club and work out. Since she didn't have to be in the office till 11:00 a.m. she could exercise and still get enough sleep. But as soon as she entered the ultra-tech gymnasium, her eyes were immediately drawn to the steam room. "That's where I'm going," she told the attendant, who gave her two towels and returned her focus to the small TV set she was watching. And then she thought to herself, *I want to sweat every last drop of that drunken, smelly, piece of shit, out of my body.*

Descending into the mist of steam, she committed herself to staying there as long as it took to be completely rid of him.

Chapter 23

"Good Morning, Cathy. Did you just get back from vacation?" asked Bob, as he shook her hand in the limp-wristed way men shake a woman's hand. "You look so… tan." He was being kind. She was much more red than tan.

Embarrassed, she confessed, with a forced laugh, "No. I fell asleep in the steam room of my hotel. I'm more poached than tan." If it was possible, his noticing her color made her even redder.

"I didn't think it was possible to fall asleep in a steam room."

"I guess it is. The attendant at the spa who woke me, says it happens all the time, especially to business people at the end of an exhausting day." As hard as she tried, all her cosmetics couldn't hide the blazing red neon sign attached to her forehead that read, "Did reeeeaaaalllly dumb thing!"

"The images this conjures up are frightening. Well, I'm glad they found you before you were fully cooked." With enough time spent on the initial pleasantries, it was time to discuss business. Bob indicated a tray of beverages on the credenza, and Cathy, following instructions from the spa's manager, drank water… a lot of water.

She had been in Bob's office many times before and it always bothered her that it was always so neat, especially as compared to hers. It always made her wonder if he did any work. Not a scrap of paper was ever on his mahogany desk, the books on the matching mahogany shelves were perfectly aligned, and the leather conference chairs were exactly the same distance from the glass coffee table. Even the vertical blinds were always perfectly angled to protect the inhabitant of the space from the harsh sunlight.

There were never any piles of papers stacked on the floor. There were never any cartons on chairs. There were never any industry magazines waiting to be read weighing down the sagging shelves. She significantly doubted that they shared the same experiences of being in the Human Resource profession.

The other mystery about his office was how he got such a big and lavishly decorated office so close to Senior Management. His title and responsibilities didn't warrant this much space, nor even his being on the tenth floor with Senior Management, but somehow he managed to do it. "Who's cock did he have to suck?" is what some of the less delicate members of HR would ask.

As they sat down - she on the couch and he in a chair facing her - there was a dramatic shift in his tone, from light and friendly to serious and determined, but with a hint of nervousness. "Cathy, a significant change in the way we do business is about to occur, and this could represent an "extraordinary opportunity" for someone, and I hope that someone is you." He paused, raising his coffee cup to his lips, to let the weight of his words be fully absorbed. He wanted her to be excited about the opportunity he was about to offer her. "Let me come out and say it, we all believe... and I'm talking for Senior Management here... we all believe you're the one for the job."

Taking a sip of water, she thought, boy am I about to get dumped on. "I'm delighted that you and the rest of Senior Management all thought about me for this extraordinary opportunity, Bob. Thank you."

Leaning back in his chair, Bob was satisfied that there had been no "departmental leaks" and that she didn't know what was coming. He prided himself on his well developed network of loyal spies throughout the corporation, and he often thought of Cathy and the others in HR that just toiled away, day after day, as naïve in the ways of the world. "I shouldn't say this since it's supposed to be confidential, but there wasn't a single dissenting voice at the Senior Management Strategy Committee meeting when your name came up. I don't think I've ever heard as many good things said about someone at these meetings. This is a real career-maker."

Or career-breaker, she guessed.

"In fact, this is the kind of assignment that will take you out of department-level activities and have you reporting directly, or almost directly, to Senior Management." He laughed his annoying phony laugh, "I bet I'll be reporting to you some day."

Playing her role perfectly, she said, "Bob, I have far, far too much to learn from you yet. You'll never have to worry about me being your boss." *But, Bob, if I was your boss, you'd be licking my ass, just like you lick everyone else's.*

Among the ladies of the Human Resources Department, Bob was known as, "The Perfect Chameleon." Whatever his bosses needed him to be, that's who he was. Among the males of the department, he was often referred to as, "Numb Nuts." You can kick him in the balls, and all he'd say is, "Thank You." But whatever he was called by those he supervised, it didn't matter to him, since in the sixteen years he'd been with the company he'd risen from Director to Senior Vice President, a feat few could match, and he'd survived five different administrations, a feat even fewer could claim.

Bob clearly saw his role as making Senior Management happy and cared little about the effects on the members of his department, or on the employee population as a whole. He would sacrifice any member of his staff, enforce any company policy, or do whatever someone from Senior Management requested, to protect his position.

Last year, a particularly bad one for the company, Senior Management declared that salary increases could not exceed 2% (at least for those beneath the vice presidential level). With inflation running at over 3%, many department managers challenged Senior Management and demanded larger increases for their staffs. Not Bob. He gave everyone a 1% raise and returned the difference to the company.

Without a doubt, and she knew it, this was a set-up. He was going to ask her to do something he didn't want to do himself since the person in the job was going to be a scapegoat if it failed. She gestured with her hands, as if to say, "Continue. I'd like to hear more about it."

He leaned forward, so she did, too, but she was laughing, inside, since this was one of his trademark gestures when he wanted to make someone feel he was taking them into his confidence. But, unusual for him, his voice had a touch of desperation, and he couldn't bring his eyes to look directly at hers. Instead, he was rather fixated on a manila folder stuffed with papers that he dropped onto the coffee table.

"For reasons of both economy and efficiency, five of the Business Affairs offices are going to be consolidated under one management: New York, Washington, Miami, Minneapolis, and London."

She sat upright and turned her eyes towards to the windows. This was big. Business Affairs was the funnel through which virtually all revenue came into the company. The people in that department decided which new business clients to pursue, what were acceptable contract terms, who would service the clients, which companies to partner with, and which pieces of equipment the company should be selling. Ninety percent of all new business the company brought in every year passed through the twenty Business Affairs offices.

For decades, each office operated independently since Senior Management didn't want any one person responsible for so much of the company's business. They feared that if one person had so much power, he or she could damage the company by leaving, or worse, threaten management with unreasonable compensation demands. The system worked fairly well for many years, though there were occasional incidents of conflict-of-interest or territory invasion. But the current economic doldrums, mandated that the company cut costs wherever it could, and focus on the departments and people that were proving to be successful.

Cathy didn't have to ask, but she did. "Who will be the head of the five offices?"

"Samantha Dulak."

From a purely dollars and cents point of view, she definitely deserved the position. Her office was one of twenty, yet under her management it grew to 12% of all revenue brought into the company. The Minneapolis and Washington D.C. offices each represented about 7%. The rest brought in less than 5% of the business. But from an employee morale point of view, which is what Cathy was most concerned about, this could be a disaster. It was Samantha that she was investigating based on Alex's accusations. It was Samantha who so many former employees feared.

Her mind returned to this "extraordinary opportunity" she was being offered. Was she going to have to fire the VP's who headed the other four Business Affairs offices? She really didn't know the people in charge of Washington, London or Miami, but she knew Paul Rhodes, the head of the Minneapolis office quite well. In fact, she had found him and spent quite a bit of time convincing him to leave the company he was with in Austin to move to Minneapolis to take this job. She knew his wife and children very well and had been invited to dinner at their home several times. Undoubtedly, he would be given a generous severance package, so they wouldn't be financially troubled in the short term, but what a disruption to a successful career. It could take years before he was back on track.

Cathy looked at Bob and said, "So, what does this have to do with me?"

"The combined offices will have over 500 employees, and Samantha feels that it should have its own Human Resources Department... completely separate from the rest of the department in New York."

The shoe... no, the boot... the ski boot... is about to drop.

"And Senior Management believes it should be you heading up this department."

Bob was perspiring. He didn't perspire often... not in front of "underlings," and his tone was desperate to convince. Again he spouted the keywords he rehearsed before the meeting: "great opportunity," "visibility to Senior Management," "significant contribution to the future of the company," and on and on. She stopped paying any attention to him. This didn't make sense. Her responsibilities now were far, far greater than being in charge of one department with 1,000 people to serve. Right now she had responsibility over ten offices that serviced over 11,000 employees. From that point-of-view alone, this could be seen as a major step backwards. No matter how he sugar-coated it, the company seemed to be taking authority away from her. As a lump rose in her throat and she fought back tears, she reflected on her performance reviews and how she'd never had a negative rating.

Like many large corporations, THCC avoided firing poor performing women, minorities, and older employees for fear of potential "wrongful discharge" lawsuits. By just squirreling them away in distant offices or giving them new jobs with undesirable responsibilities, they hoped that the humiliation would lead them to quit, or at best, vanish from the corporate vision. With watery eyes and a crackling voice, she interrupted whatever he was saying, "Be straight with me, Bob. Am I being demoted? Does the company want to get rid of me?" She wiped the moisture from around her eye with the napkin that sat under her glass of water.

Panicked, realizing he had positioned this incorrectly, Bob reached out, putting his hand on her arm, desperately trying to correct the wrong impression. "No. No. Quite the opposite. No. No, not at all. In fact, this position comes with a nice raise and someday a shot at a Senior VP title."

Recovering her composure, she began to wonder if the reality was going to be worse than what she imagined. "Why does management want me? Why not Eddie? He's in the New York office and he's worked with

Samantha for a while. He knows what she needs much better than me."

This isn't going well, Bob thought, as he grasped for a way to turn this conversation around. When he imagined the discussion, he pictured her practically jumping up and down with joy at the opportunity. It had never occurred to him that she would be in tears. And now, as the good Human Resources professional she was, she was asking probing questions that would force him to talk about things he'd rather not. Obviously having trouble coming up with just the right words, Bob mumbled, "I can't get into it, but Samantha and Eddie have clashed a bit too much over the years." Bob paused for a moment. He was concerned about giving her too much ammunition for her negotiations, but finally, he just opened his mouth and it came out. "Cathy, Samantha wants you to have the job and isn't willing to consider any alternatives."

Leaning back, Cathy looked out the window and focused on the view of the Statue of Liberty. Bob, realizing he's made a mess of this added, "And Senior Management would really... really like you to take this job, too."

This is going to be real, real bad, she thought. *My God, they're even willing to talk about a salary increase for a job of much smaller proportion, during a year in which they announced a salary freeze.* As she stalled for time to respond by sipping her water again, her mind was racing over the hundreds of implications of accepting or rejecting the position. Bob, sounding more like a used car salesman trying to sell a lemon than a member of management offering a promotion, continued detailing the job's exposure to high level information, larger budgets, and so on.

What about what Alex said? What about the 100% annual turnover rate in the department? What about comments and no-comments from employees she spoke with?

But then, an interesting thought crossed her mind, "Where would I be located?"

"You can stay in Minneapolis. We wouldn't want you to have to uproot your family. You'd have to fly back and forth every week, but that's okay with us."

A smile crossed her lips. "No. I would only take this job if I'm in New York. It can't be done from Minneapolis." They both knew that it could be handled from there, but Bob wasn't going to argue this point since she seemed so strident about it.

" Okay, that's not a problem. We could locate it in New York." Actually, Bob was surprised that she wanted to come to New York since it would be closer to Samantha. Obviously, he thought, she knows nothing about Samantha's reputation.

Realizing that this was the way out of her horrible situation at home, Cathy knew she would take the position, whatever it meant. She'd demand a contract so that if things went badly, she'd still walk away with enough money to survive until she found another job. *In fact*, it occurred to her, *it sounds like they're willing to agree to almost any demand. I better prepare a shopping list before I say yes.*

While Bob was chatting on about something, Cathy could only think that the end of her nightmare was in sight.

At last, a way out!

She wouldn't tell Fred the details. She would tell him that the Human Resources Department was consolidating to save money and that her job was going to be eliminated, so she had to work out of New York or be out of a job. She'd tell him that she would take a small apartment in New York and come back on weekends. He wasn't high up enough in the company to see what was really going on, and by the time he heard the scuttlebutt, she and the girls would be long gone. It might mean she had to give up all her furniture and things, but that was a small price to pay for getting out. Let him have whatever money was in the checking account. Actually, she realized, as the 63% owner of the house, she could sell it any time, and he had no say. She'd let a lawyer worry about that after she was out.

The only problem was the girls. She couldn't take them out of school before the end of the semester... and she certainly couldn't leave them in the house with Fred. That meant she had to stay in Minneapolis, stay with Fred till the end of June. But as long as the end was in sight, she could survive.

"Samantha has a reputation for being a very difficult woman to work with," Cathy politely and politically declared, laying the groundwork for later negotiations.

"Samantha is a brilliant woman, but you're right, she can be difficult. But it's not just her. It's a very high-pressure environment. A lot of money passes through that department and Senior Management and the stockholders are always demanding more. Only a few select people, like you, can work in that environment."

"I want to meet her before I decide."

"Well, you will. We're meeting her in fifteen minutes in the Executive Dining Room."

Taken completely by surprised, Cathy wasn't prepared for this, and she resented that Bob assumed she would go along with his proposal.

Bob, ever confident in his powers of persuasion, lifted his coffee cup to his lips and delighted knowing that Cathy was the sacrificial lamb and not him.

Chapter 24

Cathy was instantly taken with Samantha. Besides being attractive, sophisticated, and exceptionally gracious, she turned Bob into an invisible ground-hog with just a sideward glance. If a stenographer had recorded the conversation that day, his name would never have appeared.

"Circe. That's a very unusual name. What's the derivation?" Samantha asked as a way of breaking the ice. Obviously, the executive dining room didn't suffer from the cutbacks that affected the rest of the company. It had it's own four-star trained chef and there was a waiter and busboy for every three tables. Silver plated flatware was used instead of stainless steel and the starched white cotton napkins never had a stain or tear.

"It was my ex-husband's name. I kept it because of the kids." Cathy said.

Samantha nodded and mouthed the words, of course.

"It's Greek origin. I don't know what the original name was, but one of the officers at Ellis Island shortened it to Circe and the family kept it. The original name was pronounced with hard C's, but I tell everyone it's French and pronounce it sir-say."

"It does have a European feel. Catianna Circe."

Every day of her professional life – and the last few of her personal life – was a fencing match. Using words to feint, riposte, lunge, probe for truth and lies from corporate executives with hidden agendas, candidates who will say anything to get a job, employees complaining about bosses, and bosses complaining about employees. Every meeting with Bob began with an "En Garde."

But with Samantha, it was different. Maybe it was because she was a woman in management, and that created an instant bond, or maybe, it was her disarming Southern charm. In a matter of minutes, they were sorority sisters who hadn't seen each other in years. "Actually, Samantha, I wish I had used my middle name, Isabel, when I started my career. I've always liked that name more, but it would upset my father since I was named after his grandmother, Catianna. I love him dearly, but he never appreciated how difficult it was for a child to grow up with a name like Catianna. I always liked the flow of Isabel Circe. It sounds like a dancer's name. Your name, Dulak, sounds French."

"It's Czechoslovakian and our name originally had 26 letters in it. Dulak was somewhere in the middle."

Samantha laughed, recalling her father's pained reaction when she told him that this was the new family name. "I said if you don't legally change our name, I'm going to marry the first boy I can find named Smith. He knew I wasn't kidding. By the way, you don't have to be so formal with me; people call me Sam. I like it because it puts me on equal footing with all the men in the place." She looked at Bob, who just smiled and bobbed his head up and down.

As someone in Human Resources, it was second nature for Cathy to interview people, so without thinking she asked Samantha about her career.

Delighted to tell her story, Samantha explained that she started her career in the legal department twelve years earlier as a Contracts Attorney who's primary responsibility was to make certain that the company wasn't exposed to unnecessary liabilities. However, on a regular basis, without instruction or authority, she stepped out of the role of protecting the company from things that might never happen, to protecting the company from things that were happening.

It was apparent to Samantha that the contracts being sent to the legal department for approval contained agreements and obligations that were unnecessarily costing the company millions of dollars annually. Nothing illegal or suspicious, just bad business practices, such as not penalizing contractors for cost overruns or delayed deliveries, or paying far too much to vendors in advance of deliveries and losing the use of the capital for months or even years. She brought it to the attention of the head of the legal department, and he admonished her for stepping out of bounds. "We don't make the deals here, we just make sure there are no legal problems with them."

Unsatisfied with that response, Samantha, in a move that could have ended her career on the spot, went to the company's Chief Financial Officer and laid a thick folder on his desk detailing the loss of almost $50 million over a five-year period. It obviously caught his attention, as well as that of everyone up to the President and CEO of the company. Before a week had passed, she was moved into the Business Affairs Department, reporting directly to the CFO. Within a matter of weeks, it was fairly obvious that she would be heading up that department; it was just a matter of time.

It took almost ten months, but one day, Bob Evans, the Senior VP for Business Affairs, and one of the good ol' boys, surprisingly "decided" to take early retirement, and she was promoted, jumping over at least seven men who thought they were in line for the position. In the six years since she became the head of Business Affairs in New York, revenues increased 250% from that office and they climbed from sixth place to first in the rankings. Because of her success, poise and personality (not to mention her good looks), the company put her out front on many occasions, such as meetings with investment analysts, shareholder meetings, and speeches at industry conferences. She was on the cover of *Fortune*, and articles about her appeared in *BusinessWeek*, the *Wall Street Journal*, and *Barron's*.

There was no doubt in Cathy's mind that Samantha had earned the respect of Senior Management and the investment community, however, the cost in human capital... the employees in her department... was enormous.

Fascinated – no, mesmerized – by her, Cathy struggled to appear as if she was seriously considering the opportunity, but wasn't yet convinced. "Let me be blunt," Cathy politely interjected, "your reputation is of being a very... demanding woman. The turnover rate in your department is extraordinarily high."

Not a bit bothered by her reputation, actually rather proud of it, Samantha simply replied, "As you can see, I'm not a six-headed monster. I am demanding, and what we do is very intense. There is a lot of burnout, but at the same time, not many people can do what needs to be done. I'll be honest," she turned towards Bob for a moment and back to Cathy, "I think the Human Resources Department has seriously failed my department. We're not seeing the best and the brightest candidates."

Cathy turned to Bob, expecting him to be outraged, or at least argumentative, but instead his head just kept bobbing, in total agreement with absolutely everything she said. "I'm sorry to say that in public, Bob," Samantha continued, not looking at him, "but it's something I've said to you many times."

Cathy wasn't about to defend the New York office since apparently a great many things have been going on that she didn't know anything about.

"I like what you did in Minneapolis, Cathy. In the two years you've been in charge, you've turned that department around. You've brought in a lot of good people. That's why I want you working for me."

Shocked that Samantha even knew about her work in Minneapolis, she said, "Thank you for your confidence in me," and "I didn't do it alone in Minneapolis, we work as team." At the same time, Cathy's mind was calculating the pluses and minuses. This truly was a career-maker versus career-breaker position. She could become a shining star or flame out quickly... and to be quite honest, the latter was more likely. Then, Samantha said something that not only pulled Cathy back from her thoughts, but absolutely frightened her.

"I know you've spoken with a number of former employees from my department...."

An 8.0 earthquake shook the table. At that moment she realized the true octopus-like reach of this woman. Maybe Alex and the former employees were right, and she was to be feared more than respected.

Samantha wondered if Cathy had been told something by Alex that had raised a red flag, or if she had "informants" around the company who had fed her information about today's meeting. If it was the former, she really would have liked to know what Cathy had been told. If it was the latter, she was very impressed.

Meekly, Cathy lied, "I was just preparing for this meeting. I hope you don't think I was sneaking around behind your back."

Bob, who knew that Cathy didn't know anything about this meeting, perked up once he heard that former employees were contacted, and guessed it had something to do with Alex. He made a mental note to interrogate Cathy later on the subject. Then he went back to bobbing his head.

"No, don't worry about it. I'm glad you did it. It's important that you understand the type of people who will succeed and will fail in Business Affairs. Let me just say this, which I know very few people appreciate." She paused to formulate her thoughts. "Let me ask you, are you enrolled in the company's pension plan?"

Cathy nodded.

"So a fair portion of your retirement benefits are invested in company stock?"

Cathy nodded again.

"Between present and past employees, pension funds across America and around the world, IRAs and mutual funds, twenty or thirty million people have a portion of their retirements fund invested with this company.

"Every time our stock goes down one dollar because our sales are soft, one billion seven hundred twenty-two million dollars are lost from people's retirement accounts. One billion seven hundred twenty-two million dollars every time the stock drops one dollar. Who do you think the stockholders and Senior Management turn to when that happens? Not Bob (whose head was now shaking and not nodding). Not you. Me. They come to me for an explanation, and they demand that I get the stock back up. I can't do that with people who say they have to leave at 5:00 p.m. because they like to be home in time to have dinner with their families."

Sitting back, Cathy realized that no matter how high she climbed in the HR department, by comparison to Samantha, she was just a tiny cog in an enormous machine. She had never considered the enormity of this person's position, and for the first time, understood why she wielded so much power within the organization. At that moment, she felt guilty for taking her away from her responsibilities.

But at the same time, this opportunity excited her. She was an insignificant, replaceable, worker bee, and now for the first time, the Queen Bee was asking her to be a partner, to keep the beehive humming. She knew she had to be part of this. This was an opportunity. Not only was this a chance to get away from Fred, but this was her one chance to get out of a tiny, anonymous office where she would be forgotten as soon as she left it.

"Let me tell you something that we're working on now, that really excites me, and why I need your help. NASA is completely renovating its technology infrastructure. It's a $100 billion contract – that's billion with a capital B - over the next 10 years. It's the technology they'll be using for decades to come to send people to the planets and to chart the universe." Like a child talking about a new telescope she got for Christmas, her eyes widened, her face became animated, and her hands were waving, pointing to planets in the distant galaxies. "I want them using THCC computers when they send manned flights to Mars. I want NASA using THCC's computers when people can travel to the Moon like they travel to Cancun. I want them using THCC's computers when they send probes to the next galaxy to find life on other planets.

"I want people around me who not only want the same things as I do, but who are willing to work for it, even if it means missing their daughters' ballet recitals or their sons' soccer games. That's the kind of person this company needs, and that's the kind of person I think you are."

Without waiting for a response, she stood up, "Think about it. I'm leaving for London tonight. Call me next week and tell me if you want to join me. I would really love to have you on my team. I think we can do a lot together." With that she left.

Cathy's eyes followed her till she walked out the door of the dining room. For the first time in a long time, she was inspired by someone in this company's management. Samantha was more than unique, she was a woman with both a vision and the ability to see it come to life. For sure, it wasn't the smartest career decision she could make, but Cathy wanted to be around someone like her.

As if helium was injected into Bob through his rectum, he re-inflated, assuming the position of a Senior Vice President for Human Resources at THCC. Probing Cathy's level of interest for his report to Senior Management, he asked half a dozen questions (including one about Alex) and then sat back, waiting for answers from someone he thought of as a subordinate.

But, as if she had already mentally moved under Samantha's umbrella, she couldn't be bothered responding to him. She knew her answer was going to be "yes," but instinctively she knew not to let him know since it would weaken her negotiating room.

"What are you offering, Bob?"

Chapter 25

"Are you having an affair?" Chris asked his wife when she called at 6:00 p.m. to say she she'd be later than usual He was joking, but he wasn't sure what answer he would have preferred.

"It's a new client that can't come in during the day, so I had to schedule a meeting in the evening. It's the most ridiculous case I've ever handled." She must have handled a thousand divorces, he reckoned, but she took each one so seriously. It's what attracted clients to her.

"This couple was married for 25 years. Then one day he meets a girl half his age and walks out on his family."

Oh, Chris mused, *another one of society's deviants has crossed her threshold, so now I'll have to hear about men who are prone towards infidelity everyday until the final bill is paid.* "Sounds like a mid-life-crisis case. You get those everyday," Chris interjected, trying to sound attentive, while he continued to search the internet for advertising jobs.

"What's interesting about this is that his business declared bankruptcy a few years ago, so she controls all the money in the house. All the charge cards are in her name, only she can sign the checks, the mortgage is in her name."

Chris groaned, hopefully not aloud, thinking of how bad it would be if Melanie had that much control over their finances. How would he cover up all those little unexplained expenses?

"So the amusing thing is that he has to go to his wife and ask her for money so he can live with his new girlfriend." Melanie talked as if she were laying out the case for a jury. She often used Chris as a representative of the typical jury panel – not too well informed about the law, sympathetic towards the underdog, and definitely favoring the woman. She found it helpful when preparing her case. Chris hated being used that way.

"That is odd. I hope she told him to go to hell."

"Why shouldn't he get access to the money, after all it's his, too." Melanie argued. "In fact, he still earns 100% of the money brought into the household. Doesn't he have the right to get some of it back, regardless of how he spends it?"

Yet again, he admonished himself for forgetting to ask who her client was before speaking.

"Anyway, don't wait for me for dinner. I'll have a sandwich here. Love you." She hung up.

As he so often did when hearing about one of her cases, he said to himself, *What a rotten profession Melanie is in*, he shook his head. *How can she find it rewarding. It's not important and noble... like selling tampons.*

Whether it was the suggestion of having an affair, the discussion about destructive divorces, or the idea of having dinner alone, Chris suddenly thought about Barry Balin and wondered if he would want to go to dinner. "I hope he's showered recently."

Standing up, he took a quick look at himself in the reflection of the *West Side Story* poster, combed the right side of his head with his fingers, and headed down to Barry's office. It would be a rotten evening, he knew, but everyone in the office would think how wonderful it was of him.

Turning into Barry's office, he stopped, as if he walked into a glass wall.

It wasn't Barry's office any more. It was… Gary's.

Leaning back in his chair, Gary lifted his surrealistic-phallic-shaped coffee mug to his lips, and smiled widely before taking a sip. "Come to visit me in my new office?"

Chris gasped, "Where's Barry?"

"Gone and forgotten," the new occupant announced with the voice of the victor. "It's official. I'm the new Management Supervisor on the accounts formerly known as Barry's. Since I've been dong all the work, I finally got the recognition." Gary wanted to make certain that Chris knew that they were equals now.

Chris' eyes darted around the room trying to find some hint of the reality he had known only a day or two ago. Nothing was recognizable anymore, not even the artwork on the walls or the books on the shelves. Nothing was the same. Looking at Gary was too painful, so he let his eyes drift down to the coffee mug that Gary always used. It had been sent to him by one of the football magazines his client advertised in, and the message printed on it read, "Ad men know the best positions to do it in."

Backing out of the office, as if seeing a ghost, Chris raced into the Maze, abandoning caution about his path to find Candy. She would know what happened. But since he rarely approached her from this direction, once more he got lost and found himself in the Media Department's section. Fortunately, the media people were friendlier than the Creatives, and they guided him back to his secretary.

"What happened to Barry?" he blurted from ten feet away—as soon as he saw the top of Candy's kinky hair.

"You didn't hear? It's terrible. He had a nervous breakdown right in front of the client."

"Oh, my God!" Dropping into a red plastic chair, Chris raised his hand to his mouth, feeling as if he was going to throw up.

"Yesterday, the client came in for the regular quarterly review. Barry came to the meeting even though Mack had told him not to. He hadn't showered or shaved for days. When Mack went to escort him out, he collapsed on the floor and started crying uncontrollably. They couldn't move him. He was kicking and screaming. They had to move everyone out of the conference room as fast as they could and into Mack's office to finish the meeting. Mack promoted Gary on the spot and had the building's security people come up and pack Barry's things and put them in storage."

"This isn't happening! I don't believe this! Where's Barry?" It was too incredulous to believe. Barry was like the pipe-smoking professor who only registered shocked by withdrawing the pipe from his mouth for a moment or two.

"They called paramedics to come and sedate him and take him away."

"Has anyone been in touch with him? He can't be left alone." All for the love of a woman. Was she worth all this?

"He stayed overnight in the hospital. His secretary called his wife... ex-wife... whatever she is. Supposedly she's going to take him home with her. Isn't that the biggest joke of all? She can't stand him and leaves him, so he has a nervous breakdown, and she ends up taking care of him."

Chris was too speechless to say anything except, "I'm speechless!" Focusing his eyes on his secretary, he tried to decide what he could do for Barry, what the sudden elevation of a bigoted idiot would mean to the agency... to him. Was there a danger of losing the client... the biggest one at the agency... a lot of people would get laid off... maybe me. With Gary at the helm, we're sure to lose the client eventually. Come to think of it... "By the way, where is Sheila in all this? How come she didn't get promoted? She's certainly more capable than Gary and she had seniority."

"Oh my God, you should have seen what happened between Gary and Sheila right after the client left. They had this huge knock-down-drag-out fight in Barry's office. You could hear their screams all the way over in the creative department. He used the 'C' word. She called him an f'ing asshole. He yelled that he was tired of carrying her ass on this account. She screamed that the only reason he got the job was because he had a penis and that he certainly didn't have a brain. I think they would have tried to strangle each other if Sandy didn't run over and break up the fight."

"So, where is she now?" At this moment, Chris didn't know if he was more shocked by what had been happened over the last 24 hours, or that he was so ignorant of it all.

"She just walked out screaming F.U. Two of the other female account people left also."

"We're all adults here. Things like this aren't supposed to happen."

"Chris," Candy advised warmly, laughing, "stay in your office. It's safe in there."

No it's not, he knew, but couldn't tell her. *However*, he wondered, *maybe this takes the heat off me. They'll be so busy concentrating on keeping the current clients, maybe they'll lose interest in whether my client goes on TV.*

"I guess so." Shaking his head in disbelief, he tried to focus his eyes on something, anything.

Noticing that the bridal gown pictures were all gone and brochures for honeymoon spots replaced them as decorations on her desk, he asked, "How are the nuptial arrangements going?"

"Okay." Her voice was less than robust, which made Chris stop what he was doing and look at her with some concern in his eyes.

"It's not anything terrible," she whispered, not wanting anyone to hear. "I think it's just nerves."

Trying to comfort her, he said, "I was so nervous just before we got married, I broke out in hives—all over. I was so puffy and red I almost couldn't fit into my suit." It was a lie, but he hoped it would make her feel better. "I'll bring in our wedding pictures one day. You'll see, I'm the tomato in a tuxedo."

"You're kidding!" Whether she believed him or not, it didn't matter because she smiled, which made Chris happy. He turned to leave, took two steps, and stopped.

"Go to the Frog. Make a right. Then a left at the Ford Mustang memorabilia."

"What happened to the French flag? I always used to turn at the French flag."

"She was one of Bob's account executives who quit when Gary was promoted."

Chapter 26

Considering the offer just made, the investigation into the high turnover rate in the Business Affairs Department took on increased importance, and Cathy wanted to borrow an office in the Human Resources Department in New York for the remainder of the day. However, the revelation that she couldn't make phone calls to company employees without Samantha knowing about it was quite disconcerting and she didn't want to chance being caught again.

How did she find out about that? Cathy wondered. *Did one of the employees tell her? That's absurd. They were all too frightened and glad to be away from her. Could someone have overheard the conversation? Possibly, but not likely. I was in Minneapolis surrounded by my staff, not hers. Does she have a spy in my office? Do you think she checked my phone records? My God, I'm getting paranoid. That weasel Bob must have told her that Alex was coming to see me. He'll betray anyone.*

Maybe it was just a lucky guess.

Since she wasn't going to continue her research today, and since she wanted some time to think about both a compensation package and what she needed to do to get away from Fred, she decided to take the afternoon off. New York was a great city for just walking and thinking. You could go up Fifth Avenue, Madison Avenue, the Upper West Side, or down into The Village. You could go in any direction and enjoy walking in and out of stores and galleries… that is, except on days like today, when a conga line of slow-moving, picture-taking crowds made progress impossible.

Besides, going into stores and shopping wasn't very enjoyable anymore since Fred took control of their finances and demanded to know what every purchase was and why it was made. She shuddered as she heard him scream as loud in her imagination as it would be in her ears, "Another pair of black shoes! Take them back! I refuse to pay for them!"

"As if it was his money I'm spending," she mumbled in disgust.

Turning back towards the hotel, she resigned herself to working from there, but then, an idea came to her, *How about going back to Brooklyn?*

Cathy traveled to THCC's headquarters building on Park Avenue seven or eight times a year, every year for the last two decades, yet it never occurred to her to go to Brooklyn to see where she grew up. Once her parents moved to Florida, that borough had no attraction any longer. But with the recent re-discovery of her classmates, and Chris, and re-living so many memories, she felt a sudden and intense desire to see the house she grew up in and the streets she walked so often. Turning around, and accidentally bumping into a Japanese couple who had stopped to take a picture of the Atlas statue in front of Rockefeller Center, she headed for the Times Square subway station. Grand Central station was closer, but boarding the subway at Times Square meant it took her down Broadway, past the theatres she and Chris visited so often. Since her goal was to re-live her memories, it had to begin, and end, on Broadway.

Chris took her hand and held it for hours the first time in a Broadway theatre together. He said, "I love you," for the first time as they left a Broadway theater after seeing *Chorus Line.* And, he proposed marriage one cold night as they waited on the discount line for a Broadway show. He was happier, so much more alive, on these streets. She never would have taken him away from this. She still couldn't believe that he moved 3,000 miles away.

Twisting her head to look at the marquees down 48th, she laughed and uttered, "The more things change, the more they stay the same." Soon she realized that this became her mantra for the day.

With the camera in her cell phone she photographed the streets and the theater marquees that were so familiar to her and Chris. Of the theaters on 48th Street, three were playing revivals of shows that that the two young lovers had seen more than twenty years ago (different theaters, though) - *Fiddler on the Roof*, *Hello Dolly* (though this time with an all-African American cast), and *The Price*. The theaters on 46th Street had two shows they had seen from the balconies - *A Streetcar Named Desire* and *Camelot* - and the theaters surrounding Shubert Alley (between 44th and 45th Streets) were heavy with nostalgia - *Oklahoma*, *42nd Street*, *Gypsy*, and *Death of a Salesman*.

"The more things change, the more they stay the same."

She stopped on 42nd Street, causing a small vortex of congestion and cursing, to appreciate how that street had changed. Gone were the porn theaters with erotic names like *Pussycat* and *Beaver*, and in there place were the wholesome, family-oriented offerings from Walt Disney and American Airlines. The sharp contrast made her wince, as she wondered what the disinfection process was for those theaters. "If the walls could talk."

She wanted to take a picture of the entrance to the 42nd Street station, but that had changed too radically, and the crowds of New Yorkers descending into their rapid transit system weren't about to let her stop to remember that moment, so she surrendered to the flow and stepped down into the tumult of the subterranean cavern.

It was impossible to calculate how many hours they had spent on this station waiting for the next train to Brooklyn, but it astonished her, how so much remained the same. The mosaic tile that clung to the walls declaring that this was where your journey begins or ends. The chewing-gum-stained-cement and worn-out-steel staircase, the splintering wooden handrails that were thick with generations of paint. The old saxophone player who entertained the waiting crowds as they stared down black tunnels hoping for that pin-prick of light to magically appear. The Salvation Army soldier collecting for the needy. The fried donut maker filling the air with wretched grease and arteries with the same. The discount electronics store that was always having a "Going Out of Business Sale," and the clothing store that was selling "Fine Imported Silk Ties" for only $3. The faces and the names may have changed, but they were all still there, feeding off the energy of a million feet racing across one platform to the next.

There was no camera that could take a picture of all this, so she just made a mental photo and promised herself to write about it all in her next e-mail to Chris.

As the train rolled to a stop in front of her, and a small army exploded from the sliding metal doors, and an even larger army charged in, she had to admit, the subway cars were much nicer now than they were back then. Not only had they figured out how to keep the spray paint graffiti off the walls, but the trains were all air conditioned now. The memories of standing, crushed by crowds, struggling to get her hand on a pole to steady herself, seemed so comforting now, though they certainly hadn't been at the time. Even the unwelcome and unfriendly gropings from a stealthy passenger that hid behind a newspaper or book, didn't seem so terrible in memory.

The people definitely were different. New York was never a homogenous community, but the present diversity blossomed like the colors of Autumn. Growing up in New York, she was well aware of the White, African-American, Chinese, Italian, and Puerto Rican populations, but other groups seemed rare. Now, turban clad Sikhs and veiled women barely attracted any stares or curiosity. Haitians and Arabs, chattering away in their native languages, were common, as were Koreans and Pacific Islanders. Many of the advertisements that lined the trains were in Spanish, which bore testimony not only to the size of the Hispanic population, but also to their dominance in the underground world of the subways. New York had always opened its arms, and received the people of the world.

The subway was a lifeline for Chris and Cathy. It took them from where they were to where they wanted to be, from the small provincial neighborhoods of Brooklyn to the teeming metropolis of Manhattan. Everything they wanted was just on the other side of the East River from Brooklyn, and traveling underground, under the water, was the way to get there. They were always chattier on the way into Manhattan, and more somber on their way back to Brooklyn.

Exiting the subway at the Kings Avenue station was like stepping back in time.

In a world of instant communications, it was strange... it was nice... to visit a place that time seemed to have forgotten.

Snapping picture after picture with her cell phone, it all seemed the same. The grocery store with fruit and vegetables displayed on the sidewalk was still there, and little old ladies were still squeezing the melons to see which were ripe and which needed to be left out for a few days. The Jewish Deli was still there, with strings of hot dogs hanging in the window. FAY'S, a diner from the 50's and the favorite restaurant of the after school crowd was gone, but it was replaced, ironically, by THE 50's DINER, a restaurant that pretended to be from the era of its predecessor. The Brooklyn Savings Bank was gone and a Chase Manhattan branch was there instead, but it was still a bank and it was in the same building, though re-painted an electric green.

Kings Avenue still had shoe stores, clothing stores (The Brooklyn Boutique), restaurants, electronics stores, toy stores, gift shops, hairdressers, barbershops, and so on, but there wasn't a single Gap, Eddie Bauer, Ann Taylor, McDonald's, Starbucks, Circuit City, or Toys-R-Us to be found anywhere. It was still an old neighborhood street, and that wrapped Cathy like a warm blanket.

Too hard to resist any longer, she pulled out her cell phone and called Chris. Even though they had reunited via e-mail, she wasn't ready to speak with him till now. Not being able to call from work or home was a good excuse for not calling, but the truth was, she was a little frightened to call him. It had been so many years, and they ended so badly. She wasn't sure what tone to adopt and what words to say. But right now, back in Brooklyn, she felt good, and she wanted to share it with him.

With a tear in her eye, and slight, airy, catch in her voice, she said with a broad smile, "Hello, Chris, this is a voice from the past."

Not because he didn't instantly recognize her voice, but because the shock of hearing it was so great, he couldn't respond with anything audible for what seemed like an eternity. Choking for breath as if he swallowed water down his wind pipe, he finally coughed out, "Cathy! I can't believe it's you. Oh my God! This is incredible. You said you wanted to wait before we spoke, but... I'm so glad to hear from you. How are you?"

"I'm okay. It's so good to hear your voice. It sounds exactly like it did 20 years ago. I just had to call you. I couldn't wait another day." His voice was a magic carpet taking her to another world, another time, another place. His voice was joy, and happiness, and warmth and love, all rolled into one, just like it used to be. As ecstatic as a bride on her wedding day, she said, "You'll never believe where I am."

Sounding like the groom watching his bride come down the aisle, he said, "I hope you're at LAX and you want me come to the airport and pick you up. I can't believe I'm talking to you after all these years. God bless the internet."

Speaking slowly to emphasize every word, truly overwhelmed by her discovery. "I am standing in front of Kings Avenue Pizza. Remember that place next to the station. We must have eaten 10,000 calories at this place." Pressing her nose against the window, her eyes watered as she reflected on all the good times they had.

"How can I forget? That's where I dripped all that oil on my shirt on our first date. I was so embarrassed." Pulling his high school yearbook from the bottom drawer of his desk, he turned to Cathy's picture, and kissed his finger and touched her face. Re-reading, once again, her inscription - I don't know when, I don't know how, I don't know where, but at some moment, part of you became part of me, part of me became part of you. I'll love you always - his eyes began to water.

"It's also the place where you kissed me on my lips for the very first time. Though you were pretending to lick the tomato sauce off my mouth."

"Yes," his voice grew softer, "I remember that. I was so nervous. I had been wanting to do that from the first moment we met, but I was so frightened I would scare you away. I almost peed my pants." He remembered how she was so surprised; how neither let go of the kiss for a long, long time.

"You won't believe how little the neighborhood has changed. It's mind-blowing (even her language reverted back twenty-five years) to see Hassidic Rabbis walking down the street talking on cell phones now, but the street looks just like it did back then. This is so amazing. Remember that old guy who ran the fruit stand?"

"Sure. He hated when anyone squeezed his melons." Enjoying the past with her, Chris could see Kings Avenue as clearly as if he had just turned the corner.

"Well, he's still here." The sign had changed from "Dido's Grocery Store" to "Dido & Son," but that was the only change she could see.

"Maybe he wasn't so old back then. We were just a lot younger, I guess."

"Now, he's really, really old."

They laughed together, just like they used to do. She sat on a bus bench, and as if no time had passed, they chatted, talking about her kids, high school friends, her job, his job, L.A., Minneapolis, current and ex-spouses, and (which didn't escape Chris) her "insignificant" other.

"How are your parents and your sister?" asked Chris. He would have said 'frightening father' and 'pain-in-the-ass sister,' but they were re-uniting and he didn't want to spoil it. People may have changed in the past 20 years.

"The folks moved to Florida, mom past away five years ago."

"I'm sorry to hear that. She was a wonderful person. I liked her a lot."

"She liked you, too." That brought a tear to both their eyes. "My sister is still in New York, in the same rent-controlled apartment."

He couldn't resist. "Is she still a pain in the ass?"

Looking around to see if anyone could hear her, she said, "Yes, she hasn't changed. I'll tell you a secret if you promise not to tell anyone."

"Who would I tell?" He chuckled.

With a laugh, she admonished, "I don't know. I always thought you gossiped a bit too much with all the girls. That's why they loved talking to you in the cafeteria." It was something they argued about back then, and she knew he would remember it.

"That was 30 years ago. I don't talk to anyone anymore. Just tell me." He hated being teased like that and she knew it - that's why she did it.

Cupping her hand over the phone so no one could hear her, she whispered, "About ten years ago I could have transferred to the New York office, but I didn't take the job because I didn't want to be that close to my father and sister."

"He was pretty tough to be around." Chris remembered how her father would leave the room when he, a non-Jew, entered the house, how he wouldn't shake his hand - even on graduation day.

"Here I was, on a fast career track, and I didn't want him treating me like a child again. And I reeeeaaaally didn't need my sister sucking the life out of me. It was right after my second divorce and it would have been nice to be around family, but just not my family. I took a San Francisco position instead."

"Your father never liked me. I wasn't a Man's Man like he was." Time vanished, and the hurt returned.

"It wasn't that he didn't like you. He was a Holocaust survivor and he didn't want me dating a good Irish Catholic boy. Mom loved you because you were always a gentleman and you were good to me. She always talked about how you helped her carry the groceries up the stairs."

Every now and then the D Train would pass overhead and they couldn't hear each other. But, they were back together again, as if a lost piece of the puzzle was found.

Technology interceded in a conversation that probably would have gone on for hours. After about 45 minutes, her cell phone battery started to fade so they knew this incredible experience had to end. Nothing, not even discovering the secret recipe for non-caloric cheese cake, could have given either of them greater happiness than this phone call. Just before they hung up Chris asked, "So, is Thomas Wolfe right, you can't go home again?"

Cathy forced a laugh, "You can't, especially when they tore your house down to build condos on it." But, after a slight pause, with a tone that reached across the years and the miles, and sent a valentine from her heart to his, she asked, "But can you go back to the beginning and start the journey all over again?" In the moment of silence that followed, the little bit of life that was left in her battery was exhausted and they could speak no more. They were each other's "road not taken."

Both held onto their phones a while longer, looking at them as if they would have looked at each other's face. In their hands they held the past, and all it's memories, good and bad. Each wondered if in their hands was a new future. "The kids would have been beautiful," was all she could say as she dropped her cell phone into her purse. Standing up from the bus bench, and surveying the street, Cathy couldn't bear to leave the old neighborhood. She was home. It had been a long journey, but she was finally home again.

Wandering up and down the street, she stopped into one store after another. Definitely fewer Jewish store-owners and a lot more Pakistani's and Korean's, but that same warm greeting and willingness to serve transferred to the current owners from the old ones.

New clothing stores were in the place of old ones, and while the styles had changed, Brooklyn - at least this part of Brooklyn - was still months, maybe even years, behind what anyone in Manhattan would have called current fashion.

"Oh my God, it's still here!" She blurted out, as she wandered into the soda fountain. Sitting on one of the stools at the counter, she spun around, albeit a lot slower, just like she used to when she was there with Chris or a girlfriend. Without even thinking about it, she ordered her beverage of choice from 25 years ago, "I'll have a vanilla egg cream," though the $4.00 charge was a bit shocking since she remembered only paying 25¢ in the past.

As she watched the young soda jerk mix the milk, vanilla syrup, and seltzer into the V-shaped paper cup with the metal holder, she almost cried. So many images flooded back it was impossible to process them all. Chris gave her a friendship ring here. It was here that she cried her eyes out to Leslie when she thought she and Chris had broken up forever. It was here that Judy told Cathy what it was like to have intercourse. And, it was here that Cathy told Judy after she and Chris did it for the first time.

The cracked red leather seats rocked back and forth, just like they did then, and the posters on the walls for Elvis Presley movies (a favorite of the owner) were the exact posters that hung there decades ago, though they had yellowed since then, and it was the owner's son who now managed the place. The tin ceiling had been painted over several times, so the intricate details of the design were gone, but the black-and-white hexagonal tile floor hadn't changed, though it was easy to see a lot more chips or cracks.

Stepping back on the street, she noticed that the corner drugstore was gone and a much larger one had taken over the location. Stopping in front of the door, she couldn't stop laughing as she remembered the night they went out together to buy a condom for Chris so they could make love for the first time, and it was she who had to buy it because he was so embarrassed.

Mothers walked up the street, still pushing their babies in carriages.

The owner of the newspaper stand still wore gloves with the fingers cut off. The sign over the Brooklyn Beauty Salon was still gold and gaudy. And stoutly, cigar smoking men still argued about who had the better pitchers, the New York Yankees or the New York Mets.

Around 7:00 p.m., when most of the stores had closed for the evening, with their metal fences rolled down to protect their windows, Cathy wandered into the Kings Avenue Diner. This restaurant wasn't there when she lived in the neighborhood, but it certainly looked as if it came soon afterwards. Had she not been wandering down memory lane, she probably never would have stopped in since it was quite frayed around the edges, and a musty odor greeted customers walking through the door. The wood paneled walls were scratched and dented, the booths were clean but the vinyl seats cracked or torn, and even the customers looked old and tired. More than being old, they were huge. Everyone seated, and everyone serving, looked like over grown teddy bears. The Kings Avenue Diner was known for large portions - something she could see on the tables surrounding hers - and customers packed the restaurant.

"What can I get for you, Hon?" the waitress asked.

At first, Cathy thought that pretending to be from the fifties was just part of the atmosphere of the restaurant, but then she realized that this was the real thing. She wasn't pretending to sound like she was a waitress from Brooklyn in the 1950's, she was a waitress from Brooklyn, and she probably had been a waitress since the 1950's.

"I'll have some coffee while I look over the menu." The laminate menu with big, colorful pictures of hamburgers, hot dogs, spaghetti and meatballs in tomato sauce, steaks, French fries, and ice cream Sundays, just wreaked of calories. This is the way I used to eat, she had to admit. No wonder I was 30 pounds heavier in high school.

Serving the coffee and lifting her pad and pen, the waitress asked again, "What can I get for you, Hon?"

Cathy's eyes raced over the menu looking for the salads. Having a choice of only one made the decision decidedly easier. "A chef's salad." She quickly added, "Hold the Russian dressing, and can I get oil and balsamic vinegar on the side?"

Clearly annoyed that the patron didn't adhere to the "no substitutions" policy stated on the bottom of the menu, but at the same time, willing to provide superior service to this out-of-towner who didn't know the rules, the waitress indifferently offered, "I don't know where the vinegar is from. I'll just bring you what we got."

"I'm certain that will be fine," Cathy started to say, but the waitress was gone before she could utter the first couple of words.

Looking down Kings Avenue, she thought how small it seemed now. The two and three-story brick buildings that were once the center of her world, the street where and she and Chris and her friends would spend hours shopping and talking, seemed so limited and removed from the real world. At one time she just assumed she would take her place in the neighborhood and spend her life here - and that didn't seem so bad back then. Now it was an alien, and even distasteful, thought. Being here for a nostalgic visit was fine, but staying here was now inconceivable. She was a tourist, a spectator to the life that once was. The world - her world - had gotten a lot bigger, and had moved away from here.

If we never experienced the world outside, could we have been happy here? she asked the Chris in her mind. And then sadly she thought, *Maybe we could have only been happy here.*

Around 9:00 p.m. Cathy climbed the stairs of the Kings Avenue Station and took the D train back to Manhattan, exiting near her hotel at the Columbus Circle station.

With the little power that was left in her cell phone's battery, she scanned the photo's that she had taken during the day and it warmed her. But she didn't know Chris' cell phone number so she couldn't send them to him, and she didn't want Fred to see where she had been during the day, so she deleted them, and suddenly she remembered an e-mail she had to send to the payroll department to let them know about someone's Change in Status form.

Chapter 27

In her continuing efforts to purge every pore of her body from Fred's rancid touch, Cathy submerged herself in the hotel spa's hot tub, before having a salt scrub, facial, and massage. As the hot water bubbled around her neck and the tension in her muscles floated away, she couldn't remember a day she felt so satisfied. The nightmare that had been her daily existence was coming to an end. The company she devoted her life to was acknowledging her capabilities. After 20 years of moving from one city or another, she was finally coming home, and she couldn't have had a more wonderful day than visiting the neighborhood she grew up in and then talking to Chris.

At some moment, part of you became part of me, and part of me became part of you. We are one. How often had they said that to each other. Talking to him made her feel whole and complete again. The emptiness she had lived with for the past 20 years was gone now. How rare it was to meet the person you're truly fated to be with so early in your life. Maybe they met too early, maybe they both had to explore. She rubbed her high school ring. It had become the only piece of jewelry she wore all the time (though usually on a chain hidden beneath her blouse). So many memories.

The attendant tapped her on the shoulder to let her know that Antinous was ready for her. Rising from the bubbling cauldron, she wrapped the towel around her naked body and followed the attendant to the candle lit massage studio. Desperately wanting to be reminded that a man's touch can be sensitive and pleasurable, she requested a male masseuse.

"Be gentle, please," she guided, before she relinquished her body to his hands.

Just about the same time, Chris was meandering up and down the aisles of Ralph's Supermarket near his office. Chris loved going to the supermarket. To his trained eye, it wasn't just a warehouse for food, cleansers, and paper products, it was a dynamic and exciting battleground where the best marketing and product development brains in the world fought for the smallest edge over the competition.

Supermarkets operated on razor thin margins, so everything was designed to increase profitability. End aisle and in-aisle displays were usually from manufacturers who offered incentives - such as free or discounted merchandise - to the store. Products for children were on the lower shelves so the child would take them and insist that the parent buy them, while products for adults were higher up, usually fourth or fifth shelf from the bottom, since this was eye level. The worst place to be was on the bottom, where it was hard to see, and difficult for some to reach.

These days, what Chris liked most about the supermarket was that is was a good place to hide. The maelstrom he had created at the agency was in full force. Everywhere he went - the creative department, the media department, the production department, the management corridor - people were working on the preparation of a television campaign for Envira Tampons. People were constantly barging into his office to ask for clarification or stopping him in the aisle begging for instructions.

Mostly, he stayed out of the office to avoid Mack's questions: "What did the client say about the budget?" "Do you want me to go to New York with you?" "If we do focus groups, do you think we can get them to commit to a national campaign?"

Knowing he had to make a real case for going on television, Chris decided to go to 25 supermarkets scattered over Southern California, Envira's number one market, and photograph the shelves, showing how badly Envira Tampons were positioned. As a small company with only one product line, Envira always had a poor location on the shelves - usually on the bottom or second shelf from the bottom. To a marketer like Chris, this was very unfortunate, since it negatively affected sales, but under the current circumstances, it was a blessing in disguise.

Chris' argument would be that once they went on television, it would force the grocery store managers to give Envira better visibility since customers will be asking for them, and in turn, that will lead to increased sales.

The trick was just to get the president of Envira to say he was willing to look at a few ideas. If he would say it - preferably in writing - Chris could contend that he was justified in authorizing the development of the ad campaign. Of course, no one had to know that the client agreed to see the ideas until after the development had begun. That would just be one of those little facts that disappeared into cyberspace.

Since K&Q was paying his travel expenses to New York (which just happened to be the same weekend as the Kennedy reunion), he was certain he could convince the client to spend an hour looking at some ideas. As he often said to his clients, "It's our responsibility to come up with new concepts that will help increase your sales - especially when you don't ask for them." Who was going to pay the bill for the development of the campaign was another issue, since clients were usually invoiced for time spent by the agency in developing the creative. Chris just hoped he had another job by then, though he was feeling less confident after his conversation with the executive recruiter yesterday.

"With your resume and unique experiences, I'm having a hard time picturing who could take advantage of your special skills," the head hunter diplomatically explained.

"But you put me in this job ten years ago," Chris undiplomatically replied. "You told me it would be good for my career!" It didn't really matter how loudly he raised his voice, the recruiter was not going to do anything for him. He was stuck, and needed more time to get situated somewhere else.

As he turned the corner of the feminine hygiene aisle of the supermarket, he tried to approach it as a woman would. Stooping down a bit to make himself a little shorter and pushing the shopping cart with one hand, he held a small video camera at eye level. He planned to make a composite video of his experiences in the feminine hygiene aisle, showing how slowly or quickly the Envira Tampon's box came into view. In most stores the boxes were buried so far in the corner, or behind an in-aisle display, that he had to get within inches of the product before he could find them.

At this supermarket, Envira wasn't in a particularly bad position, actually, it was a rather good position. So for the sake of his argument, and his video (and his career), he moved the boxes into the worst position he could find and re-recorded his entrance into the aisle. It was dishonest, "But, what he hell," he rationalized. "We've gone this far, we might as well go all the way." An amusing thought crossed his mind. *What if this all works out? What if they like the idea and decide to run the TV commercial? What if it actually increases their sales?* "It's not impossible."

As he returned the boxes to their original locations, out of the corner of his eye, he could see someone watching him. It must have been quite a sight - a six-foot, one hundred and seventy five pound male, stooping down in front of boxes of tampons, re-arranging them with unusual intensity. *Should I explain myself? But that would mean I was guilty of something, and why should I feel guilty. I wasn't doing anything wrong. Anyone could walk down any aisle of a supermarket and pick up any item. Just because tampons are traditionally a female item, it doesn't mean a man couldn't look at a box, or even purchase the item. Maybe I'll just stand here pretending to read the sides and backs of the boxes until whoever it is just moves along.*

Boy, this looks real stupid. Now it looks like I'm standing here and comparing the ingredients of tampons. I wish whomever it is would just move along and let me finish what I'm doing.

But, the other person in the aisle didn't move.

Okay, that's it. I'm just going to put the boxes back on the shelves and continue up the aisle.

He replaced the boxes, and turned to quickly walk down the aisle and out of the store, and suddenly he was eye-to-eye with the other person in the aisle... it was another man!

To his surprise, rather than being stared at with suspicion, Chris was being looked at with compassion. There was a look of relief in this other man's eye. No, more than relief, there was an instant and special bond between them. Clearly, this short, stout, balding shopper was grateful that he had found one of his Band of Brothers.

Surreptitiously, looking up and down the aisle, as if he were about to steal the Crown Jewels from the British Museum, this soldier on a special mission snatched a box of tampons - scented, heavy flow - from the shelf and shoved it deep into his basket, surrounding the humiliating box with fruits and vegetables. Looking back towards Chris, relieved that this odious mission was accomplished, the little man nodded towards Chris. Not just a nod of acknowledgement, but a nod that said, "Victory." The bond between them was strong. They would carry it with them to their graves. Chris smiled back and wondered if there was a marketing angle in this somehow.

They exchanged that special, silent glance that men share after victory in battle, and each started to moved off in opposite directions.

Just at that moment, another shopping cart thrust its way into the aisle, and shattered the moment of male bonding. It was a woman. Seeing two men in front of the tampons, one with a camera and a tampon box, the other with suspiciously arranged fruits and vegetables, she stopped short. Her eyes shot from one to the other, trying to detect their sick motives for being in the feminine hygiene aisle. "Perverts!" the scowl on her face screamed. "Decadent perverts who liked to touch women's products in aisle 4," would have blasted over the loudspeaker at that moment if she had the microphone.

With feet planted firmly behind her shopping cart, dead center in the aisle, she stared down at the two interlopers to the women's private sanctum. She wasn't going to surrender this aisle to these sicko's, and she wasn't going to let them sneak past her.

Chris thought he could explain the four boxes of tampons still in his arms by saying that he was stocking the shelves, but having the video camera made that story somewhat doubtful. Turning to his brother male, he could see panic in his eyes. He had been so close to a clean get-away, but he didn't move quickly enough. Now he was a deer caught in the headlights of this on-coming shopping cart.

Abandoning his comrade, he raced down the aisle, not stopping to pick up the grapes that fell out of his basket.

Now alone, Chris smiled the smile of defeat, dropped the boxes and his camera into his shopping cart, turned, and followed his brother to the check-out counter.

Once again, the men lost the battle of the sexes

Chapter 28

The e-mail read:

Hey, everybody, remember Dr. Nestor's speech at our commencement - I think he titled it - the Road Ahead - or something like that - I looked up what he said in the yearbook and he said -"With this diploma you've now taken your first step on the road towards your goals. Make it an interesting journey."

Well I think its time we all fess up and report on how we did on our private journeys - since I'm bringing it up, I'll be the first one to admit that I got lost somewhere -remember I wanted to be a filmmaker - I'm sure you'll all remember that I was pretty obnoxious about it - wearing a French beret and all that shit - anyway, to support myself until I was discovered I took a job as the head of audio-visual services at a high school upstate - without boring you with the details, I'm the principal at that school - not a bad detour but I certainly didn't get anywhere near what I was aiming for.

Let's hear from some other people- I'll be at the reunion.

Mark

***

Good suggestion, Mark... here's my story.

I didn't get anywhere near what I intended to do but it worked out sooooo much better. Some of you folks may remember that my dad was an accountant in Borough Park - he probably did the taxes for some of your parents. Anyway, The plan was that I would get a degree in accounting and join him and that's what we did for a couple of years. But one year when the economy went into the toilet I had to leave the business and a head hunter placed me into the accounting department of a plastics company (sounds like a scene from The Graduate). I did pretty good and rose up to become the CFO, which - here's the joke - got purchased by General Electric and because their guy quit over some corporate bullshit, I ended up being the CFO of that division. A couple of years and promotions later I'm a super, senior, executive, wahoo VP.

I have to laugh, especially when I read some of these emails. If everything had gone the way I planned, I'd be sitting in a small office in Bklyn helping you folks (at least the ones who stayed) do your taxes. BOY, I'M GLAD I DIDN'T REACH THE GOAL I LAID OUT FOR MYSELF.

I'll be at the reunion - look for someone who is bald, overweight, wearing an Armani suit, with an American flag in his lapel.

Rob

***

Actually, I did exactly what I wanted to do. I became an investment banker at Goldman Sachs. I was the youngest woman ever to be a vice president with that company. When that happened I couldn't imagine anything greater in life.

I'm not at Goldman Sachs any longer. I'm not an investment banker any longer. I'm married now. Living in a small town in Colorado. My husband manages the ski resort. I do some bookkeeping. Two wonderful kids.

I couldn't be happier. I won't be at the reunion.

Sally

***

i always wanted to be a teacher - i am a teacher - i can't imagine any nobler profession on earth - i'll try to be at the reunion

maxine

***

Mark, my impression of Dr. Nestor's commencement address is that he wasn't talking about obtaining some business goal that we set for ourselves, but that the future was not knowable. I was never certain if he felt that our destinies were pre-ordained, or at least out of our control. As much as we all used to talk about determining our own futures, isn't the reality that we can't do that, isn't the reality that we're driven or pulled by forces outside of our control. I think that is what Dr. Nestor was talking about.

Sophie

***

Remember how we all used to call Sophie, Sophocles.

Actually, I partially agree with Sophie. I don't think Dr. Nestor was talking about what kind of job we get. I don't think our destinies are pre-ordained or out of our control. I think Dr. Nestor was saying that we can never know our destiny – it's out there, like the horizon, and every twist 'n turn alters where we end up. Who we marry… You take this job and not that. The President declares war (remember those days) and you get drafted. You fall in love with the woman sitting next to you on the plane and your marriage is ruined. You miss the flight and you're happily married (Now you know why I'm on my third marriage, btw.) Your company is bought and you get fired. As much as we want to say we control our fates and our futures, the truth is that we can only control what we are doing that minute, for in the next minute the world changes. All we can do is make the journey interesting. That's what De Nestor said… make the journey interesting. I don't know about my destiny, but I do know I will be at the reunion.

Jerry

***

I know you'll call me a hopeless romantic, Chris typed, but I still believe that we each have only one great love that we are destined to be with. You may never meet that person, or she may be sitting next to you in math class, but there is someone, for each of us, out there... waiting.

Chris re-read his contribution to the discussion several times then decided not to send it. If somehow Melanie accidentally saw it, it would cause a problem at home, and if Cathy saw it, she might be embarrassed.

The poet in him celebrated that they broke up so many years ago, because – up to the final moment - their love was pure and not tainted with arguments about money, children, plumbers, laundry, and houses. He remembered reading about an engaged couple, that, on the night before their wedding, jumped out of an airplane without parachutes, holding onto each other. Very sad, very romantic. They knew it would never be as good as it was that moment.

He read over a few more contributions to his class's discussion of destiny, but then Melanie called him to breakfast, so he shut down the computer and headed for the kitchen.

At the same time he was sipping his morning coffee, Cathy was sitting at the boarding gate of United Airlines, waiting for her flight home. The euphoria of the last couple of days had vanished like smoke from a campfire. The awful reality of returning to Minneapolis was in front of her and all she could think about was fear, pain, violence, abuse, and rape. She fought each step she took down the jet way, knowing that tonight he would force himself into her, and she'd have to groan in pretense of enjoying her own humiliation and subjugation?

Six more weeks, she told herself. *There's only six more weeks till the end of the semester and our move to New York, and then it's over.* But it would be six more weeks of living in hell. The people behind her in the jet way were annoyed at her slow pace, but they could see tears rolling down her cheeks and they forced patience upon themselves. A pretty young flight attendant with a small diamond engagement ring on her left hand asked, "Is everything okay?"

"I'm okay. Thank you for asking. Just some very sad family news." She asked herself, *How do you explain to someone just starting out in life, how terrible it can be?*

Trying to focus on her daughters, her source of joy, couldn't stop the flow of tears. Maybe because the end was in sight, and all her emotions could finally be released, or maybe because for a few days, she was free of her terrible burdens and couldn't imagine submitting to them again. Whatever the cause, she couldn't stop crying, and other passengers noticed, imagining stories, such as "Her husband must have just died," or, "She's probably coming from visiting her mother in the hospital."

As the plane approached Minneapolis, her shields kicked in, and like the warrior she had become, she stopped crying. Splashing cold water on her face and applying more makeup, it only looked as if her eyes were red from the dry air in the plane. Fred had sent her an e-mail to say he would be picking her up, which meant that he may or may not be there, but in any case, she didn't want to show any vulnerabilities.

Given a choice, she hoped he wouldn't show up so she could have another hour to herself before confronting him, but as she stepped into the terminal, Fred lunged in front of her, almost knocking her backwards, and shoved a bouquet of flowers in her arms. Embracing her tightly, he released her from his grasp long enough so he could give her a long passionate kiss. "God, I missed you. The house is so big and empty without you and the girls there."

People all around the gate smiled as the two lovers were re-united.

With his arm around her all the way to the baggage carousal, he rattled on and on about how wonderful it was that she was home, that he missed her so much, that he never appreciated how he missed the noise that the girls made and on and on.

What's going on? The flowers. The hugs. This is the way it used to be, but that was a long time ago. Far more skeptical than hopeful, she had to wonder, *Is it over? Is this terrible period finally over? Did something click in his head? But the more doubtful side of her dominated. I bet he thinks I'll have the power to give him a promotion.*

Watching the baggage go round and round on the carousal, she stepped back, hoping to understand what just happened. He was smiling. Not that sadistic smile she saw so often, but a smile of happiness. The anger that he wore on his face like a chest full of medals was gone, and the only smirk on his face was that of a kid with a secret. Though it was only 5:00 p.m. he suggested that they not go directly home, but instead go to dinner at her favorite Italian restaurant, the Marco Polo, so they could catch up. He wanted to hear everything about this new job, about her new boss, about the people in New York. Still startled, she agreed, though she wasn't a bit hungry. Besides, talking about her new job was a great opportunity to start laying the groundwork for her escape.

When they got to the restaurant it was obvious, he had stopped there before he went to the airport to make arrangements. A table in a dark, secluded corner was waiting for them, with an open bottle of wine and a lit candle dripping down an old Chianti bottle. As they walked into the restaurant, they were escorted to the table without any hesitation, and immediately the waiter poured the wine.

Puzzled, she raised her glass to his toast, "To your return and this wonderful new opportunity for all of us."

For all of us?

They sipped the wine, but he raised his glass again, and held it there, so she did the same. Touching his glass to hers, he softly said, "I want to apologize for some of the things that have happened between us over the past few months."

Her wine glass almost slipped from her hand, but she was able to recover quickly before spilling anything.

"I'm not proud of some of the things I've done. I think I've been very frustrated at work, and I've taken some of it out on you."

Was this horror finally coming to an end? Could this be? Could this really be? This horror started so suddenly, could it end suddenly, too. Is it truly possible? But maybe...

"Now you'll be working out of the New York office," he continued, "which sounds exciting, and I want to hear all about it. But I'm concerned about us..."

Us? I bet he just wants a job in the New York office, her skeptical side concluded.

"We have a good thing going, and I don't want to lose it." Sliding around the red vinyl booth, he leaned over and kissed her lips. Closing his eyes, he took a deep breath and blurted out, "Cathy, will you marry me?" Relieved to have finally gotten the words out, his eyes opened, and sitting back, he waited for Cathy to leap across the table and hug him, screaming, "Yes, yes, yes!"

As if they had just dug her out of a thousand year old grave in the North Pole, she was mummified. A passing doctor might have stopped to see if she had stopped breathing or if her heart stopped beating. She didn't sip her wine or put her glass down. She didn't smile, gasp or frown. She didn't blink her eyes or close them. She didn't focus on him or away from him.

Thinking that it was cute that he caught her completely by surprise, his smile only widened. Sipping his wine to let the full effect of his proposal wash over her, he leaned backwards, again preparing himself for the huge kiss that was inevitably coming. After a few moments, as she put her glass down and stared at the wine inside it, clearly in contemplation, he leaned forward and asked again, "How about it? Would you like to be Mrs. Mardred?"

At one time, eons ago, she certainly would have said, "Yes!" At one time, she was even looking forward to it. But that was long before the bruises, the bloody noses, and the Saturday Night Fucks. Now she didn't know what to do. No way would she accept, not now, but she didn't want to take a chance that saying, "No!" would cause an ugly scene. But if things could be back to the way they used to be... maybe there was a chance for the future... after a lot of therapy. Stalling for time, trying to exude a sense of delight, she breathlessly offered, "Boy, you certainly know how to surprise a girl." The candle flickered as she let out a heavy sigh.

Having never imagined that she would say, "No," he still smiled that her reserved response was more from shock and less from rejection. "I'm not insecure about us, but you're going to be spending most of the week in New York and I'm still here. I know you have to take this job, but I would like something permanent between us, something that says we're committed to each other even if we can't spend every night together. Say, yes, and make me the happiest man in Minneapolis tonight."

This can't be, was all she could think. *He actually believes we're happy together? That I would want to be with him after all that's happened.* This moment was beyond her ability to comprehend, but her shields snapped into place again, and the computer in her brain was quickly calculating the effect of saying "No" vs. lying and saying "Yes."

From the corner of her eye, she could see the restaurant staff, who had already been told what he had intended to do, huddled together, as if waiting for a signal, so they could burst out in song.

"Well, is it yes or no?" His tone filled with impatience. He couldn't fathom why she didn't jump at the opportunity. His fingers moved wildly around the wine glass that he held with both hands, as if they wanted to make a fist, but were being prevented from doing so.

Still stalling, "I'm in shock. I never assumed we'd get married. Only that we'd live together. At some point don't they consider people living together as married?"

"Everything's in both our names anyway. This would just be formalizing it," he stated, as if he were a lawyer offering his opinion on the subject.

That's the problem, she thought, *I put everything in both our names.* "We don't need to formalize it. Why not just keep things the way they are?"

Pulling back, his eyes turned to ice, and that look, as if he was targeting a prey, emerged on his face.

That was the wrong thing to say, she quickly realized, and groped for something that would calm him down. She had to find something else to say, fast.

Seeing that all was not going well, the restaurant staff began to disperse from their position since the prearranged signal launching them into song didn't appear to be forthcoming. "You're embarrassing me in front of the entire restaurant staff." The anger in his voice had the staccato sound of arrows piercing the target.

Because it was still early and the restaurant wasn't very busy, there wasn't the usual clatter to mask their voices, so the few other patrons who came in for the Early Bird Specials could hear their exchange in full. She imagined what they must be saying: "At her age, you'd think she'd grab the first man she could get." "A good looking guy like that. If she doesn't want him, my sister will." "He may be the last offer she'll ever get. If she doesn't say 'yes' pretty soon he may stop asking."

Grasping the edge of the table as if he was about to crush it, he tried one more time, "We're at the age when we don't need to make a big thing out of it. We can get married this weekend or next weekend. But I'd like to do it before you start spending more time in New York."

She no longer had any belief in his redemption.

Raising her glass up to him and smiling, trying to appear as if she was truly delighted by the proposal, she offered the best explanation she could think of. "I know this sounds crazy, but I want to talk to the girls first. Getting married again isn't just about me, it affects them, too."

Releasing his tight grip on the table, he had to concede, it made sense, so the anger dissipated from his eyes and he took another sip from his glass.

"You know, the girls and I have been through a lot together, and after all, you would be their father. We go as a group. So let me talk to them first." As the words came out of her mouth she knew it was a mistake. Putting the delay on the girls meant he would blame them when she finally said, "No," which meant, he might turn on them. It was a stupid mistake, but she couldn't think of anything else to say.

She picked up the menu, signaling that she felt the discussion was over, and when he reluctantly picked up his, she breathed a sigh of relief. The crisis was averted for now, but she feared, it was only for now. She worried that what she did set the stage for another, potentially far worse, crisis.

"I think the girls like me. If they say yes, will you say yes?"

"Please, let me just talk to the girls. I really don't want this to become a you vs. them thing." *Stupid, stupid me!*

Dinner was painful. Despite her explanation, and his appreciation of why she couldn't accept on the spot, he felt rejected, and throughout the evening repeatedly begged, "Lets just do it," and "Lets make the commitment."

Barely eating and forcing a loving gaze and seductive smile, she suffered painful heart attacks as she thought of the danger she just put her daughters into, and how six weeks until her escape plan was launched was now much too long. Lifting her glass often to toast their relationship, she hoped he would fall asleep as soon as they got home (assuming he didn't get them killed driving home first), but the two bottles of wine that he mostly drank at dinner wasn't enough. She decided to engage him in sex. She'd have to make it as long and satisfying for him as she could, but that would put him to sleep for the night, and give her some time to think.

She kept her hand in his lap as they drove home, and as they walked into the house, she whispered, "Hurry upstairs," into his ear before she licked it. She quickly undressed and slid into bed, waiting for him to drop himself on top of her.

As he entered their bedroom, he didn't undress, but stared at an object in his hand. He wandered over to the bed.

"Who is 310-555-1255? That's in California"

Chastising herself for forgetting to sanitize her cell phone's call history, she raised herself up on her elbows and trying to appear nonchalant, offered, "It was a job applicant for a programmer's position I'm trying to fill in the software group."

"You spoke to him for 45 minutes. Why were you using your cell phone?"

She laughed a phony laugh, "I was interviewing him while I was walking down Fifth Avenue. First interview I ever did while I was shopping. Now come to bed." She reached out to touch his arm, but he quickly withdrew it.

He turned his back, which made her think he was going to the bathroom, until she heard, "Kingsley & Quincy? What kind of business is this?"

She held her breath.

"An ad agency?" He sounded genuinely hurt, "You lied to me. Who's at this ad agency that you spoke to for 45 minutes? You never talk on the cell phone for 45 minutes." And, in the poorest imitation of Daffy Duck in all of the Midwest, he asked, "Were you talking to one of your... high school friends?"

Her first instinct was to elaborate on the story and say the programmer worked at the ad agency, but she knew the lie would be exposed quickly, so she confessed, "Well, yes," she said, purposely dropping the sheets so her breasts were revealed to him. "I know how you feel about me being in contact with them so I didn't want to tell you that I was talking to an old girlfriend who now lives in California. I thought..."

The hand that yanked her from the bed and threw her across the room, was so swift, all she saw was a blur. With his large hands, he pushed her face into the brick of the fireplace, screaming, "You piece of trash! You lied to me, you bitch! Are you cheating on me? Are you fucking one of your old high school boyfriends? Is that what this is about? Is that why you don't want to marry me? I can't believe you made such a fool of me tonight in front of everyone at the restaurant!"

He released his hand from her head, and expecting him to strike her again, she shrunk inward, protecting her face with her hands. But instead of hitting her, he took is anger out on the cell phone and threw it across the room, aiming for the open window, but he missed and it hit the arm of a chair instead. Grabbing her robe from the closet and throwing it on top of her, he screamed, "You lying bitch! You can sleep on the floor tonight. I don't want you in my bed!" With that he climbed into bed, without even undressing, and quickly fell asleep in the drunken stupor she had been hoping for all night.

Touching her face, she ran the tips of her fingers over the ridges created by the contours of the bricks. Nothing seemed broken, and there was no blood. Trying to focus on something, anything, just to make certain her eye wasn't damaged, she looked at the street light outside the window. She was comforted that there was no damage to her vision.

Curling up into the corner behind the chair, afraid to move, afraid to turn on a light, afraid to cry, she remained as motionless as long as she could. Pulling her robe over her head, she feared he would explode again if he woke up in the middle of the night to go to the bathroom.

She didn't know how long she remained in that position, or if she had fallen asleep at all, but at about 3:00 a.m. she felt brave enough to emerge from under her robe and silently crawled towards the cell phone, lying on the floor about ten feet away.

Silently, easing her way into the bathroom and locking herself into the shower stall, she dialed Bob's office. With two bath towels draped over her head, and her hand cupped over the phone, she composed herself as best she could and spoke in as professional a voice as she could muster. "Bob, sorry I wasn't able to return your calls sooner. I took some time off to consider the position, and I just wanted to say that I'm very excited by this new opportunity, and gladly accept the position. I have a few projects to close out here and I can start in about two weeks. Thank you for thinking of me and please thank Senior Management for its support. I'll call you tomorrow and we can start sorting out the details."

It no longer mattered that she was losing her leverage regarding a raise and promotion, she just wanted to get out of this house.

Chapter 29

Fortunately, Fred had to leave early the next morning so she had time to erase the evidence from last night. Unfortunately, she had become too experienced in covering up bruises, so no one would suspect what her home life was really like. While she showered, while she dressed, while she drove to work, while she sat at her desk, she repeated over and over to herself, "I will do anything I have to, to get me and the girls away from that pile of shit as soon as possible." With the cold determination of a general planning an invasion, she plotted her course out of the Hell that her life had become.

First, to her doctor so he could examine her eye and head to determine if there was any permanent damage - as well as to record the bruises for use in any legal situations.

Then to her lawyer's office, so he could prepare the escape route. On graduation day, she and the girls would move to New York, permanently. All assets she held jointly with Fred would be frozen, so a court could decide how to divide them, and all joint credit cards would be closed. The house would be put up for sale and the proceeds placed in escrow, again for a court to decide the disbursement. Then, she contacted a realtor in New York and instructed her to find a three-bedroom condominium.

A protective order would be issued in both Minnesota and New York preventing him from coming near them, and she researched private protection services that carried real guns, and weren't afraid to use them. Her lawyer suggested filing a civil suit against him and suing for ten million dollars, which was an intriguing idea except it would mean that the connection between them would linger on for years, and all she wanted was never to see him again.

Finally, she called the head of the South St. Paul office where Fred worked. Since she didn't want to leave a message with the receptionist or a voice mail that the branch manager, Stanley, might mention to Fred, she dialed the number ten times during the day before he answered the phone.

Surprised to hear directly from Cathy, actually, surprised to hear directly from anyone at the Minneapolis office, Stanley was, literally, falling over himself trying to make a good impression.

After the initial pleasantries, Cathy, in a tone reminiscent of a newlywed planning a surprise birthday party for her new husband, said, "Stanley, first, I need this call to be strictly confidential. No one, and I mean no one, can know that it ever occurred." For someone who frequently suffered from feelings of isolation and insignificance, the thought of having a VP from corporate call and wish to share something in private with him was such an honor, such a compliment, such a surprise, that he would have agreed to absolutely anything. "You have my word on that."

In Stanley's personnel folder that Cathy had on her desk, she noted that he was often referred to as a "boy scout" by his supervisors, so she knew he could be trusted. "Thank you, Stanley. This is very awkward for me. I'm not used to asking for favors, but I need a big favor from you."

"You have my word." In his excitement, he dropped the phone, but was able to catch it before it hit the ground. It was as if he was an astronaut and was just selected to go to the moon. Standing, because he thought that made him sound more professional then when he sat, he wanted to scream at the top of his lungs, "They know I'm here! Someone at corporate knows I exist!"

"As you probably guessed, it's regarding Fred." Actually, Stanley didn't guess that at all, but once she mentioned it, he wasn't surprised since it was a well-known secret that the two of them were living together and would be getting married someday. Deflated, because the call wasn't about him, he sank into his worn and torn chair. Obviously, this wasn't the "official recognition" from someone important at corporate that he had thought it was. No one was asking his advice on a new product launch, or sharing a business secret with him, or advising him in advance of major changes that were forthcoming. It was just one woman trying to do something for her man. It was like a soldier on the front lines of battle who finally got a letter from home and it turns out to be a solicitation for a donation from the Veterans of Foreign Wars.

"What can I do for you... and Fred?" *The guy's a jerk*, Stanley thought. *I can't imagine the attraction between them. But Cathy is a vice president and anything she wants she has to get.* Resigning himself to do whatever she asked, he took a yellow pad and pen from the top drawer of his dented metal desk and prepared to write down the information.

"Again, this is very awkward, and I apologize for saying it again, but this has to remain strictly confidential."

Grunting acknowledgement, Stanley knew he was going to hate to do the favor that he was about to be asked.

"Fred's self-esteem has been suffering for quite a while. He has this feeling that his career is going nowhere; of being stuck in the same old job year after year."

Stanley thought, *it's probably because he's a major asshole and his career is going nowhere.*

"I'll be honest," Cathy continued, "he's more than a bit jealous of my position. The fact that I travel a lot and meet with Senior Management on a regular basis. I was just wondering if there was something we can do for him that would make him feel better about himself." Both knew - and both knew the other knew - that there was a job opening for the Wisconsin territory, and that it was a much more important position, with much more travel and income potential, than Fred's current position.

There was no point in pretending, so Stanley said the words he was expected to say, "Well there is one position available, but quite frankly I don't think it really fits his background." What Stanley wanted to say was that the Wisconsin territory was far too important to turn over to an idiot like Fred.

"In what way, Stanley? I think Fred is a quick learner and very adaptable." She knew she was putting him on the spot.

Trying to be polite, and political, he answered, "Fred seems to work best with small businesses that don't require a great deal of handholding. The Wisconsin territory has some of the company's biggest clients - the University, Johnson & Johnson, Rockwell - I'm not sure if his style would work with them." Fred handled clients that the company didn't even know that they had or wouldn't even know if they lost them, like small businesses that purchased a new $49.95 modem once every three years.

"I'm certain it could work out, if he was given the chance," Cathy insisted.

It's one thing to be a mouse, and another to know you're a mouse, and Stanley knew exactly what he was. Knowing he couldn't resist her request, he made one last effort to object to Fred's promotion and save his dignity. "Cathy, I would love to help you, but Fred really isn't one of our top salespeople. He's not even in our top ten." They both knew that there were only twelve salespeople in that office.

But she wouldn't be deterred. "I think you'll be surprised at how good he can be. He just hasn't been motivated these last few years." But, if not, and you have to fire him in a few months, that's okay with me, Cathy said to herself, because I'll be long gone.

For appearance's sake more than anything else, Stanley again began to object, but Cathy interrupted, "Stanley, I would consider this a great personal favor if you would do this." The words "personal favor" were richly expressed, so there was no doubt that there would be some benefit to the executor of the personal favor.

She repeated the words "personal favor" several more times until Stanley finally understood that they were not just discussing new responsibilities for Fred, but they were discussing his career, too. He had no particular desire to stay in the small South St. Paul branch and harbored aspirations of moving to the Minneapolis office for many years. He also knew that Cathy was not only a good friend to have in Minneapolis, but that she was someone who would, and could, fulfill her obligations.

Believing that she wasn't making empty promises, he stood up, and looking at his reflection in the glass protecting an old *Gunfight at the O.K. Corral* poster, he said, "Maybe, you're right, Cathy. This might be good for him... and the company. Let me think it over."

"Thank you." She allowed a moment to pass to make certain that he accepted the idea fully, and then added, "Since I've embarrassed myself once today with you..."

Stanley knew the other shoe was going to drop.

"I hate to be pushy when I'm asking for a favor, but, I'm leaving for New York tomorrow, and it would be great if we had something to celebrate tonight, if you know what I mean."

Since he had already conceded that he was a mouse, and that he would give Fred the job even though he was the last person on his staff who deserved it, Stanley had to agree. Why not make it today and wallow in the full humiliation of the decision. More than worrying about Fred, he was wondering what he could possibly say to the half dozen people in the office that truly deserved the promotion. At least, he could make the case that Fred had been with the company the longest of anyone in the office, and deserved an opportunity to prove himself. Flopping back down into his chair, he suddenly had a strong urge for some cheese.

In a voice that wreaked with boy-do-you-owe-me-big-time, Stanley offered, "I think you'll have reason to celebrate tonight."

Thanking him sincerely and profusely, she hung up.

The next call was to the Public Relations Department. This would be easy since the head of that department was a woman and they shared the bond of struggling against the good ol' boys network. "Betsy, could you do me a favor? Could you invite Stanley Kleiner from the South St. Paul office to the reception the company is having at the museum next week?"

"It's only for vice presidents and above. Is he a vice president?" Betsy was surprised, but would do it without hesitation since Cathy was the one asking.

"I'm certain he will be one day." *A lot sooner than he should be*, she thought. "He's been really nice to Fred and I'd like to do something special for him. I think he'd really enjoy meeting some of the Minneapolis people."

"I may get some flack for this. Can you make him promise not to get drunk and embarrass himself? Some of these guys come in from the field and they can't resist all the free food and liquor. Does he have a tuxedo?"

"I'm sure he does." Cathy conjured up an image of Stanley standing on top of the dessert table dancing with a lampshade on his head.

"Okay. I'll put an invitation in the mail today."

"Thank you, Betsy. I owe you one for this." But added, "Since the reception is next week," her voice dropped to a more conspiratorial octave, "could you send him an invitation by e-mail - today."

That piece of shit she lives with must be in big trouble, Betsy concluded, but only said, "Consider it done."

The Great Escape, as she began to call her plan, was going smoothly.

Finally, as she was about to write an e-mail to Chris, she noticed he was online. As much as she wanted to talk to Chris, to hear his voice, there were spies and gossips everywhere. From now on, all they had to say to each other would have to be in the form of digital dots when she was in the office.

Cathy: Hello

Chris: hello... I was afraid I wouldn't hear from you today

Cathy: very busy - transfer to NY has me in limbo - some
mornings I wake up and don't know what city I'm
in.

Chris: I used to feel that way when I was handling the
advertising 4 a hotel chain... I get confused... r you
2 or 3 hours behind me

Cathy: It's actually 2 hours ahead when I'm in MPLS and 3
hours when I'm in NY. You still don't have a sense
of time. Do you wear a watch?

Chris: no, still don't wear a watch

Cathy: Don't you think someone in business should?

Chris: I tried it for a while. when I wear a watch I'm always
looking at it

Cathy: That's what watches are for

Chris: I got too stressed .... always worried about being
someplace on time ... drove me crazy... I'm better
off without one

Chris: how r things going with the new job????

Cathy: Incredible. I haven't really started yet and they've
already offered me a promotion

Chris: that's great :))))

Cathy: It's a big compliment... puts me in a very important
position. I'm more than a little frightened by the
whole thing. I know I do my job well but now they
want me to take on a lot more responsibility. I don't
know if I'm up for it

Chris: you can do it... you're great at what you do... my
god, look how far you came along... you started as a
trainee 20 years ago, now you're running the place.

Cathy: not quite running the place... but it is handling the ops for a critical department.

Chris: you're a real big shot now... maybe you can get me a job in your ad department

Cathy: Trust me - I'm not that big a shot. Hey, before I say anything else, thanks for sending the Agatha Christie Collection to me... she's my favorite mystery writer.

Chris: I remembered that... when I saw them in the bookstore window I said it was a perfect gift 4 your birthday, and then I remembered that I forgot your birthday... some things never change...

Cathy: The very fact that you remembered that your forgot my birthday makes me very happy. You couldn't have chosen anything that could have made me happier.

Chris: whats Fred have to say about the move to Nyc

There was a real long pause in the conversation, which made it obvious that he touched on a delicate issue. Originally, he had assumed that they were headed towards marriage, but the little references he'd been picking up made him doubt it now. He might be bringing up something he shouldn't, but he intentionally asked, to test his theory.

Chris: r u there?????

Cathy: yes, someone just walked into my office. (She lied and Chris knew it.)

Cathy: (He could feel the words slowly being typed.) Actually, I'm leaving Fred.

Chris: (Trying to decide what to say, he gravitated to the cliché.) I'm sorry to hear that. (He wasn't sorry at all.) somehow I got the impression you two were headed towards marriage

(Maybe there's another chance for us, he thought.

Maybe getting together again at this time is fate, as if we missed our chance when we were supposed to take it, and now we have another chance.)

Cathy: He thought so too (She looked in a mirror and could still see a slight discoloration of her skin where he hit her. Unsure if she should admit to this, she decided to confess all.) he proposed

Chris: and ??????? (He watched the computer screen like a sailor watches the compass of his ship.)

Cathy: there's no way I would marry him... I didn't want to hurt his feelings so I told him I'd have to think about it. (Through tears in her eyes, she, once again, chastised herself for blaming the girls for a delay in her response.)

Chris: sorry 4 asking but it sounds confusing... he thinks you 2 should get married and you think you should break up...

Again there was a long pause. He regretted saying what he did, but he was driven to do so. If there was a chance, no matter how miniscule for them to be back together, he didn't want to miss it.

Chris: forget what I said... I shouldn't ask... It's none of my business

Cathy: No. its okay.. If I can't talk to you. who can I talk to?

Her poised fingers didn't want to depress the keys to type the words. She signed on to tell Chris how excited she was about her new job, but instead the truth about the horrors of her life were leaking through the cracks in the dam she had built around herself. If she didn't sign off now, right now, she knew she would tell him everything. If she signed off now, she could continue to suffer silently and alone.

Cathy: It's just no good between us... the fact that Fred doesn't understand there's a problem between us, is the bigger problem... he sees everything from his point of view... he's getting what he wants so everything must be okay.

Chris: Im sorry... its so sad when that happens

Cathy: I've always said I need a sensitive person - someone
like you - but instead I always seem to end up with
these muscle bound idiots that think everything is
resolved with their fists :(
After the rape... I felt I needed protection so I ran
into the arms of someone big and strong... what I
didn't realize is that it wasn't my body that needed
protection... it was my soul... and that couldn't be
protected by someone who shouts a lot and thinks
sex is just a quick in and out
I can't believe I made the same mistake again... i
can't believe I'm telling you all this... I thought
Fred was different. I thought he was sensitive. I even
remember comparing him to you.

From the moment they came back into contact, Chris could only
reflect on how wonderful everything had been between them and he
seethed in a jealous rage that some other man was enjoying the absolute
ecstasy of her soul and of her body. Reading the words over and over he
couldn't imagine how this man, and her ex-husbands, wouldn't just revere
her and cherish everyday with her.

He was about to respond with some uninspired piece of wisdom,
like "It's not your fault," but then suddenly one word seemed to pop out.
With fear and doubt, he typed his next question. But before he sent it, he
stared at it for what seemed to be an eternity.

Chris: does he hit you?

There was an even longer pause, and before the screen changed, he
knew the answer.

Cathy: I'm so embarrassed.

She was crying. He touched his computer and he could feel the tears
and that made him cry to. Even though he hadn't seen her face in decades,
he knew exactly what she looked like right now. He remembered how she
had cried, and how he had cried, the day she boarded the plane to go to
California. He stared at his reflection in the computer screen, horrified to

think that the woman he loved was in such pain and being beaten by some pig who didn't respect her. Conjuring up images that he couldn't bear to think, he rubbed his eyes as if to make them go away.

Chris: he's hitting you!!!!!!!!!!

Cathy: yes.......

Her responses were slow and he knew how painful it must be for her to be telling someone.

Chris: how often has he hit you?????

Cathy: 10 times... maybe more...

Chris: he's hitting you and you stay there?!?!????

Cathy: I'm so embarrassed... I shouldn't have told you

The stone walls of the prison that held the truth of her existence, the pains of her daily life, the humiliation, the desperation, the fears, and the hatred collapsed. She no longer had the strength to hold her shame captive and fight against the degradation of her soul. Had she not been sitting in a chair at that instant, she surely would have fallen to the floor. Though, like the exhaustion after making love, it was satisfying to finally share her secret.

Chris: don't go back!!!! Stay in NY!!!!

Cathy: its finally coming to an end - everythings going to
be okay - I just need a few more weeks till the girls
are out of school – I'm okay now.

What had happened to her? How did she get into this situation? Chris' mind raced in circles trying to understand what from her past could possibly have lead to this present. Was it the rape? Was it breaking up with me? Was it her father? Thoughts of her father taking sexual advantage of her coursed through his head.

Chris: LEAVE!!!!! NOW!!!!

Tightening his hand into a fist, he pounded his desk as if it was Fred's face.

Cathy: Its okay.... I know what I'm doing.

Chris: can we talk? can I call you right now?

He used to squint his eyes and watch her face as they made love. It gave him so much pleasure to see her smile as he eased himself inside her. Now he had visions of an over-sized, hairy ape, hitting her if she didn't perform perverted sexual acts.

Cathy: NO! YOU CAN'T CALL ME! Tooo many people can hear everything I say. I know it sounds bad but I'm okay. I'm moving to NY soon - away from him. He wont be able to touch me. It'll just be a few more weeks. You'll see - everything's okay

Chris: (He wiped his eyes with the back of his hand.) it's a few more weeks of him hitting you!!!!!!!

Cathy: NO! I arranged it so he'll be out of the house most of the week. we're together only on weekends and he's out golfing most of the time. We really aren't together tooo much SO CALM DOWN. Everything is okay.

Chris: he's making you have sex with him. (He was so repulsed at his own images of them having sex that he withdrew his fingers from the keyboard and wiped them on his pants.)

Cathy: I know it's tough for you to hear this and... trust me... I hate to say it... but I can live with that... if it keeps peace in the house, it's a small price to pay. As soon as we're out of the house, I'm getting a restraining order so he can't visit me.

Chris: i cant believe this... i can't believe you're living with a man that beats you.

Chris: Please tell me. I need to understand.... when did it start???

Cathy: Shortly after we moved in together - 7–8 months ago - I can't even remember what happened but he shoved me into a wall - I remember him laughing a lot - thinking it was funny - he kept telling me I tripped

Chris: I'm incredulous... i didn't think this happened to educated white women

Cathy: It happens to everyone. I'm not alone - but it's coming to an end. Just a few more weeks.

Chris: (It was impossible for him to imagine how she could willingly go home every night, knowing what waited for her.) I think you should call the police. if you don't, I will.

Cathy: DON'T YOU DARE!!!! Now stop that. All I need is for the Good Ol' Boys around here to find out I'm just a punching bag for them to snicker about in the bathroom and I'll be on the street looking for a job in no time

Chris: You're letting this guy beat the shit out of you so you can keep your job? Listen to yourself... i think you're losing your grasp on reality! YOU CAN'T GO HOME!!! even if it's just for the weekend

Cathy: Will you support me? I have no money He has control of everything. I can't afford not to have a job. Besides, I have to go home. The girls are there and I can't leave them there alone.. It'll all be over soon. I'm moving to NY and the girls and I will be safe

Chris: has he ever hurt the girls????

Cathy: No. I'll kill him if he does and he knows that.

Chris: this is unbelievable. what do they say?

Cathy: Fortunately, the girls have never seen him hit me... everyone just laughs because they think I fall down a lot (She touched her latest bruise as if to say, the only thing that falls down is his fist on my face.)

Chris: You did nothing to deserve this.... i just can't imagine you being involved in something like this Please let me call right now.

Cathy: NO. I CAN'T TALK TO YOU FROM THE

OFFICE. There are people all around. I'll call you from my hotel. (Though no one was right outside her door, she was still unnerved by Samantha's knowledge of her telephone calls.)

Cathy: Talk to me about something else. The reunion Are you coming to the reunion?

Chris: how can i talk about the reunion when i know what's going on in your life

Cathy: knowing you care is the most important thing to me. Sometimes I think I'm all alone and if he kills me tomorrow no one would care.

Cathy: I mean except for the girls... of course, they care... but he successfully scared the few friends I had

Cathy: Just being able to tell you, to talk to someone, feels so good. Ive kept so much inside. Its like I've been in a dark, dark place and I didn't know how to get out. You can't imagine how good it is just to talk to you and know you care.

Cathy: now tell me, will I see you at the reunion.

Chris: yes, yes, yes... I'll be there... this is no good... I can't leave you in that house... you have to let me do something.

Cathy: There's nothing you can do. I'm taking care of it all. I really have to run now. Thank you so much for being there for me. it was good to finally tell someone. I'm really happy that it was you I shared this with. We'll be okay - its just a few more weeks

Chris: I wish I could put my arms around you and hug you once again... i'm here to help in anyway I can.

Cathy: I know that - thank you - I love you Chris

Chapter 30

"I wish I never had kids," the 42 year old attorney from St. Paul confessed. "I love my kids, but it's meant I've had to live my life for them, and I couldn't live my own."

Probably the newer members of SPAT were shocked by the admission, but since she repeated the same comment every time she showed up, anyone who attended the meetings for more than a few weeks had heard her whines and woes before.

SPAT stood for Single Parents With Teens. Obviously, the abbreviation should have been SPWT, but since the attendees felt that they "spatted" with their children much more often than they "spwtted," SPAT became the official designation.

SPAT was the brain-child of Sol, an enterprising restaurateur whose location near office buildings meant that he had a weekday clientele, but few weekend customers. Since, as he said, "I still have to pay the rent on weekends," the entrepreneur created reasons for people to come his place. On Saturdays, the restaurant filled for Kid Lits (book readings for kids) in the afternoons, and the evenings were devoted to Saturday Night Singles. Sunday nights rotated between Divorce Decree Discussions (where lawyers compared recent divorce settlements) and Single Parents With Kids, where, frustrated parents could come to share their horror stories with an empathetic audience.

Group dynamics were always fascinating. While Sol knew how to get people into his restaurant, he didn't know what to do with them while they were there (other than to serve them food), so once the people showed up, he disappeared into the kitchen. Some of the more aggressive (which may have been why they were single) attendees decided that everyone would sit in a large circle and each person had to say something: whether it was about an incident that occurred during the week; some deep inner thoughts; or, some other kid related problem. SPAT had no dues, no membership forms, no websites. The price of admission was that you had to participate, and twice a month, anywhere from 15 to 25 single parents were willing to pay that price.

At some point, and no one could remember who brought it in, a basketball appeared, and it became the ritual for it to be passed from person to person in the circle and whomever held it had to speak. "The ball's in your court," everyone would call out as the orange ball was handed to the next person.

Cathy was really an interloper at these meetings. Other than not spending enough time with her children, she really didn't feel like a failure as a parent. However, Fred, who criticized her as a rotten parent, found this group for her and insisted that she go. Since it meant two nights a month out of the house, and away from him, she was glad to attend; though fabricating confessions every two weeks was becoming more difficult.

"The deal was he would finish his MBA and then I'd apply to medical school, and depending on where I got accepted, we'd move to that city," a weary Nancy sighed. Having come directly from the hospital after completing her shift as an emergency room nurse, she was still wearing her sea-green scrubs with her ID badge dangling from a cord around her neck.

Few romances ever blossomed from the SPAT meetings, especially since the women usually outnumbered the men three or four to one. But, more importantly, this was where single parents came to bare their souls and share their frustrations, and that didn't really make for good dating chit-chat. The group didn't laugh very much, nor have animated conversations about life, love, or politics. There was a lot more silence and nodding in agreement.

"But then he got this incredible job offer in a city that didn't have a good medical school, and it was impossible to turn it down. 'We could save enough money in a couple of years to pay for your first year of medical school,' he would say. So he took the job and we moved. Then we got the BMW's because we had to look successful, and the house because it was a great investment, and he got promoted and couldn't quit. And, I know you're all going to say this is a stupid thing for me to say, but, one day there were kids and school and pick them up and drop them off." There was a long pause as she massaged the basketball, and dropped her head a bit to hide the tear that was rolling down her cheek. "And then one day there was Leslie, who was interesting and dynamic, and not staying around the house all day baking cookies and driving kids to soccer. Leslie was a lawyer. She was out there in the world doing things, defending innocent people against large corporations, stopping polluters, not just shuttling kids around, and worrying about school projects and play dates. So he left me and the kids for Leslie and moved to another city, which ironically has great medical schools. I moved the kids to Minneapolis to be near my parents. I still hope to go to medical school someday, but at this rate, my kids will be graduating before I will."

The basketball that now carried the sweat and tears of two dozen worn-out-with-worry moms and dads bounced into Cathy's lap. "The ball's in your court now," a weak echo bounced through the empty restaurant.

"I really love my job," Cathy confessed, tracing the seams of the warm and wet ball with her finger tips. "I worry that the kids are suffering because of it..."

At just about the same time that Cathy was sharing her woes, Chris and Melanie were snuggled on the couch watching, for the thirty-third (or maybe it was the sixty-sixth) time, *The Way We Were*, Melanie's favorite movie in the whole wide world. Actually, she was snuggling and Chris was finishing an egg roll from the Chinese take-out that they had for dinner. While she put her head in his lap, and he rested his slightly greasy hand on her shoulder, his concern was that if she didn't fall asleep he would have to have sex with her. She always liked to have sex after *The Way We Were*.

Maybe I should pretend to fall asleep, he wondered. *What did I do the last time we watched this movie?* His stomach was full, he had drunk a little too much wine, and was feeling good. He just was not in the mood for her kind of sex tonight. He was also more than a bit worried that, with his defense's weakened by Merlot, he might call out Cathy's name. *Wouldn't that be funny*, he thought, *that after all these women, the one I get in trouble with is Cathy, and I haven't even had sex with her in over twenty years.*

By the end of the movie Melanie was asleep on the couch. Chris covered her with a blanket and went into the bathroom, where he brushed his teeth and masturbated, and then got into bed and went to sleep.

Chapter 31

A week later, everything was going extremely well. Fred was ecstatic about his promotion. "The territory's a mess," he delighted in telling Cathy. "It's a real mess... needs lots of TLC. I was thinking of turning it down because of all the travel, but Stanley begged me," he bragged. "He must have said a dozen times, you're the only one in the office that can do what needs to get done." *Thank you, Stanley, thank you, thank you*, Cathy cheered, quietly tapping her thumb and forefinger together.

Fred explained, as if it would be disappointing to Cathy, "At least initially, I'll be on the road more than I'm home, but at the end of the day, it's better for all of us." Cathy couldn't agree more. "Besides, you'll be in New York a lot, so at least I won't have to be home alone as much." Cathy fought back the jubilation and tried to look upset yet understanding.

In South St. Paul, Stanley was amazed at how quickly and significantly Cathy made good on her "implication" that he would benefit from the gesture. Not only did he sincerely enjoy the reception at the museum with management, but the message wasn't lost on him that this was a "vice president's and above" function and he was the only non-vice president present. He committed to himself, and to Cathy, to make certain that Fred succeeded in his new position.

Her move to New York was going well, too. Her new office was going to be a very large corner office with a great view and new furniture. Considering how small and shabby her space was now, she was really looking forward to the transfer, though it began to concern her that the company was being too generous. When this company takes that much care about someone, there's bound to be a questionable reason.

The realtor said she would be ready to show Cathy a few "great condominiums" that were just coming onto the market, so chances were quite good that she and the girls would have a place to move into fairly quickly. And, much to her delight and amusement, she found a moving company that specialized in "significant separations." The END Moving Company (this acronym was actually the owner's initials, Eric Nelson Dickerson) guaranteed that no "evacuation" would take longer than two hours. They were available 24/7, and they didn't charge while "waiting for the signal" no matter how long it took. They had warehouses hidden in three states, their trucks had no markings of any kind, and they swore to uphold Mover-Client Privilege to the same extent as lawyers and doctors did.

Feeling happy about how everything in her life was going, she e-mailed Chris.

Chris,

I've been thinking about those years long ago a lot lately. It's too bad we can't go back and start again... put some mistakes aside. I don't know if we would have succeeded as a couple, but I know it's very unfortunate that we didn't have a chance to try - I blame myself for that. My rape counselor said I had to get back to my normal life, that if I altered my life because of the rape, then he won.

Well, I guess... he won... whoever he was, since I lost you and went on to two unhappy marriages. I think I never really got over that miserable event and that it altered me permanently - I even can trace problems with Fred back to the rape.

I know the reason it was difficult for you to come to Minneapolis then was because you started a new job and you were in a play - but I think inside - I didn't want you to come because I felt damaged... I was broken somehow... I wasn't good enough any longer... I took the assignment in Texas without even telling you because I felt that I could start all over there - no one knew me. No one knew that I was spoiled merchandise. I know it's a stupid thing to say - but that is how I felt at the time.

I guess what I'm saying... and have wanted to say to you for the past 20 years... is that I don't blame you for not being there with me then. I remember saying to you "I'm okay. I'm going to counseling. There's nothing you can do." I know if I had said "Please come and be with me" you would have been on the next plane... I didn't leave Minneapolis and didn't answer your letters or return your calls because I was angry with you... I didn't want to talk to you because I was disappointed in myself... I don't know why I was, but that's how I felt.

After reading your e-mails, I suspect we both feel the same way - that we really wished we had a chance to be together back then... I guess we'll always have to wonder.

But maybe this new connection between us will give us both a chance to say things that have been bottled up inside all these years... I know that would be refreshing, and I welcome the joy of finding an old friend - someone who I could tell anything to - once again.

Forever,

Cathy

Reading her e-mail on his Blackberry while sipping a mocha frappuccino at Starbucks, Chris raced into the bathroom and cried into toilet tissue. He could have gone to Minneapolis. He should have gone to Minneapolis. He didn't go because... he didn't even know why he didn't go. He was in pain about what happened, and he knew she was in worse pain, but he just couldn't bring himself to go and deal with the situation.

But the pain he felt today was far worse than it was two decades ago, for now he realized that he had been punishment for his actions, or lack of them, of twenty years ago.

Unrolling more toilet tissue and pressing it against his eyes, his legs crumbled under him and he sat on the toilet bowl, wishing he could flush himself away.

Chapter 32

Much to the misfortune of the 43 year-old attractive blonde attorney who was standing behind Chris just when the traffic signal blinked WALK, WALK, WALK, Chris saw a penny and bent down to pick it up. Tripping over him and starting to fall, she dropped the cup of coffee in her hand and instinctively reached out to balance herself. Unfortunately for Chris, the only thing she could balance herself on was his shoulders, and by pushing herself upward, she sent him to the ground, where he sat in a small pool of spilt coffee and dirty street water.

Two passersby moved towards him to help him get up, but he waived them off, and mouthed the words, "Thanks, I'm okay." He felt the sewage-destined water soak through his pants to his skin, and he could only enjoy the moment as symbolic of his life at that moment.

She gasped in horror, but the sight really was too funny, and she couldn't resist laughing a bit at Chris' expense. Placing her attaché case on the ground and wrapping her hands around his arm, she tried to help him up, repeating over and over, "I'm sorry. I'm so sorry."

"No, no. It's my fault," Chris gallantly declared, as he rose up. "It's going to be a rotten day at the office and this is as good a way to start it as any."

As she removed her hands from his arm, it didn't escape either of them that this was one of those funny stories couples tell when asked, "How did you two meet?"

"I'm sorry. I didn't realize you had stopped." Bending down to pick up her coffee cup, she tossed it into a trash can. A quick glance at his left hand revealed no wedding ring. "I didn't think anyone stopped to pick up pennies anymore." *He's kind cute*, she thought. *Sense of humor. This could work.*

Surveying the damage to his clothes, he joked, "I'm trying to cut down on caffeine, so I only buy coffee when I save enough pennies that I pick up." Never having used that line before, he admired how well it worked since not only was it witty, but it was the perfect opening for an inviting response. Slipping the penny into his pocket where it joined three others, he twisted his head just enough to see if she was wearing a wedding ring. *No ring, good looking, obviously a professional.* "I'm sorry," he apologized once again, "it's my fault. I'm just glad you didn't fall over, too."

Picking up her cue, as if she had memorized a script written for such situations, she took a tissue from her purse and tried to help brush off some of the debris from his suit. "It must be a long time between lattes. Can I buy you a cup of coffee to apologize for ruining your suit?" Her smile was warm, her lips were tempting, her laugh was infectious, and her body was delicious.

A smile erupted on his face and just as he was about to say, "There's a Starbucks around the corner," a ten-ton block of ice fell from the sky, hit him on the head and crushed him into the gutter ooze. *If he went with her, he'd be cheating on Cathy.* Staring nowhere in particular, he didn't seem to be able to move in any direction, or utter a single word.

When he didn't jump at her offer, it was clear to her that the moment had passed, and it was time for each to go their separate ways. Checking her Blackberry, she hastily declared, "Oh my God, I've got to get back to the office. We'll have to do it some other time." With that she turned and walked away.

It took a full two seconds of thorough consideration before he called out after her, "Excuse me," and then he quickly walked over to her.

"I'm sorry, I'm being rude. My mind is on a client presentation and I'm wondering how I'm going to do it looking like I was sleeping in the streets." They both laughed. "I'm Chris," he said, extending his business card to her.

She smiled because she genuinely thought he was nice and wanted to go on a date with him. "I'm Abby... Abigail..." She took his card and gave him one of hers.

"What a lovely name. Abigail Adams is my favorite First Lady." He thought that was a good line since it showed he had a grasp of history.

"Christopher Columbus is my favorite explorer."

They spent a few more minutes chatting, and he promised to call her when he got back from New York. They shook hands, not firmly, but gently, and held the grip a few seconds longer than would be expected. With that she turned and went into the nearby building.

Just holding her business card, he felt as if he was cheating on Cathy, and he even considered tossing it into the trash. Even though he promised himself never to call her, he put her card in his pocket and continued to his office. Though from that moment on, she was pretty much forgotten.

The next three weeks each began with him thinking about his presentation to his client, and wondering if he and Cathy would enjoy being together, in every sense of the word. By the end of the three weeks, there was little else he could think of besides Cathy.

It was much the same for her.

Over the next twenty-one days, she visited her favorite boutiques and department stores at least six times, and bought four new outfits. She spent hours trying to match the perfect blouse with the perfect suit with the perfect shoes. She had two skirts shortened, and then decided they weren't short enough, so she had them shortened again.

For the first time in her life, she visited a Victoria's Secret to buy something special... just in case. While she liked the way she looked in lace panties, she told herself, there probably wasn't going to be the "appropriate" occasion to wear them... but she bought them anyway. "Is there a certain etiquette," she joked as she looked in the mirror of the Victoria Secret's dressing room and ran her fingers up and down in the valley between her breasts, "for asking a married man to sleep with you?"

"Is it better," she hoped no one could hear her, "to be subtle; like, ask him to come to my room for coffee? Or should I be straightforward about the whole thing and negotiate the arrangements... 'your room or mine, what time?' Maybe, since he's married, he and his wife have a system of letting each other know when they're in the mood, like turning a light off or pulling on an ear lobe. Maybe I should just take his hand and put it on my breast and see what develops." Sliding her hand over her flesh, she tried to imagine what his touch would feel like.

A dozen times a day - between appointments, in her office, in the lady's room - she could be heard talking to herself, asking should I do this or what if he does that? She had her make-up re-done with three different product lines and finally decided on the cosmetics from Bobbi Brown, since the look was more natural and didn't use high fashion colors that would draw attention to the color - and away from her.

During that three-week period, Chris found himself wandering into the Thrifty Drugstore near his office on five separate occasions. Sooner or later, after he picked up toothpaste and mouthwash, or soap and dental floss (none of which he really needed), he'd find his way to the aisle with the condoms, but would stand there, confused, studying the different brands like a kid studies the candy in a display case. What do you buy: ultra thin for better sensation, ribbed for that special feeling, or stronger to be safer?

For all the women he'd been with, he'd never had to wear a condom. They all took birth control pills, or wore patches, or something. He and Cathy never really used them when they were teenagers. Her mother, realizing what was happening, and though disapproving, quickly put her on birth control pills. (Her father never knew.) Besides, hadn't she had menopause yet?

"Maybe she's not expecting me to do anything. Maybe this is all a figment of my imagination. Maybe I'm kidding myself about the attraction between us. Maybe I should forget about this." He said these words to himself a hundred times a day, sometimes louder than other times, but it never stopped him from wanting to be with her, and he finally bought a selection of condoms, which he hid in a box for shaving cream.

During this time, Melanie was retained by a new client. A Hollywood producer had left his wife while she was pregnant with their fourth child, married and impregnated his new wife, cheated on and divorced her, and finally moved in with a new girlfriend. To get out of paying child support, he declared bankruptcy and had all his assets transferred to the new girlfriend. Melanie's clients were the two ex-wives.

Sadly, on several occasions during this period, Chris found Candy crying at her desk. "Nerves," was all she would say, but her constant melancholy was evidence of far greater problems. On the bright side, she continued with her wedding plans.

During that three week period, the last three women who worked for Gary resigned. From the maze, the Australian flag, the collection of stuffed rabbits, and the Jasper Johns art posters all disappeared. Gary's only comment on their leaving was, "Great tits, no brains."

During those three weeks, Chris begged Cathy, again and again, to leave Fred.

Chris: Hi, r u there?

Cathy: For you... always...

Chris: i wanted to mention that on the same day of the
       Reunion my client is having a 50th anniversary/bon
       voyage dinner party. It's a formal dress kind of
       thing... I have to be there for an hour or so to make
       my presence felt... can you come with me?

Cathy: Are you asking me out on a date :)

Chris: I guess so.... appropriate for a Reunion Weekend...
      wouldn't u say?

Cathy: Of course I'd love to attend. I hope I'll be
      appropriately dressed. I only have one cocktail dress
      I can wear... we'll be a bit overdressed for the
      reunion...

Chris: I'm certain anything in your wardrobe would be
      appropriate... besides, I've rarely seen my clients
      without food stains on their ties so i doubt there'll
      be many fashionistas there.

Though they were typing, they could hear each other laughing and
they spent a considerable amount of time reminiscing about how nervous
he was when he asked her out on their first date, and how he spilled food
on himself, and how she knocked over a glass of water on him. Finally,
exhausting the memory, there was a slight pause, and he asked...

Chris: can we talk???

Cathy: If you think about it... that's one of those
      expressions that has 3 or 4 meanings. If you mean...
      can you call me on the phone, the answer is NO!
      and you know that. If you mean, can we openly and
      honestly communicate with each other, the answer
      is... haven't we always.

Chris: I see ur in a giddy mood

Cathy: I think I'm going stir-crazy from staring at a
      computer screen all day. I have this theory that the
      computer electrons suck the consciousness out of
      people and eventually they become vegetables.
      Maybe I shouldn't say something like that while I'm
      working at a company that sells home
      entertainment electronics

Chris: sounds like you have been on the computer much too
      long today... maybe you should go out and
      interview someone...

Cathy: I think I'm almost finished for the day on this project. What's new?

Chris: I've been reading websites about domestic violence and it's very frightening... i didn't realize it was such a problem... i'm VERY worried about what Fred is doing to you!!!

Cathy: So much for being in a good mood. You don't have to remind me about him

Chris: i guess I always thought it was a problem among minorities and Hispanics.... i'm worried about you and the girls

Cathy: Believe me, I'm worried about us too

Chris: you have to move out... immediately

Cathy: with what? Are you rich? Can you send me money?

Chris: you can't stay in that house

Cathy: I'm getting us out.... just a couple more weeks

Chris: that's a couple of weeks of him treating you like a punching bag!!!!!

Cathy: I was hoping to forget about it for one day

Chris: Cat, i love you so much... it hurts me that you go home to that pig every day

Cathy: I love you, too, and knowing you're there and that you care is the most important thing you can do for me right now. I need to be loved. It makes me feel worth something to someone.

Chris: you are loved... very, very, very much

Cathy: Thanks for your concern about my girls and me - and thanks for caring. It's ok. its almost over. Talk about something else

Chris: I spoke to a counselor on one of those domestic violence hotlines... she's waiting for you to call her

Cathy: CHRIS, I TOLD YOU I WILL TAKE CARE OF
THIS

Chris: You need help!!!! you can't take care of this alone!!!!!
She said she can help you... move you into a shelter
until you can find a place to live...

Cathy: LIVE IN A SHELTER!!! I'm a VP at THCC. I can't
live in a shelter. I really appreciate your concern.
Stay out of it now!!!!

Chris: Please call her... she can help you

Cathy: Enough Chris!!! thank you for your concern but I
will take care of this!

Chris: you haven't been able to take care of this till now...
what makes you think you'll be able to in the future

Cathy: CHRIS STAY OUT OF MY LIFE!!!

Cathy: (after a long pause) Sorry, I didn't mean that. You
don't understand what it is to be a VP at a
corporation like this. If anyone gets a whiff of the
fact that my life is in shambles I'll be out on the
street looking for a job

Chris: they can't fire you because you're being abused at
home

Cathy: YOU DON'T KNOW CORPORATIONS!!!!! I've
seen it dozens of times.. Women passed over for
promotions because people suspect - not even know,
but just suspect - they're pregnant. Women kicked
off projects because the men don't want to put up
with someone's PMS mood swings

Cathy: We've passed on many good female candidates
because they just got married and the men around
here think they'll either leave soon to start families
or follow their husbands to his next job

Chris: That has to be illegal! they can't do that!!!!

Cathy: Of course it's illegal, and they do do that!!! I've been
fighting against that for years but my victories are

few compared to my defeats. Now Im a VP I can
finally do something about it.

Cathy: if people here found out what was really going on in
my life, the sharks would be circling. I wouldnt be
able to do my job. I'd be the butt of every bathroom
joke in the place, Sooner or later they'd ask me to
leave because I was "ineffectual" or something

Chris: pleeze call her...

Cathy: No! STOP badgering me!

Chris: (After a long pause) sorry... I was just trying to
help....

Cathy: I'm sorry. I really appreciate what you're trying to do
for me and the girls. I know it's out of love. But you
have to trust me - I know what I'm doing. it's all
going to be okay. Trust me, please. I love you

Chris: I love you & it hurts me to know whats happening to
you

Cathy: Thank you for trying to do the best thing for me.
Please, e-mail me the contact information for the
counselor. I cant call from here. I'll call her when I
can. I promise

Cathy: I love you, Chris. You really don't know how much
being able to talk to you means to me. I feel as if we
were never apart

Chris: I love you too... its never changed for me... I just
want what's best for you and the girls. I love you
very, very much

During those three weeks, Kingsley & Quincy Advertising's creative
department presented their concepts for Envira's campaign to the Creative
Review Committee.

The process of creating a campaign was very straightforward. After a
series of briefings by the Client Services personnel, the project was
simultaneously assigned to several creative teams. Each team could take

whatever direction it wished (with the consent of the Creative Director), and at one point all the ideas were presented in a "creative shoot-out" to a committee consisting of the agency's senior management, the department heads, and the Client Services team. Everything was open for discussion and anyone could contribute ideas.

Three campaign concepts for Envira were presented about one week before Chris was to go to New York, which made everyone uneasy.

The first campaign concept focused on the "Envira Cycle," as they called it, which depicted the lifecycle of an Envira tampon. As the copywriter explained, the campaign would show the tampon starting as a product of nature, then being used by a woman, and eventually returning to nature as the natural fibers disintegrated.

The TV spot would be an animation, the art director explained, pointing to the rough illustrations in the storyboard. The first frame was a tree that, when chopped down, was made into absorbent tampons, as depicted in the second frame of the storyboard. The next frame was of a smiling woman presumably wearing the tampon, and the last frame showed the tampon dissolving and fertilizing a new tree. The copywriter pointed out that there would be no narrative, just music, with a religious chant kind of sound.

The Creative Review Committee members were always in a bind when they heard a truly rotten idea like this one. Should they be honest and say how bad it was, incurring the hostility of the Creative Department, or should they waste time and try to discuss the idea as if it had merit, which meant that the Creatives might not truly appreciate how bad it was, and might try to save it.

All eyes turned to Chris. By tradition, the account's senior manager was allowed to offer the first opinion since he, theoretically, was closest to the client and could speak for the client. Chris hated this spot and knew the client would, too, so it was perfect for the plan he was executing. *The problem*, he argued with himself, *is that the idea is so bad, if I defend it, it may raise some suspicions in the room that something is amiss.*

In the end, he took a tepid approach to his criticism. "It's not accurate, so we could run into legal issues. Envira's tampons don't start as trees, they actually start in a bubbling chemical vat where recycled paper is dissolved and blended."

"Paper starts as a tree," the copywriter defended, clearly annoyed that something as trivial as legal considerations were going to interfere with the brilliance of his concept. But, his comment was ignored by everyone since they could all grab onto this as an acceptable excuse for shooting the idea down – and, at the same time, they were all impressed that Chris was able to shoot such a deadly arrow that they wouldn't be obligated to offer opinions on the creative.

"I love the phallic symbol in the first frame," Gary offered, quite seriously. Everybody looked at the drawing of the tree on the storyboard.

"Gary, you see phallic symbols everywhere you look," Chris spit out in disgust.

"Since you've been married forever, you may not know 'wood' is slang for an erection," Gary intellectualized his prurient comment, while the rest of the staff laughed and rolled their eyes.

The second campaign faired no better. The copywriter contacted one of the "rent-a-celebrity" services and came up with a list of female sports figures and actresses that were available, yet not very expensive. It was a very short-lived campaign idea, since for every bargain priced female celebrity, there were at least three people in the room who had never heard of her, and, most importantly, not one was associated in any way with environmental causes.

In advertising there is an expression, "When you don't know what to do, throw the company's president on the screen." So that's just what the third creative team did. It started with a long shot of Envira's president and slowly moved to a tight close up. He would speak of the company's commitment to tampons, and underneath the narrative, softly at first, then building to a crescendo, was stirring patriotic music.

Those who knew the president of the company, a short, fat, squeaky-voiced Eastern European with a thick accent, couldn't stop laughing. The women in the room, whether or not they knew him were revolted by the thought of this hard-to-understand grandfather figure telling them about which tampon to use. The other Creatives in the room were so embarrassed that this was the best they could do, dared not defend the idea. Looking around the room, one could see writers and art directors sinking below the edge of the conference table, pushing their chairs backwards into the shadows, or burying their faces behind easels and yellow pads.

Chris was elated, though he painted a pained portrait on his face. Broadcasting from the satellite between his ears, he tried to get the words humiliation, embarrassment, useless, failure, horrible, and hopeless to the antennas on everyone else's heads.

"So, what do we do now?" Mack asked in frustration, clearly reflecting the thoughts of everyone in the room. "We have only one week left till the presentation."

"If we had gotten better input from the account team," Sandy weakly offered the standard defense of a failed creative, "we would have had better concepts."

Enraged by this accusation, Chris opened his mouth to speak, and had no intention of being gentle, but Mack cut him off before the first syllable was spoken. "That's bullshit, Sandy. You had the input. I saw it all. I heard it all."

Sandy dissolved into thin air.

"Look, this isn't a tough one," Mack continued, throwing his hands in the air. "It's a simple recycling story. What did you call it, Chris?"

"A challenge to the mothers of the nation to do something for their children," Chris enunciated each word, making his best effort to sound important.

Mack repeated the line twice, though not with Chris' passion. "I read the same memos you read in which Chris used those words, and I heard him say them at the kick-off meeting. Not one of the campaigns presented here today reflects that message. Can't you come up with something that shows disgusting garbage dumps that turn into children's play grounds with a little recycling?"

"Oh, God," Sandy found his voice again, "don't tell me you want a Cat-Steven's-Where-Can-The-Children-Play," kind of thing?"

Insulted that his idea was being shot down from his vaporous creative director, Mack looked at Sandy and smiled, "Yes, that's exactly what I want. And you have one week to turn it into a campaign."

Chris actually sided (silently) with Sandy on this one. Not only was it a bad idea, but there were probably twenty advertising campaigns that took that approach over the past decade. Poor Sandy, he looked like a circus clown that had a frown and a tear permanently painted on his face. Everyone in the room turned towards Chris to let him shoot it down. But, instead, he shot back a look that said, "You know you can't argue with Mac once he makes his mind up."

Not wanting to say anything that could be quoted later and used against him, but at the same time delighted that the horrendous creative campaign was being generated by the president of the agency, so any failure rested at highest levels of the agency, Chris stood up, smiled broadly, looked Mack directly in the eye, and gave him a big thumbs up.

Delighted by his own brilliance, Mack marched out repeating, "I like it. Where can the children play?"

"But that's so trite," Sandy whimpered after Mack left the room, just to make sure his words were on the record.

"That's the campaign," Debra declared, patting Sandy on the back, as she left the room to meet her lunch appointment, the sales rep from a TV station in Atlanta. The Creatives rolled their eyes. This was a campaign concept they themselves rejected weeks ago.

Everyone abandoned the members of the Creative Department, who found new strength to attack Mack and the rest of the agency's management once everyone left the room. In Chris' mind, things couldn't be better. The least creative Creative Director in the entire city was going to give creative direction to Creatives who hated him, and he had been assigned by the President of the ad agency. He didn't know how he had masterminded all of this, but for the first time, he truly felt that the storm winds that were coming were going to blow right over his head. How desperately he wanted to tell Cathy of the brilliant plot he had created; how intricate, how intriguing, how complex, worthy of an Agatha Christie story.

By the end of those three weeks, Cathy was exhausted by arguing both sides of the "Should I sleep with Chris debate." By the end of those three weeks, she didn't know if she was going to be seduced or if she would be the seducer; if she would allow herself to have an affair if he became romantic, or if she should be aggressive or meek.

But most important of all, during those three weeks, Chris called his client several times to discuss the concept of going on television with Envira Tampons, and much to his surprise and euphoria, the client said, in writing, in an e-mail, "Yes, I would be interested in seeing some ideas for a television commercial. If it's a good idea maybe we can pull together a little budget for it."

A secretary walking down the Client Services corridor heard shouts from behind his closed door, "Thank God! Thank God! Thank you, God!"

Chapter 33

"A secretary... why is it so hard to find a good secretary?" Samantha complained. "It's not rocket science. All they have to do is type and answer the phones."

Cathy started to say that secretaries were probably the most underrated jobs in any corporation and that good secretaries were worth their weight in gold, but Samantha cut her off with, "My God, a trained chimpanzee could do this job."

Wanting to say, "With an attitude like that, no wonder you can't keep a secretary for more than four months," but she didn't. Instead, she reminded herself that her investigation into the high turnover rate in the Business Affairs Department hadn't progressed very much and it definitely was something she would have to resume before she hired anyone for the department.

"Here's the situation," Samantha steamrolled, moving onto the next topic without allowing a response to the previous one. "I'm going to be spending quite a bit of time in the Washington, D.C. office over the next six months. That bid for NASA is coming up and I have to be there to shepherd it through. I'm going to tell everyone that you're in charge of the New York office in my absence. You impress me. You can handle the job. In a few months, we'll get you more money and a new title. Besides, I think everyone will be much happier dealing with you than with me."

Once she got going, Samantha had a machine gun approach to shooting out instructions. A shopping list of "To Do's." It was all one could do just to take notes quickly enough, never mind ask questions or respond. But as she was listening to this last instruction, Cathy stopped writing because it suddenly occurred to her that she was just given a promotion and a raise. Samantha seeing the change in Cathy's face, wanted to let her enjoy the moment, so she raised her coffee cup to her lips and sipped.

This wasn't just a small step up the corporate ladder, this was an elevator ride to the top floor. *As Samantha's representative, I would be working directly with the President, CEO, and COO,* Cathy realized, *and I wouldn't have to go through layers of flunkies, like Bob, any longer. A few weeks ago I was stuck in a tiny office interviewing candidates for accounts receivable clerks, now, I'll talking with the President and CEO about revamping NASA's technology program.*

As they stood up to leave, Samantha finished by saying, "When I come back, I really would love to interview some candidates for a secretary."

Returning to her office, Cathy surveyed the overstuffed chairs, Indonesian wood burl desk with matching credenza, hand crafted wool carpet from Persia, and the twenty-foot wide windows with an unobstructed view of lower Manhattan. Standing at the window, watching cruise ships sail past the Statue of Liberty, she whispered, "Samantha would have taken a knife and cut Fred's balls off if he ever hit her. I wish I was more like Samantha."

After a few moments she returned to her computer to write to Chris and tell him about what had happened. Opening the e-mail that was waiting for her, she read:

Cathy,

I can't tell you how glad I am that you're safe in nyc… the
thought of you being in Minneapolis, within his reach,
drives me insane… more than you can ever imagine. As the
weekend approaches I get so worried and can think about
little else… I wish I were free to fly to Minneapolis and
make sure you're safe

It seems to me that a sequence of unfortunate events
occurred starting with that horrible event in Minneapolis 20
years ago… I cant help wondering that if there had been no
(I have difficulty saying the word since I'm frightened it
provokes unpleasant memories) rape or if I had come to
Minneapolis to be with you, would both our lives been
different??? would you and I be happily married at this
moment, talking about what college our children would
attend or where we were going to take our family vacation

I know this isn't about me, but I feel very guilty… I guess
the nuns did a really good job on me

I'm sorry for what I did to us, Cathy… I wish I had come to
Minneapolis when you needed me… I think our lives would
have been different.

C

***

Chris,

First, don't be afraid to say the word rape. My crisis
counselor said that by making the word "meaningful" it
puts the incident in a special place - it's important to
trivialize it and not make it so meaningful, so the word rape
should be used like any other word.

And don't apologize or feel guilty. You didn't set a series of
events into motion. Things happen. I might as well blame
the college recruiter from THCC who interviewed me and
offered me a job in the Minneapolis office or, I might as well
blame my parents for insisting that I go to Stanford so I can
get a good job after college or, I should blame my teachers

for giving me good grades.

No one's life is pre-determined and then suddenly something comes along and knocks it off track.

Who could say that you and I wouldn't have been victims of an act of violence in NYC? Or, I hate to say this - there was no guarantee that we would have had a happy life together. Maybe (I don't think so), but maybe, you and I would have ended in divorce

Let me say it, and I hope you're not bothered by this, I truly wish we had gotten married and had the chance to find out if what we had was special. But things didn't work out that way. I've thought about you a lot over the past 20 years and my feelings for you have never changed. I just put them someplace under "M for Memories."

Cathy

P.S. Besides - and let's be honest here - it's a good thing you didn't come to Minneapolis since we both know you would have gotten lost and God knows where you would have ended up. It's better you stayed in NY.

***

Cathy,

I've thought a lot about you for the last 20 years too and my feelings haven't changed either... I look at my life now and I wonder if all marriages deteriorate into two people tolerating each other... worrying about the plumbing, the dry cleaning, the mortgage...

sometimes I think it's good that you and i didn't get together because now I can always hold you up as an ideal... I can always have something to smile about... we had a pure love.. and it's good to know that something like that exists... since I don't have it now.

As the weekend approaches I'm getting more and more upset that you are going back to Fred. I know what your first husband would have done. He would have taken a gun, flown to mpls and shoved the barrel into Fred's mouth, all the while screaming "You ever touch her again... you even brush against her in bed... and I'm coming back here and blow your fuckin' head off!"

I wish I was more like him.

C

***

Chris,

That's why I divorced him. it's not more violence I need in my life, its more tenderness. Your first instincts were right - I need a big hug. I need to know that I'm still worthy of being loved - that I'm important to someone. I used to get that only from you. My father could never bring himself to hug me and tell me he loved me -my husbands weren't good at that either once they got out of bed - certainly Fred can't. Only you could sit with your arm around me and make me feel safe and happy.

It's not the bruises that hurt so much - they heal- it's the feeling that I'm no good - that somehow I deserve what's happening to me - that I'm damaged merchandise and not worthy of anyone's love.

I so desperately need your sensitivity and not some Dirty Harry imitator threatening people.

Cathy

***

C,

You never have to worry about being loved. ..I've loved you from the first day I met you and thats never changed. I feel as strongly about you today as I did all those years ago... and you never have to worry about feeling unworthy or damaged. What you're doing for the sake of your children is remarkable... I can't tell you how much esteem I hold you in... I hope someday they understand the sacrifices you've made on their behalf. Youre a wonderful woman. I wish I was with you now to show you how much I respect and love you

That pig you live with cant take away your dignity. He can only bury his deeper and deeper into the dung he exists in… I don't understand how you and he ever got together, but I hope his life and his death are painful

I love you, Cathy. I always have and I always will

Forever and ever,

C

***

C,

Thank you. Without your love, I don't think I could exist right now.

Know that my love for you is as strong as it has ever been.

I don't know when, I don't know where, I don't know how, but there was a moment when part of you became part of me, part of me became part of you. You've been with me always, and that has given me strength to continue.

I owe you more than you can possibly imagine.

I am yours forever,

C

Chapter 34

It was a perfect New York day.

For a population held prisoner by the snow, ice and rain for five months, the warm blanket of the sun was a new found freedom. People shed as much clothing as they could, and sat, stooped, and lay anywhere they could to soak in the rays of the sun. Sitting on benches, businessmen took off their suit jackets, loosened their ties and rolled up their sleeves. They ate their lunches with their faces turned towards the sun. Mothers pushing carriages stripped away layers of blankets so their babies could feel nature's embrace. Children dressed in the skimpiest shorts and t-shirts threw off their shoes and ran across the new grass. Everywhere you looked, people stretched out on the grass, climbed on the rocks, spread out on the benches. It was a day of two-hour lunches and distracted employees who couldn't focus on anything but what was outside the office window.

Strolling down a cobblestone path that led nowhere, Cathy shed her pain and allowed her spirit to be free; one in perfect harmony with the many around her. She allowed herself to smile at the boys who defended the castle that was once a rock against the onslaught of girls. She imagined Erin and Erika riding their bicycles along the path, and that felt good. She laughed at the squirrel that scampered back and forth across the footpath, struggling to remember where he put his dinner. She stopped to listen as a teenage girl shared with her best friend the absolute depth of her love for a boy named Arnold.

It made her remember how she used to tell her girlfriends about Chris.

Meandering among the trees, hoping to get lost for a long, long time, she touched one tree after another. Many, many years ago, Chris had actually carved their initials into a tree (they had just seen that in a movie) and she wondered if she could find that tree again, and if it still had their initials on it. It's probably overgrown by now, she conceded, but looking for a sign of her past was a pleasant way to forget about the present.

They had come to Central Park so often when they were in school – it was their escape from the cement sidewalks of Brooklyn - that it was hard to remember which landmark was near the tree. They called it a "special tree," she remembered, and it took them well over an hour to find it. But all these years later, she couldn't imagine why the tree was so special and how they selected it. Though, ironically, she did remember that when they found the tree and carved their initials into it, Chris turned to her and said, "This is a very special tree. It holds all our love, and if anything terrible ever separates us, we'll both come back to this tree and be joined together again."

That shallow little heart and the initials that he carved with the Swiss Army knife he carried in his backpack was probably buried by sap or suffocating under ivy by now, but it didn't stop her from looking. They had come directly from the movie theater on 72nd Street and walked straight into the park. Turning to the left, like they would have done on their way to the subway station, she tried to retrace their steps. But it was hopeless. She was wearing the wrong shoes for this hunt through the trees of Central Park, and finding herself near the carousel, she called off her hunt, sat on a bench, and watched the children go round and round, imagining that they were racing across the Arabian desert on magic steeds.

And then, she remembered the new cell phone she held in her hand, and sadly, why she was wandering down a path in Central Park in the first place.

She shook her head and thought, *I used money I hid from my insignificant other who abuses me to buy a cell phone with pre-paid minutes so no one at the company for which I am a vice president and have spent the past twenty years can trace my calls. Because I'm worried about my boss's enormous spy network, I'm sitting on a bench, hidden behind some trees, in a remote corner of Central Park, and I'm about to call ex-employees whose names I scribbled down on napkins while pretending to be eating lunch at my desk so I can look through resumes of secretarial candidates that I'm reluctant to hire since my boss burns through them like the tobacco in a cigarette. That about sums it up.*

Despite all her efforts, her investigation into the problems in the Business Affairs Department had not gotten any further, even though she was calling people who were no longer with the company. Every call was just more of the same - fear.

"Why are you calling me?"

"Who told you to call me?"

"I just want to forget I had anything to do with that company!"

"The worst year of my working life!"

And then there was the call to a young woman who had been Samantha's secretary for five months. "No man has ever used the 'C' word with me. The way she tossed it around you'd think it was my first name."

Dropping the phone into her purse, Cathy just couldn't believe they were talking about the same person she worked for. To Cathy, Samantha was a dynamic leader that inspired her to do more. To absolutely everyone else, Samantha was the devil, and a vulgar one at that. *Is this what's going to happen with Samantha? Is she going to turn on me one day?* She had pinned her all her hopes on this woman, and really couldn't bear another let down. She was taking this job to get away from an abuser, not to find a new one.

What should she believe? Was this such a unique situation in which, truly, only the rare few, the best-and-the-brightest could survive? Or, was she just a powerful bitch with a humongous ego? Though, and she paused for a moment, there's something nice about being around someone who was strong enough to put fear into the heart of every executive in one of the largest corporations in the world. It's actually nice being on the side of the stronger than the weaker for a change.

Glancing up at the trees, she smiled, *it's sort of like being the evil Sheriff of Nottingham and not Robin Hood.* It was a terrible thing to admit, but she was tired of being the victim, of being beaten time and time again.

The more she thought about herself as a victim, the more she realized that it was not just about Fred, but it defined her life with the company, as well. Her salary grade was always a step or two below those of her male peers. When they were getting 10% raises, she was getting 3% or 4%. Her office was always just a little smaller than it should have been, and she was always given the least desirable spaces. Her office in Minneapolis had a huge pillar running through it, and there were a lot of junior executives - male junior executives - who had better spaces. And, let's be honest, while there was no doubt the promotion to vice president was well deserved and too long delayed, it only came amidst an investigation into discriminatory practices by the U.S. Department of Labor.

And, those transfers from one city to the next. They were never offered as promotions, only instructions to go here or go there. Go solve this problem or that problem. There was no doubt that she did very well by the company, but the company certainly squeezed every penny they could out of her.

At that moment it occurred to her, *Maybe I'm taking the wrong approach to this issue. Maybe I should try to understand why this department succeeds and who succeeds in it. Maybe I need to understand why Samantha succeeds. After all, there are some people still in the department that have been there for years. Maybe this really is a place for a rare breed of person. Maybe I'm such a person.* Watching the quickening pace of the horses revolving around the carousal, in a rare moment, she praised herself, "Maybe I am one of best-and-the-brightest."

Heading back to the office, she weaved her way through the stream of meandering mothers, and exited Central Park.

This is a landmark day, she recognized, and decided to remember it. The day she went from being the lamb to the lion. At that moment she had an overwhelming desire to call her girls and say, "Don't worry. Everything will be okay. Mommy has taken care of everything." But she couldn't call them, they were still in school, so she just sent a text message to each of them that said, I luv u :).

Chapter 35

Cathy's newly found bravado didn't survive the hour. When she called her voice mail she found four panicky messages from Stanley Klein. "We have a problem," Stanley exploded as soon as she returned the call. "We have a very big problem."

"What is it?" As if she didn't know.

"Fred. I've gotten three complaints from customers about him. I can't ignore them." He was a little man and his little world was caving in on him because he made a deal with the devil.

Speaking matter-of-factly, as if this was not something to get too excited about (even though her heart started beating at a thousand times a minute) she calmly asked, "What kind of complaints?"

"He's far too aggressive – he's practically threatening clients. Cathy, these are important clients we've been selling to for years. I can't afford to lose them, or I'll be out of a job. I'm getting enough heat over this whole thing as it is." His voice rose in anger, something he could not have done to a corporate vice president only a few weeks ago. But she was no longer a corporate vice president, she was a co-conspirator in a plot to deceive, and her title no longer demanded the respect it used to.

Just three more weeks, she chanted to herself. *Just a three more weeks.* "I'm certain he's overly eager. He just wants to prove himself to everyone. He puts a lot of pressure on himself."

Pulling the phone from her ear, she could feel his perspiration coming through the wires.

"At this point I don't really care what his problems are. I've got to pull him out of the territory and send him back to the order desk." With panic swallowing every syllable, he was a fountain of incoherent sentences about Fred screaming at clients and demanding clients buy more than they needed.

This is very bad, Cathy acknowledged, but only to herself. He had to stay in that position and on the road for twenty-two more days. A sharp pain pierced her forehead and she didn't know if it was a headache from the stress, or an anticipation of where Fred's first punch will fall. "He's not used to working with this type of client, Stanley. You have to give him a chance." One year Chris took her to midnight mass at St. Patrick's cathedral on Christmas Eve, and while she couldn't appreciate the religious significance, she found the voice of the monsignor very soothing and uplifting. It was that voice that she tried to imitate when talking with Stanley.

"I can't take a chance, Cathy, no matter what the benefit is supposed to be for me. He told one client that unless you sign an order now, he'll be put them down at the bottom of the list and they'll have to wait six months till they get anything from us." Stanley was screaming, and there was no way to calm him down.

Oh my God! What an idiot! This whole thing's going to explode! I'll never get out of that house now! How could I ever have gotten involved with someone so stupid?

She was now a lone mountain climber, standing underneath Stanley's avalanche of complaints and fears. "I'm sitting on ten thousand units in the warehouse and that idiot is telling customers that they can't have any for six months unless they sign today."

"Look, Stanley..."

Cutting her off, "Cathy, I'm in survival mode here. Our deal is off."

Taking a tougher tone, taking a Samantha tone, she declared to Stanley, "It's too late, Stanley! We started this together, we're going to finish this together or you, me, and Fred are all going down together!"

Shocked by her sudden burst of strength, Stanley remained on the phone in quiet. He was the meek territory manager of modem sales again, and she was the corporate vice president again.

Impressed by her ability to put an end to his tirade of complaints, she backed away and took a more conciliatory tone. "Look Stanley, you're in sales. Let's make this a win-win situation."

Still angry over how things unfolded, and believing he had been set up for failure, he conceded his tone, but he would not concede his position. "The only way I'm going to win is to get him out of my office. You're in Human Resources. Transfer him somewhere."

Trying to appease him, knowing there was no way she could transfer Fred, that no one would take him with his record of bad reviews, she lied, "Okay, I'm going to do that. I promise. I'll find a place for him. But it's going to take a couple of weeks, Stanley. We can still both come out ahead on this if we don't panic. Stick with me on this and you'll end up a vice president." There was no way in the corporate world that she could get him promoted, but he still had his dreams, and was willing to listen. "Stanley, we don't have a choice. All our careers are at stake here. Let's work together."

There was silence, and than a mouse's squeak, "How?"

Thank God, I gave him a taste of the good life, she thought. *He wants more of it. Typical man, they're so easy to bait with ambition.* "For the next couple of weeks why don't you travel with him in the territory. Say that it's mandated by the company that anyone new to a territory can't travel alone for the first month. It's a new rule and you just got your head handed to you for not knowing about it. I promise, Stanley, I just need two, maybe three, weeks to get him out of there."

She could hear him considering it, more importantly she could hear him realizing that he had no alternative. Another squeak, "Okay." Remembering that she was his only ally and supporter in the Minneapolis office he wanted to smooth things over, and so he made a friendly, but reminding, joke, "After this, I should be a Senior Executive Vice President."

She joked back, relieved, "I'm sure someday you will be."

They both breathed a little easier.

After he hung up, her next thought was, *this is going to be a rotten weekend*. She had to get back to Minneapolis immediately, before Fred got home, to make sure the kids were safe. On the way to the airport in the corporate limousine, she checked the Minneapolis weather on the computer that was built into the back of the driver's seat. "Thank God, it's going to be sunny all weekend." Hopefully, he'll vent his anger on the golf balls and not on me. Though a pain developed between her legs when she thought about the excruciating and degrading Saturday Night Fuck she could expect from him.

"Three weeks," became her mantra for the weekend. "I just need to hold it together for three more weeks.

Surprisingly, that weekend wasn't terrible at all - except for the Saturday Night Fuck. He didn't want to admit to Cathy about the problems in the territory (and he assumed she would never hear about something at his level), so he pretended everything was going superbly. Before heading to the golf course, he even manufactured some compliments from Stanley: "The clients love you," and, "You're the best thing that ever happened to this territory."

Chapter 36

Monday morning Cathy stayed out of the office, and using another pre-paid cell phone, she continued her investigation into the Business Affairs Department. On her seventeenth call to a former employee, when she expected more of the same, something unusual occurred.

Beginning the call, as she had all the others, she explained in a rather mundane, clerical voice, "I'm doing a Retention Survey of former employees of the company. We want to know why people leave so we can correct any deficiencies, and hopefully, retain good people like yourself." It sounded believable, something the Human Resources Department would do.

Expecting yet another rude response, or at least an abrupt hang up, she removed the phone several inches from her ear, but quickly pressed it against her ear again when a young girl named Tiffany cautiously said, "You know the terms of the settlement prevent me from speaking about my experiences in the department."

But the surprise in Cathy's voice when she said, "Settlement?" was obvious, and they both knew that ultra-confidential information was just revealed. In that one word, their worlds would be forever changed.

Realizing the gravity of her mistake, Tiffany, in tears, pleaded, "Please forget I said anything. I could get in a lot of trouble. I assumed since you're a vice president in Human Resources, you knew. Oh my God, I'm sorry. I shouldn't have said anything. Please, I'm begging you, don't say anything to anyone. I just had baby." In genuine fear that every word she said only worsened the situation, she slammed the phone down as if it had been a poisonous snake in her hand.

"Settlement," Cathy snickered to herself with satisfaction, as if she just found gold after decades of digging at the bottom of an abandoned mine. In a low voice, she practically sang the words, "I think I found the money." Proud of herself, wishing she could call Alex and say, "Ah ha! I found it even though you gave me nothing to work with," she walked along the path that bordered the river, thinking, *what a beautiful day. The sun is out, the sky is blue, the air is warm, and I'm very, very good at what I do. I truly am one of the best-and-the-brightest.*

Satisfied with herself, she also wondered if maybe her search should stop here. At this point, she knew nothing that could endanger anyone's standing in the company, including her own, and there were much more important things to do, such as finalizing the details of the Great Escape.

Tossing the cell phone into a trashcan, she admitted it was an easy choice. *Give up the search for the truth and become the second most powerful person in the most important department of one of the world's largest corporations, or continue the search, become a whistleblower, expose hypocrisy and cover-ups among Senior Management, and end up out of work, living with a pig that beats the shit out of me.* "Hmmmm, tough choice."

Her mind skipped ahead to a future in New York, in a position of power, without Fred, without the fear of going home at night. Maybe Chris, maybe not Chris. Maybe somebody else. Maybe nobody. Maybe just her and the girls. *That wouldn't be so bad. At least, for a while. You can be single in New York and still enjoy your life. Maybe she could hook up again with some of her old girlfriends from Kennedy High School. Wouldn't that be funny.*

And despite everything she'd heard, she really liked Samantha; maybe the two of them could become friends and go to restaurants and the theatre together.

As she drove back toward the office, still congratulating herself for unraveling the "follow the money" mystery, she made a mental note to herself to read Tiffany's employee file to see what she received a settlement for. But as she was thinking about how to retrieve the file, a thought occurred to her: Alex and Tiffany didn't work in the Business Affairs Department at the same time. He couldn't have known about the settlement, so his "follow the money" clue couldn't be referring to her.

Maybe it was general knowledge in the department. Too many people talk way too much about things that should be private. Though, you could tell from the genuine panic in Tiffany's tone, she wasn't going to blab to anyone, not even a best friend, about her settlement.

Desperately wanting to see Tiffany's employee file, but knowing that her movements on the computer could be traced, she thought, *I could search Tiffany's file, and no one would be suspicious, if, at the same time, I pull the records of all former employees of the department for the past five years. God, I'd have to look through hundreds of employee files so no one would know that I was actually looking at just one record.* She also asked herself, "Was I just very lucky that I found the one person who had a settlement out of the hundreds that have left the department or did I just find one of many? How would Alex have known about them? He was in Strategic Planning. That's senior enough to see the budgets. There's something in the budgets that he knew was out of line."

While she had no access to the Business Affairs Department's budget from Minneapolis, she could access it from New York and no one would question why she was looking at them. After all, she was the de facto number two person in the department.

Today was a good day. She felt good about herself. Even if she wasn't going to do anything with the information she found, since it would ruin the Great Escape, she enjoyed the challenge. She, single-handedly, against "the greater minds" in Senior Management, was going to solve this mystery with the scantest of clues, just like Sherlock Holmes and Ellery Queen.

That night, as she walked through the door to her house, she was actually smiling and decided to take the girls out for pizza at Pompeii's.

As she opened the door, Fred crash landed in front of her as if he had dropped from the ceiling, "I hope you're smiling because you decided to marry me?" Fred had been patiently waiting for Cathy and had arranged a romantic evening for the two of them.

Pre-occupied with events at the office, for one pleasant moment she hadn't even been thinking about him. So when he suddenly appeared in front of her, she almost fell backwards.

She gasped. He laughed.

"Aren't you supposed to be in Milwaukee?" The utter panic in her voice was clear. In less time than it takes to blink, she pictured him doing something completely stupid, getting fired, damaging her career, and worst of all, ruining her escape plans.

Knowing in his heart that her panic was an expression of her concern for him, he bent over and kissed her. "That's a fine way to greet the love of your life." As much as he enjoyed surprising her and seeing her confusion, he did offer an explanation. "Stan says I'm doing a great job and he wants to turn some major accounts over to me, so we're going to travel together for the next couple of weeks so he can introduce me."

Gently taking her arm, he led her to the living room, which was golden in the glow of twenty or thirty candles. A small fire was burning (even though it was a warm evening) and the aromas of the wood and scented candles perfumed the room. Preparing a picnic of cheese, sausage, French breads, and red wine, he spread a blanket in front of the fire and placed two cushions next to each other, facing the flames. Soft violin music, that spoke of love and passion, filled the air, and he quietly whispered, "Come sit with me in front of the fire. I told Esmerelda to take the girls to dinner and a movie, so we have at least three hours alone together."

"But it's a school night," she protested.

"I know. But I wanted tonight to be special. I have something I want to say to you."

She didn't like this. She didn't like this at all. The last time they had a romantic dinner, she ended up sleeping on the floor, holding her bruised head... yet she had no choice but to drop her attaché case, gush with enthusiasm, "Oh, how lovely," and return the kiss. She let him lead her to the pillows, kneeled down, and mimicked him in raising the wine filled glass in front of her.

"I know I'm a real jerk sometimes," he confessed, "and I want to apologize for everything that I've ever done or said that has ever made you unhappy." He leaned over and kissed her fingers where she held her wine glass. She kissed his lips, because she knew that was what he would expect.

No master could ever trust a loving dog that had bitten her, and if Cathy forgave him now, she would live in fear of the day he turned again, as he surely would.

"First, I want to thank you for everything you've done for me in relation to my new job." Stiffening with fear, she saw her plotting to get him field sales job exposed, but she relaxed when he added, "I know that your being home when I'm on the road means you're lonely and have to keep the house up on your own. I just want you to know that I appreciate it."

Doing everything she could to prevent herself from bursting out laughing, she wondered exactly what he did to help maintain the house? Pick up his empty beer cans?

"We haven't talked about marriage for a few weeks. I wanted to know your feelings now that you have had time to think about it." Again he bent over and kissed her lips. His was the voice of a man in love who desperately wanted to be with his absolute soul mate.

Once again, she was completely taken by surprise and didn't know what to say. After the horrible events of that evening, she thought it was a dead subject (and delighted that she wasn't dead). She lifted her wine glass to her lips to prevent him from kissing her again.

Her silence was a bit annoying, but he was willing to overlook it since he knew he was catching her by surprise. "I still want to marry you. Will you be my bride?" This was the voice that drew her to him when they first met. When he wanted to be passionate, his words were like notes on a page of music. He could have been reading the employee manual, but she would have closed her eyes and drifted up to the clouds. Yet, his voice had a strength, and she knew he would never let her fall down to earth and hurt herself.

How often he charmed her with that voice. She would have followed him anywhere then.

She opened her eyes. That's how it once was. It wasn't like that anymore. Now, her only memories were of blood and pain.

What she meant to say was, "No, I haven't really thought about it," but all that came out was, "No."

He fell backwards, as if a Roman soldier had pushed a lance through his heart.

Realizing that she had better soften her response... very quickly... she added, "No, I haven't thought about it. After the events that evening, I didn't think it was a subject between us anymore." She was nervous, and she began to perspire. She could only hope he would think the drops of water forming above her ears were from the flame making her hot.

It was a good response. He withdrew the lance from his heart and leaned forward, smiling, "You silly fool. Of course, I want to marry you. I love you."

Since she couldn't think of anything to say, and certainly didn't want to say "Yes" or "No" to his proposal, she pushed the picnic aside and forced herself on top of him. Kissing him aggressively, on his lips, on his neck, on his ears, as if she wanted to be with him forever. She ran her hand up and down his thigh, opening his pants and massaging his penis. Between her kisses, he whispered, "I wasn't very nice to you that evening. I apologize. I should have never reacted that way. I'm ashamed of myself." He sounded so sincere she almost believed him, but she was more worried that he would press her for a response.

Leaning back, letting Cathy slide his pants down, he whispered, "Have you asked the girls what they thought about me as their father?"

Running her tongue down his chest on the way to his penis she cursed herself again. Stupid, stupid, me. How could I ever have brought them into this mess? She groaned as if to say, "Not now. Don't talk. I just want to enjoy your body as I've enjoyed it before." But, after he groaned from pleasure, she did mumble, "No, not yet."

"Please do," and with those words he lay back, enjoying the feel of her wet tongue on his body. She loves me, he knew, she wants to marry me. Why else would she want to give me so much pleasure? After he came in her mouth, he pulled her to him and delicately, passionately, undressed her and inserted himself into her. For her, there was no pain this time, but as always there was no pleasure. As soon as he was done, she pretended to fall asleep in his arms.

Chapter 37

Another lecherous, lascivious, licentious, low-life client that wanted to get out of paying alimony for Melanie, and another night of being a bachelor for Chris. He had to admit, as much as he was convinced he would never marry Melanie again if he had the option, he really hated eating alone so often. Wandering down to the mall, trying to decide which restaurant to go to, he strolled passed Meriwether's Bookstore, where a small crowd had gathered around the entrance, clearly waiting for an event to begin.

A lovely young (pity, too young for him) redhead with a splendid body, flawless skin, and tortoise shell reading glasses, tapped him on the shoulder and slid a piece of paper in his hand. Fixated on her white teeth and tight tank top, he completely missed what she was saying, so he nodded, since it seemed to be the appropriate response. Taking him by the arm, she thrust him into the middle of the small crowd that was moving through the doors that had just opened. On the inside, another young lovely (also too young) ushered him to a seat, and before he knew it, he was a sardine in a small auditorium, anxiously awaiting the arrival of...

... of who?

Looking down at the piece of paper he still grasped, he read that he was here for a presentation by Dr. H. Troy about her new book, "The Roadmap of Your Life."

"Why not," he whispered to himself since he didn't want any of the intellectuals filling the room to think he wasn't one of them.

The Chairman of the Philosophy Department of one of the local universities introduced Dr. Troy, and then turned the podium over to her. A somewhat big woman, she took the microphone and stepped away from the podium. She sat on a stool that was placed center stage, almost like a folk singer performing in an intimate coffee house.

"Good evening. Thank you for coming.

"I want to tell you about a patient of mine. For the sake of this presentation, we'll call him John and say that he is a Baby Boomer. The reason I want to tell you about John is that he is representative of many people that I see in my practice and that I speak to since my book was published.

"John graduated from a good college, raised a family, and worked hard his whole life. He is a sales manager at a large corporation, and is now seeing his career wind down. To some degree that's his decision, and to some degree it's just part of the process of being in a corporation that breathes in new, young, energetic employees every year, and exhales older, tired, more expensive ones.

"John is depressed, so after a certain amount of badgering from his wife, he finally agreed to see me. When I asked him what was bothering him, he said the following... and I want to capture his words as exactly as possible since they really define the feelings of many, maybe even some in this audience. He said...

"My life feels so small, so insignificant. I thought I would be somebody important. I thought I would be at the Oscar Awards, or be invited to the Presidential Inauguration. I thought corporations would send me to China and Europe to work on special projects, or maybe I'd be sent by the United Nations to Africa to study the economy of some starving nation and make recommendations on how to turn it around. I thought I would be invited to lots of parties filled with celebrities.

"I just thought my life would be bigger. I didn't think I'd spend my life in front of a computer during the day and a TV set at night.

"When I asked him what he did to move his expectations forward, I got a blank stare.

"Were you active in the Democratic or Republican Party in your community, I asked him. He said no.

"Did you volunteer at any philanthropic organizations, working with the board of directors to raise money? No.

"Did you look for a job where you might meet celebrities or diplomats? No.

"Did you write articles that appeared in the important journals and newspapers that would express your views, and possibly get you invited to speak at forums and conferences on the subject? No.

"Did you do anything other than sit in front of a computer during the day and the television at night to advance your dreams? No, he admitted. Who had time to do any of that between work, and the house, and the kids.

"So, I said, why are you unhappy. You got exactly what you pursued in life. You didn't go after anything, and that's exactly what you got.

"To which he said, I just thought they would find me and invite me to do something.

"Obviously, he didn't remain a client very long." There was some laughter in the room.

"As I said, John is not alone in his feelings. Many people, men and women, tell me that after a lifetime of work and raising a family they feel so small, so empty, so inadequate. Many ask me 'How did I get here?'

"They say this as if they woke up one morning and suddenly found themselves in a job they didn't seek, sleeping next to someone they never met, paying a mortgage on a house they didn't buy, or feeding children they never had. They say this as if it's all new to them.

"They got there, I tell them, because that's exactly where they wanted to be. Personally, I don't understand why they're so surprised, and the fact that I tell them this probably explains why I am being invited to fewer and fewer cocktail parties." Another mild laugh from the audience.

"Every time you get in the car, you have a destination. You're going to work, to the store, to the movies, to the doctor, to visit a friend, returning home, wherever. You're always going somewhere, and you know where you're going. No one gets in the car, starts the engine, takes their hands off the steering wheel, and lets the car determine which way to go.

"However, when most people set out on life's journey, they usually don't have a destination, and they let the road take them.

"People, when thinking about their lives, can basically be separated into three groups.

"I call the first group, which is definitely the largest, the River Rafters. They don't really have a destination other than saying they want 'a good life.' They know the river is going to come to an end someday, and they hope it will be a beautiful smooth lake. But between the rapids at the top of the river and the smooth lake at the bottom, they surrender themselves to the river and their only navigation is to avoid the rocks and the whirlpools.

"As they come to the end of the ride, they look around and see a very uninspiring place. Instead of a beautiful tree-line lake with views of the mountains, somewhat like Lake Tahoe, they find that the river ended in a muddy pond on a flat, featureless plot of land, maybe like east Texas. They look around and they ask 'How did I get here?'" Some laughter.

"River Rafters are easily identified, like a bird, by the sound of their, 'I should have beens.' I should have been a teacher. I should have been a pilot. I should have been an astronaut. I should have been a cowboy.

"The second group, which is smaller, I call the Brando's, after

Marlon Brando from his performance in that wonderful movie, *On The Waterfront*, where he tells his brother, 'I could have been a contender.' These people have a goals, have dreams, know where they want to go, but are not willing to make the sacrifices, so they never pursued them.

"You can tell the Brando's by the sound of their excuses. My favorite is, 'If my wife didn't get pregnant.' I don't think I need to elaborate on this one. But there are many other excuses to go around. If my husband made more money, if my mother didn't force me to get married, if I had been able to take music lessons, if society didn't discriminate against whoever you are, and so on. The most honest excuse I ever heard was from a young man who wanted to be a surgeon. He blamed 'Not being smart enough.'

"Whatever the excuse, and there is always an excuse, they never pursued their dreams, but they always hoped they would be realized.

"Sadly, these are the unhappiest people of all. They harbor a great deal of resentment – towards themselves, their families, their employers – because that which would make them happiest is just out of reach. Failed marriages and participation in therapy sessions are highest among this group.

"And then there are the people who know where they want to go, and set out to get there at all costs. I call them the Captain Kirk's. For all you younger people in the audience, Captain Kirk was the commander of the Enterprise on the very first Star Trek TV series.

"If it means working during the day and going to school at night, they do it. If it means having two or three jobs, they do it. If it means driving an old car and wearing old clothing they do.

"Someone I admire very much is a 59 year old jazz pianist who, though very talented, never achieved significant recognition nor financial success. She said very early in life, right after she graduated college, that she wanted to play the piano everyday of her life. This meant that, at 59, she still has to have a roommate to help pay the rent, that she wears clothes given to her by her friends, who fortunately have expensive tastes, and that she drives a 13-year old Honda.

"It doesn't bother her that her fellow ivy league graduates are all making six figure salaries, or that the people whose homes she entertains in spend more on flowers than she makes in a single year. She is quite happy.

"I met her ten years ago in a coffee shop and have kept in touch with her since. Over this period, she's had three serious relationships with men who would be considered successful by any standard, but the relationships all ended when the men couldn't deal with her happiness. One way or another each said, 'If I'm going to be unhappy, so should you.'

"In my book, which is available from Meriwether's right after this presentation," the audience laughed. I suggest an exercise. It is creating a Roadmap of Your Life, and hence the title of the book.

"Literally, on a piece of paper, plot out the path your life has taken.

"It can start anywhere, but I always suggest beginning from the day you left high school, so write down that date at the bottom of the page, and then write the goals you set for yourself when you left school at the top of the page. The exercise is to follow the path of your life and see if it takes you to your goal.

"Draw a straight line from high school to your goal and let's see how often you strayed from the path.

"Is the college you went to on the path or did it take you off the path? If it took you off the path, draw a line deviating from the path. Did that first job after school keep you moving towards your destination or did it put you on a different path altogether? Draw a line. If it was just a detour and you got back in the right direction, draw a line getting back to your main path.

"Did the second job keep you moving in the right direction? Did it put you on another course all together? Did it put you back where you wanted to be? Did you establish a new goal for yourself?

"New jobs, new cities, new investments… write down every major event in your life and decide if it moved you along in the right direction, became a detour, or maybe became a parallel road, always keeping you at arm's length from where you want to be.

"I think what you'll find is that every significant action you took had implications you didn't foresee, and you had to react to them, which may have taken you on a journey away from the one you wanted to be on.

"I had a student who was a wonderful writer. Her goal was to write for the New York Times and win a Pulitzer Prize for international reporting. As you can imagine, before you get to work at the New York Times you have to write for some smaller newspapers and prove yourself. When she graduated seven years ago, that's exactly what she did. She recently came back to visit me. About four years ago, she bought a condominium because it would be a good investment, and a new car about a year after that. The combination of the mortgage and the car loan were more than she could afford on a small newspaper reporter's salary, so she took a job at an investment company writing annual reports for public corporations. She says someday she hopes to go back to working in newspapers, but I wonder if a few years from now she'll be interested in taking a 75% cut in her salary, or if she'll be ready for a larger condo or another new car.

"One perceptive student once asked me, can the destination change? Of course it can; in fact, it would be very surprising if it didn't. The more we're exposed to the world, the more we learn about ourselves. Of course the destination changes, and that's okay. The question always is, are you headed on the path to your destination or are you just letting the river take you wherever it goes?

"Let me conclude by repeating the question most people ask me, 'How did I end up here?'

"And let me answer that by quoting Buckaroo Bonzai, a character from one of the least appreciated movies of the 1980s, 'No matter where you go... that's where you are.'

"Thank you." And with that, she slipped off the stool and returned the microphone to the podium.

Vigorous applause greeted the conclusion of her lecture and lots of people pushed to the front of the auditorium to talk with her about their own situations.

Chris stayed in his seat, held captive by her words. She had pegged him correctly. He strayed far from the path he once set out on and now was so far from his destination he couldn't be happy. He definitely was a Brando, an actor he greatly admired. He once knew where he wanted to go, but he never really committed himself to get there. And, he was embarrassed to admit, he blamed everyone but himself for the reason he didn't reach his destination.

He barely slept that night thinking about the lecture, about his wife, about all the extra-marital affairs, about Cathy and that critical period in their relationship, about his life. It was all very disturbing. How do you evaluate your own life?

He had bought Dr. Troy's book right after the lecture and he committed himself to immediately reading it, drawing the roadmap of his life, and getting his life back on track.

Chapter 38

"Resistance is futile! Compliance is mandatory! You must submit!"

The computer-generated voices of Fred's favorite science fiction movie shook the house, like the Rap music kids blast from their car stereo's. Every corner of the house vibrated with explosions as beings from other planets dismembered and destroyed whole civilizations with laser swords and photon spears. Using all the power of their home entertainment center, Fred stood with the defenders of Earth and suffered every blow and explosion common to man-vs.-alien combat.

Fearing the noise would disturb the girls, she often asked him to lower the volume, but her requests were a speck of cosmic dust colliding with Fred's colossal titanium spacecraft. Her only hope was that since their rooms were on the opposite side of the house, they didn't hear it too much. Fortunately, for the next few days, they were staying at a friend's house and wouldn't be subject to the complete disintegration of Earth if Fred couldn't save the planet.

"Come watch this, Hon," he shouted above the din. "This guy has a handgun that can fire 100-megawatt's of electricity."

"No, I have to get to the airport." Going now meant she would be sitting around the airport for four hours, but it was one of the few acceptable excuses she had that saved her from having to sit with him and watch the Guts 'n Gore Channel. On far too many occasions, just to keep the peace, she had sat with him in front of the 60-inch plasma television screen and watched creatures from one world inflict incredible mayhem and cruelty on creatures from another, just because they could.

"I'll drive you," he offered in the loudest voice he could, barely twisting his head from the screen. As usual, it was an empty offer and they both knew it.

"Thank you, but I have a cab waiting." Over the past few months she developed a technique for a "pretend kiss." She would get close enough to his ear to make a puckering sound then quickly brush his cheek with her ear. As she leaned forward to pretend to kiss him goodbye, she had the misfortune of the sudden demise of a creature from the fourth planet in the third galaxy, so he bent his head backwards and with his right hand pulled her head towards his, kissing her, forcing his tongue into her mouth.

Wanting to spit in his face, but smiling as if she enjoyed his stale beer and tobacco tasting saliva in her peppermint tasting mouth, she shouted, "Esmerelda is taking the girls to mall and then to a friend's house, so they won't be home for a couple of days."

Yet another creature with reptilian-like skin and a glowing weapon appeared, so he returned to the violence in front of him. Gathering her bags, she stepped out of the house, actually a few minutes earlier then she needed to be, but she was out of the house and away from him.

She really loved the house and the neighborhood they lived in. Olympic Estates was one of the wealthiest suburbs of the city, and many senior executives from THCC lived here.

Reflecting the name, the original homes in Olympic Estates were designed as if they were taken from the Acropolis in Greece. White marble homes with lots of columns and white marble statues of Zeus, Hermes, Athena and the other Gods on the lawns, rooftops, and entryways. While the homes weren't authentic reproductions they were so convincing that schoolchildren who were studying the ancient world were often taken on field trips here to see Greek architecture.

But since the owners of these homes weren't ancient Greeks living along the sun-drenched Mediterranean coast, but rather Americans living in the Mid-Western Snowbelt, the houses gradually changed over the years. One owner painted his house blue and another gray, and another added a wing that could vaguely be called Trashy Colonialism. One owner, who wanted her children to have a safe place to play, filled in the spaces between the columns, and another, who apparently did not believe in consistency of style, added a white picket fence.

Of the original homes, few survived modernization. Only one house, the symbol of Olympic Estates, the one owned by the original developer, never changed. It sat on top of a small man-made hill, bigger and higher than all others. It actually was a close, but smaller, replica of the Parthenon, and there were twenty-six columns and twenty-six statues surrounding the home. Even though it changed hands several times, each owner accepted the responsibility and maintained this home as it was built, despite the difficulty in finding capable craftsman when needed. Built in a circle, all roads lead to the center of Olympic Estates where this symbol of democracy and American entrepreneurship rose up above all else.

Cathy's home, which was built about ten year before she bought it and thirty years after Olympic Estates was founded, was an interesting combination of Modern and Art Nouveau styles; lots of glass and metal, yet surprising soft with a curving facade. Fascinated by it from the moment they drove up, she loved that it was filled with discovery and complexity. You couldn't just look at the front of the house and be satisfied that you had seen it all. You had to walk completely around it, and even then you wouldn't have the sense of having seen it all. With each step there were new views and new experiences. The sides weren't perfectly identical to each other and nothing was perfectly proportional.

The architect who designed it had an incredible understanding for the use of glass and its reflective properties, so the house never looked exactly the same twice. Depending on the height of the sun in the sky, the density and type of clouds, the angle and warmth of the light, the house could look anywhere from a bright yellow to a dark gray. After she first moved into the house, there were many occasions when she was distracted by her thoughts, that she would drive right past it, not realizing that the dark blue house she was returning to was the same warm green one she left only twelve hours earlier.

An incredibly unique feature of the design, even for glass houses, was that no two adjacent panels of glass were perfectly aligned. It actually made the house rather difficult to sell since prospective buyers assumed that the mosaic-like surface represented poor construction and were adverse to buying something in that condition. Fortunately for Cathy, the low level of interest meant that the price was relatively low, too, and therefore, more affordable. Fred wanted to pass on it and look for a house in a less expensive community, but Cathy insisted that they buy it so she could send the girls to the local schools.

Researching the architect, she read that he sought to reflect the parallax of time and space in his designs, and the use of reflective glass with varying orientations on the skin of the house, let you see where you are, where you've been, and where you're going - your past, your present, and your future - all at the same time.

"That is bullshit," Fred declared, offering his well-articulated opinion of the architecture. But, since Cathy's contribution to the purchase price was far, far greater, and since in those days he was concerned about pleasing her, he agreed.

Regardless of the style, all homes in Olympic Estates were large, with each sitting on a three-quarter acre lot, with wide separations between houses, as if each was a distinct object of art. When Olympic Estates was first built, it was less like a real estate development and more like a sculpture garden. The original homes were now some of the smallest, and the newer homes were built with less interest in outside appearances, and much more concern about maximizing the amount of square footage inside the house. At 4,500 square feet, Cathy's house clearly wasn't one of the largest in the community.

One of the features that she didn't think about when they bought it, but had came to appreciate, was that the unusual shape of the house kept Esmerelda and the girls at a good distance from her and Fred. Intended to give the parents some privacy, she hoped it prevented them from ever seeing or hearing the violence.

Speeding passed her house, the Macedonian taxi driver slammed on his brakes and threw the car into reverse when he saw her standing on the curb in his rearview mirror. Smiling, he didn't get out to help her with her bags, nor opened the door for her.

The route to the airport from Cathy's house was about 25 miles, but because there were no major highways, the trip took an unusually long time. While the wealthy people of this community prided themselves that they had the political influence to keep out urban development, such as high speed roadways ("they bring crime and a different element of people"), they didn't realize that they made it incredibly difficult for themselves to access downtown Minneapolis, where most of their wealth came from, as well as connections to interstate highways, airports, and railroads. It was a slow and circuitous route to the airport through city streets, which bothered her when they first moved into the community and she was worried about making a plane. But now, it gave her an excellent excuse for leaving the house well in advance of her flight, so she was actually rather delighted about it.

Not surprisingly, the road that connected Olympic Estates with the rest of the Minneapolis metropolitan area was called Olympic Boulevard, and in the years just after the creation of a community for the very wealthy, developers took the opportunity to build communities for the semi-wealthy and wealthy-wannabes. Hoping to share in the luster, the developers of the adjacent communities continued the Grecian theme, so one cluster of homes was called the Aegean Islands and another the Ionian Islands. There was an Ithaca and a Delphi, as well as a Rhodes and Mykonos. The streets, of course, also maintained the ancient civilization feel, Athena and Apollo Avenues ran East to West, while Hermes and Hercules Highways ran North to South, and Corinthian and Cyclops Circles didn't really go anywhere.

The first of these communities modernized the Olympic Estates design, which meant they were white, ranch-style homes adorned with a few columns on either side of the entry. But as the years passed, the communities grew and merged with each other, and as the interest in maintaining the artificial appearance of ancient Greece waned, sooner or later, anything but Grecian became the acceptable style.

The homes along North Olympic Boulevard actually reminded Cathy of the houses in Golden, Colorado, the Denver suburb in which she had lived. Large-sized homes on clean streets, with expensive cars in the driveways, and bicycles and toys scattered over manicured lawns. In Golden, she and her husband had bought a Federal style house that was basically a ranch style with a semi-circle of columns surrounding the entry, and the only difference that seemed to exist with the homes on either side of Olympic Boulevard was that her house was painted blue with white columns, while these were white with white columns.

Olympic Boulevard was quite wide and the retailers closest to Olympic Estates still appealed to the very wealthy, as well as to those that wanted to look as if they were very wealthy. Department stores, such as Saks Fifth Avenue and Neiman Marcus, still defined the class of retailers that populated the street, and designer shops such as Salvatore Ferrigamo, Bally's, Polo, and Gucci, attracted customers with money and/or taste. Many of the community's housewives spent their days strolling up one side of North Olympic Boulevard and down the other.

Hermes Highway was the unofficial dividing line between the wealthy and those that served the wealthy, and while there were no signs to that effect, it was quite visible the instant the street was crossed. South of Hermes (SOHE) was where the servants and craftsmen lived when the folks at Olympic Estates were to be catered to. Even with the creation of so many more communities, homes and streets, SOHE remained the province of hardworking, blue-collar laborers. Like the neighborhood in

Brooklyn in which she grew up, the homes here were row houses and duplexes, with no pretense of any design sense, least of all Grecian. These were very functional units offering individuals the minimum amount of square footage to survive comfortably.

She remembered when her father declared that they could finally afford to buy a house, how rich they felt finally owning a home. It seemed so big then, an incredible amount of space as compared to the apartment her family lived in. And, best of all, if she jumped off the bed, there were no neighbors downstairs to disturb. How many hours she thought that that they now had it all and there was no more to want in life.

As they approached the airport, the taxi crawled along South Olympic Boulevard, a predominately Afro-American neighborhood of drab and indifferent apartment buildings and stores. While not a poor neighborhood, it wasn't as spotless as the ones further north, but there was a lot more activity on the streets. The lawns may not be as impeccable, nor the streets spotlessly clean as North Olympic, but the neighborhood was alive, like Brooklyn when she was growing up. People weren't cloistered in their private castles, they were outside talking about politics, jumping rope, roller skating, reading newspapers, and arguing about who was the best Minnesota Twins pitcher. Grocers put their fruits and vegetables on display in front of their stores, hoping old ladies wouldn't squeeze them and kids wouldn't steal them. Street vendors sold belts, ties, umbrellas, and CD's from cartons piled on the sidewalk. This was an exciting community, not just anonymous taxpayers. She missed the electric energy that was here and it made her more anxious to get to New York and see the people that charged her spirits back then.

Her cab got stuck behind a bus that was loading and unloading passengers, so they had to sit for a few minutes before they could finally get on the short stretch of highway that would take them into the airport. Looking across the street, she glanced at a young couple, both in their early twenties, waiting for a bus heading to downtown Minneapolis. They reminded her of Chris and herself at that age. They looked so much in love and had such hope for the future.

As they laughed and chatted, their bodies never lost touch with each other. The fingers of one were always intertwined with the fingers of the other, and with his right hand he would, occasionally, stroke her fine back hair. With her hand, she would touch his arm or his leg as she told her story with great animation. Her hands waved in the air and he hung on every word, laughing, smiling, so glad just to be with her. They were two beautiful people, very much in love. They belonged to each other.

But Cathy wondered if they could ever have a happy life together.

She was dressed in a black suit, obviously inexpensive, but still a suit, and carried a Louis Vuitton (probably a knock-off) purse. She wore a white silk blouse with colorful silk scarf tied around her neck and a matching silk handkerchief in the suit jacket's pocket. The perfect corporate uniform, with just the right touch of personalization to accent her beauty. Her shoes were clearly several years old, but they were polished and perfectly matched to her outfit, and the briefcase she carried was more appropriate for a high school student than a businesswoman, but at least it was a briefcase, which meant that she was in some type of junior executive position.

By contrast, her boyfriend wore the familiar uniform of the clerks in the Delphi Supermarket chain. His gold-colored jacket was neatly pressed, but stained, and he wore it over a clean white t-shirt, denim jeans, and well-worn basketball shoes. He could have been wearing that outfit ten years ago, and if he stayed at the store, he probably would be wearing it ten years from now.

In the seconds that she had to study them, Cathy constructed their story. They were high school sweethearts, she went to college and was now working at a bank or insurance company, on track to be a VP someday. He may have completed high school, but never went to college, probably hanging out a lot on street corners with his friends. He's probably had a string of odd jobs, such as delivering groceries, but once his girlfriend graduated from college and started on a career path, he realized that if he ever wanted to marry her, he'd have to get a real job. With no real skills, what else could he do, so he took a minimum wage job at the supermarket. While he talks about becoming a store manager someday, he sees that everyone who is promoted has a college degree and a lot more business sense than he does.

The Number 10 bus that travels to Minneapolis's financial district pulled into the stop and Cathy could no longer see the young couple. In her mind, she imagined them embracing and kissing good-bye. A few seconds later, she boarded the bus to head to a different, more attractive, more exciting world. As the bus finally pulled away with an explosion of black smoke, he was left standing alone, watching the woman he loved get farther and farther away with each passing second. After a moment or two, his head dropped a bit, the smile vanished from his face, and he shuffled off to the store to stack shelves and bag groceries.

Her cab was also enveloped by a cloud of black smoke as the bus in front of it finally pulled away from the curb and they were allowed to get on the highway to speed the last few miles to the airport. Over the past 20 years she'd been to this airport a couple of hundred times, and each time she entered her eyes turned to the Olympic Airways billboard with its invitation to visit that Athens. No matter how many years passed, no matter how many times she looked at that billboard, and no matter what her marital status was, every time she saw that billboard she remembered that she and Chris were going to go to there on their honeymoon. Chris so desperately wanted to see the birthplace of comedy and tragedy that he wouldn't consider any other destination.

And because she never went with Chris, she'd never been to Athens, even though her second husband wanted to go there on their honeymoon. She swore only to go with someone she truly loved, and she knew even then that it really wasn't him.

"Fort-two dollar," the Macedonian cab driver announced as the taxi pulled up to the departure level of the United Airlines terminal.

Cathy opened her Bottega Venetta handbag and instantly knew something was wrong. Her reading glasses had fallen out of the case, her lipstick was rolling around the bottom of the bag instead of being in the small side compartment, and, her wallet was upside down.

Fred. It had to be Fred. It couldn't have been the girls. They know better.

"Fort-two dollar," the driver with limited English speaking abilities repeated.

With the dread of knowing the unpleasant experience that was about to occur, she opened her wallet, and true to her worst fears, it was empty. In preparation for her trip, last night she had put $200 in her wallet, and now there was not a single penny. *When do I stop being a victim*, she thought. *Twenty-five miles from home, and he can still hurt me. No matter where I go, no matter what I do, I can't get out of his grasp. He'll destroy me before I can get away from him.*

Annoyed, at her inaction, the cab driver announced yet again, in a somewhat louder voice, as if she didn't English, "Fort-two dollar."

Noticing the small display of credit cards logos on the window, she passed her corporate American Express card to the driver.

"Cash better than credit cards," he grumbled.

"No cash," she sighed.

Begrudgingly he took it, ran it through a portable credit card imprinter, and passed it back to her for her signature.

Embarrassed, she added a $15 tip to the fare and passed it back to him after she signed it. Exiting the cab, she shook her head and wondered, *will I ever be free of him?*

Chapter 39

"What do you think of the name Dick?" Samantha was in somewhat of a giddy mood, highly unlike her, but around Cathy she could lay down her defenses and be more casual. There were times when it was clear who was the boss and who was the underling, and there were times when they were two friends just chatting. Most conversations included both relationships and it was often a burden on Cathy to figure out which Samantha she was talking to at any given moment.

"Actually," Cathy laughed, "I've always wondered how Dick came to be the nickname for Richard. You would think anyone named Richard would want to be Rich or Rick, not Dick."

"If I was a man, and I was called Dick, I would change my name. I can't imagine anyone walking around and willingly being called the nickname for a man's genitals. You might as well just call someone Penis instead of Dick." Considering what an ogre she was supposed to be, she and Cathy laughed a lot at the absurdities they found around them. What frightened her was that she and Fred laughed a lot, too, when their relationship first started. "Can you imagine if someone named Richard was a real jerk, 'You're a dick, Dick.'"

Their instant bond, their ability to sit with each other for an hour or two at time, made it clear to everyone in the department, and in Senior Management, that they had become a team and the veil that sheltered Samantha now was extended to Cathy. No memo had been sent, no e-mail written, no voice-mail recorded, but as if it had been ordered, it was now known by all that Cathy was to be "protected, respected, and feared."

There are many ways to measure ascendancy in a corporation. One is the out-pouring of the weasels, like Bob. Literally, out of nowhere, they made their presence known to her, with sudden drop-ins to her office, with e-mails soliciting her opinion, with invitations to their homes, to dinners, and most importantly, to corporate events held exclusively for Senior Management.

Strategy meetings suddenly couldn't be conducted without her presence, and she never had to ask twice about getting a painting hung or a piece of furniture moved. Her assigned parking space was taken away, replaced by the executive valet service, and the executive kitchen, with its tuxedo-clad waitstaff was available to her 24 hours a day.

There was an unpleasant reaction to her sudden ascendancy in the corridors of the company. People envious of her rise began to speak unkindly of her, and in the employee's cafeteria, expressions could be heard, such as, "Everyone sells out sooner or later, it's just a matter of price," and, "I knew that her Miss Perfect attitude was just an act to get herself promoted."

While "friends in the company" shared the rumblings they heard with her, she was enjoying the benefits of her promotion too much to be disturbed by whispers and hushed tones. It didn't take too long before she couldn't hear any of them at all.

"Why are you asking about the name Dick?" Cathy had to ask between laughs, sipping the wine that the waiter just poured.

"Oh, my significant other insists on being called Dick and we had a bit of a row about it last night after I introduced him to some people at a party as Rich." The two had a final laugh on the subject and then turned to business. "How is the hunt for the perfect secretary going?

Cathy produced a manila folder with five resumes. "These are all people currently with the company who applied for the position. As I'm sure you know, company policy is to encourage advancement by current company employees first, and all job openings are posted internally for two weeks prior to being offered to the public." It occurred to Cathy that whatever the company policy was, it probably didn't apply to Samantha.

"I understand that was one of the policy changes you fought for over the years. It's a good policy," Samantha acknowledged.

Cathy was delighted to have Samantha's approval, explaining, "As you also know, employees are only allowed to apply for positions after they've spoken with their supervisors, so no one is sneaking around behind anyone's backs." Unspoken was that hiring from within also meant that the candidates knew Samantha's reputation and wouldn't be shocked by anything she did. Secretaries hired from outside the company usually lasted a shorter time.

"I like the policy of hiring from within," Samantha added. "It's been a major boost to my career. I probably have you to thank for where I am today."

"It also has given me the opportunity to have an honest discussion with the supervisors regarding the candidates' capabilities. You'll be happy to know that 26 people applied for the position, but these are the only ones I feel were worth interviewing. The others didn't have strong enough skills." What Cathy didn't say was that virtually every supervisor she spoke with admitted to warning the employee not to consider a job in the Business Affairs Department and to wait until another opportunity came along, but these 26 still wanted to proceed since there would be a significant salary increase.

Samantha paged through the folder of applicants. "I like all five. Excellent selection. Please set up interviews for them."

Again, Cathy was delighted that she had pleased Samantha with her first assignment.

Samantha spent the rest of lunch going over a number of issues. It wasn't lost on Cathy that this was extremely confidential information and Samantha seemed to share it without hesitation, though, since they were in the Executive Dining Room, she did speak in hushed tones and was difficult to hear at times.

The $20 billion bid for the NASA project was going well, but NASA's management team was not pleased with THCC's choice of personnel assigned to the program, which meant that some senior level technical people would have to be replaced. She was going to suggest to Senior Management that these people be transferred to New York City Transit System project.

"Sounds like a good idea," Cathy naively offered, clearly not understanding the dynamics.

"Except we don't have an ice cube's chance in Hell of getting that business."

Suddenly, she understood that Samantha was going to be ignominiously ending the careers of several long-term, loyal employees without the slightest concern for their families, futures or seniority. Cathy's initial HR instincts were to object to the move and suggest that an alternate solution must be available, but then she thought about how good it would be for the company to get the NASA business, particularly in this economy, and how many jobs would be saved and new hires brought on, so she withdrew her silent dissent. Besides, she reasoned, there was no way she was going to change Samantha's mind with a pep talk about employee loyalty.

"We're buying a small company that has a unique process for making semiconductors that can be used in notebook computers and cell phones."

While Samantha went on to describe the benefits of the acquisition to the company, Cathy realized that she had just been given "inside information." If she bought stock in that small company, with whatever little money she had squirreled away from Fred, she could realize a profit of 50% or more in just a matter of weeks, and considering the debacle of her financial situation, that money would be very much appreciated.

It also occurred to her that since the acquisition had absolutely nothing to do with the functioning of the Business Affairs Department, Samantha's sole purpose in telling her about the acquisition was to give her the opportunity to invest. But in her own careful way, Samantha maintained plausible deniability, since she claimed that the acquisition would open lots of new avenues for THCC in the pursuit of new business.

"Last, I have to ask you to prepare the separation packages for the current managers of Minneapolis, Washington, Miami and London offices."

Cathy didn't know the managers of the other offices, but she did know the manager of the Minneapolis office.

She had struggled to convince Paul Rhodes to join THCC in Minneapolis, and he certainly was popular with his staff. This time she had to offer some resistance, "I don't really know any of these people except Paul. He's been quite successful in turning that group around, and it may be worth retaining him."

"Of the group, he is clearly the best. I thought long and hard about it, but in the end, I don't believe he and I would work well together. Rather than struggle through months of infighting, which will only end in the same conclusion, it's better to get it done now, so it looks like a departmental layoff, and not later when it will be seen as incompetence. Everyone saves a bit of dignity this way." It was obvious she really had given some thought to this, and it was surprising to Cathy that she was even the least bit concerned of how the layoffs would look to others inside and outside the company.

"You really don't think you two can work together?"

"I'm certain I can work with him, but I don't believe he can work for me. It's better this way."

The discussion was over, and Samantha moved on to another subject. She talked about minor operational issues - office equipment, location of desks (as opposed to people), her preferences in office supplies - all things Cathy could make note of while only half listening. She was still bothered by the Paul Rhodes decision. This wasn't a faceless engineer from another office, this was a real person - a very decent person - and his career was now going to be seriously disrupted, maybe even destroyed.

Lunch abruptly ended when, as usual, Samantha announced, "I'm late for a meeting." She popped up, grabbed her purse and briefcase and was gone, saying something about "meeting later to finish the discussion."

Cathy sat for a few moments sipping her coffee, counting the number of careers that were about to be ruined. For someone who came from Human Resources, the body count was getting uncomfortably high. It was easy to say that everything was being done for the benefit of the company, but who was the company if not the sum of the employees. She also wondered, once again, if she was saving herself from the nightmare of her existence, or just trading one nightmare for another?

Eyeing a penny on the carpet, she bent down and picked it up. Playing with it in her hands for a moment or two, she looked outside at the blue sky and the heavens beyond and said, "Mama, I hope you're not watching me now." She dropped the penny into a small pocket of her purse where it joined six others she had found.

"Sixteen days left to go," she mumbled to herself as she made notes of all the layoffs and transfers she had to execute in the next 72 hours.

Chapter 40

"Do you remember we carved our initials inside a heart on a tree in Central Park?" Using pre-paid, disposable cell phones, Cathy called Chris whenever she could sneak out of the office for twenty or thirty minutes. And, while they talked about their work and whatever crisis was occupying their energies, they still hadn't exhausted the past, and more often than not, they explored their shared memories.

"Wow, yes, I remember. It was just before you went away to college. I haven't thought about that for years." Even more than she, he wanted to re-live the past; recapture the happier, simpler days. "What made you think about that?" Standing up, he stepped from behind his desk and over to the window to look out at the horizon. The past, and maybe even the future, was just out there, just out of reach, on the other side of the line that separates earth and sky.

"I was killing time between meetings, so I took a walk in Central Park and I remembered we carved our initials in a tree after we saw it in a movie. I wanted to see if I could find the tree, but I couldn't remember where it was. Funny the things you suddenly remember."

Without a moment's hesitation, he brought the past to the present,

"It was right next to the carousal. I think it was on the west side... or the north side... I get those two confused."

Shaking her head, she was so embarrassed that she couldn't remember what he so easily brought back to life.

"Remember, we both used to ride on that beautiful white Arabian stead that seemed to be leaping off the earth and right up to the stars, and every time we'd pass the tree, we'd toss flowers we picked during the day at it." He paused for a moment to swallow; she wiped her eyes with the back of her finger. "Remember how that Greek guy who ran the carousal used to scream at us, 'Don't do that. Who do you think is going to have to clean up all those flowers.' He had no romance in his soul."

Yes, she remembered now, and had to reach into her purse for a tissue to catch the memories rolling down her cheeks. "Why did we carve our initials into that particular tree?" She could hear his sniffles as he tried to hold back the flood of sorrows, too.

In a voice, so soft and so inviting that it could have come from a violin, he said, "It was actually two trees that grew from the same spot in the ground. At the base you could see that they were two trees, but as they grew, they bent and twisted and intertwined around each other so much that they could never be separated. They were so close, they looked like one tree and not two. We used to say they were in a passionate embrace, and that they were like us. When we carved the heart with our initials, it crossed over to both trees."

Ashamed that she couldn't remember something like this, she could barely say the words between the swallows, but she wanted to let him know that she didn't completely forget about that tree. "We said it was a special tree."

"Yes, we said it contained all our love, and if something ever terrible separates us, we should come back to the tree, and we'll become one again."

She couldn't hold back the free flow of tears any longer, but somehow said the words, "Maybe it wasn't you who should have come to

Minneapolis after the rape, but me who should have come back to you, and our tree." She regretted her words as soon as she said them because it was about the reality that separated them, and not the wonderful memories of their being together. For many years she blamed him for not coming to her, but until now she never blamed herself for not returning to him.

They listened to each other cry for many, many minutes. It wasn't about their memories that they cried, but about the memories they never had because they didn't come back to their special tree when something terrible separated them.

Finally, one whispered, "I love you."

"I love you, too," the other breathed.

And they put their phones away to be alone with the thoughts.

Chapter 41

"'Cluck, cluck, cluck,' says the chicken…"

Lying on his couch, Larry read aloud the script for a commercial he had just received from his agent.

"'How are you today, Mr. Chicken,' says the farmer. 'Cluck, cluck,' responds the chicken. 'I see you've finished your dinner,' the farmer says. 'Cluck, cluck, cluck, cluck.'

"That's four clucks… I wonder if they meant it to be that many clucks or did the typist just get carried away by the riveting dialog?

"'Did you know, Mr. Chicken, that your dinner is made of only the best organically grown grains that come from specially certified farms in Northern California?

"Isn't that where they grow all that marijuana? Maybe that's what they're sticking into those special grains," Larry editorialized.

"'Cluck,' the chicken responds with delight…

"How does a chicken cluck with delight?"

"'So if you eat every bite of your delicious food, one day you'll be a

Real California Chicken.'

"And get your head chopped off," Larry added. "If I were that chicken, I'd kick the farmer in the balls and get my ass out of there.

"Maybe I'm reading it wrong. I have to get inside the farmer's head. Who am I? I grew up in Wisconsin on a dairy farm. My father was a farmer, like my grandfather and great-grandfather. My grandfather emigrated to the United States from Poland and had to pass through Ellis Island. Our family name was Wjzwalouzkowski in the old country, but the ignorant immigration officer changed it to Smith.

"My grandfather walked... barefoot... in the snow… across the country till he found a piece of land to call his own. He bought the land with the money he hid in his teeth and through hard work has grown those tiny two acres into a 1,000 acre agribusiness complex. My father and I don't speak to each other anymore. He has never forgiven me for selling off the cows and buying chickens. I just hated waking up before the crack of dawn to milk those smelly beasts.

"I studied agribusiness at the University of Wisconsin, but I never graduated because I found the coursework too difficult. However, I did develop a fondness for classical literature, so in my spare time I read the works of Aristotle for relaxation."

Picking up the script he read the lines again, "'Well, Mr. Chicken, how are you today? The chicken replies, cluck, cluck, cluck, cluck.'"

Throwing the script down and his hands up, he yelled, "Who writes this drivel? Did they really pay someone to put this crap on paper? And what's a Real California Chicken? A chicken that surfs?" Frozen in place for a moment, Larry quickly grabbed the envelope the script came in and looked for a note from his agent. "My God!" he suddenly realized, "The agent didn't say which part I'm supposed to read for. I could be that plump, God-forsaken chicken.

Well, you know what they say, 'There are no small parts, just small actors.'" With that in mind he stood up, closed his eyes, touched the fingers of his right hand to his forehead, and repeated, "I am a chicken. I am a chicken."

Assuming the pose of a chicken - hands behind his back, arched forward, bobbing head, and high steps - he pranced around the living room, pecking at the arms of the torn furniture, and practiced his clucking. Sometimes he clucked once, sometimes two, three or four times. He clucked with delight, with melancholy, with passion, and with horror. He stepped on the couch, knocking off the Indian blanket that covered the holes. He walked on the coffee table, kicking off the pile of magazines. He practiced standing with one leg on the dinette chairs.

Flapping his wings as fast as he could, he was about to attempt a dramatic flight from the dinner table to the couch, when the phone rang. Realizing that chickens, and humans, can't fly, he morphed into the pose of a ballet dancer, and pirouetted his way to the phone. He prayed, "Please God, make this is an offer to star in the re-make of *Gone With The Wind*." As he reached for the phone, he worried to himself, *I think I'm talking to myself too much.*

Into the receiver he announced, "Hello, this is Laurence Oliphant, actor extraordinaire."

"Larry!" The voice was loud and enthusiastic, but a brief moment of silence followed. "This is a voice from the past. It's Chris... Chris O'Dess."

Staring at the phone, speechless, Larry felt like clucking because he couldn't think of what else to say. This was a voice from a lifetime ago. Dozens of split second images flashed through his mind. He could see them laughing together, drinking together, double dating, on stage, lying on the grass on the campus quadrangle, pretending to be med students as they tried to pick up girls. Dozens and dozens images from the dusty photo album of his memory were instantly found again.

"Oh my God! Chris! I can't believe it's you! It's been years! How are you? Where are you? Are you in New York? Oh my God. This is incredible" He had to put his hand over his heart to stop it from exploding from his chest. This wasn't just a voice from the past, this was the voice of the closest friend he ever had. This was the voice of someone he used to call "the other half of the egg." At one time they were so close, they used to swear they were twins separated at birth (which happened to be another line they used when trying to pick of girls).

"I'm here. I'm here in New York."

"This is incredible! I can't believe it. It's so great to hear your voice!" Tears welled in his eyes and rolled down his cheeks. He started to wipe them away, but stopped because they were tears of such joy that he wanted to feel them. "How'd you find me? Can we see you?"

"My New York office pulled some videotapes of talent to consider for a commercial. All of a sudden your face popped up on the screen. I couldn't believe it. I jumped up and screamed, 'I know this person.' I had our producer track you down through your agent."

"That's great! This is wonderful. Will we be able to see you?"

"I'm in New York for a few days to present to a client..." Larry couldn't see them, but he could hear the same tears of joy in Chris' voice.

"This is great. When can we see you? Mandy will be so happy to see you. What are you doing tonight? I can't wait. It has to be tonight." Larry couldn't stop blabbering away.

As soon as he had a chance to inject a word into the conversation, Chris said, "I can do tonight. Actually, I'm pretty close to you. I have your address from your agent. I just have to finish a few things here. I can be over in about an hour. Is that good for you? We can all go to dinner. My treat."

"I can't believe this. This is so incredible. Just get over here whenever you can. I won't tell Mandy. It'll be a surprise. God, she'll go crazy when she sees you."

For the next hour Larry raced around the apartment making it as presentable as possible. Since he was at home during the day when he wasn't performing or at casting calls, he tended to spread out. Dishes he used didn't get washed. Open soda cans remained where they last touched a flat surface. Magazines, books, scripts, and newspapers grew into piles on the floor, as did worn clothing, waste paper, and pillows from the couch.

When Mandy came home at night she usually straightened up the disarray her husband had created, but some days she was just too tired and couldn't be bothered. The past week was filled with those kinds of days, so the apartment was a perfect reflection of the shabby building and trash-strewn neighborhood they lived in.

After making the one bedroom apartment as neat as he could, Larry charged into the back of the closet in the hallway to try to retrieve long-forgotten memorabilia. So, as soon as he finished putting things away, he was pulling other things out and leaving piles on the floor again.

Almost to the hour, there was a knock on the door, and Larry shouted from the bedroom, "Come in. It's unlocked." Chris opened the door slowly, ready to embrace his dearest friend from years ago, but the room was empty. It was like getting off the plane after a round-the-world flight and having no one there to welcome you home: a bit surprising and very disappointing.

Suddenly, from the bedroom, there was a shout, "Catch!" and a sword flew at him threw the air. Instinctively, just as he was taught decades earlier, Chris caught the handle of the sword. Did he just walk into some kind of trap? Did Larry bear some grudge against him all these years and now wanted to settle the score?

It took him a moment, but he recognized it. "Oh my God! This is my sword!" Because their college didn't have large budgets for performances, the actors often had to buy their own props and make their own costumes. There on the handle was his name. This was the sword he used to defend the honor of a thousand maligned maidens and to save the throne of England from the barbaric Saxon invaders (and, then later again, from the barbaric Norman invaders). Water welled in his eyes.

From someplace outside of Chris' view, Larry sprang through the air, somersaulting over the couch, whipping the sword first to the left and then to the right. Pointing his sword at Chris, he called out, "Romeo, you swine! The hate I bear thee can afford no better term than this - thou art a villain! Boy, turn and draw."

It was Romeo and Juliet. Twenty-something years ago Chris played Romeo to Larry's Tybalt. Struggling to remember the lines he spoke, he opened his mouth and a few words burst forth. "Alive... in triumph... And Mercutio slain! Away to heaven... something, something... fire-eyed fury be my conduct now... something... for Mercutio's soul is but a little way above our heads... and something like... Either thou or I, or both, must go with him"

The metal of their slightly rusted swords clashed and sparks flew. Parry, thrust, parry thrust. They moved into each other and growled. Pushing himself away, Larry/Tybalt challenged, "Thou wretched boy that didst consort him here. Shalt with him hence."

Circling the couch and waving their swords wildly, Chris/Romeo cried out, "This shall determine that." Metal hit metal again, and again. They may have forgotten the words they spoke, but neither forgot their well practiced sword moves. A picture frame was knocked over, magazines fell to the floor, the pillows from the couch went flying through the air, but that didn't stop the aging swordsmen from re-creating (or trying to) the fight that received a standing ovation from their small coterie of friends and family in the audience of the college's basement theatre.

Forgetting his next line, Larry improvised, "Thou are the dog shit under thy feet, Romeo."

Parry, thrust, parry, thrust, his muscles elegantly responding to the grasp of the sword as if a day had not passed since his last fencing class. "Thou art the slime that rises to the surface of thy own cesspool."

As a swordsman, Larry was never very good, and he began to run from the fight with exaggerated prancing steps, weaving figure-eights around the furniture. "Romeo, you are none better then the scum that floats in the Jacuzzi of a singles' health club!"

"Tybalt, you are herpes in a senior citizens' home." With that slur, Chris poked his sword into Larry, who acted out a prolonged death (his death scenes were quite famous in the school's theatre department), eventually falling over the back of the couch, knocking a picture frame off the table.

Chris, with arms raised, sword held high, took a victory lap around the room, and when Larry finally recovered from his wounds and popped up from the couch, the two embraced, laughing to the point where they both almost fell over.

"I don't think Shakespeare ever referenced herpes in a senior citizens' home." Releasing the embrace, Chris sniffled and wiped the water in his eyes away.

"He didn't mention Jacuzzis and health clubs, either."

The two stepped back and studied each other. Chris poked Larry's stomach, indicating it had grown. Larry rubbed Chris' hair between his fingers, indicating it had grayed. During college, Larry was obsessive about his weight and shape, and Chris had always been obsessive about his hair.

"God, Mandy will be so happy to see you. She could use a good smile."

During college, Mandy, Larry and Chris were an inseparable threesome. They met in their freshman year while working backstage on a college play, formed an instant bond, and practically lived together for most of their academic years. Even though they had their own rooms in the dorm, it wouldn't surprise anyone to find all three sleeping in one bed together. They ate at least one meal a day together and it was understood by all that to invite one to a party was to invite all three; or, to tell one a secret was to tell all three. It was a running joke that they were all re-incarnated, and at different times in the past they were each the lover of the other.

This threesome was good for Chris. With Cathy some 3,000 miles away, he was often lonely, but having Mandy and Larry meant he had friends to share his time, his woes, his thoughts and his fun with. And, even though he wasn't completely faithful to Cathy, she was always in his thoughts and his decisions were always made with her in mind.

Sadly, sometime in their senior year, with the real world looming large in front of them, something changed. Suddenly, they couldn't be a threesome any longer. As it almost inevitably had to happen, Mandy's affections shifted from Larry to Chris and she offered herself to him, physically and spiritually.

He couldn't accept. He wanted her as a best friend for life, but not a single day as a lover.

Rejection, humiliation, insult, injury, betrayal. For the three thespians, their comedy became a tragedy, and they could no longer be together... not in the dorm room, not in the classroom. Chris left the Theatre Department and switched his major to Advertising & Marketing. Almost a decade passed before they would be in contact with each other again, and that was only because of an accidental meeting. Long ago, a few electronic birthday cards were exchanged, but that was long ago. Nothing other than that, till today.

"What do you mean that Mandy could use a good smile?" Chris always worried about her. It's a burden carrying someone's love when you rally don't want to.

"You know, things have been a bit tough for us. Money-wise, and things." Taking a tour of the room with his hands, his voice dropped to barely above a whisper. "You see how we live. She's been real good about supporting my acting career. Never made a stink about me not bringing in enough money and things. She's a real jewel. I owe her a lot. She stuck by me when most other women wouldn't have."

Sitting in silence for a few moments, both reflected upon the reality that hung over them like a storm cloud. Larry was Mandy's second choice and even though decades had passed, she never felt the great passion for him that she had for Chris. When he rejected her, she clung to Larry for survival, desperately seeking the arms of her "first love," even if it wasn't her "great love." And, Larry, who had been melancholy and lonely as his two closest friends drifted away from him, was overjoyed to have her back in his life. In a simple ceremony at City Hall, with no friends or family in attendance, they got married the day after graduation.

Sadly, a great passion never blossomed, but they stayed together anyway. He chose a profession that offered rare moments of satisfaction amid years of dejection, and he desperately needed her encouragement. She feared, more than anything else, being alone, and as the years went by, that fear only intensified.

Always the actor, Larry knew when a pause in the conversation was too long, so he popped up and practically bellowed, "How rude of me. I haven't offered you a drink yet. They're going to kick me out of Charm School if I forget my manners one more time. We have some cheap Mexican beer that I get at the Mercado or Diet Coke."

But before he could leave the room to go to the kitchen, the door opened. It was Mandy returning home from work. Chris stood up and stepped in front of her as she pulled the key from the lock. She couldn't say a word. Her head bobbed back and forth between her husband and the great love of her life. Her keys dropped from her hands, but she didn't notice. She only stared. Chris smiled and started to say, "Hello, Mandy," but before he could utter the first syllable, she ran into the bedroom crying.

Not certain what her feelings were, Larry prayed that she was happy to see Chris (he knew he was), and not resentful of the surprise. He feared that bringing long gone memories into the living room would bring sorrow with them, but he so wanted Mandy to have something to smile about that he thought it was worth the chance.

"I've always had that effect on women," Chris joked, "except for the running into the bedroom part."

The two men stood staring at the door, knowing she was going to come out eventually, but it seemed to be taking an awfully long time. Larry mumbled, "Maybe I should go in there and see if she's okay," but he was thinking, I hope she's not angry at me for surprising her. They chuckled a little, shrugged their shoulders, and turned their heads back and forth a bit. Finally, the sound of the doorknob turning broke the silence.

Once she re-emerged, she flung her arms around Chris as if he were the life raft from the Titanic. Her tears couldn't hold back and she wouldn't have wanted them to. He hugged her back, and she remembered his touch and how much like a woman it made her feel. Burying her face deep into his shoulder, she couldn't pull away from him for what seemed like hours. Chris, letting her tears flow onto his shirt, pressed his head against her hair.

Because of the awkwardness of standing there, holding tightly onto another man's wife - especially of this man and of this wife - Chris mumbled a few phrases about how great it was to see them and who could believe all the years have gone by, but she never heard a word. She just held him and cried into his shoulder and re-lived the wonderful years. The years when everyone looked forward to a wonderful future.

In that embrace, all her wishes, dreams, fantasies, should-haves, could-haves, swirled like a tornado, and finally, she could fight against it no longer. The reality in which she lived, a life without great passion, comfort, or fulfillment, bellowed behind her eyes and the pain became too great. The tears of joy became tears of sorrow and self-pity.

Sadly, the change could be heard, and understood, by both men, and feeling incredibly embarrassed, Chris wished he had never sought out his old friends. Releasing him from her grasp, Mandy, with far too many feelings to cope with, kissed Chris, passionately, on his lips and ran back into the bedroom, not to re-emerge, even though she knew she would never see the man she wanted to be with for a lifetime, ever again.

The initial ecstasy of the reunion soured, and now there was the uncomfortable obligation to spend a reasonable amount of time together and make conversation. Once again, the two college cronies stood in silence staring at the bedroom door. It's not that they expected it to open again, but neither could think of what to say or do now.

Having dealt with his, and his wife's, emotional highs and lows over the years, Larry had a surefire way of dealing with difficult situations.

"Pizza! Let's call in a pizza." Grabbing the phone, Larry dialed without looking up the number. Chris began to protest, mumbling that he had to cut this short... client meetings in the morning... calls to make back to the office... there'll be another time... But Larry wouldn't hear of it, and he placed an order for an "I am Spartacus Special" (it had absolutely everything one it) to be delivered "Pronto!" Breaking out a couple of Mexican beers, Larry transitioned - as he had so many times before - from one scene to the next. "You haven't mentioned Melanie. How is she? Any kids?"

"She's fine. Still works all the time. She's a divorce lawyer so she has this unending stream of scummy clients. Thank God they're just idiots and not murderers. No kids. We just never wanted them. I don't know if we're just selfish or we knew we wouldn't be good parents, but we never even talked about having them. How about you guys?" Trying to decide whether or not to mention Cathy, he was thinking that at this point he should just leave. What he thought would be so wonderful was turning into the worst evening of his life.

"No. We tried. Something's wrong with one of us and we never had the money to find out who. We couldn't afford any of those in vitro things." His voice softened, "Mandy really wanted a baby badly. She cried a lot during those years. We tried to adopt - even a Black or Hispanic kid - but none of the social services agencies would take our application seriously." Forcing a laugh, "I guess they have a rule about taking a kid out of poverty and putting him back into it." Then, broken by the tear he had to swallow, he confided, "Whether it was going to be a boy or a girl we were going to call it Chris... after you." He took a long swig of beer and then opened another can. "We joked about being a threesome again."

Pulling the beer can from his lips, Chris heaved a sigh, "When did it all change?"

"When did what change?" Pretending not to know, Larry knew exactly what his old friend was talking about since it was a question he asked himself every day, maybe every hour, since Chris walked out of his dorm room for the last time. The more they talked, the more they remembered, and the more they remembered the more they realized how far away they were from where they had been, and where they had wanted to go.

They both remembered how they used to talk about creating art, and not just making money, how they swore to have lifetimes filled with love, passion, excitement and purpose, and not just get by every day. They used to be surrounded by friends like a general with his army, but now they were as alone as King Lear.

Picking at the pieces of the "I am Spartacus Special" and drinking more beer, they counted fifteen shows they worked on together - six dramas, six comedies, and three musicals. Every now and then, one of them would lapse into the role of a character and struggle to remember the lines of the play or the words to the song. Somehow, they hoped, that 25 years would just vanish, and there would be no distance between yesterday and today.

As some point, Larry grabbed his guitar, and began strumming the song from Camelot that he sang to Mandy on the college's main stage, "If ever I would leave you..." When he finished there was a silence, that neither could brush away with a joke or a memory. Camelot was the last show the three ever performed together. Larry as King Arthur, Mandy as Guinevere, and Chris as Lancelot. It was soon after that performance that Chris changed his major, and became a stranger to his two closest friends in the world. He never told Cathy why he abandoned his friendship and she respected his desire not to talk about it.

They sat in silence for a few more minutes. Larry pretended to tune his guitar. Chris pretended to look through songbooks. It's hard to say how long they sat, but Chris finally broke the stillness with, "I've really got to go."

"I'll walk you to your car," Larry offered, both sad and glad this reunion was ending. There were many wonderful memories but there were awful reminders, too.

"I'm just around the corner. You don't have to come with me."

"You're not a local. It would be a good idea for me to walk with you." Local gangs had a habit of taking advantage of outsiders that wandered into the neighborhood.

Walking down the street, stepping over the garbage that never seemed to disappear, Chris, hoping he could be honest with his one-time best friend, finally said, "I was a bit surprised - delighted - but surprised, to see you both together. Years ago I went to one of those college fundraisers that they hold in L.A. and ran into Meghan and Mark. It's hard to believe that they're still together. Anyway, they said you two broke up. I wanted to call you, but you moved back to New York and I didn't know how to get in touch with you."

"We did break up," Larry confessed. "She left me. She came back to New York. If I wanted her, I had to come back here, too." A moment passed, then he asked, "Did Mark tell you why we split?"

Uncomfortable, but not wanting to lie, Chris acknowledged, "I heard it had to do something with a young co-star."

Larry stopped, turned to his friend, "We were doing Miller's *After The Fall* at one of the equity-waiver theatres on Melrose. We fell in love. Her name is Sabrina, and she's 16 years younger than me."

"What happened?"

"We met and fell in love. It was that simple. I guess it's impossible to keep that kind of thing secret from your wife very long. Mandy basically said I had to choose and that she was moving back to New York. I could stay or follow. It was up to me to decide."

"Did you decide you didn't really love Sabrina?" Chris questioned, each word mouthed hesitatingly and only slightly above a whisper.

"I loved Sabrina then, and I love her today. A day doesn't go by that I don't think about her." He paused for a moment to stifle a tear. "Saturday nights are the worst. There hasn't been a Saturday night in the last ten years that I haven't wondered who's she dating. If she's enjoying herself with someone else as much as we used to enjoy ourselves. If she's making love to him. Don't ever call me on a Saturday night because chances are I'm depressed."

"But you left her?" It was blunt and he knew it was painful, but he was driven to ask.

Glad to be able to talk about it openly to someone, he paused for a few moments, and finally admitted, "I've thought about that a lot. I still do. I was frightened." Larry was an actor without a script and clearly having trouble expressing himself.

"Of what?"

"I was frightened of everything. I was frightened she wouldn't stay with me when I got older and sicker. I was frightened I wouldn't be able to perform in bed and she would want someone younger. I was frightened I'd be too old to be a good parent to the children she wanted to have. I was frightened that I wouldn't be able to live with somebody else after all these years of living with Mandy. Mostly, I was frightened I'd lose me.

"I truly enjoy my life and I don't want that to change. And quite frankly, I owe a lot to Mandy. She let's me be me. She supports me in whatever I do. That's very rare and I didn't think I would have had that with Sabrina. Acting is all I've ever wanted to do," Larry said with a heavy sigh, trying not to sound apologetic for never changing after college. "Sometimes I take stupid parts in commercials, but most of the time I'm doing the parts I want to do - even if it's for no pay. I'm happy being who I am."

"You couldn't do that with Sabrina?"

"Sabrina was at a different point in her life. She wanted a family and big house to raise children in. She wanted a husband that would go off to work everyday and make a good salary. She wouldn't live like this." In a sweeping gesture of his hand he pointed to a neighborhood of people living on the street because their apartments were too crowded, of overflowing trash cans because nobody cared what the streets looked like, of Mercado's with half rotten vegetables and day old bread because they're cheaper than fresh.

"I couldn't ask her to live like this. I was scared." The anguish on his face revealed how difficult it must have been for him to leave Sabrina; how tortured he was by the conflict between his heart and his head. "It's funny, it's not the physical relationship that I miss the most. She had a lot of energy and a lot of drive. Maybe she would have forced me to be a success."

"You can't be a success with Mandy?"

"No. I don't know why, but with Mandy, this is who I am and where we'll always be."

They reached the Toyota Avalon that Chris had rented and turned towards each other. As an actor, Larry knew there was a need for a good closing line, so he declared, "Mandy and I can spend hours together just walking around the city. We still spend Sundays reading the New York Times, and working on the crossword puzzle together. We still like going to plays and movies together, and discussing them afterwards. We still laugh together on occasion - which most married couples can't say. I don't know what you call it, but I was afraid to lose all that. I was afraid that 'Love wouldn't conquer all.'"

Before Chris drove away, he embraced his friend and they held onto each other for a long, long time, as if each was the other's touchstone to the past. While they pledged to stay in touch, they both knew that they shared a history, but not a future. Chris got into the car and drove away.

Chapter 42

Cathy's second husband was a Forensics Accountant who worked for the U.S. Treasury Department. He, along with a detail of armed agents from the FBI, would seize the financial records of companies suspected of either evading taxes or conducting illegal activities and then he would analyze the data, looking for evidence of wrongdoing. His work was interesting, she remembered thinking, too bad he wasn't. He made love like he was entering data into a computer.

"Patterns," he used to tell Cathy was what he searched for, "and then any variation in the pattern. A company never has more than $50,000 in it's corporate checking account for five years, then one day it suddenly pops up to $100,000. Maybe they just signed a new contract, maybe they didn't. Look a little deeper, and that $100,000 pop comes the first week of every other month. A little peculiar, don't you think? Maybe nothing illegal, but certainly worthy of investigation."

She chuckled a bit as she remembered that he would only wear clothes that were solid colors - no designs or patterns. "I don't want anyone to see a pattern in me," he once proclaimed. "But isn't avoiding a pattern a pattern unto itself?" she responded, to his annoyance.

"So that's what I'm looking for," she mumbled to herself, "patterns and variations from them." After pretending to read seventy-six employee files she finally got to Tiffany's. "Now what pattern am I supposed to find?"

"There's a beauty in numbers," her ex-spouse used to say. "They're like a line on a map, taking you from one place to another. They're not just electronic dots on a computer screen; they mean something. That number was put there because something happened. Someone spent a day working and got paid for it. A company bought enough raw material so they could refine it and sell it for a profit. One company bought the services of another. If you stare at the numbers long enough, you can almost see the people working on the shop floor and in the office."

"You're very good at what you do." She remembered asking him once, "What's the biggest clue that something is wrong?"

Thinking about her question for a few seconds, he replied, "When I close my eyes and I can't imagine what people did to justify the money they received." He told her about one company he was investigating. It had 50 employees and reported that it was selling, on average, 1,500 units a month. "However, when I visited the factory, it was clear that 50 were far too many employees to produce 1500 units. The company couldn't afford 50 employees and all that machinery just to produce 1500 units. When I ran the numbers, it was clear that they needed to produce 5,000 a month in order to stay in business. Where were the other 3,500 units, and where was the money for having sold them?"

Cathy stared at the computer screen, looking at Tiffany's file again and again, and nothing stood out as unusual. Yes, she was hired at a higher than normal salary for a paralegal, but she came to the Business Affairs Department with excellent references. Everything in her application was in order: references, typing test, background check, driver's license check. The company used an executive recruiter - Richard Anthony, Inc. - to find her, which wasn't unusual for paralegals, and in the two years she was with the company, she received glowing reviews of her performance. She regularly received salary increases and bonuses, somewhat higher than the norm, but again, not unusual for the Business Affairs Department. (If Samantha wants it, Samantha gets it.) Nothing in her file seemed too extraordinary. There were no patterns.

Having now spent between 60 and 70 hours on this investigation she was ready to give up. While it was clear - between Alex, Tiffany, the high turnover rate, the panicky ex-employees - that something was not right, at this point, she couldn't imagine anything else to do. Besides, abandoning her search now would be the smart thing to do. Without further evidence, she could assume that Alex was blowing off steam and Tiffany - well, Tiffany could have been anything. Maybe it was a sexual harassment thing involving any of the 50 or 60 men in the department. Samantha doesn't necessarily have to be the cause of every problem.

Maybe it was a medical thing. She could have sued over carpel tunnel syndrome. The HR trade magazines were filled with stories of secretaries suing their employers for repetitive stress problems. Who knows what her problem was. It may have even been...

But then she stopped her ramblings.

Tiffany's file says she's a paralegal, it occurred to Cathy like a firecracker exploding over her head. But if she was a paralegal, why is there a typing test in her file? Paralegals don't take typing tests.

She opened Tiffany's file again and reviewed her application. She had been a secretary at a law firm, but that doesn't qualify someone to be a paralegal, certainly not in the Business Affairs Department.

While she didn't know why there was a settlement, she now knew how they were paying people off. *Pretty smart. They changed Tiffany's professional status and inflated her salary. This has Samantha's thumb print all over it. No one else could have thought of this, or had the temerity to do it. I don't like it, but you have to be impressed that she was able to pull this off.*

Then the second explosion occurred. Even Samantha couldn't do this alone. It had to be done with the consent of others. The legal department would have drafted up an agreement, the payroll department would have had to make the adjustment, the accounting department would have had to issue a check. Others would have known about it, including Senior Management.

Again she had to remark at Samantha's handiwork in funneling money to this young girl without it appearing as if there was a legal settlement. But like a Chinese puzzle that suddenly becomes obvious once you see how the pieces were interlocked, so too did the elements of this mystery become unraveled.

According to the electronic records, Tiffany was brought into the company by an executive recruiter - Richard Anthony, Inc. - yet according to her application Tiffany had responded to a classified ad placed in the New York Post. But what was really interesting was that Richard Anthony, Inc. was paid $30,000 - almost a full year's salary for Tiffany at the secretarial level - as its fee.

Why is Richard Anthony, Inc. getting paid this money? How is this firm involved in this whole situation? With Samantha controlling and altering the records at will, who knows what was going on. Maybe he's not a recruiter, but is really an outside lawyer that Samantha used so she wouldn't have a record of it internally.

Still making it appear as if she was orienting herself to her new position, Cathy called the departmental secretary temporarily assigned to her, "Could you bring in all vendor contracts. I'd like to review our relationships." A perfectly natural request for the VP in charge of operations. It shouldn't raise suspicions.

But thwarting her investigation, her secretary responded, "It'll take me a couple of hours to get to it. Since Samantha doesn't have a secretary, she asked me to type the proposal for the New York City Transit Department." A couple of hours. Cathy didn't want to wait a couple of hours, but she couldn't supersede Samantha's request, so she thought she'd take a chance and ask directly about Richard Anthony, Inc.

"Never ask the question you want them to answer," her ex-husband often said as he was relating the ingenuity with which he conducted his investigations. "When you ask them a direct question, they know what you're looking for and they start maneuvering to make certain you don't find it. Let them tell you what you want to know, but never ask them."

"I have a message from an executive recruiter named Homer & Associates. Have we ever worked with them?" Cathy casually asked trying to sound as if were an irrelevant matter.

"No. No, the name is not familiar. It's not one of our regular recruiters," the secretary innocently responded.

"Who are our regular recruiters?"

"Well actually, we only use two - Wordprocessing Pros and Mr. Samantha," the secretary responded with a giggle. Realizing how foolish that was, she added, "Oops, I shouldn't have said that. I'm very sorry." She was genuinely very embarrassed.

Trying to sound as if she was joining in on the joke, she asked, "Who is Mr. Samantha?"

"I'm sorry, I shouldn't have referred to him that way. It just slipped." In this department, a slip like that could be career ending and she knew it.

"It's okay, Carole, I won't tell anyone." She forced a laugh. "But who is he?"

"Samantha lives with a gentleman named Richard Anthony. He's an executive recruiter and we use his firm a lot. Wordprocessing Pro handles all secretarial and clerical positions, and Mr. Anthony handles all the rest."

Trying to make amends for the faux pas, she offered, "Should I call Homer back for you?"

For a second she had forgotten her ruse, but, fortunately, it came back to her quickly. "Homer? Oh, no, I'll take care of it. I'm sure it's just a general solicitation." She hung up the phone.

So, he's the Dick she was talking about. This is all getting very odd. Now let's pull up the budgets and see how much he received last year. Since she had full access to departmental budgets, and since there would be no questions about her interest in them, she opened the password-protected files and was unconcerned that someone could track her online movements.

One and a half million dollars, she read to herself. Staring at the screen she once again recalled the words of her ex-spouse. "These aren't electronic dots, these are people working. These are companies doing something to make a profit; imagine what they're doing and decide if it makes sense." One and a half million dollars didn't make sense. That would have meant that he filled virtually every opening in the department, including the secretaries and clericals. No, a million and a half dollars doesn't make sense.

"So that's it," Cathy concluded. "This whole thing was about skimming some money from the corporation by funneling money through her boyfriend's firm." But no sooner had she settled on that conclusion, then she dismissed it. No, that's not her style. He's a line item in the budget. Everyone would see it. It would be too easy to get caught. Besides, she's not interested in money, she wants power. This is an arrangement that is sanctioned by Senior Management. Money is flowing through his firm, but for what purpose?

Maybe he is a legitimate company vendor. She had to call him to get a feel for the amount of work he's doing for the company, and without a doubt, it would get back to Samantha. So, once again, she had to waste precious hours and create a fog, which meant calling all their vendors. Under the guise of introducing herself, she called the advertising agency that handled their recruitment ads, the promotions firm that handled their exhibits at job fairs, the imaging firm that received and scanned the resumes sent to the company, the people who handled the recruitment portion of the website, and finally, the two recruiting firms.

"Good afternoon, Dick Anthony speaking." She was more than a bit surprised that he answered the phone himself. A recruiting firm that generated a million and a half dollars of business would have a full clerical staff.

"Hello, Richard," she didn't want to call him Dick after the conversation she had with Samantha. "My name is Cathy Circe. I just joined the Business Affairs Department at THCC and I will be responsible for the operational aspects of the department." She decided not to mention Samantha's name because she didn't want to make it seem as if she knew about their personal relationship.

Enthusiastically, as if talking to an old friend, he responded, "Yes, yes, Sam mentioned you." Cathy was shocked that he made absolutely no attempt to pretend that he had a purely business relationship with Samantha. He felt invincible, that he was also protected by Samantha's shield.

"Yes, well, I was just calling to introduce myself to you since we would be working together."

"That's very nice. It's a pleasure to meet you... at least meet your voice." He laughed at his own humor. Quite casual, she thought, toward a million-and-a-half dollar client.

"I gather your firm does a lot of work for our department."

"A fair amount." He certainly wasn't making an effort to impress his new contact.

"Do you specialize in any particular type of candidate?" Following her ex-husband's advice she was trying to ask questions that wouldn't raise suspicion.

"No, we're pretty much generalists. We work in all categories... not clericals, of course," he hastily added with a certain snobbishness.

Searching for just the right way to gauge his company's size, but without making him aware of her interest, she said, "I would welcome the opportunity to come to your office to meet your staff. I generally believe in a close working relationship with our suppliers. I really prefer to think of you and your staff as partners, instead of just vendors."

She waited to hear his response, concerned that he might have figured out what she was probing for. However, he answered quite candidly and seemed unconcerned about any implications his reply might give. "Actually, you're talking to the whole firm. It's just me. But I would welcome the opportunity to take you to lunch in the next week or two."

"Bingo," her ex-husband used to scream when he knew he caught the perpetrator, and she screamed it, too, internally, because she got what she was looking for.

There was no way a one man recruiting firm could generate enough business to earn a million and a half dollars a year. The company was definitely using his firm to funnel money somewhere and for some purpose. She continued the conversation, as if she was really interested in his capabilities, and as soon as it was completed, she pulled the files of all the employees that were supposedly hired by Richard Anthony Inc.

Thirty-two names in the last twelve months. As she flipped through the records, seventeen certainly seemed legitimate. They were still in their positions, and their signed letters of employment agreed with their applications which agreed with their computer records.

But fifteen, an alarming fifteen, had hidden contradictions: positions and salaries were out of sync with the rest of the department, dates on applications seemed to overlap, the wording in performance reviews was written in different styles, and some were internal transfers, so there would be no recruiting fee.

Yet, Richard Anthony, Inc. received an oversized fee for finding each one.

One record in particular caught Cathy's attention. Richard Anthony, Inc. received a $75,000 fee for hiring a junior analyst with no experience. This was quite extraordinary considering that the employee's salary was listed as $50,000. As she studied the fifteen records, the pattern held true. Employees seemed to "suddenly and retroactively" received salary increases, and they were being paid as fees through Richard Anthony, Inc. Whatever she felt about what was going on, it was a very clever method of paying settlements.

She wanted to test her theory, but it would require a boldness and possible exposure if she got caught. However, to finally resolve this mystery she was gambling that all the ex-employees would have the same reaction as Tiffany and would beg to keep the settlement quiet.

She picked up the phone and randomly called three of the fifteen ex-employees. "Hello, my name is Cindy Phillips with the Business Affairs Department at The Home Computer Company." There was always a haunting silence on the other end of the phone. "Apparently word about your settlement has leaked out and it has caused some embarrassment to the management of the department and before we accuse anyone I want to get the facts."

Her bet paid off. Fear gripped each of the ex-employees. "It wasn't me. Please, God, you have to believe me," begged a former project manager from the department.

"I don't know how it got out. I never said a word to anyone. Please tell Samantha it wasn't me," pled a former real estate analyst.

"Oh my God, I don't want any trouble. I didn't tell anyone about the settlement, I swear," cried a former secretary.

While she didn't know why so many people were paid settlements, she now knew that a lot of people for a department of that size had been paid off, and she knew how it was being processed so it wouldn't be obvious to internal or government auditors. The Board of Directors, stockholders, clients, and the vast majority of management would never know that there was a problem in the company. Samantha's reputation would stay intact. On paper, no problems existed in the Business Affairs Department - only excessive generosity.

But the next question in her mind was, "Now that I have this information, what do I do with it?" I would be a whistle-blower without a whistle.

There's no point in going to Senior Management since they're in on it. There's no point of exposing the information to Samantha since she's the one perpetrating the cover up. There's no point in going to the Board of Directors since they would look at a million dollars paid in legal settlements as the cost of doing business.

Not knowing what to do with the information, she even began to rationalize it. Samantha is making settlements with people who have claims against the company and doing it in a manner that doesn't involve the legal department and the courts. Maybe its not the "official" way it should be done, and maybe they pay too much to too many people, but for a multi-billion dollar company, this is pocket change, and these settlements prevent the cases from becoming distractions. It's actually pretty quick and efficient.

But no matter how she rationalized it, something seemed wrong... hidden funds being shuffled through third parties... too many settlements... falsified employment records. All this was being done to protect Samantha and keep the Business Affairs Department functioning. Scanning her luxurious office, staring out at the unobstructed view of the Statue of Liberty, touching the wood of her desk and the leather of her chair, she concluded that the only real question was, "Do I want to work for someone that creates so many problems for employees and then covers them up."

She didn't have an answer, but she looked at the calendar and said, "Fourteen days to go."

Chapter 43

Reunion fever was building. With just days to go before people who hadn't seen each other in decades reunited, a certain giddiness pervaded the cyberspace.

Hey, how about we form a 'support group' for the reunion... anyone who has gained more than 10 pounds can join. We can encourage each other to get back to how we use to look.

Judy P. (Not to be confused with Judy M.)
***

Can we expand the support groups into sub-support groups... those that have 10 - 20 lbs to lose... those that have 20 - 30... 30 - 40... I'm embarrassed to tell you which I belong too.

George (the formerly slim, trim quarterback)
***

How about a support group for those that have lost our hair... maybe we can establish rules regarding comb-overs, ratio of hair on the head to hair on the face, and so on.

Jerry "The Duke"
***

How about some prizes. We all can chip in. categories could be:

• Those who actually did what they said they were going to do in the yearbook. (I've lost that one already… i said I was going to be a cowboy and I turned out to be a dentist.)

• Those who married their high school sweethearts (and stayed married)

• Those whose parents still tell them that they have potential. (Mine gave up on me years ago after I performed a root canal on one of them.)

Dr. Stanley (I presume)

***

How about a category of those who look the most like their class pictures

Amy (the taller Amy)

***

Maybe we can do a salute to the great couples of our class:

- Jerry & Peggy

- Peter & Susan

- Larry & Lori

- Bob & Barbara

- Jack & Susan

- Jack & Lori (Yes, it's the same Lori of Larry & Lori… she got crazy for a little while)

- Jack & Alice

- Jack & Marty (Don't worry, ladies, he's not bi-sexual - Marty is short for Martha)

- Jack & Margie

- Jack & Sally (They really were never a great couple)

(I guess we now know why Jack was named class Romeo.)

Sally

Chapter 44

It probably wasn't the smartest idea for Chris to arrange to meet the great love of his life and the vessel of all his hopes, dreams, and wishes, for the first time in over twenty years at a client cocktail party, but then again, it was the absolutely first opportunity they both had and he didn't want to delay even by one minute.

Staring at the oversized doors to the Grand Ballroom, he was trying to hide from his clients behind a silk palm tree, yet, at the same time, have an unobstructed view of entry way.

But since it was the day that he tried to convince a roomful of aging Eastern European-born scientists that the route to incredible wealth was by advertising on television using the lackluster campaign that his ad agency had created, they sought him out and he had nowhere to hide. "Do you really think we can sell five million boxes of tampons a year?" Oscar, one of Envira Inc.'s founders, asked Chris as he balanced a mountain of food on the tiny plate from the buffet table.

Distracted, and trying to maneuver their position so he would have a clear view of the entry, Chris offered with confidence, "You saw the numbers in my presentation. If Envira is willing to invest in a more aggressive advertising program, including TV, we can do it." Oscar's eyes were spinning like a slot machine in Las Vegas.

"If we could get to five million boxes a year, someone would surely want to buy us out," Oscar mused, calculating his share of the sale, and Chris eased himself away from him.

Another partner grabbed Chris from behind, slapped him on the back and declared, "Great presentation," but didn't stay to chat because there seemed to be a sudden opening in the crowd at the bar.

It had been a long, grueling day. The presentation wasn't a typical one, where creative ideas were presented and budgets discussed. At this presentation, Chris had to draw a straight line from running the TV advertising created by his agency, to taking the company public, increasing the stock price, and finally being bought at a premium price by one of its bigger competitors. It wasn't an advertising campaign that he presented, rather, he plotted a roadmap to riches for the owners.

"I like what you said today." Joseph Arimather, the Vice President of Manufacturing for Envira, caught Chris before he could find another phony tree to hide behind. "But I bet we could sell 10 million boxes if we just flood the market with coupons. That would make the supermarkets take notice of us."

Chris never cared for Joseph. He spit when he talked, especially when there was food in his mouth, like now, and it never bothered him to interrupt someone else's conversation if he wanted to say something, regardless of how irrelevant it was. Focusing on the comings and goings through the doorway, Chris responded, "The problem is, if you flood the market with coupons, you cheapen your brand, which means you shave your margins so you won't increase your profits. Then customers only buy when they get a coupon and are unwilling to pay the premium price. We have to tread lightly here. We still don't have a strong enough customer base." Trying to still be respectful, yet trying to get away, Chris gestured that he wanted to head for the bar and get a drink.

But Joseph caught him like a fish in a net and continued, "I admit I have very little experience in marketing, but I can tell you, if we get up to ten million boxes, the cost efficiency we gain in the manufacturing process will more than make up for the cost of the coupons and we won't need expensive television advertising." At some point, Joseph realized Chris was ignoring him so, insulted, he moved away, unnoticed.

Seeing the executives from Envira in tuxedoes was like watching a roomful of penguins at a Cinco de Mayo celebration. They were just so out of place. Except for tonight, they were completely uninterested in their appearances and he often referred to meetings as being on the inside of a Jackson Pollock painting. Unusual combinations of plaid, twenty year old ties, color combinations that would put a peacock to shame, were all part of the corporate wardrobe

Turning to look into one of the framed mirrors that lined the room, Chris used his fingers to brush some strands of hair off his forehead. In the reflection, he saw Cathy enter the room.

She was exquisite… a Grecian statue dedicated to the God of Beauty.

He always thought she was the most beautiful woman on earth, even with those extra five pounds she always wanted to lose, but he was not prepared for the flower she had blossomed into. So elegant, so sophisticated, so regal. Had a rumor spread throughout the ballroom that the Princess of Monaco had entered the room, no one would have disputed it.

As she stepped into the room, and hesitated, searching for Chris, the doorway framed her, like a work of art, and every man and woman turned to see this masterpiece that just entered the room.

Bereft of the gaudy jewels and splashy gowns of so many in the room, she stood in stark contrast by the sophistication of the simple long black dress that clung to a body that had just been taken from the cover of Vogue magazine. Simple and elegant, yet sensuous and tempting without being cheap.

The roomful of women, most of whom were now twice as heavy as when they got married, stood a little more erect, breathed their stomachs in a bit more, and twisted their bodies to a more "slimming" angle. The roomful of men, equally overweight, all wondered which of them had acquired a new "companion," and they all fantasized that they would be able to do so, too, once the company was sold and they were rich.

His eyes met hers and he was eighteen years old and at the senior prom, again. He could not imagine that someone so lovely could be intended for him. At that moment, nothing mattered. Not Envira. Not television advertising. Not his wife. Not his job. Nothing mattered, but Cathy. At that moment, he committed himself to being with her forever and no cost would be too high.

Scanning the sea of aging, balding, overweight men, she wondered if Chris had become one of them. In all their e-mail exchanges they purposely didn't send photos of themselves, as if both were content to live in the past. But, as she turned her head to the right, there he was. She should have guessed that he would look exactly as he did. Terribly vain about his hair and his body, even in high school, he never would have let himself expand as most of the men in the room had. He was still drop dead gorgeous. Oh, the children they would have had.

Like a boat in a gentle breeze, she sailed towards him, and the crowd that stood between them parted, as if driven by the Red Sea winds.

He didn't move. He couldn't move. He was just so captivated by the way she glided across the floor, and how every step accentuated her lovely shape. He knew this moment would play over and over and over in the cinema of his eyes forever.

When she was about six feet from him, he raised his right hand towards her, and her left hand slid into his, like a ballet dancer reaching for her partner, and the two embraced. The missing pieces from the jigsaw puzzle of memories snapped into place, and it was a complete picture, again. From that moment, there was barely a second that her hand wasn't intertwined in his, his arm caressing hers, their arms around each other on the dance floor, or the tips of their fingers playing touching games. They were entwined around each other like two trees that grew on the same seed.

Neither knew what to do. To cry, to laugh, to smile, to speak, to not speak, to touch, to not touch. There were far too many emotions to control and this certainly was the wrong place for them to meet again after all these years. But nothing mattered right now, but each other.

The party was to celebrate the 50th wedding anniversary of the company's president, but for them it was the wedding they never had. They were in love, and everything was a blur swirling around them. As they moved around the room from buffet table to dance floor to bar to quiet corner, they never left each other's glance. They never allowed anything to stray between them. There was great jealously in the room at this perfectly matched, gorgeous couple, but there was joy, too, as people hoped that their own children would find the same happiness these two had.

"Chris, aren't you going to introduce us to your wife?" From behind, Chris heard the familiar voice of the president of Envira. The two would-be lovers smiled, enjoying the mistaken identity, but then Chris realized that the Envira people knew very little about him as a person, and while they knew he was married, none had ever met Melanie, or even heard her name. The obvious assumption, particularly after the sensuous embrace and romantic glances, was that Cathy was Mrs. Chris.

"Cathy, this is Mr. and Mrs. Herastein. Hymie is the Founder and President of Envira, Inc." Chris said, moving the hand that wasn't holding onto Cathy back and forth between the two. "And this," indicating his wife, "is Esther, definitely the woman behind the man." Cathy smiled, bowed her head gracefully, and graciously extended her hand.

"You two make such a lovely couple," Esther said.

Neither Chris nor Cathy made any gesture or uttered a word that would have indicated they weren't a couple. Instinctively, they knew what a problem it would be professionally if the client thought Cathy was Chris' "friend" and not his wife, and no one would believe that this was just a high school reunion. More importantly, for that night, they wanted to be Mr. and Mrs. O'Dess, and were glad that all the guests thought so.

"This is certainly a significant occasion," Cathy congratulated. "Thank you for allowing me to be part of it." While he enjoyed every nanosecond of being with her, Chris had to wonder, when did she go from being a girl from Brooklyn, to this Princess of European royalty. She was always friendly, but now she was enchanting. She was never clumsy or awkward, but now moved like a prima ballerina. Gripping her hand a little bit tighter, she feared that maybe they were no longer a perfect fit, that he was still a boy from Brooklyn, and she surpassed him.

"We all think very highly of Chris," Hymie said. "He's the one who's going to make us all rich." Behind Chris' smile was his concern, if he still had a job by the time he got back to L.A.

"Men are always talking about being wealthy," Esther declared. "We didn't stay married 50 years because we had a lot of money." Esther was one of the woman who was twice – maybe even more than twice – her size as when they got married, and while Hymie didn't gain that much weight after 50 years of marriage, they still looked like they belonged together.

"You must tell me what the secret of a long marriage is." Cathy released Chris' hand and gently touched Esther's arm because she felt a special bond between them. A collective gasp could be heard from every corner of the room. No one touches Mrs. Herastein! She was ice. She was cold. No one spoke to her, unless she spoke to you.

Esther raised her left hand to show Cathy the tiny diamond ring, which she still wore, that Hymie gave her when he proposed marriage. Then Esther giggled and showed her the huge, not particularly tasteful, but huge, diamond ring that he gave her last night.

Cathy lavished such praise over both rings that Esther pulled Cathy aside - one of the few times the younger couple lost touch of each other - and spoke softly, "A relationship must build over time. It builds on a foundation of struggling together, of working together, of trying to get somewhere together. The harder the struggle the better. Don't let things come too easily or you won't learn to rely on each other. We had nothing - we had less than nothing - when we got married. Now we have 50 years of happiness together."

Esther raised her voice so the men could hear, "God willing, I'll dance at your 50th anniversary party." Hymie made a joke that they'd all be doing their dancing in wheelchairs.

The four stood together in an impenetrable circle for more than half an hour. The older couple told the younger what it was like to grow up poor in Eastern Europe during horrible times, and how they saved each other's lives, physically and spiritually. The two women talked about clothes, recipes, having children, decorating, hard times, men, good times, travel, and everything else that instant friends have to say to each other. The two men talked about business, company gossip, plans for the future, what happens after Envira sells, and how it feels to watch your children grow. They chatted away more like parents and their grown children than business associates and their wives.

Surrounding the small circle was a wary cadre of corporate executives that spied on the four with suspicion, and loathing. They didn't like the president becoming so close to, and visibly enjoying, this outsider. He was just a vendor and shouldn't be occupying so much of Hymie's time. Several tried to become part of the small group, but were instantly repelled. Most just circled it, hoping to be asked to join, but none were.

Eventually, the older couple recognized they had other guests to attend to and would have to circulate. Esther hugged Cathy, whispered something in her ear that made Cathy smile broadly, and kissed her on the cheek. Hymie shook Chris' hand firmly and patted him on the back, once again congratulating him for the good presentation. Then the host and hostess of the party meandered toward some guests that were gathered near the buffet table.

Chris wrapped his arm around Cathy's shoulders, and she pressed against him enjoying the warmth. They didn't say anything to each other for a few minutes, they just wondered if they would have had a 50th anniversary had they gotten married. Finally he asked her, "What did Esther whisper to you that made you smile."

Cathy giggled, covering her lips behind curled fingers. "She said, 'I want to make all those stupid women watching us jealous, so smile and pretend I'm saying something amusing to you.'"

"I think she likes you," Chris laughed. "Esther isn't the friendliest person in the world."

Throughout the course of the evening each of the executives of Envira and their wives managed to drift over to Chris and Cathy. Clearly, the wives had the assignment, "Find out who this Cathy is and why did Esther Herastein find her so interesting?"

Even Chris became an object of curiosity. Everyone in the room knew him. Many had been in today's presentation. But they had never seen Hymie spend so much time with anyone in casual conversation. He usually couldn't stay in one spot for more than a few minutes. He'd turn and walk away when he was finished, even in the middle of a conversation.

While, for obvious reasons, they steered away from discussions relating to their relationship - how they met, how long they've been married - no matter who they spoke with, everyone came away saying they certainly were a couple in love. Chris found that the only way he could have Cathy to himself - and avoid the probing questions of jealous executives and their wives - was on the dance floor, so they spent as much time in each other's arms, swaying and swirling to the sounds of the orchestra, as they could. They never took their eyes from each other as they glided around the room, and they never stopped smiling.

About midnight the guests started leaving, and Cathy and Chris knew it was time for them to leave, too. They acted like lovers all evening, and they both wanted to, and intended to, continue the feeling once they left the party. But even after such a perfect evening, they both were more than a little nervous.

Chris was worried about his performance in bed… being good never seemed so important. She was nervous about what he would expect. The last time they made love, they were still young and experimenting. Decades later, they'd both matured and crossed many boundaries.

Her skin tingled with anticipation of his touch. She could feel it in her breasts as her dress rubbed against her nipples. She could feel it between her legs as her loins became warm and wet. She desperately wanted his love. She desperately needed to be loved. For the past 20 years she had been used by men for their personal gratification. Today, now, she needed to be loved.

He wanted to please her. She wanted to please him.

As they entered the hotel room, she took his hand and led him to the bedroom, and in that moment, all fear and doubt disappeared. They were high school kids again, back in Brooklyn, and in love. They kissed, and they didn't stop kissing. They went straight from the front door into the bedroom and lay down together, as they did so often, so many years ago.

The very first time they made love, it was awkward. It was messy. It was juvenile. But the last time they made love, it was tender, it was satisfying, it was romantic.

As if no time had passed, he knew where to put his hands to stimulate her, how to use his tongue to excite her, and how to hold her against him so they could feel each other. Unlike the other men she had been with over the past two decades, he didn't rush to shove himself inside her. He made love to her as if he was a woman, because he knew that putting himself inside her was only one of the pleasures to be enjoyed.

She lay back as his warm, wet tongue massaged her nipples and circled her breasts. He ran his tongue down the full length of her body, inside her thighs, between her toes. Coming back up her legs, his tongue rested inside her vagina, and delicately massaged the area that had been so often bruised by the men in her life.

She rolled over to put his penis in her mouth, but he softly whispered, "No, just lay back and enjoy," and she obeyed. There have so few times over the years that she could have actually done that.

As she closed her eyes, drifting somewhere in time between what was and what is, she was taken back to the night of their high school prom. With four other couples, they rented a limousine to take them to Manhattan for a "private prom" after the official prom was over. As a gift, one of the parents reserved a suite at the luxurious Iliad Hotel and filled the room with foods and beverages from around the world (Australian lobster tail, sushi, New Zealand lamb) so the night would be memorable to friends who would soon go their separate ways. The parents also had all the beds taken out of the suite and replaced by lots of straight-backed chairs.

By this time, Cathy and Chris had already made love for the first time and were getting to know each other's bodies better. While some of the other couples hid in a corner under a blanket to have sex, Cathy and Chris spent the night holding onto each other, in an embrace that couldn't be broken by anyone.

At dawn, they changed out of their formal clothes and left the hotel and their sleeping friends. Holding hands, they meandered through the trails of Central Park, watching squirrels racing across the grass, looking at the buds blossoming on the trees, until they found themselves at the edge of the lake. It was too early for the rowboats to be out on the lake, and a soft breeze barely created a stir on the water's surface.

Chris picked up two stones, placing one in Cathy's hand. Instinctively they both tossed the stones into the water a few feet in front of them, and that was the first time he said to her, "Like the ripples in the water that blend into one, so will our two lives become one." It became a ritual that they performed often over the next few years.

As if he knew this was the moment she wanted him closest to her, Chris slid himself inside her and they became one, tightening their grip around each other, passionately pressing their lips together.

"I love you," she whispered, feeling as if she was on a magic carpet, floating above the clouds. This was the way it was supposed to be. This was the way it used to be.

"I love you," he whispered in return, and she knew it was true. For all the men she'd been with, he was the only one that made love to her, that made her feel as if he was a warm blanket wrapped around her. For hours, he held her, touched her, caressed her, massaged her inside and out. She had never known such attention, such passion.

After a while, they fell soundly asleep in each other's arms, and neither rolled away from the other's grasp. They were safe from the world. No happiness could be greater. No want was unsatisfied. It was what love was meant to be.

They slept that way for almost four hours. Her eyes opened first, so she rolled over to be face to face with Chris. He always had a young, somewhat feminine face. People described him as pretty (sometimes, too pretty). Time had changed him. He no longer looked like a boy. The lines revealed too many experiences and worries, but he still was incredibly handsome.

Feeling a change in his universe, Chris began to open his eyes. She leaned over, licked his ear, and whispered, "Do you think we should eat something?"

He chuckled, "Not exactly the first thing I expected to hear from you after last night, but the point is well taken." Grabbing her, he kissed her again and again.

"Would it stroke your male ego if I told you how incredible you were, before asking about food?" They laughed the same laugh of twenty years ago, which made them both cry a little.

"There's a tray of fruit and cheese in the refrigerator. It's complimentary from the hotel for THCC management." She began to climb out of the bed in the direction of the kitchen, but he stopped her.

"No, I'll get it." With that he jumped off of the bed. "I'll make some coffee."

He put on some weight since college, but not much, maybe ten pounds, she guessed as he ran around the suite naked. He still had a great body. His chest and arms were really built up.

She lay back with a grand smile, realizing that the last time she had three orgasms in the same evening was with Chris just before she moved to Minneapolis. Since then, she was lucky to get one in before the guys pulled themselves out of her.

She was well beyond the ability to have children any longer (a hysterectomy took care of that), but when she felt the warmth of Chris' sperm, she had the incredible sensation that life was beginning inside her body again… that the time lost to them was erased… they could begin their dreams of having a baby again.

Chris returned with the tray, and sitting on the bed, wrapped in the sheets, they fed each other and replenished their strength.

Giggling like a teenager, she said, "You've learned a lot since we were last together." It was obvious that they've both become much more mature in the art of giving pleasure.

Blushing, he offered, "It's just that we belong together in every way."

"That may be true, but I don't remember you being quite this… passionate. Somebody must have taught you a thing or two." He leaned over and kissed her, pushing a small wedge of cheese into her mouth.

She reached for his penis and it began to stiffen. Getting giddy, she dripped strawberry jam on her nipples and lay back on the bed. He removed the tray from the bed and leaned over, licking the jam, and then using his tongue in wide circles around her chest. He put his fingers inside her, and when she was wet again, he slid himself inside her again, and they stayed that way until they were both too weary, and once again they fell asleep in each other's arms.

"I don't think I've been off this bed for twenty-four hours except to pee," she laughed, when they woke up. He released her from his arms as she sat up to look at the clock. "What time is it?"

Cathy twisted so she could see the blue light of the clock. "Well, I'm wrong, we've only been in bed for twenty-one hours." Kissing him, she added, "I think we missed the reunion."

She kissed his chest and lay back down in his arms. "God, so many missed orgasms," she said.

Nodding, he simply whispered, "Yes."

In that one word was the truth that they now both knew for certain, that they'd spent the last twenty years with the wrong partners; that they should have been together; that they'd lost the best years together; that the children they should have had together would never be born.

It made them both cry.

She went into the bathroom to start filling the tub for their bath. He took the opportunity to see if Melanie left any messages on his phone. There was one, but it wasn't from Melanie, it was from Candy.

In a voice of wild desperation, she shrieked, "Get back here immediately! Mack's on the warpath! There's a meeting here 9 a.m. tomorrow morning. You'd better be here. No excuses. This is bad. This is really bad."

In two hours Chris was showered, packed, and on a plane to Los Angeles.

Chapter 45

The meeting started quite well, a real textbook example of a sales pitch.

As they walked into the office of the new purchasing agent, Fred caught sight of a picture of Tony holding a trophy for winning a bowling tournament. Since bowling was one of the many sports that Fred tried (unsuccessfully) to master, he still had enough knowledge of the game to carry on a conversation.

Exactly at the moment when the "warm up" phase of the conversation should end, Fred smoothly slid into a discussion of the university's needs. It was so subtle and so well timed that Stanley leaned back in amazement. In all the years, he had never realized how good his employee was, and he admonished himself for not recognizing the man's talent's sooner. If this had been a training class, he would have stopped it right at that moment and graduated the student on the spot.

Whether this purchasing agent was just more verbose than the last, or whether it was Fred's ability to make him feel comfortable, Stanley couldn't tell, but he had called on the university many times before and he was never able to get the information about hardware and budgets that this man was now giving to Fred.

"We've got about 12,000 computers hooked up to the internet, maybe 12,100 or 12,200," Tony revealed, "and we have to do something to give them better access."

As Tony spoke, Fred maintained a silent and concerned focus, hanging on his every word. If he could have, Stanley would have stood up on his chair and shouted, "Yahoooooooooo!!!! Twelve thousand units!!!!"

Not only would this be the biggest single sale this company ever made for the new modem; not only would it put his branch office well over quota for the year, even though the year wasn't halfway over; not only would this be the first piece of business from a new and gigantic client; but this - along with Cathy's support - would be a lock on a vice presidency.

He shook his head in disbelief. This was all thanks to Fred. Fred had been working the territory and heard a whisper - literally - in a bar, that the students and faculty were disgruntled by the antiquated technology on campus and the administration committed itself to doing something about it before the start of the next semester.

Stanley just couldn't believe how everything had worked out. Two months ago he was managing a small office with a handful of second-rate salespeople. There wasn't a chance in the world he would have promoted Fred and the thought of him ever becoming a vice president - well it just wasn't a thought. The only expectation he had was to finish his career with the company in the next few years and enjoy his retirement. He planned to back move to Wisconsin, watch the Packer's in the winter and go fishing in the summer. The biggest upset he experienced over the past few years was that during a couple layoffs, the company had never offered him early retirement.

Now, after all these years of being an insignificant cog on the assembly line of the company, suddenly a vice presidency, in the Minneapolis office, was a real possibility. Stanley's mind wandered to the future and all its potential, not to mention the dramatic increase in salary and benefits that would accompany his vice president's position.

With one ear, he heard Fred say, "Tony, we have just come out with a product that I believe you'll agree meets all - not just 99% - but all your needs. It'll speed up access at every one of those twelve thousand computers. It will cost the university millions of dollars less than all other technologies, and it can be installed on every computer in less than a month."

Once again, Stanley was flabbergasted at how well Fred was doing. Even though he knew it wasn't his idea, he was the one who actually promoted Fred and he congratulated himself for his decision. After all, he reasoned, I could have said "no." I didn't have to promote him. Ultimately, it was my decision.

He listened, like a proud father, as Fred presented the case for THCC's new modem. The THCC Explorer was based on a new technology that compressed analog signals, which meant that five times as much data could run through an existing telephone line as compared with current modems. This meant faster internet connections for the same computers, and best of all, the phone lines were already in place. It was very clean and very cost effective.

"We're thinking about installing one of those Wi-Fi wireless networks so people can sign on to the internet from anywhere," Tony mentioned. He didn't actually say "We're thinking...," what he did say was, "We're tinking...," which Fred thought funny, but managed to suppress any outward sign of amusement. Tony's accent was unmistakably from somewhere in New Jersey and he looked like the casting department's idea of "a mafia hit man type."

"Wi-Fi networks are good, but that means every computer has to have a wireless networking card installed, so you not only have the cost of the cards, which aren't standard for every computer, but the hardware installation expenses for the system. If you have any computers that are more than a couple of years old, network cards may not even be available so everyone isn't going to be able to get online."

Stanley caught his jaw before it hit the floor as he listened to the parry and thrust of the conversation between Fred and Tony. The client offered a good reason not to buy THCC's modems, and Fred addressed and dismissed them. In fact, he was doing so well that Stanley began to tune out of the conversation and began thinking of routes he could take from his home to the office in Minneapolis. There was a train he could take, but that meant not having a car and if he still had sales responsibilities, he'd probably need his car everyday. But then again, it depended on the position he would be elevated to, maybe he wouldn't still be in sales. Maybe he would be more on the marketing side, or the management side.

"What do you think about a broadband hook-up, like a T-1 line or DSL?" Again he said "tink" instead of "think" and while he didn't show it, Fred wondered how such an idiot could have risen so high in an organization and be responsible for millions of dollars of equipment purchases.

Once again Fred masterfully dismissed another reason not to buy. Everyone was smiling, the conversation was serious and animated. The buyer was ready to make a decision. As he glanced over, he noticed that Fred was pulling out an order form. It was a little pre-mature for an order form, he thought, since they hadn't even done a proposal, but since Fred was handling this so well, he had no intention of interrupting.

"Over 60% of the computers on campus are at least three years old. Since we're going to have to replace them in the next couple of years, we're wondering if it pays to replace them now and stick a Wi-Fi card in each and be done with it."

Stanley sat back and waited for Fred's response... but, there was none. He turned to look at Fred, and all he saw was a blank stare. For the first time in the meeting, Fred, clearly in pain, struggling to think of something, couldn't come up with a reasonable response. Since Stanley hadn't been listening to the flow of the conversation, he had no idea where they were in the discussion and couldn't offer any help.

Had Fred said, "Let me run some numbers for you and come back next week with a proposal," that would have been a good response.

Had Fred said, "Next year Intel is coming out with a new chip, which means that if you buy new computers now, they'll all be out-of-date by next year," that would have been a good response.

Had Fred said, "Even if you bought our modems now and threw them away in two years when you bought your new computers with network cards installed, you would still save millions of dollars," that would have been a very good response.

But what he did say was, "That's the stupidest thing I ever heard. Instead of paying $100 for a new modem, you're going to spend a $2,000 on a new computer. Anyone with half an ounce of intelligence about technology would know how ridiculous that was."

Tony, who clearly was the author of the thought, clasped his hands, almost as if each hand was holding the other back from punching Fred in the face. Stifling his anger, he uttered, "It can't be as stupid as some two-bit modem salesman telling a purchasing agent with a ten million dollar budget that he doesn't have an ounce of intelligence. I think (tink) you should leave now," Tony suggested.

Stanley's mouth opened, but he couldn't think of a way to save the sale. He started to lean forward and speak, but a strong arm from Fred pushed him back in his chair.

Slamming the order form on the desk in front of Tony, Fred spit out, "Just sign the order form and we'll leave."

"I'm not signing any fuckin' order form, you asshole. Get out!"

Fred, at over six feet, four inches, was an imposing figure. He stood up, and looking down at Tony, threw a pen on top of the order form. Unfortunately, the felt-tip pen bounced and hit Tony, leaving a six-inch line on his highly starched, tightly buttoned, white cotton shirt.

The three of them froze, staring at the blue line. Tony's hands started to form into fists, and he gnashed his teeth together as if he had just bitten the head off a rattlesnake. Fred realizing it was a mistake to throw the pen, but saw no reason why the order form shouldn't be signed, lamely offered, "I'll buy you a new shirt. Now just sign." No one stared at that thin six-inch line in greater shock and dismay than Stanley, for that line was the separation between a vice presidency for one of the world's largest corporations and being the manager of an office of mediocre modem salesman.

Tony, who was only five feet, eight inches tall, but weighed well over three hundred pounds and played center on the Ohio State football team the year they won the Rose Bowl, stood up and went face to face with Fred. "Get the fuck out of here right now or I'll toss you out the window." Anyone looking in the office would have thought that there was about to be a battle between a basketball player and a sumo wrestler.

Stanley, who was also five feet, eight inches tall, but weighed only 152 pounds, tried to thrust himself between the two warriors, but Fred cast him aside like a toothpick.

Thinking that Fred was now going to turn and push him, Tony tightly grabbed Fred's right arm, with a tourniquet-like grip.

Feeling the life being squeezed out of his arm and thinking that he was about to be the subject of a fist in his face, Fred shoved the heel of his left hand into the Tony's nose, breaking it and sending blood splattering over the order form, the white shirt, the black pants, the carpet and the desk.

All the years between growing up in the rough neighborhood of East St. Louis and the genteel farmlands outside the window of his office at the university, vanished like steam from a shower and Tony swung his fist at Fred, smashing his chin and sending him flying over the two guest chairs, landing on top of Stanley, who wrapped himself around Fred, screaming, "Stop! Stop! Stop! Stop!"

A dozen or so other employees of the university's purchasing department rushed over to Tony's office to see what was going on, stopping suddenly by the incredulousness of the scene they were witnessing.

Someone got the first aid kit and started treating Tony's nose. Someone else called the emergency room at the medical center to let them know that they were on their way over. A third person called security, which arrived promptly and escorted the two salesmen to a holding area where they waited for the police to arrive. Having heard about all this from one of the witnesses, the head of the Purchasing Department called the university's lawyer and instructed him to press charges.

Between being held at the university's security office, the police station, and then the drive back to their homes, Fred and Stanley were together for over fifteen hours since the first punch was thrown. In all that time, they never said a word to each other. Stanley couldn't think of anything but strangling Fred, but since he would have been easily overpowered, he kept his words and thoughts to himself.

As Stanley dropped Fred off at his house, he said, "Don't even think about coming into the office again. I never want to see you again."

Chapter 46

Walking through the agency doors, he instantly knew a crisis was looming. Everything looked the same as it had a few days ago when he left for New York, but it felt as if some alien being had sucked the life out of the place. The silence was as loud as fireworks on the Fourth of July.

Ad agencies, even this one, were very vibrant places; production people racing up and down the hallways screaming at anyone who stood in the way of getting an ad delivered on time; impromptu meetings between creative, media, and account people occurred a hundred times a day outside one office or another; supervisors argued with their assistants about why something hadn't been done correctly; and the phones... the phones were constantly ringing.

It was too quiet, much too quiet.

Doors were closed up and down the corridor, and people popped in and out of their offices as quickly as they could. No one lingered in the hallways to chat. No one stood around the coffee machine concocting the perfect brew. No one spoke and only a rare few whispered.

At first, he thought it was all about him - that the Big Lie had been exposed and he was going to be crucified, then fired, but then he wondered, how could anyone know that he was a fraud. Not only did his meeting with Envira occur late on Friday, but the presentation went exceedingly well. They were actually considering going on TV. They even liked Mack's ridiculous idea for a commercial. Besides, he hated to admit, "Not that many people care about me here."

Immediately heading to Candy's station, he froze at the entrance of the maze as if he just realized he had stepped on a land mine. Everything was gone. The flags were gone. The stuffed animals were gone. The handmade signs were missing. The posters of cars and distant destinations vanished. Everything was gone. The partitions had no personality anymore. It was just a sea of tan fabric. It didn't look like an advertising agency anymore. It looked like an insurance company.

The rats in the maze had their own communications grapevine and someone on the fringe sent a message to Candy that her boss was here, so she popped up instantly, and scanning to see that it was safe, she called to Chris, "Stay there, I'll come to you."

Candy didn't look well at all. She obviously had been crying a great deal and was more disheveled than usual, but this wasn't the time to talk about personal problems. Chris had only a few minutes before he would have to attend the management meeting. "What's going on?" he whispered.

Leading him to an empty office, she closed the door behind them. "It's bad. Really bad. You know all the women who used to work for Barry Balin, and quit once Gary became their supervisor..."

"Yes, what about them?"

"They're suing the agency. They filed a multi-million dollar class action suit against Gary, against Mack, and against the agency. They're claiming sexual harassment, as well as job discrimination based on gender." Shaking his head, Chris said to himself that he knew it was going to happen one day - it was obvious every time Gary's foul mouth was heard.

"Mack got served with papers as he was giving a tour of the office to a new business prospect. I've never seen an explosion like that. He was screaming and yelling. The new business prospect literally ran down the hall, and as soon as they left, he marched through the maze tearing up signs, pulling down posters, kicking stuffed animals. Everyone's just hiding now. I haven't seen Gary all day. I think Mack threw him out the window."

What does this mean to me? How do I take advantage of this? Chris considered.

It was hard to take it all in. There were lots of implications and consequences to a company when something like this happened. *Would Envira, a decidedly feminine product, find it too uncomfortable to keep its account at an agency in the middle of a sexual harassment suit? If the suit was big enough, could it bankrupt the agency and force it to shut down. Gary's sure to get fired so is his client up for grabs?*

His eyes rested on the digital clock on the building across the street. It was time to go to the meeting. "You're right, this is bad," he said as he picked up a pen and paper, and opened the door. But before stepping out, he turned to her and in a more gentle asked, "Are you okay?"

"We're having some problems. I hope we can work them out," she sniffled. Tears welled in her eyes. He wanted to give her a hug, but they both knew he couldn't stay. No one dared to be late for this meeting.

It wasn't a conference room anymore, it was a war room, with the officers waiting to be briefed. Pictures, maps, charts, profiles, and lists, were all tacked to what were once pristine walls. The room wreaked of stale food as piles of boxes that once had food in them overflowed the few tiny trash cans, and an army of coffee cups and soda cans lined up on the conference table waiting for their orders to march.

The partners and lawyers were all there; hovering around the conference table, studying documents, making notes, whispering to each other, eying people around the room and deciding who was on the team and who was likely to be a traitor.

Chris was the last one to enter, and it was clear that there was hate in Mack's eyes. He clearly would not accept any challenge or lack of loyalty.

The news of Chris' success in New York was irrelevant today. Whether or not the agency did a television commercial, was of no interest to anyone, so he slipped into his usual chair, which was whatever seat in the room was farthest from Mack. Unfortunately, and surprisingly, this placed him close to Gary, who was sitting in a dark corner - ironically, the same chair Barry Balin sat in a few weeks ago. Visibly shaken, Gary's perspiration soaked through his clothes and a rainstorm of fear ran off his face. Wiping his face, he slipped lower and lower into his chair, trying to hide below the level of the table. Hoping to stay out of Mack's view, he slowly maneuvered his chair behind Chris.

The silence lent an eerie feeling to the room. The low-level buzz of most meetings was gone and all that could be heard was rustling pages turning and the scratching of pens writing. Everyone was hunched over, staring down at the table, at their hands, at the floor, anywhere as long as eye contact with anyone could be avoided.

In a tone that spoke of the pain, the agony, he was suffering because his former employee... no, his friend... stabbed him in the back, like Brutus to Julius Caesar, Mack said, "This agency is under a vicious and unwarranted attack." The pain in his face looked so sincere, you'd think he was rehearsing for a part in *Hamlet* or *Macbeth*. "A group of ex-employees, all who happen to be female, are suing the agency for sexual discrimination and harassment."

As Mack uttered those words, Chris couldn't help notice that of the thirteen people seated around the conference table, Debra, the head of Media, was the only woman, and heads repeatedly turned towards her, as if to say, "It's one of your kind. Can't you control your people?"

Taking advantage of the moment of silence, one lawyer reminded everyone that everything they had said or will say, everything they had done or will do, everything they had written or will write, whether on paper or a computer, was suspect and could be questioned in court. Someone with a suspicious mindset might have thought that the lawyer was suggesting that people destroy any documents or files that could be used as evidence against the company before they're requested by the opposing counsel.

As was explained, the women who had originally worked for Barry Balin, and now reported to Gary Accolon, had filed a class action suit on the grounds that Gary's lewd and sexist remarks made the office environment too unbearable for them to work in. As it turns out, the women were diligent in keeping records of his offensive remarks, especially the secretary who sat just outside the coffee room, and every filthy joke or reference to a woman's body parts were detailed in the court papers. As the lawyer explained, "The one positive about the sexual harassment claim, if there is a positive, is that Gary never touched any of these ladies, and he never propositioned them. He is just a lewd and disgusting individual."

Also, meticulously recorded in the legal papers was the hiring and promotion history of K&Q over the past five years, and the cases of discrimination based on gender was much more serious. Sheila Loewe, who had been Gary's peer, working for Barry Balin, actually had more experience and an excellent employment record, so she was making the claim that she wasn't promoted based on gender. Thinking about the last ten years, Chris' recollection was that he had never seen more than two women in the eleven senior positions at any one time. More often than not, though, there was only one woman in management, and it was always the Media Director. Whenever a position had to be filled, Mack would declare, "I want the best person available. I don't care if they're male, female, black, white, or purple. I just want the best person." Remarkably, the best person always seemed to be a white male.

John Spencer, the senior partner of Farragut & Nostrand, the law firm representing the agency, stood up to address the assembled group. "Let me begin by making a statement that some of you may resent, but I feel it's my obligation as your attorney to say these words. First, everything you say to me is protected under client-attorney privilege, so feel free to be completely honest with me.

"Second, it is grounds for immediate termination with no opportunity for severance should any information about the case put forth here today, or in any future meeting, or in any written document - whether electronic or hardcopy - be discussed with any person not in senior management of this agency or in the presence of a representative of Farragut & Nostrand. I am passing out a written statement to this effect and I would like everyone to sign and date it immediately, so we can proceed. Anyone who cannot in good conscience sign this statement, please leave the room immediately. You will be escorted out of the building by the security guard that has been hired by your firm."

Their eyes darted back and forth as the prisoners-of-war trapped in the conference room just realized that their escape plan was discovered. With no hope of getting out, they all quickly signed the statement and handed them to the junior attorney that circled the room.

"Good," Spencer continued, delighted with the fear – and submission - he saw in everyone's' eyes. "I want to discuss our strategy for handling this legal challenge and what is required of you. First, we are hoping we can settle these cases in arbitration. You should each assume that you will be called, please make Brian Herman (he indicated the junior attorney) aware of your travel schedules, and also please advise anyone you're meeting with that you may have to cancel any meetings at the last minute, however, you cannot explain to them why under any circumstances." A few of the people in the room began to object, and there were some rumblings about the lack-of-professionalism, but Mack stared them all down.

Spencer continued, "We will attempt to separate these charges into two different cases. The first case will be in relationship to the sexual harassment charges. We believe we can negotiate a minimum settlement with the young ladies. Four of the five women are in early stages of their careers, and they weren't earning a significant amount of money. We're going to try to buy them off with a year's salary, a recommendation, and an apology from Gary for any comments that they found offensive.

"If need be, we'll terminate Gary and re-instate all the young ladies."

The news of his death was a shock to Gary, and for a nanosecond, he rose up in his chair to assume a defiant posture, but as soon as that moment of bravado evaporated, he sank back into the shadows. Though no one was the least bothered at the thought of Gary being sacrificed, everyone in the room was taken back by the cold, calculating manner in which they were all being addressed.

"We will be taking the position," Spencer detailed, "that senior management was never fully aware of the problem, and now that they are, they are reacting swiftly and decisively." It was a complete lie, but that was irrelevant to the attorneys. "Is there anybody who cannot support that position?" This wasn't a question, it was an announcement, and anyone who objected would have no future at this agency. The eyes in the room immediately turned toward Debra, since it was automatically assumed that she would side with the women. But she nodded her head in agreement with the attorney and mouthed, "I can support that."

Then eyes moved toward Chris. More than anyone else in the room, he had criticized Gary's behavior and language, and had actually brought up the subject to the agency's management on several of occasions.

This was a major dilemma. If he supported this position, it was an outright lie, and if he lied on the witness stand it would be perjury and he could go to prison. He had to laugh a bit, internally, of course, because the last time he was in a dilemma in this room, he was spouting lies like water from a fire hydrant in July.

He nodded his head in support, but not very vigorously.

Unknown to Chris, but not to Mack or the attorneys, the young woman who sat outside the coffee room door and wrote down Gary's obscenities, also took notes about Chris' frequent criticisms of Gary for his language, and consequently, Chris was going to be one of their star witnesses.

Spencer continued, "Good. The discrimination based on gender is a far more serious challenge to us."

Because it's true, Chris thought.

"The young lady in question seems to have been a very effective employee. She received excellent reviews and had good relationships with her clients. Naturally, we're going to try to settle with her, too, but I doubt she will accept. I'm told that her husband is a very successful investment banker and her salary was insignificant to their household income. She's bringing this suit more for principle than for money, which makes things more difficult.

"We have decided to take the position that while she was a good worker, the management of this agency didn't feel she could be a successful manager. In effect, being in the number two position is the best she ever could have hoped for." Everyone in the room knew Sheila was well qualified for the job, and it didn't sit well with them. But supporting Sheila meant sacrificing their own careers, so as Spencer's eyes went around the room, they all nodded in support, with minimum levels of commitment.

"What I need each of you to do today is go through your files and pull out absolutely anything that can be used in this case to either defend or deny these claims. I don't care how remote the information may seem, even a handwritten note that says 'Good job' can be used as evidence. This includes all, and I emphasize the word all, documents that were written by or sent to any of the women involved in this lawsuit. I want all this information forwarded to Brian Herman by tomorrow. Do not make copies of any documents. If you have a document that you feel you must continue to have in your files, please discuss that with my office before making copies. Is this understood?" Once more, all nodded their heads as if they were on the dashboard of a car.

After Spencer sat down, the Chief Financial Officer for the firm stood up and presented some gruesome realities. The agency was not financially prepared to handle the suits, and if the claims were sufficiently severe, it could force the agency into bankruptcy. The liability insurance coverage the agency carried was woefully inadequate for this type of situation, so the bulk of any settlement would have to come out of the agency's pockets, which weren't very deep. No one in the room, except the partners, the CFO, and the lawyers knew that the information being presented was false, and that the agency was in far better shape than was being presented, but Mack thought that this would be a strong motivator, encouraging people to work harder to save the agency.

Mack closed the meeting with a locker room pep talk, the spirit of which the dispirited attendees had difficulty absorbing. In just over an hour they'd been threatened with the loss of their jobs, informed that they were irrelevant and expendable resources, distrusted, humiliated, and ordered to function on the distant edges of ethics, all for a foul-mouthed sexist who thought of women only in terms of tits and ass, and two partners that gave women no credit for brains.

All in all, this was not an inspired army that stood behind the Purveyor of Evil in their battle with the "Forces of Good." This was an army that wanted to be on the other side of this fight, but were too afraid to cross the line.

Just before Chris reached the door, a hand fell on his shoulder. It was Mack. "We need to talk." The hand pressed him down into a chair, and then they waited. As the lawyers, and everyone else, left the room, he could hear the voice of his former supervisor, The General, blasting in his ears, "Hit the dirt!!!!! Incoming!!!! Incoming!!!!" Chris didn't need a Broadway marquee to tell him that this was a genuine Mission Critical Moment. Without a doubt, he was going to be asked to do something significant, and he prayed that it wouldn't be illegal.

"Let me ask you, Chris, what's your take on this gender discrimination case?"

This was going to be a hard issue to circumvent, and there was no middle-of-the-road position. As Mack expressed it, either you're with the agency, or you're with the bitches trying to bring us down. In the past, Chris had always been able to avoid a strong commitment he couldn't in all good conscience defend, but this time it would be different.

"Like everything," Chris was groping for just the right words to say, "there are two sides to this."

"Oh," Mack already didn't like the answer. "What are they?"

Hoping to stall his response long enough until he could decide how to benefit from the situation, Chris knew he was obliged make some sort of committal statement, but he also knew he had to set the stage for some deal to be made. "While I don't believe this agency has ever consciously practiced gender discrimination..." It was obvious Mack didn't like the idea that there was going to be a 'but' in this sentence. "...but, if you just look around the room at the management meetings, women are obviously under-represented." Mack's anger swelled up like a balloon about to burst, but he kept it under control.

"Do you know of any cases in which a better qualified woman was passed over for a less qualified man based solely on gender?" Mack was using all his energy to hold back his famous... infamous... hot temper, which Chris had been on the receiving end of much too often.

This was the pivotal question in the case and answering directly was to make a commitment on one side or the other. Since he hadn't gotten anything out of this conflict yet, it was too early in the conversation to take a firm stance. However, he did know that if he answered honestly he would have flatly stated, *Yes, lots of deserving woman have been passed over for your golf-buddy assholes like Gary!*

As an actor, Chris had learned to use silence to his advantage, clasping his hands in front of his lips, he seemed to barely breathe, as if seriously pondering the question. He would have stayed that way for an hour if he had to, but as he anticipated, Mack couldn't wait another second for a response so he charged in with, "We're not discriminating against anyone at this agency. This is just one of those professions that doesn't attract high-level female executives. The media department seems to attract qualified women, but the rest of the profession has been dominated by men since the industry began. Go into any other agency and you'll see it's no different." Mack could rationalize anything to himself.

Obviously this wasn't true, but there was no point in arguing.

"We all need to pull together on this issue if the agency if going to survive. And I called you in here to ask if you're going to be on the team."

Mack was nothing if he wasn't direct, but in truth, it would have been more honest if Mack just asked him if he wanted to keep his job or not.

Yes... no..... up... down... black... white. This was it. "Of course I'm on the team," it seemed safe to say. "I've been on this team for ten years now, and I have no plans of changing horses mid-stream." Actually, Chris was never a great sports fan, so he always mangled athletic expressions when he tried to use them to make a point. But he kept using them, just to let folks know he was one of the guys.

"Good, I knew you were." The air in Mack's balloon seemed to release just enough so there would be no explosion.

Chris started to lift himself from the chair so he could leave the room, but Mack's large hand on his shoulder pushed him back down for a second time. "We've been going through the personnel records of Sheila Loewe, looking to see if maybe she had a valid claim. We forgot that you were her supervisor about three years ago."

Ambush!!! Ambush!!! The General screamed. "Just for a short time. When she was a junior account executive on one of my accounts," he cautiously let slip.

"As it turns out, you're the only person still with the agency that directly supervised her. That makes you an important person in this case." Mack's grin was back and that focus-on-the-target-look was returning to his eyes. "What did you think of her when she was working for you?"

At first, Chris groaned to himself, *Oh my God! I'm in the middle of this shit.* But as he was bemoaning his fate, it suddenly became clear that Mack just dealt him four aces, and it was his turn to bet. *What do I want? More money? A promotion? A bigger office?* Again, Chris embraced the craft of silence.

"We pulled your reviews of Sheila from her personnel file. You rated her very highly."

"I don't recall what I wrote. That was a long time ago." Until he decided what he wanted, he planned to remain as uncommitted as possible.

"Well, let me ask you this. Did you rate her highly because you thought she was very good at what she did, or did you give her these high grades because you wanted to encourage her." Clearly, an attempt to put ideas into Chris' head, and hopefully words into his mouth.

Mack went on, "I know there have been occasions where I gave someone a good rating, thinking they would want to live up to that expectation. Sometimes they did and sometimes they didn't. In fact, as I was just talking with Bob and Alex, they indicated they've done the same thing at times. Chris, have you ever rated someone higher than they deserved?"

So this is what agency's strategy would be... and this was The Moment. The agency wanted Chris to say in court that even though he had rated her highly, it was for motivational reasons; that she really didn't deserve the excellent ratings she received from him. In no uncertain terms, the partners in the agency wanted Chris to lie, to perjure himself, in the arbitration hearings, and in court. Chris thought, *I wonder if I can get them to make me a partner, if I do this.* Balancing on the fence, he conceded, "I'm certain I must have rated some people higher on some points over the years."

Mack leaned back and smiled. He could feel Chris coming on board. While he knew it was going to cost him something, for the first time in many years, he really respected Chris' gamesmanship. "I guess the question is this. Have you ever rated Sheila Lowe higher then she deserves?" Mack leaned forward and looked Chris right in his eyes.

How should I play this? Chris wasn't ready to show any of his cards, just yet. "To tell you the truth, I would have to re-read her reviews. I just don't remember."

Exasperated that he didn't get an immediate answer, but knowing he couldn't push this critical person too hard, Mack agreed, "That's fair." Sliding Sheila's employee file to Chris, Mack added, "The other point you may want to consider is her management capability. Did she really have any?"

"Again," Chris said reminding Mack that the price wouldn't be cheap, "I'll have to spend some time thinking about this."

"Unfortunately, time is a bit of a problem. The lawyers really need some kind of written statement from you by end of day tomorrow. Do you think you can do that?"

"I'll try." Chris headed to the door, declaring that he was ending this meeting, which made him feel powerful for the first time in years.

Back in his office, reading through Sheila's past reviews, he wondered: *What should I do? It's nice to be noble, but it'll get me fired.*

Opening a word processing document on the computer screen, he stared at a blank page, hoping some inspiration would come. Finally, he wrote: Sheila was an excellent employee, was shafted by the management of this agency, and deserves everything she can get. Sitting back, reading the statement over five or six times, he deleted the sentence from the screen. "So much for the truth."

Then he wrote: Sheila Loewe was an inadequate employee who I gave high grades to because she used to give me blow jobs under the desk. *They'd love me to say something like this.* He deleted the screen.

Let's get serious, he commanded himself: Sheila Loewe worked for me as a junior account executive. She was an excellent employee. (*That'll scare Mack.*) However, her responsibilities at that time were mostly clerical and involved almost no original thinking. (*That's lie number one.*) In fact, on several occasions when I was asked if she was ready for promotion, I expressed deep concern to Mr. Mack. (*If I'm going to lie, I want him down here in this with me.*) I recall one conversation when she was being considered for promotion, that we specifically discussed whether she had the basic instincts to be a manager.

Can I really do this? Can I sink this low?

At that moment Candy walked into his office, closed the door, and sat in the chair opposite him. He twisted the computer screen away from her. It was clear she had been crying, but she also had a determined look on her face. There was a distinct reason for her being there and she wasn't going to let her personal situation stand in the way of accomplishing that task.

Without the usual pleasantries, she blurted out her question. "Who are you going to stand with on this, Chris, the boys or the girls?"

"Is that how everyone sees it?"

"Yes." Candy was being unusually direct, and her usual pleasant demeanor had completely vanished.

"Are you here on your own or have you been sent by the..." Chris was going to say the "rats in the maze," but thought better of it, so he changed his words to, "...the other women in the office."

"Everyone's curious, Chris, where you'll stand on this issue. You're the most decent person in all of management, so we all think you'll be honest. But some people have doubts. They say you've always done anything you've had to do to save your own ass. They say you always put yourself first. I know that's not true, but we'd all like to know where you stand."

Again, though unconsciously, he began to use silence as his response. As much as he liked Candy and felt badly about her present situation, he was offended by her inquisition, and the comments being made about him by everyone. It's been a struggle just being here all these years, now the people he depended on and trusted were doubting him and criticizing him.

He stood up, which had always been his way of indicating he wanted whoever was in his office to leave. She stayed seated a few seconds longer than she normally would have, waiting for an answer, but out of respect for him, she left his office with nothing to report back to the other women.

Returning to his computer, he mumbled to himself, "So, it's the boys against the girls."

Chapter 47

The house was dark when Cathy returned home, but since it was after midnight, it was no surprise. The girls and the housekeeper would be asleep so she entered very quietly, hoping not to wake them. Fred was in Wisconsin this week, so she actually could look forward to a good night's sleep.

But how could she sleep, when she was as giddy as a high school teenager once again.

She was in love and the man she loved, loved her back. He made her feel like a woman, something that she hadn't felt in many years. His touch reminded her that sex could be beautiful and the joining of two bodies, heavenly. Her heart felt free. Her spirit felt free. She had escaped the underground world she had been living in and had come into the sun. It wasn't just a light at the end of the tunnel, it was like stepping out of a dark cave onto Broadway, with its bright lights, theatre marquees, and animated billboards.

No more would she have to fear evenings and weekends. No more would she have to sink under the water of her bathtub and wish to stay there forever. No more would she cry out in silent pain as a man lay on top of her.

Ten more days, and her body would be as free as her spirit now felt. The nightmare was almost over.

As she locked the door behind her and turned to silently walk up the stairs, her eye caught a strange blue light in the corner of the living room. It vanished, came back, then vanished again.

As she approached it, she saw the outline of a seated figure, and gasped at the thought of a burglar in her house. *How could he have gotten in? The alarm was still set. The absolute one time she really needed Fred, where was he?*

Carefully, inching back toward the alarm system, hoping the intruder didn't see her, she raised her hand to press the Silent Panic button and alert the Olympic Estates Security Force. But, then, as her eyes adjusted to the darkness, the shadowy figure took shape. She called out to him. "Fred?"

The mere utterance of his name carried a dozen questions. *What are you doing here? Are the girls okay? You're supposed to be in Wisconsin. What's wrong? Do you know about Chris?*

Pressing the keypad of her cell phone every few seconds to illuminate the screen, he responded, "You have some messages on your cell phone." The devil was in his voice. Looking at the blue screen, she could see it indicated that she had twelve messages. *Shit! I forgot to take my cell phone!* She had become so used to using pre-paid disposable phones in New York, she completely forgot to take the one the company pays for.

"I'll listen to them in the morning." *This isn't good. This isn't good at all. Something happened.* Hoping to cool him down, she placed her hand on his face. "I missed you. Let's go to bed." *Maybe a quick ejaculation will calm him down. I'm still pretty sore down there, but I can live with that.*

"I think you should listen to your messages," he commanded, which frightened her, but she had no choice, so she put the phone to her ear and played the messages. The first three messages were from the office reminding her about meetings or reports due.

But the fourth message...

The fourth message was from one of her closest friends from high school. "Hi Cat, it's Maxine. I'm so sorry you weren't able to attend the reunion. We all had such a great time. When I saw your name tag, I got so excited that we would finally hook up again after all these years. Bummer. I was so hoping to see you. I wanted to tell you about the new man in my life. There must have been over 100 of us there. You wouldn't believe what some of the people look like. I took some pictures. I'll e-mail them to you. As it turns out, I'll be in Minneapolis some time in July. I'll let you know when and maybe we can hook up there. I'm really disappointed you didn't show up. Hopefully, I'll get to see you soon."

Still feeling a little bit like a kid who just got busted for staying out late, she started to say, "It's unfortunate I missed the main reunion, but..." She was going to say that a bunch of the "in crowd" from high school went out together for dinner before the reunion and were having such a good time they never made it to the official reunion.

Fred cut off her explanation by saying, "Why don't you listen to the next message?"

Surprisingly, Fred wasn't screaming about being lied to and his hands weren't curling up into fists. Putting the phone to her ear, she moved as slowly as a death row inmate walking down the corridor for the last time.

"Cathy, where are you?" She recognized Stanley's panicked voice. Clearly in tears, he was begging her to call him immediately. "This is my fourth message. Where are you? Oh God, what a disaster! Call me immediately! Any time of the night! Please, I beg of you!" Now she wanted to hear the rest of the messages. The next two messages were woeful pleadings by Stanley for her to call as soon as possible, not matter what time of the night it was.

Listening to the last message, she dropped the phone and looked up at Fred. "You punched a client?" In a louder tone, "You punched a client because he wouldn't sign a purchase order? I can't believe you did that. How stupid could you be?"

"Why did Stanley call you?" He maintained a cold but laser focused tone. "What's going on here?"

"Nothing's going on except you just got yourself fired and THCC in the middle of a lawsuit." Frustrated and angry that all her plans for escaping this nightmare were rapidly disintegrating, she forgot all the cautions she usually exercised when talking to him and just yelled. Everything she struggled for over the past twenty-five years - her job, her title, her house – were incinerated. It will all come out. She'll be out of work, too. What would she and the girls do then?

"This is all you're doing, isn't it?" Anger was beginning to creep into his voice, and his eyes half shut as if he was aiming at her.

"No one forced you to punch a new business prospect but yourself," she screamed. The battle to keep her emotions under control was lost.

"I wondered why I was promoted to that territory. Other people deserved it more than me. I wasn't ready for it and everyone knew it. What did you do?" Even in the darkness of a room lit solely by reflections from the outside, she could see his face tensing up.

"I did nothing but recommend you. I thought it would be good for you to get off the order desk and into the field." She didn't have the energy to be angry any longer. She didn't have the energy for anything anymore. Everything was ruined. Nothing mattered anymore. Fred didn't matter. Tomorrow she would just walk out with the kids and find a place to stay. Maybe go to a shelter. Maybe go to her father in Florida. After all the years, and all the moves, and all the promotions, she would probably have to get a job as a secretary and live in a small apartment. She had nothing now. No money. No future. Some lawyer will have to work out the details of the house. Maybe she'd come away with something. Who knew what debt Fred had gotten them into.

Finally, he unleashed his artillery. "You knew I wasn't ready for the field! You knew I needed more training, but you conspired with Stanley to get me out there so I would fail!" Barrage after barrage vibrated the house to its very foundation, so there was no doubt everyone would be awake.

In a counter-attack equaling his, she blasted, "You've been working for the company for twenty-five years, how much more training do you need before you do something right?"

In the darkness, she never saw the fist that slammed into her stomach.

In the past when he hit her, those were always for some form of sadistic pleasure, or a frustration at not being able to find the right words, so his abuse, though painful, was restrained. But now, he was humiliated, plotted against, failed, cast out, and reduced to insignificance by some old bitch. Now he had no reason to show restraint. Now he was unable to show restraint.

Once again, he was the World's Heavyweight Champion, and once again the same Challenger dared to enter his ring. With his first punch he had her hung up on the ropes. With his second, third, and fourth, he pummeled her again and again and again in the stomach, in the chest, in the chest. She couldn't breathe or stand erect.

Catching her before she could drop to the floor out of his reach, his Goliath-sized hands clung to the clothes of her back. Bringing his hand down on her face like an evangelist in a battle with the Devil, he smote her with all his fury. He needed to destroy she who defiled his very soul. Once, twice, three times, he slammed his fist into her face. His gold-plated high school football ring tearing at her skin like razorblades, pressing into her flesh and shattering the small bones of he face.

When she was little more than a wet bath mat, soaked in her own blood, he tossed her, like a dead rat, into the red brick fireplace, as if touching her made him dirty.

"How dare you talk to me like that, you piece of shit! You think you're so desirable! Well let me tell you, no one else would have you! You're lucky to have me! You think you're so special! You're old and ugly! You're a rotten fuck! You're nothing!"

As if he was throwing a spear into at her to keep her nailed on a cross, he thrust her cell phone at her, hitting her in the chest, right above her heart.

"You fuckin' liar! Who were you fucking at that reunion you didn't go to? You were fucking that ad agency guy weren't you! I'll get him, too! You fucking whore! I can't believe I wanted to marry you! Thank God I found out what a piece of shit you are. I want you and those stupid kids of yours out of my house tomorrow."

At the point when he could do no more to hurt her, he grabbed the keys to her car and charged out of the house, screaming, "The worst day of my life was the day I met you! All this is your fault!"

Upstairs, Esmerelda did as she was instructed to do if she ever heard a violent argument between them. She gathered the two girls, who fortunately were too sleepy to hear the ruckus, and brought them into her room. Closing the solid core, wooden door, she slid the three, five-inch bolts that Cathy had installed on the door, turned on the prepaid cell phone she had been given for emergencies, and waited for either the "all clear" from Cathy or an attempt by Fred to get at the girls. As the yelling continued downstairs, she dialed 9-1-1 and kept her finger on the send button, ready to press it at the first sign of danger to the children she helped raise.

Gasping for air, between swallows of her own blood, Cathy lay down to die.

It wasn't the pain - she was beyond pain – she could feel herself slipping into a coma. As life drifted away, her last rational thought was that she wanted to say goodbye to Erin and Erika. If she could only hug them one more time, kiss them good-night one more time, she would be ready to leave this world.

At least she could leave this world knowing she had prepared for even this emergency. As soon as Esmerelda and the girls were in the custody of the police, they would use the emergency money that Cathy had hidden for them to take the girls to Denver, to their father. *Don't pack... just go...*

Good-bye Erika, Erin...

The little light she could see through her blood-filled eyes, grew increasingly dim. The faces of her daughters grew fuzzy.

It was finally over... no more beatings, no more pain.

Chapter 48

Cathy didn't die.

The excruciating pain that she now felt in her face, her chest, her stomach, woke her up and declared that she was still alive.

Wishing she was dead so she would never have to endure this again, but glad she was alive to protect her daughters, she lay motionless on the floor. She wanted to cry, but was unable to through the blood. She wanted to wipe the blood from her shattered face, but was unable to raise her arm from beneath her twisted body. All she could do was command herself to breathe.

Spitting blood into a small red pond, she tried to clear her lungs, but more air, brought the reward of more agony. It would have been easier to just stop breathing altogether. Now she could only think about the girls and the need to get them to safety. If he could do this to her, there was nothing that would stop him from attacking them. She had to breathe. She had to get help.

Motionless, unable to see through the red curtain that filled her eyes, she lay there for an hour... maybe two... worried that he would return and hunt down the children.

"Es...." She tried to call out to Esmerelda, but it was little more than the squeak of a mouse. "Es...."

Breathe in... breathe out... breathe in... breathe out... hurry... he'll be home soon... oh my God... this can't be happening... breathe in... breathe out...

Rolling over on her side, she could see the blood-blurred outline of a lamp, shattered into pieces on the floor beside her. There was the vase of fresh flowers drowning in its own pool of water, a shoe, a picture frame, and in the distance, the reflection off a silvery object. She tried to focus her eyes, blinking as often as she could. It was her phone.

If only I could get to my phone, she told herself. He'll be back soon to finish what he started. He'll be back soon to kill me and the girls.

But it was hopeless. It was too far away. The tears mixed with blood as she knew the brutal deaths of her daughters was imminent and she was powerless to stop it.

Imagining him tearing down the safety door in Esmerelda's room with the ax he kept in the garage... bludgeoning the three of them to death with the edge that he sharpened often... the guilt for having exposed her daughters to such life threatening dangers was more painful than anything he did to her.

How could I have done this to them? How could I have been so stupid?

She had to try to save them, regardless of the pain, or die trying.

With her toes she could feel the sharp edge of the black slate around the fireplace. Pressing her left leg against the stone, she heaved herself towards the cell phone, moving only a few inches closer. She tried to tell herself that no matter how horrible the pain was, it truly could be worse, and she passed out again for a few moments.

Coughing up blood woke her. She gasped to breathe. The warm blend of phlegm and blood traced a path across her cheek and dripped from her chin onto the carpet, but she didn't have the strength to raise her arm to wipe it away.

In the reflection of the moon light that poured into the room, she could see the darkness of the stain from the blood that poured out of her body, and she knew, soon she would bleed to death. She had to save the girls, now, while she still had some strength.

Her shoe was still on her right foot, so twisting her body, she dug the heel into the carpet and tried to propel herself forward. But the carpet proved to be a poor support and her legged slipped outward, kicking a picture frame, but not moving her forward even an inch.

Rolling back onto her stomach, she reached forward with her left hand, digging her nails into the thick, wool Berber. She had to do this. She had to do this now. Soon there would be no strength left in her body. Soon he would return to spit on her dead body and to kill the girls.

Please God, give me the strength.

She pulled herself six inches closer to the phone... and then she rested. In a funny way, it was comfortable just lying here. The carpet was warm and wet, and closing her eyes, she could dream of happier times.

A home movie of Erin and Erika played behind her bloody eyes... coming home from the hospital... the first step... the first birthday party... the first day of school... the first report card... She couldn't let their story end, not now, not so young.

With a great second effort, she again dug her nails into the carpet and pulled herself forward another six inches along the rough wool carpet that was sandpaper to her wounds.

Please God, help me.

Swinging her left leg back and forth, hoping to brace it against a piece of furniture for a big push forward, her foot only found a broken vase and a toppled pile of old magazines. She stretched her arm forward as far as she could, and again dug her nails into the carpet. Pulling herself forward six inches, she rested, then went another six inches before rest. Reaching forward yet again, she dug her fingers into the carpet, but before she could pull herself forward she felt the sudden, sharp pain of a nail at her finger tips. "Damn," she laughed with a gallows humor, "on top of everything else, I now have to get a manicure." Her arm was too weak to pull her forward anymore and she rested on the spot, closing her eyes.

Don't let me die, yet, God. Please, not yet.

But there was no rest until the children were safe, so again, she swung her left leg back and forth, searching for a sturdy support to press against. This time she found a wooden leg and pressed against it. But sadly, it was only an end table, too light to be of any assistance and it fell over with a loud crash.

"Es...," she tried calling out one more time, but her plea was drowned out by the blood she swallowed.

Soon, God. You can take me soon, but not yet.

Flaying with her right leg, she finally found a sturdier launch pad, and catapulting herself forward with the ferocity of a wounded lion desperate to protect its cubs, she flew through the air another seven or eight inches. Landing on her right side, an arrow shot right up her spine, and all the pain she felt as she was being beaten was re-lived.

Crying out, she begged, "Help me... help me, somebody... please God, save me... I can't do anymore." Blood and tears and mucous poured out of her body, and she knew that all she had to do to end this agony was to lie down, and let herself drown in the lake she created beneath her lips.

Any minute... he'll be back any minute... the girls.

Raising her head, she could see the reflection of the cell phone... it was almost in reach... but too far... It was hopeless... she no longer had the strength to move forward.

Fifteen minutes passed, maybe more, maybe less, but she opened her eyes again.

Flaying her left leg back and forth, she was able to latch on to another piece of furniture, she pressed forward one more time, screaming out to her daughters, "I love you."

It was close... she could almost touch it... just a little more... one more push...

One last time, she dug her nails into the carpet and pulled herself forward again, just enough so she could wrap her hand around the phone and pull it towards her. Holding the phone as dearly as when her new born daughters were put in her arms, she couldn't see the numbers on the keypad through the blood in her eyes, but like a blind person, felt the numbers and dialed 9-1-1.

Spitting up blood, with hardly any life left in her breath, she pleaded, "Help... please... help... ambulance... police."

She did it. She saved her girls. She could die now.

Dropping the phone, she closed her eyes and drifted to a place away from pain, and rested there. In the background, she could vaguely hear the crackling sound of the emergency operator calling out, "What is your address? How many people are there?" But that too faded into the mist that surrounded her body.

Ironically, GPS locator technology on her cell phone, which had been pioneered by THCC twenty-five years earlier, pinpointed the location of the house, and within 10 minutes, Cathy was on a stretcher being wheeled by paramedics into an ambulance, and police found Esmerelda and the girls and let them know that they were safe.

Chapter 49

Clutching a manila file close to her breast, Samantha power-walked down the aisle to Bob's office. It was highly usual for her to leave the fiftieth floor and visit someone on a lower floor, so when she offered to come down to see Bob, it was obvious he had something she wanted. Having become so used to being commanded to come up to see her, this sudden change made him feel powerful, but it also frightened him, because whatever she wanted from him would be "big" and he didn't know if he could deliver it, or worse, what it would cost him to deliver it.

Breezing passed the people on the lower floor, it seemed so crowded to her. It was hard for her to believe that people actually sat in six-by-six cubicles, and mid-management level offices were only ten-by-ten. A dark beige industrial carpet complemented the light beige walls and divider panels, and posters by famous artists hung on the walls instead of original art. Metal file cabinets lined the hallways instead of the wooden ones she was used to seeing, and vending machines substituted for the corporate chef.

So this is how the other half lives, she smirked, quietly admitting to herself, *this is how I used to live.*

She loved the corporate chess game of out-thinking and out-maneuvering one's opponents to get a better title, more power, more money. More importantly, she understood how to play the game better than anyone else. The most important rule to remember, she told Cathy one day over lunch, is to never ask for what you're asking for. Once they know what you want, they can position themselves against you. Always have them pointing their spears in the wrong direction. It's like politics, everything's about something else. Little did Samantha know that Cathy's second husband gave her the same advice a decade earlier.

She hated the thought of having to ask something of him, but as the Chairman of the Compensation & Promotions Committee - or The Committee, as everyone called it – Bob's vote on certain issues was critical, and this was one of those rare times that Samantha actually needed his support.

Bob was so easy to manipulate. He was so obvious and had one, and only one, focus – make Senior Management happy – so it was easy to use that as a bludgeon against him. She knew her request today would be unpopular, so coming down to see Bob, instead of having him come up to her, was the first move of her pawn. Whenever he was in her office, he was always able to avoid commitments by claiming he left information back in his office. This severed him from his favorite excuse.

"A lamb to the slaughter" was the only expression that she could think of to describe the coming meeting, and there was no doubt in her mind who was the lamb.

As she was about to walk into his office without knocking, Bob's secretary hastily, but meekly, called out. "He's having a meeting. It's going to end in a few minutes. Please have a seat." She indicated a small waiting area outside Bob's door. But Samantha couldn't sit; she could only pace, passing within inches of his wooden door.

From inside, she could hear men's voices and there was lots of laughter with phrases like, "punching bag," "always seemed so prim and proper," "must be desperate at her age," "divorced twice," and "Who knew she liked it so hard?"

While she never heard them mention a name, surely it was Cathy they were talking about - laughing at - and that only made her sharpen her teeth for the kill. "Get up," she commanded the secretary, who stood without a second's hesitation or concern about surrendering her desk.

Samantha sat at the secretary's desk, put her hands on the keyboard, opened a new word processing document and began typing immediately and rapidly.

"Wow, I never thought you knew how to type," the secretary offered in genuine surprise.

"How do you think I began at this company?" Samantha responded with the air of a professor telling a student, you can be anything you want to be and don't let anything hold you back.

Bob's meeting broke up a minute or two later and the men strutting out of Bob's office - all VP's - couldn't help but notice Samantha at the secretary's station. Since they were in a jovial mood from their meeting, and since there were six of them, they felt sufficient bravado to toss some humor at Samantha. "I like the way you look there."

"A perfect fit."

"Another promotion, Sam?"

"Getting back to your roots?"

Smiling, without saying a word, Samantha stood up and stared down the gaggle of vice presidents and they tripped into themselves as they hurried down the hall like a stampeding herd of buffalo.

Parasites that fed off the company and added nothing to it is how Samantha thought of Bob and these other middle managers. They stir up enough paperwork to make themselves look needed and they exist because they never do anything badly enough to get themselves fired. It pained her greatly that her efforts in securing new business were going to clothe and feed these blood-sucking, insignificant and invisible vermin.

The good thing - the only good thing - she contended, about parasites, like Bob, was that deep down, somewhere beneath their bombastic self-promotion, they knew they were parasites and feared that it would be discovered, which undoubtedly would cost them their careers.

Having a weakness like that meant that it could be exploited.

Deleting the electronic file she just created, Samantha turned to the secretary and said, "If that phone rings, I don't care if it's the President of the United States, don't you dare interrupt my meeting or I'll have you transferred to my department."

Knowing that Samantha could have it done with the snap of a finger, the secretary blurted out, "Yes, Ma'am," in abject fear.

"Come in, Sam," Bob called out. Indicating a chair for her to sit in. She obeyed, even though it was obvious he was placing himself in a position of superiority. "I'm glad you're here, there is something I want to talk about with you. But why don't you tell me what's on your agenda first." As the gallant gentleman, he waved his hand towards the file she clutched in her arms.

"No, Bob, it's your office. You go first." Samantha looked at Bob and the scent of lamb roasting over an open fire filled the room. While he was smart enough to know that every conversation with her was a chess match, he wasn't smart enough to make any smart moves to thwart her, so he blurted out his concerns as if he was talking to one of the gaggle who had just left the room.

"It's Cathy. With all the events of the last couple of days, I can't see how we can keep her in the company." He was using his "regret" voice which was well honed by all his years of performing layoffs and terminations.

Like Scarlett O'Hara trying to resist Rhett Butler, Samantha offered a weak defense, "But she's been with the company longer than you or I. How can we just turn our backs on her - particularly at this time?" She would have brought the back of her hand to her forehead, just like Scarlett did, to express the torment that this posed to her, but she thought such a gesture would be too humorous, so she just let her head drop a bit, and shifted her gaze to the floor.

"I feel badly, too." Sensing there was no real objection on Samantha's part, he threw his hands into the air, trying to appear as if he had fought hard for Cathy, but had been overruled by a higher authority. "But she can no longer hold the respect of her peers and subordinates, not to mention Senior Management."

Without saying a word, she let her body collapse, in what appeared to be total defeat.

"I'm going to propose to The Committee that we give her two years salary and keep her on our medical plan for a full year," Bob continued, proud of the generosity he was offering, since it really wasn't out of his pocket.

Samantha sighed, nodded, mouthed the words "Thank you," and continued to look at the floor.

Surprised that agreement was so easy, After all, they were both women, and they stick together on these things. Bob concluded by saying, "She's been loyal to the company and we have to do right by her."

Knowing Samantha, Bob assumed that she had already decided it was in her own best interest to let Cathy go and that was why she didn't offer any real objections. Having expected a terrible argument, he sat back in his chair and wondered how he would describe the meeting to Senior Management, so he would look more heroic.

They sat quietly for a few moments, as if at a memorial service.

Finally, after he felt the appropriate amount of time had passed, Bob asked, "Why did you want to see me, Sam?"

Unfolding an organization chart of the new Business Affairs Department under her management, she slid it in front of Bob. Quickly scanning it to see if there was anything unusual, nothing popped into his head. It looked like every other org chart of a multi-location department in the company. "It looks good. Is there anything in particular you'd like me to notice?" He couldn't imagine why she even brought it to his attention, which should have been a warning to him, but he wasn't smart enough to realize it.

"Well, actually, yes." She pulled her chair closer to the desk and using a solid gold, Mount Blanc fountain pen, she pointed to the box of the Director of Operations. The head of each office reported to this one position, and this position was the only one that had a direct line to Samantha. Clearly a critical and powerful position, it was the one that Samantha had offered Cathy. "I think this position should be a Senior Vice President and not just a Vice President."

Leaning back, he never took his eyes off the Director of Operations box. Something was beginning to smell wrong, but he couldn't put his finger on it. "That makes sense," Bob offered. "Since everyone who reports to this person is a vice-president, he (and then quickly added) or she, should be an SVP. I don't think there would be any trouble getting that through The Committee. I'll bring it up this week when we meet."

"Thank you, Bob." Samantha said, folding the org chart and putting the cap back on her pen, clearly signaling that the meeting was over. But, as she was standing up, she accidentally knocked the folder she had strategically laid on the corner of his desk onto the floor and a dozen or so papers fell out. Kneeling down to gather them all, she made some jokes about still being clumsy and that's why she wasn't a baton twirler in high school.

What made Samantha so effective in negotiations is that she would let people do the mental calculations for themselves. She would make a simple suggestion, a harmless request, an off-handed remark, or considered opinion, and then, in the silence that followed, would let her prey consider the implications. It usually took a few minutes for people to realize that something significant had just been said (or not said), but once they took the first step in agreeing to her position they were trapping themselves in a room with no exit.

Bob clearly was no mental giant, and waiting for him to realize something significant had just happened always took a lot longer than most, so she had to re-drop the files she picked up and laugh at her own clumsiness to the point where she couldn't think of anything else to criticize herself for. Finally, Bob cocked his head, and pointing a finger towards Samantha asked the question she was waiting for. "Why did you come down here to ask me that? You usually send a memo to The Committee when you want a title change."

She always enjoyed watching people's eyes as they started to calculate the meaning of her remark. She could see the glare into space as they mentally raced through the options that, in reality, didn't exist.

"Well, Bob, I'm glad you asked." With that she pulled out the page she had just typed and slid it in front of him. It was sheer joy to watch his face go from curious to uncomprehending to absolute horror. With a shaky, terror-stricken voice, he squeaked, "You're writing a letter to the President of the company asking him to have me work for you?"

"After the layoffs we just went through, other than Cathy, you're the only senior person in human resources." Just like in *A Christmas Carol* an apparition entered the room and climbed onto his desk. It was the ghost of Executives Past. Wearing a suit that had passed through a paper shredder, he carried a laptop computer that had a baseball size hole through it.

Brushing the roasting lamb with barbecue sauce, she said, "Bob, without a doubt in my mind, you're the most qualified SVP in the company. In fact, you're the only SVP with operational and human resources experience in this office." Staring in horror at the apparition his head began to shake from left to right, and muffled screams gurgled from his mouth, "No! Oh no! No!" His hands grabbed the arms of his chair, then released them, then grabbed them again, then released them again. The apparition reached and put his hand on Bob's shoulder, and in a voice echoing from the very center of the earth, bellowed, "Come with me."

As if it had been written with poison ink (poison laser toner), he pushed his chair as fast and as far away from the letter on his desk as he could get. Smashing into his credenza, a picture of his wife and two sons fell over, but he made no attempt to pick it up. Images of a horrendous future, ending in a humiliated termination, crossed his eyes. He couldn't imagine any fate worse in this company than the one presented to him now, and worse, he knew if she deposited the letter on the President's desk, it would be approved without question or hesitation.

But Bob wasn't a completely stupid, nor powerless, person. He couldn't have survived five changes of administration had he been completely unaware of the way the wind was blowing. He knew that there was no way he could work for Samantha, but he, also, knew that there was no way that she would want him working for her.

"What do you want?"

"Cathy." Samantha needed to say no more.

Closing his eyes, imagining the wisp of smoke that his career had become, he nodded his head. He didn't even have the strength to say the words.

When he opened his tear-filled eyes, the apparition was gone, but he knew it would be back as Senior Management expressed its displeasure that he didn't do their bidding properly. But in the spreadsheet of his mind, he calculated that he had a better chance of surviving Senior Management's disappointment than working for Samantha.

Getting out of his chair and walking to the window, as if he was about to jump, he wondered how he would present this to Senior Management. After all, he had never really challenged them as openly before and had no idea of what their wrath would be.

Samantha wished she could be present when the other parasites found out that Cathy - the woman they all laughed at - was now being promoted above them. For a moment she thought that having all of them transferred to her department would be a just punishment, but in the end, she decided it would be such a waste of time, and she was certain they would do more harm than good.

She gathered her papers and quietly left the office. She was always very good about letting her prey drown in their own self-pity. Though, before leaving the lower floor she stopped at the secretary's desk, whose wide-eyed look of panic betrayed her fear that she had done something to infuriate this woman. In a charming voice that bespoke of Samantha's proper upbringing, she said, "You're safe. You don't have to work for me."

With another scalp on her corporate spear, Samantha returned to the fiftieth floor from whence she had come.

Chapter 50

What should I do? Chris asked himself again and again.

No matter how many times he weighed the pro's and con's, the scales never changed. He could sell his soul for money, or he could keep his honor and watch his already-pathetic career take a final nosedive.

"What whistleblower ever ended up winning the Noble Prize?" He challenged himself to answer, "What's left for a has-been advertising executive?"

The irony of the whole situation was just so amazing to him. Sheila Loewe's husband was a very successful investment banker, and her salary was, literally, pocket change. The job was only meant to be intellectual stimulation, give her a sense of identity all her own. She even remarked to Chris once that she didn't want to become one of those rich men's wives who called themselves interior designers, but spent most of their time gossiping over lunch.

But, the fact that she was wealthy didn't change the fact she was treated very badly by the agency. Simply put, she was an excellent employee with great management potential.

"If I lie about her, I'm degrading himself. But I've been degrading myself for ten years just working at this shit hole," he mumbled as he walked along the ocean's edge.

What would Capt. Kirk do? Stepping back in time to his training as an actor, he tried to project himself into the character of one of his favorite TV roles. *Capt. Kirk always seemed to find a seemingly unavailable alternative. When presented with two unappealing choices, he always ingeniously found a third acceptable one. What is the third alternative that I'm not seeing?* No matter how he struggled with the issue, no acceptable choice ever presented itself.

It was getting late, so, unresolved, he headed for home.

Unfortunately, when he got home, he no longer had time to think about Sheila Loewe, and the Kingsley & Quincy Advertising Agency. Melanie was sitting at the kitchen table, tears rolling down her face, as she read the letter she had just opened.

"You fucking pig! You asshole! Who's this whore Cathy you're fucking!"

A fleet of Klingon ships had surrounded the Starship Enterprise and were pounding it, again and again, with photon torpedoes. "You prick! You don't fuck me, but you fuck every cheap whore you can stick your dick into! I warned you, if you ever fuck someone else you're out of here. Now, get out! You fucking piece of shit."

Battered and bruised, gasping for air, he couldn't believe that she found out about Cathy. *How could she have known? It was one time. In a city 3,000 miles away. She doesn't know how to get into my private e-mails. I threw everything in the washing machine or sent it to the dry cleaner as soon as I got home. She couldn't have smelled Cathy on me. There are no marks on my body. Who could have told her?*

"You fuck! I never thought that story of you having one brief affair all those years ago was all there was to it! You've been fucking whores all these years behind my back! Get the fuck out of here! You pig!"

Maybe it was time to finally put an end to all this cheating. Maybe it's time to finally confess my unhappiness and get a divorce. These affairs have to end.

The lying. The cheating. It's getting too exhausting. They're not as much fun as they used to be. This is the last one. Cathy's the one I've been waiting for my whole life, and I can have her now, and she's available. It's time to tell Melanie that the marriage is over. No reason to tell her about all the other affairs. Let her think I've just fallen in love with my childhood sweetheart and that I'm being stupid and having a mid-life crisis. It's time. No more sneaking around. No more stories.

But when there was a pause in her bombardment, instead of being honest, he did what men do. He denied it. "What are you talking about?" Chris tried to keep his voice at a normal volume, and sound both incredulous and wounded at the same time. "I'm not cheating on you. I didn't sleep with anyone."

"You fuck, you've been lying to me all these years and I know it. Why should I believe your fucking lies now?" With one wave of assault coming after another it was hard to sound like the calm voice of reason, especially when he knew that his torpedo tubes were empty and she had all the ammunition.

Finally, he exploded, and the neighbors up and down the hall heard him and opened their doors to see what was going on. "What are you talking about?"

Thrusting the grenade she held in her hand into his face, she screamed back, just as loud and just as disturbingly to the neighbors. "This, you fucking asshole. You're so ashamed of me that you have to introduce your bimbo to your precious tampon client as your wife."

The note, handwritten on very expensive, personalized stationery, read:

Dear Cathy,

I am writing to thank you for attending Hymie and my 50th Anniversary Party. I truly enjoyed meeting you, and I think you and Chris make such a wonderful couple. You remind me so much of Hymie and me when we were first starting out.

In the Jewish religion there is a belief that we each have one person we are fated to be with. It is called Basheert.

I can see that you and Chris have each found your Basheert, your destined one, in each other. I wish you both a long, happy life and many children.

Please call me next time you and Chris are in New York, I would love to go to lunch with you.

Love,

Esther

P.S. Enclosed is a recipe for cheesecake that I think Chris will love

In the two seconds that Chris had to decide how to respond, he decided to go the Shakespearean mixed-up identity comedy route, and he laughed. But as soon as the first chuckle left his lips, he wondered if it was a good idea because two nights ago they watched, for the tenth time, Chris' favorite movie, *Shakespeare in Love*, and he was afraid she might recognize the strategy.

"It was all a terrible mix-up." He was afraid that his attempts to sound light-hearted were sounding too artificial, but he was waist deep in the river now and the tide was too strong.

"A bunch of us got together for a drink before the reunion and I asked Cathy if she would go with me to the Herastein's cocktail party for an hour, so I would have someone to talk to. Mrs. Herastein is just being gracious."

Pretty good explanation, he congratulated himself, and she seemed to be buying it, though not completely, so he added, "I asked you to go with me to this party. I told you how important it was for you to be there. You said no, you couldn't get away. You had a deposition or a court date or something."

The Basheert-thing and the cheesecake-thing were still bothering her, but she was calming down. "You're going to a party with some bimbo, telling everyone she's your wife, and you're blaming me?" Her face was red, and she kept wiping the tears with the back of her hand.

"She's not a bimbo. She's someone I went to high school with. I just wanted to have someone to talk to while I was there. I told you I was going to go to the reunion after I stopped into the client's cocktail party. Let me show you her picture." Photos from the reunion were being posted on his school's alumni website and, banking on the fact that there was someone unattractive that he could point to, he quickly entered his password (Cathy) and signed on.

"And what were you and the high school girlfriend doing that people thought you were married?" The tears were stopping. The shouting had ended. He knew he could survive this assault. The starship Enterprise had broken free from the Klingon trap and was heading home, a bit wounded, but still intact.

"Stop that. Everyone at Envira knows I'm married," he lied, "so they just assumed she was you. It was that simple. I hadn't seen her in thirty years so I guess we really enjoyed seeing each other."

"It sounds like you and she were having a very long and personal conversation with Esther, but you couldn't tell her this wasn't your wife?" Having lost the battle, she was still trying to score some hits.

"No, I couldn't, as a matter of fact. It would have been embarrassing to my client. It was a large group, and it was very noisy. I couldn't hear what the conversation was. And the Envira guys were pulling me aside to talk about my presentation. I told you how important this presentation was. Actually, I think it's all kind of funny. By the time I realized what had happened, it would have been very embarrassing for Esther, and I didn't want to do that. Since I doubt you'll ever go with me to one of their functions, I figured they'd never know that Cathy wasn't you. It really was just a silly mistake." *God, I am good.*

"I find it hard to believe, very hard to believe," she emphasized, "that you would have looked like you were fated to be together according to some old Jewish legend if she was just doing you a favor by being there." Having a career filled with nothing but unusual stories, she was becoming more accepting of this one, and her normal composure seemed to be returning. She knew she was guilty of ignoring much of what Chris talked about every night since it often seemed so irrelevant, and it wouldn't have surprised her if he really did ask someone to attend the cocktail party.

Opening the photos from the reunion, he quickly scanned them to find the most homely, gray, fat alumni he could. Poking the screen at Judy De Vine's picture he declared, "That is Cathy."

Melanie moved closer to the computer and studied her closely. She had to admit, if Chris was going to cheat on her, he wouldn't do it with this woman, but why would anyone think they're a good looking couple. However, looking at this picture of someone 50 pounds overweight, it was pretty obvious why the subject cheesecake recipes came up.

Watching Melanie staring at the screen of his computer, it suddenly occurred to him that she could zoom into the badge that the woman in the photograph was wearing and see that it was Judy and not Cathy. It also occurred to him that he wasn't in any of the pictures, so he had to get her away from the computer as quickly as possible. He thought he should start a romantic "making up," but as hard as he tried, he couldn't get an erection, so he abandoned the idea.

Pulling her away from the computer with the announcement, "I have to write an important e-mail to Mack." But he added as sort of a wag-of-the-tail in the Klingons' face, "You delay court dates everyday of the week for your scum clients. The next time your husband asks you to delay a court date for something that's important to him, maybe you should consider doing so."

The argument was over. They each went to their corners and sat in silence. What she wanted to say was, "If I find out you're sleeping with somebody else I'll ruin you! You won't have a penny left to your name!" But she chose not to.

He would have loved to have gotten that letter to Cathy, but he knew he couldn't. In fact, he would have loved to get any letter to Cathy, but he didn't know how to do it. She'd been out of touch since he got back, and he was worried.

Actually, he did have to write to Mack regarding the K&Q case, so he sat down and typed:

Mack,

After thinking about the situation regarding the former employee in question, let me say that I agree in principle with your thinking. However, I have to respectfully disagree with the corporate attorney's instructions to put my thoughts in print. My wife, who you may recall is also an attorney, suggests there are legal and strategic reasons for not committing to paper. Not only would a pre-meditated reversal of Sheila's reviews seem suspicious, but it could become part of the discovery process, which could work against us. Her opinion is that my admission of different feelings about the employee would seem more genuine if it happened spontaneously when asked the appropriate question by K&Q's attorney, in front of the arbitrator. According to my lawyer-wife, who is representing me in this matter, and whose advice I therefore must adhere to, having anything in writing could be damaging. Upon her advice, I also must ask you to delete this e-mail.

Chris

While he was thinking of telling her about it, he actually never mentioned the case to his wife, but the stalling tactic seemed to work. The next day in the office Mack patted Chris on the back, and gave him a thumb's up.

Chapter 51

With half of her face covered in bandages, and with severe swelling and discoloration blurring her vision, Cathy could see little more than a blur of a tall person standing in front of the window six feet away. Raising her hand to her face to try to understand why she couldn't see out of her right eye, her fingers scrapped against the fibrous gauze. With the little strength she had, she explored the bandage, moving her left hand to the top of her head, and down almost to her chin.

Where am I?

As her senses slowly returned, the antiseptic smell and blurry image of lights on medical equipment, made her realize that she was in the hospital. She hadn't died. She was alive.

Blinking several times, she tried to focus with the one eye that wasn't covered, but the painkillers that filled her system guaranteed she would only be able to open her eyelid no more than halfway. Trying to make the features of the form that stood by the window of the room, she called out to the one person she wanted to see more than any other, "Chris?"

The slim form moved towards her, and around to the left side of the bed, so the light from the window reflected off her face. Bending over the uncovered eye, the form said, "Good morning, welcome back to the land of the living."

"Sam?"

"I flew in last night when I heard what happened. Why didn't you tell me you were having trouble with Fred? I would have helped you. Castrating men is my specialty." Samantha was still reveling in the joy of what she had just done to Bob.

Cathy could half understand the words, but was comforted by the reassuring sound of Samantha's voice.

"You're really drugged up. You've been asleep for a couple of days," Samantha explained knowing that Cathy was completely confused. "You're at Avalon General Hospital." She wanted to burst forth with the good news about Cathy's promotion, but knew this wasn't the right time.

"Girls?" Cathy whispered. As the memory of that awful night came back, she had to know if she managed to save them or if her worst fear was realized.

"Right now, they're on their way to see their father," Samantha explained with great satisfaction that she was able to take care of matters efficiently. "I spoke with the principal and he understood completely. Their grades won't be affected. And I spoke with their father. You're right. He is quite boring. How could you ever have married him?" She laughed, but continued her explanation. "They were here earlier this morning to say good-bye. I told them you would call them as soon as you woke up."

"Fred?"

The smile of Athena, the Goddess of the Hunt, crossed her face. Clearly, she was delighted by what happened to the scum that so badly hurt her friend. "With any luck, by now, he's been raped by every prisoner in cell block C." Becoming more serious, she described with delight what would happen to him. "He's never going to hurt you again, Cathy. You have my word on that.

"They picked him up at the bar at his golf club. He's in jail right now and he goes before the judge tomorrow morning. If he can make bail, they'll let him out. But that might be a bit tough considering my lawyer friend froze all his assets. And as you can imagine, he doesn't have a job. Come to think of it," she really enjoyed detailing this part, "he doesn't have a home to go to either. There's a restraining order that prevents him from going anywhere within 500 feet of your home, and I placed an armed guard there with instructions to shoot to kill if he comes anywhere near the house."

Cathy couldn't see the joy in Samantha's face as she described how she was systematically destroying the slime that was so brutal to a defenseless woman. "He's actually better off in prison. At least, he'll have food and a roof over his head."

Cathy raised her hand to the bandages, as if to say, "How bad is it?"

"The worst of it is a break in the bones around your nose and eye. As soon as the swelling goes down they'll be able to operate. Fortunately, everything is operable and there's no permanent damage. I asked the surgeon, who's single and rather cute, by the way, if he could take out that little bump in your nose that you've always hated, and he said he would. The arms and legs are just pretty bad bruises. The swelling and discoloration will go down over time. You'll be here for several weeks, so just rest. I'm taking care of everything."

With that reassurance, Cathy fell back into a healing sleep.

Chapter 52

The day of the hearing Chris went to the arbitrator's offices in Santa Monica, where he had to wait in a lounge area with the fifteen other employees of the agency. By now, it was clear to all that he was the key to the agency's defense, and word had gotten out that he would be taking management's side in this controversy, so no one wanted to sit near him.

Kingsley & Quincy's lawyers didn't contest the fact that Gary was foul-mouthed and created an uncomfortable work environment - there were far too many witnesses against the agency on those claims - so they were willing to settle on those issues. It would cost some money, but a little belt tightening here, and a layoff or two there, would make the financial impact less painful.

But on the charges of discrimination based on gender, they had to stand firm since this could result in a settlement of millions of dollars. The agency management was willing to admit it didn't do a particularly good job recruiting women executives, and as part of its case it presented a plan to correct that. However, they flatly refused to acknowledge the charges of discrimination based on gender against Sheila Loewe.

Each side was able to selectively use aspects of the agency's personnel files to support its claim. The agency contended that job-hopping was common to the advertising industry, and that the women – and men - who were ready to move up frequently jumped to other ad agencies. After all, being relatively small, Kingsley & Quincy just never had many opportunities for promotion. Supporting their claim were executive recruiters (the ones that they used over the years), all of whom detailed the high turnover rates of the profession.

Sheila Loewe's lawyers called as witnesses ten women who left the agency because they felt they couldn't be promoted. However, for every woman that claimed discrimination based on gender, the attorneys representing K&Q, made a strong argument that the person who ultimately was promoted, and who happened to be a male, had more qualifications for the position.

Sheila was the glaring exception. At the point Gary was promoted, she had several years more experience, and her performance reviews were consistently better than Gary's. She even received more compliments from the client than Gary.

While in the agency, she had had two supervisors - Barry Balin and Chris O'Dess. Barry, still in a depression over the break up of his marriage, was considered an unreliable witness, so that left Chris. If Chris could blunt Sheila's claims that she was clearly the better candidate for the job, the agency might be able to win the case, or at worst, get out of the whole mess with a small financial penalty.

Both sides knew the importance of his testimony, and they carefully prepared their questions to elicit the most favorable responses. When it was decided by the arbitrator that Chris would be called after the lunch break, Sheila leaned over to her lawyer and whispered, "I don't like this. Mack is smiling too much."

Chris sat alone at a table in the building's cafeteria. Pretending to be doing important work for his Envira client, he was actually searching the internet for any mention of Cathy. It had now been over a week since they were together, and he hadn't heard a word from her. Disgusted by his own actions, he scanned obituaries in Minneapolis newspapers, fearing that Fred might have beaten her to death, or that she carried out her pledge and shot him to death. He searched Google for "domestic violence, Minnesota" wondering if something would come up on some blog about an incident involving her. Fortunately, he didn't find anything about her being brutalized or dead. Unfortunately, he didn't find anything about her and didn't know what had happened to her.

Before going into the hearing room, he stopped into the men's room to check his appearance. As he was combing his hair, Mack entered, checked to be certain they were alone, and walked up to Chris, pulling an envelope out of his jacket pocket.

"Mack," Chris said, "I'm not sure this is a good idea." Flashing through a hundred grade B movies, he thought there was money in the envelope. "I don't think we should be talking." Mistakenly, Chris had thought he was safe in the arbitrator's offices, and now, trapped by Mack in the bathroom, with no witnesses, made him physically frightened.

"This is not about the case. Regardless of what's happening here, we still have a business to run." It was about the case, and Chris knew it. Mack had barely mentioned Envira since this whole lawsuit began. "I'm a little concerned about what's happening on the Envira account."

"What do you mean?" Stepping back, Chris felt Mack's hand grab his arm and pull him closer.

"Do you know who a Joseph Arimather is?" Chris could smell the egg salad that Mack had for lunch on his breath.

"He's the VP of Manufacturing and Marketing at Envira. Why?" *This is bad.* Mack had never heard Joseph's name before.

"Well, he sent me this note." There was that smile. The hunter had his prey in his sights. "He says he's in charge while the president is on his second honeymoon. A six-month trip around the world, as I understand it. He has formally instructed the agency to halt all spending immediately, and to cancel all media and creative development. He also," Mack paused for emphasis, "wants to know why he received an invoice for $74,369 for creative development since they never asked for the development of a TV commercial. Apparently, you told them that it was the responsibility of the ad agency to present ideas to them that we think can help their business." Silently the hunter lifted his rifle, placed the crosshairs of his scope over the heart of the mighty beast, and squeezed the trigger.

The bullet charged out of the barrel and hit Chris dead center in his chest. "He also made some rather disturbing remarks about you. He wants you off the account."

The color drained from Chris' face, and he dropped back against a sink. Wiping his hand across his mouth, he muttered something about Mr. and Mrs. Herastein being away for a couple of months on a second honeymoon, and when he comes back, everything would be okay... but he knew it wasn't true.

"Well, let's talk about this back at the office." Then Mack added in a friendly voice, after a slight pause, "...after your testimony." Releasing Chris from his grasp, he washed his hands and headed for the bathroom door. Placing his foot at the base of the door so no one could come in unexpectedly, he added, "Now that you're no longer working on that tampon account, maybe you can take over for Gary, since he's no longer with the agency."

Mack left Chris standing alone in the center of the men's room. His face had gone white. His breathing came in short, rapid gasps, and the sweat dropping from under his arms was turning into a rainstorm. He read the letter over and over, staring at it in disbelief. *Exposed. He was exposed. Everything about the Big Lie was known. It was over.*

Looking at the postmark, he realized that it was almost a week old. Mack had this, literally, in his back pocket and was going to bludgeon Chris with it. He had planned this little encounter. A little insurance to make sure things go his way. That's why Mack wasn't upset about not receiving a written statement. "I can't believe this!" Chris hissed, "That fucking asshole doesn't trust me and is using this letter to blackmail me."

Well, that settles it, was his first thought. *If he thinks I can't be trusted just wait till he hears me tell the truth.* For ten, maybe fifteen seconds, he was committed to honesty and moral justice.

But, *Wait a minute, he just offered me a promotion and a raise. He wants me to take over Gary's account. That's funny. It should have been mine all along and now it is. There's some sort of justice here.* He had to give credit to Mack. It was easy to underestimate him because of his bald, pudgy appearance. But he was cunning, and by offering Chris the promotion, he was protecting his flank from surprise attacks. The General would be impressed.

Without a doubt, Mack wanted Chris as a comrade in arms in this battle, not a hardened adversary. If Chris lied for the agency, Mack wouldn't want some disgruntled ex-employee talking to the district attorney telling tales of coercion, he would want his co-conspirator right there next to him.

Lunch was over and it was time to go into the arbitration room.

The doorway to the meeting room opened onto a twenty-foot long conference table. The arbitrator's back was to him, and Chris was expected to sit at the far side of the room facing the arbitrator. On the left as he entered, were the agency's partners, its attorneys, and Gary Accolon.

On the right, sat Sheila Lowe and her attorney. She tried to make eye contact with Chris, but that drew a reprimanding stare from the arbitrator, so she dropped her face into some papers.

As he inched towards his seat, Chris' eyes swung back and forth between the two sides of the table. On the left, the scum of the earth. On the right, a nice, decent, very competent employee. On the left, my career. On the right, someone who doesn't need a job. On the left, people who only think of themselves. On the right, someone who worked hard, and was always willing to help others. On the left, those who think workers are just drones who should be eaten when they no longer served their purpose. On the right, one of those drones.

On the left, Chris sadly concluded, *is my car, my condo, my clothes, my future. On the right is someone I'll probably never see again the rest of my life regardless of what happens here today.*

As Chris slipped into his chair, the arbitrator began, as he had done for each witness, by summarizing the charges being brought against K&Q and explaining the legal nuances of the case. Chris really wasn't listening. His mind was still playing ping pong across the conference table, weighing the arguments for supporting one side or the other.

Images of the past twenty years in advertising, particularly the last ten at K&Q, floated in front of him. A lot of late nights sitting around eating pizza and trying to come up with a creative idea. The celebrations at the launch of a new campaign, and the gallows humor (and alcohol) of the creative postmortems when things flopped. The camaraderie of a team working together. The industry parties. The satisfaction of knowing that you're good at what you do. *Even this presentation to Envira was a thing of beauty,* he told himself. *I had everyone in the room hanging on my every word.*

"Chris. Chris?" The arbitrator had begun asking questions, but he didn't hear them because he was lost in thought.

"I'm sorry, I was just... I'm sorry. I didn't hear your question. Would you please repeat it."

"Would you please describe the nature of your working relationship with Sheila Loewe. "

"Sheila was an assistant account executive working on Pick Up Styx, the Chinese restaurant fast food chain. I was the account supervisor. She and two account executives reported directly to me."

"Was she an assistant account executive on the account when she first started reporting to you?"

"No, she was an account coordinator." So far so good, Chris thought, since this was all a matter of record in her personnel file and both sides had the information.

"Did she receive a promotion from account coordinator to assistant account executive while reporting to you?"

"Yes." Still information from the records

"Did you support that promotion?"

"Yes." Chris thought that by not elaborating he couldn't be accused of helping either side. He didn't dare deny it since he wrote a memo recommending her for the position.

"Is it not true that she was promoted after only three months as an account coordinator?"

"Yes." Still facts.

Sheila, her lawyer, and even the arbitrator were getting a bit frustrated at the brevity of Chris' answers. The agency management and their lawyers were satisfied that Chris was "on the team."

"Would that be considered a short period of time before someone receives a promotion?"

Again, Chris knew that both sides had all the records so there was no point in committing. "Yes. However, others have done it, too. It all depends on the needs of the agency."

"How long did she report to you?"

"A year and a half."

"Under what circumstances did she move from reporting to you to reporting to Mr. Balin?"

The interview was getting closer to the point where he would have to take sides, but he hoped he could remain factual and non-committal if he just kept his answers to a minimum. "The agency got a new piece of business and she moved onto the account. It's very common in the agency business."

"Did she go over to the other account as an assistant account executive?"

"No, as an account executive."

"So, she was promoted?"

"Yes." Again, a matter of record.

"Did you support that promotion."

"Yes." Another memo from him supported that promotion, too.

"Did you feel she was more deserving of the promotion to replace Barry Balin than Gary Accolon?"

A very direct question. All eyes stared straight at him. He pondered his response for a few moments trying to decide what the safest response was. He needed to come up with the most middle of the road answer that he could think of: never worked with Gary... didn't know the demands of the client... never really spoke with Bob about Sheila...

Realizing that Chris was going to be a difficult witness, the arbitrator sat back and turned him over to the two attorneys.

Chris sighed with relief. He never really had to take one side over the other. All he did was report historical facts. No one could accuse him of lying based upon what he said here today, nor could he be attacked for supporting the men of management against the women workers.

Glad that John Spencer, K&Q's attorney, was going first, Chris sat back and prepared himself for some softball questions.

However, that wasn't Spencer's strategy. He wanted to destroy the enemy's best weapon and to stomp on their bodies before they had the chance to re-group. "Tell us, when you made these recommendations for promotion, did you have any hesitation or concerns about Sheila's ability to perform the tasks."

A six month old puppy dog that was kicked in the face with the boot of its master, couldn't have looked as woeful. Desperately wanting to cry, but afraid to do so in front of everyone, he pretended to sneeze into a tissue.

Everything was falling apart. His wife didn't trust him. Cathy had disappeared. Envira was gone. Everyone at the agency hated him. There was no Susan anymore. And now he was going to either be the tool of his own destruction or of somebody else's.

Too much. Too much to deal with. Why me? What did I do to deserve all this?

Chris' eyes drifted around the room hoping to find something to rest on. The meeting was being held in the legal library. It was a good choice of rooms for this meeting. There was a wall of law books behind Sheila and her lawyer, as if to say, in this room, the full weight of the law is being meted out. Behind Mack and his team were floor-to-ceiling glass windows, with a magnificent view of the Pacific Ocean.

Chris wondered if he should have brought his own lawyer to the meeting, but then it occurred to him that he didn't need to hire a lawyer, he could have brought Melanie. But at that moment he also realized that he never even told her about all that was going on, that he might need legal assistance... he also realized that he never thought about his wife very often... especially since he Cathy was back in his life.

Cathy... boy, is this ever not the time to think about Cathy.

"Chris, would you like me to repeat the question?" Spencer asked.

There was another long moment of silence, which was getting very annoying to both sides. Chris tried to recall if any of The General's military idiom's could help him here. But there was none that he could recall. And Captain Kirk seemed to have no more solutions for him either.

"Chris, would you like me to repeat the question?" Spencer asked again.

Those on both sides of the table looked at each other, and then to the arbitrator, hoping that she would force Chris to testify.

"No." Chris responded.

Everyone in the room was a little puzzled. He didn't want to have the question repeated, but he didn't want to answer it either.

"You don't want me to repeat the question?" Spencer asked.

This was it. This was the commitment of a lifetime. The biggest commitment he made since saying "I do."

"No. Because 'no' is my answer."

Irritated at the semantic game, Spencer challenged, "Which

question did you just answer?"

"You asked," Chris spoke slowly so everyone would know where he stood, "if I had any hesitation or concerns about Sheila's promotions, and I'm responding, 'No.' I didn't have any concerns about her ability to perform the tasks required."

Sheila and her attorney smiled, while the agency's team went into controlled chaos.

Grasping at a straw, trying to understand how his key witness, whom we was convinced he had in his pocket, could be answering questions that supported the opposition, Spencer sought to clarify, "Isn't it true that the positions she was promoted to were more clerical in nature?"

"Quite the contrary, they required a great deal of managerial capability and original thinking," Chris responded with confidence in his voice, "qualities that Sheila demonstrated superbly. Her work was superior and she deserved the promotion, certainly much more so than Gary did."

Spencer sat down. Sheila's lawyer decided he had no questions to ask, and Chris was excused. He left the room by passing behind Sheila. He turned his head so he wouldn't have to look at anyone on the other side of the table.

Chapter 53

Returning to his office immediately after giving his testimony, Chris just wanted to collect his personal items, delete personal information from his computer, and get out quickly so he wouldn't have to see Mack again. It was time to just put this place, and everything that happened, behind him.

And, if truth be told, he also came back to collect the accolades of his fellow employees (especially, the women). After all, he was the biggest loser in the whole affair. He was out of a job, wouldn't be able to get a reference, and certainly, wouldn't be able to duplicate this salary at another job. There was something Knights-of-the-Round-Table about it. In the name of a woman's reputation, he sacrificed his life (well, his career). That should be worth a pat on the back, or a kiss on the cheek. But when he got back to the agency, he found he was a total pariah. He was nobody's hero.

After Chris testified, the lawyers for K&Q decided to forego any further arguments and just talked settlement. At some point, Mack exploded and declared that, thanks to Chris, half the agency would have to be laid off because of the amount of money they would have to pay out.

Someone (a male) standing in the corridor overheard the comment and called someone at the agency (also a male). From that moment, the male dominated agency was blaming Chris for all the terminations that were coming. "Those bitches are going to walk away with millions of dollars, and I'll be out of a job," was the curse that raced down the corridors, and grew and grew until it was known by all that, thanks to Chris, the agency was closing down.

As Chris strode down the hallways, doors closed as he approached, gossip-mongers dispersed as he appeared, and even the Rats in the Maze slid down out of sight.

One woman, who didn't identify herself, left a note on his desk that read, "Thanks, from all of us women. We appreciate what you did for us, even though it doesn't seem like we do right now."

When he went to the coffee room to collect his favorite cup, he had to laugh. The handle had been broken off and it was already in the trash.

Ironically, the settlement reached by Sheila Loewe and the other women was very modest and would have very little impact on the agency's financial performance. Much to the distress of their lawyers, the women weren't as much interested in financial reward, but rather fought this battle for principle. Seeing Gary kicked out of the agency was the greatest reward, though they did allow themselves to accept half a million dollars.

The reality was that the savings on the salaries of Barry Balin, Gary Accolon, and the women who left, coupled with the elimination of bonuses and salary increases for the next year or two, and a few strategic layoffs, K&Q could easily cover the cost of the settlement without a significant effect on the agency's profits. The Envira account was gone, but it was never very significant, so it wouldn't be missed.

Chris looked out his window for the last time. What an odd turn of events. One day you have a good paying job, respect of the people around you, and the next day you're out of work, collecting unemployment, and hated by everyone. All I did was give a very good employee, a very good review, three years ago, and now I'm out of a job.

With all that was going on, he hadn't had much time to think about Cathy, but he was worried. It had now been over a week and he hadn't heard a word from her. He stopped calling her office since the secretary recognized his voice, and none of his e-mails were returned. He had absolutely no way of getting in touch with her - he didn't even know where she lived.

As worried as he was about her, he had to smile at what Mrs. Herastein said about them being perfect for each other. What was the word she used? Cathy was his Basheert - his destined one.

Sitting on the floor, emptying out the bottom drawers of the file cabinets and building a replica of Stonehenge from sample boxes of Envira tampons, he was suddenly struck by the looming figure of Mack in the doorway. Sliding slowly behind his desk in fear of physical violence, he searched with his finger tips in his box of possessions for anything that could be used as a weapon.

"I cannot believe I'm about to say what I'm going to say." His angry, but controlled, voice announced. "On advice of counsel, because of your advanced age and because of your long working relationship with this company, I am not going to terminate your employment since it would appear as if I am taking retribution on you and would expose the company to another harmful lawsuit."

As shocked as Mack was, Chris was even more so and he released his grip on the ballpoint pen that he was prepared to use as a weapon if attacked. Mack wasn't so much speaking these words as reciting a script given to him by his attorney. Shoulders dropping, shaking his head, he continued, "Furthermore, in light of the situation with Bob, Gary and Sheila. I'm promoting - I can't believe I'm saying these fucking words to you - I'm promoting you to their accounts." It was hard to say who was in greater disbelief at that moment.

"However," Mack declared with a clenched fist that was absorbing all his hate, "there will be no increase in salary. You have no chance whatsoever to get a bonus, and you'll have to make do with whatever remnants of a staff are left. You get to hire no one and I don't give a fat rat's ass if that means you work 100 fucking hours a week. If you don't like the deal, quit and make me the happiest man on earth. In fact, I think I really hope you fuck up royally on this assignment so I have a legitimate reason to hang your ass on the wall."

Walking away from Chris' office, he instructed, "Tomorrow morning, you and Sandy get your fucking asses down to San Diego and you do whatever you have to do to make the client happy again, and I don't care if it means you got to suck every dick in the place."

Chris wasn't sure what to do. Jump up and cheer that he still had a job, cry that he still had a job, just walk out because this place was so disgusting, or maybe, just leave and go find Cathy.

He had to talk to someone about what just happened. Cathy was incommunicado. Melanie was probably in court. Susan - he didn't want to start up with her again. Candy... Candy... Where was Candy?

Suddenly, he realized, he hadn't seen or spoken to her in days. She called in sick three days ago, but no matter how sick she was, she always checked in with him everyday.

He buzzed her desk to see who would answer. It was Lillian, Barry Balin's former secretary. Clearly, she was quite upset, and had conflicting feelings about Chris. She was very surprised, and delighted, that he supported Sheila and the other women, but she fully expected him to be fired. Now that he was assigned to Bob's account, he would undoubtedly bring Candy with him, which meant that she, a single mother, was out of a job. Not sure how she felt towards Chris, she explained to him curtly and professionally that Candy had called in and said she was taking all her vacation days and sick leave, and wouldn't be back for three weeks.

Dialing her house, the phone rang twenty or thirty times before she finally answered. "Candy, it's Chris. What's going on? How are you?"

Incoherent, she obviously had been crying for a long time, but pieces of phrases burst through the gasps, sniffles, and tears. "Over." "Break up." "No wedding."

"I'm coming over right now!" Chris asserted.

"No, don't, don't" she begged.

"I'm coming over right now." Slamming the phone down so she couldn't convince him not to come over, he rushed out the door.

As he raced past the gold leaf scripted words Kingsley & Quincy Advertising Agency, he did what he did every time no one was around, he stuck the middle finger of his right hand in the air, and with a silent bravado declared, "Fuck you, you assholes!"

At her apartment, Chris had to ring the downstairs buzzer for five minutes before she finally let him into the building. When he knocked on the door, she kept yelling, "Go away," but he wouldn't, and she only opened the door when he threatened to have the police kick it down.

The apartment was in total disarray. As soon as he walked in he was assaulted by the foul odor of excrement and urine. Candy had four cats, and hadn't cleaned their litter boxes in more than week. The cats were eliminating everywhere and on everything. There were piles of tissues, paper towels, and bathroom tissues that Candy had been crying into and didn't care where she dropped. Food and beverage containers were spilling their contents onto the counters and the floors, and pillows, blankets, clothes, and towels were strewn everywhere. It's as if she had taken everything she owned, threw it all up in the air, and left it where it landed.

Passing through the living room, he could see Candy, lying in bed face down, crying into a pillow, wearing the white wedding dress she was supposed to be married in. As he got closer to her, it was painfully obvious that she hadn't taken it off for days. Sadly, it was torn, stained, and twisted.

There were no words he could say to make her feel better, and he knew it. He just wanted her to know that she was loved by many people, so he sat down on the bed and rested his hand on her back. He said some soft things to her. "Everything will be okay. Things will work out for the best." It wasn't so much the words, but the gentle, caring tone of his voice that mattered.

She curled up in his arms because she needed to be held by a man. He could feel the warm wet tears as they ran down her cheek and onto his finger tips. He stroked her head, and pulled her closer. She wanted to forget the thousands of nights she slept alone with no one to hold her, no one to be warm next to her.

She turned to him and kissed his lips. He kissed hers because he didn't want her to feel that a man was pulling away from her again. She rose up and pushed him backward onto the bed, slipping her hand into his pants and touching his penis.

He started to rise up, but she begged, "Please, please."

He didn't want to have sex with her, but she so desperately needed to be loved, to be touched, to feel wanted, and she needed that right now, from someone who truly cared about her, or she would die. So he made love to her - but he needed help - he needed to pretend that he was with Cathy. Closing his eyes, he drifted back decades. He wanted to remember the overwhelming passion he felt the first time he fell in love. The tree they carved their initials in. The pebbles being tossed in the pond. The first time he was inside her and they truly became one.

The rush of semen surged from his body to hers, and she began to cry, whispering, "Thank you."

He kissed her a final time on her forehead, eased himself out of her, got dressed and called her cousin. He waited till she arrived so Candy wouldn't be alone. Then he went home.

Chapter 54

"I heard what you did," Melanie said as he walked though the door.

Astounded at how fast she found out that he slept with Candy, he was too exhausted to lie any longer, especially after today.

If she wants to kick me out, so be it. But how did she find out? Did Candy or her cousin call here as soon as he left to tell Melanie? But that was only thirty minutes ago, and why would they call? Maybe she's been having me followed by one of her private investigators. Isn't that amazing. After all these affairs, I get caught the one time I have sex because I'm trying to make someone feel better.

Gently taking his hand, Melanie pulled Chris into the bedroom, pulled him onto the bed, and kissed him with a passion he hadn't enjoyed in many years.

She's kissing me because I slept with Candy?

"Lillian told me what happened. She called to ask me if my firm was hiring secretaries. I can't believe you didn't tell me you were having problems like this. All you ever said was there was something to do with a television commercial."

He mumbled a few phrases about not wanting to upset her, but before he could finish, she kissed him again, with a love and respect and a passion that evoked many happy memories.

"The women at the agency are all astounded that you took Sheila's side and endangered your career." What was left unsaid was that Melanie, too, was astounded at his sacrifice.

Opening his pants she began to massage his penis.

Oh, my God. Not now, he screamed silently. Recalling the day he had slept with Melanie and two girlfriends, he prayed for an erection. He knew if he thought about Cathy it would help him get hard, but he was afraid that if he thought about her he would call out her name, so he tried to get hard thinking about the early years with Melanie - but it wasn't happening.

He thought that maybe if he started detailing the arbitration hearing, she would get interested in that, from a professional point of view, and forget about the sex. "But I didn't get fired, I got promoted." He started to tell about his conversation with Mack (leaving out the part about him having to suck the client's dick), but she cut him off.

"That doesn't matter. When you testified you thought you were going to be fired, but you did it anyway."

Sensing that he was still soft, Melanie dropped down on her knees, pulled his pants off, and began to suck on his penis. It was working.

Chapter 55

"It sounds like you got yourself into a real mess this time," Cathy's father accused in the gruff and distancing voice that she had known all her life. "What did you do to get him so upset?"

There was no point in explaining. Cathy could only cry. She didn't have the strength to argue with him, yet again, and she was now very angry with her older sister, Jane, who had called their father and told him what had happened. She passed the phone to Jane who scolded him with a child's voice. "Daddy, what did you say to upset Cat? She's in a very delicate condition."

While they were growing up, Cathy was always the scholar in the family who could be counted on to do the right thing and be completely self-sufficient. Jane, perhaps because she was the first child their parents had after the Holocaust and she represented the re-birth of the Jewish people, was the delicate flower of the family, and given all the attention and care any child could wish for. She was a very needy child, which followed her into adulthood. And to this day, she still expected and received the assistance of the entire family, in any and all forms.

Even as Cathy lay in a half-conscious, pain-killer induced stupor, she could hear her sister chatter on and on about how great it would be that they'd both be living in New York City; how Cathy could baby sit for her boyfriend's kids and give them a chance to take vacations with him without dragging the kids along; how Cathy could help her pick out clothes since her taste wasn't as good as her sister's; how Cathy could use her expense account to take her out to expensive restaurants that she couldn't afford; and, so on.

Her first week in the hospital was a big blur. She remained in a half-awake, half-sleep state thanks to the medicines that slowly dripped through the intravenous tubes into her arm. Her most vivid memories were of the nurse placing ice packs on the swollen areas of her face and body, and of shining lights into her eyes. She remembered Samantha being there, but didn't really hear anything she said, and her sister kept appearing, then disappearing then appearing again.

When the paramedics lifted Cathy onto the gurney to take her to the hospital, she was clutching her cell phone so tightly that she fought with them when they tried to pry it from her hand. Even as she was being treated in the emergency room, she held onto it firmly, and anyone who tried to take it from her met stiff resistance. She would only give it to Samantha, who, when she scrolled through the phonebook to find her sister's name, knew she hit pay dirt when she reached, "Pain In The Ass."

With a little reluctance she scrolled down further to see how Cathy might have referred to her, but to her relief she was just listed as Sam. (One time when Fred was checking the phonebook and saw a man's name, he became enraged and started to scream about her cheating on him, but Cathy convinced him to call the number and it was Samantha's office, so he apologized. For that reason, she never put Chris in the phonebook.)

Fred, of course, was in the phonebook under his name. Knowing that he checked the registry of calls often, she couldn't have taken the chance to put in something like "Piece of Shit," or "Woman Beater," but she did make a small statement about the nature of their relationship. He wasn't entered into her phonebook as a knowing and friendly Fred, but as Frederick Mardred, someone she barely knew and with whom she had no relationship.

Also, to express her feelings towards him, she assigned the last speed dial number - 99 – to him, as if to say, "He's the last person on earth I ever want to call." She purposely assigned the speed dial 98 to the city's animal shelter, as if to say, "Even bastards and bitches are better than you." A silent, but amusing protest.

When Samantha called Jane to let her know that her sister was in the hospital as a result of a terrible incident, she understood what made her a "Pain in the ass." It was as if Cathy had purposely moved in with a violent woman-beater just to cause discomfort to her. "Oh, I guess I'll have to come to Minneapolis," Jane sighed at the difficulties this would cause her.

"I think your sister would appreciate it," Samantha suggested. "I would stay, but I have to be in Washington, D.C. for a meeting tomorrow."

"That will mean I have to use up my vacation days," Jane mused weighing the value of going to Minneapolis to be with her sister versus being with her latest boyfriend at a casino in Atlantic City. "I guess I have to do it for the sake of the family. It always falls onto my shoulders."

"Your presence here will certainly help your sister recover faster." Samantha always had the ability to insult people in a way that they never knew they were being insulted.

"Okay. I'll be there tomorrow." Jane was resigned, one more time, to accepting the burdens of the family, especially when every excuse she made about the enormous expense of coming to Minneapolis was washed away by Samantha. She had agreed to use her frequent flier miles to pay for Jane's airfare, and since she would be staying at Cathy's house and using Cathy's car, there would be no other costs.

Standing beside Cathy before heading to the airport, Samantha summarized, "A woman beater in Minneapolis, a pain in the ass sister in New York, an ice pick for a father in Florida, ex-husbands in Texas and Colorado. Have you ever considered a job in our Alaska office?"

Before leaving the hospital, Samantha stopped into the security office and handed the six-foot-five, 295 pound, blue clad, ex-marine, five, new $100 bills. "The piece of shit who beat my friend so severely that she's in room 1001 has somehow made bail. If my friend leaves the hospital without being disturbed, there will be five more of these for you. If that excrement comes to the hospital to harass her and suffers great pain while you eject him, there will be ten more of these for you."

Placing the $500 in his shirt pocket and buttoning it securely, he smiled, "Your friend will not be disturbed." As she left, it occurred to him that he hadn't been to the tenth floor in a while so, with blackjack and handcuffs in his pocket, he began what became a very frequent routine.

As Samantha rode to the airport, she wondered about the kind of power some men have over women. She would have left Fred in jail, but feeling sorry for him, his ex-wife provided the funds to bail him out. Not realizing why he was in jail (she assumed for drunk driving), and thinking that being in jail would interfere with his ability to pay alimony (she didn't know he no longer had a job), she wrote a check against the equity line of credit on the house that used to be theirs.

But Samantha wasn't going to let him roam the city free to prey on Cathy. Before he could leave the courthouse, he was served with a restraining order, forbidding him to go anywhere near Cathy, the kids, or the house he used to live in. He was also served with a civil suit for $10 million for the brutality he exercised against his now-former girlfriend.

His first words as he left the jail were, "No fucking bitch and no fucking lawyer are going to tell me I can't go into my own house." But true to her word, Samantha hired an armed guard to prevent him from entering. As Fred quickly learned, this was no donut-munching, toy-pistol carrying, rent-a-cop. The six-foot, six-inch, ex-Navy Seal protecting Cathy's house had only to stare down at Fred with his cold steel gray eyes, and Fred inched his way back to his car and drove away.

After ten days, the swelling on Cathy's face was down considerably, and the doctor had reduced the amount of pain killers she was receiving, so Cathy was awake. Hearing her sister talk on and on about herself, her job, her boyfriend, and what they could do together, made Cathy wish she was still drugged. While she was glad for the company, she wasn't ready for the new world of a closer relationship with her sibling.

Jane, true to form, found the hospital depressing, and since her sister really couldn't engage in animated conversation, decided to go shopping in the Mall of America several hours each day. Even though she had told Samantha that she didn't have the money to fly to Minneapolis, stay at a hotel, or rent a car, she apparently had money for four new pairs of shoes, a wool coat, three wool sweaters, a dress, a pants suit, and leather gloves. "Can you imagine," Jane enthusiastically offered during her daily fashion show for her sister, "I live in New York, the fashion capitol of the world, and I'm buying clothes in Minneapolis."

After two weeks, Jane was exhausted, had exhausted her vacation time and credit limit, and so decided to return home. "Though I hate to leave that hunk guarding the house," she said with regret as she stopped by the hospital on the way to the airport. "That's what I call a real man." And then she added. "Though I won't miss that house. I've never seen a house that changes color. Do you know how many times I've driven right past it?"

By the eighteenth day of her stay in the hospital, Cathy felt strong enough to call Chris on his cell phone. He was on his way to San Diego, to begin the lengthy and delicate task of rebuilding the agency's relationship with Barry Balin's, then Gary Accolon's, sporting goods client.

"Oh, my God! Where have you been? I've been so worried. I called your office over and over, and all they would say is that you're out of the office. I didn't want to leave a message, but I think they recognized my voice. Are you okay? Where are you?" All the worry, all the fear, and all the longing that had been building up came pouring out in a flood of panic.

"He hurt me, Chris," she cried softly into the phone. "He hurt me real bad."

"I was afraid of that." Tears welled in his eyes, too. "I was so scared that he...," Chris was about to say, beat you to death, but thought better of it. Instead he said, "...put you in the hospital, there would be no way for me to know. Where are you now?"

"Avalon General Hospital." Her tears increased as she re-lived the pain of the attack.

His eyes bleary from the tears, and too tormented to worry about the traffic on the road, exited the San Diego Freeway at MacArthur Boulevard.

"Tell me what he did?" Grabbing a tissue, Chris wiped his eyes and blew his nose.

"He hit me. Over and over and..." The memories were still vivid, and they frightened her even as she said the words. She could hear Chris' crying and his inability to speak.

"I go in for surgery tomorrow," she struggled to control her voice, to calm both Chris and herself.

"For what?" Chris asked quietly.

"You know that bump in my nose that I've always hated?" Her voice was mix of forced laughter and swallowed tears. "Well, I'm finally going to get rid of it."

A loud plane landing at John Wayne Airport obliterated Chris' voice so he had to wait a few long, painful moments to ask, "He broke your nose?"

"And a few other bones in that area." She touched the bandages that covered the side of her face.

There was a long silence and the two lovers could hear each other breathing and weeping.

He shifted his transmission into drive and started moving towards the entrance to the airport. He committed himself to not making the same mistake twice. He was going to be near her, this time, when she needed him. Nothing in life was more important than being with her now. This would be the start of a new life... with her... his intended... he had to go… today… now.

"Chris, can you come here? Just for a day or two… for when I get out of surgery? I'm so frightened. I don't want to be alone," she pleaded.

Melanie knew he was going to be with a client and pretty much out of touch for several days, so whether he was in San Diego or Minneapolis, it didn't make a difference. But the client was expecting him, and Sandy, without a doubt, would squeal on him to Mack and he surely would be out of a job. Even he if told Melanie he had to stay in San Diego over the weekend, she wouldn't question it. But, there would be no way he could bury the cost of a Minneapolis trip on his expense account, and if he used their personal charge cards, Melanie would find out since she paid all the bills.

After a long moment, he meekly whispered, "I wish I could be with you. I really, really wish I was there right now to wrap my arms around you. But, I can't just leave. I have a new client, and Melanie…" He cried, but this time it was for himself. He was failing the woman he loved, when she needed him most. She was in great pain and he couldn't comfort her because he was putting the life he claimed to detest first. All the words of love spoken, all the wishes and hopes, all the dreams of a future, all the memories vanished, gone forever.

Chris bypassed the entrance ramp to John Wayne Airport and pulled into the empty parking lot of a Pick Up Styx Chinese restaurant, and wiping the tears away with his sleeve, he called out to her.

The phone dropped from her hand and fell to the floor. Feeling horribly alone, Cathy rolled toward the window and stared at the drifting clouds. "Mama, I wish you were here with me. I miss you very much."

A tiny voice could be heard from the receiver, "Cathy, Cathy. Are you there? What's the number there? I'll call you every day. When do you get out of surgery? Can I call someone to find out how your surgery went? I love you."

Chapter 56

A month after her surgery, Cathy stepped out of the limousine that would be bringing her to the office everyday and entered the lobby of the THCC building in New York City. As she passed through the revolving door, a small welcoming committee - Samantha Dulak and the same six-foot, six-inch, ex-Navy Seal with steel gray eyes - were there to greet her. Presenting her with a bouquet of fresh flowers, Samantha warmly embraced her friend and said, "Welcome back. We missed you."

Tears welled up in Cathy's eyes, not because the flowers were so beautiful or the welcoming committee so grand, but because someone had been so kind to her. While she was recovering from her surgery, Samantha completed the sale of the Olympic Estates house and the purchase of the New York condominium, had The End Moving Company move her clothes and possessions to the condo, hired a decorator to unpack and make the condo ready to live in, enrolled her children in an exclusive private school, arranged to have a company limousine transfer her between her home and the office everyday, as well as her children to and from the school, scheduled an appointment for her at The Garden of Hedon Sensuality Spa, where her hair was colored and styled, and her body refreshed after a long stay in the hospital, and, the most enjoyable part, embroiled Fred in such a financial and legal quagmire that he was working for minimum wage at a fast food restaurant and living at the YMCA in downtown Minneapolis.

"This is Rod," Samantha introduced, pointing to his Navy Seal tattoo. "He's our new Head of Executive Security." And then she leaned over and whispered into Cathy's ear, "Believe me, his is a very, very appropriate name, in case you're ever interested." Cathy giggled like a 16 year-old schoolgirl.

As they stepped into the elevator, Samantha pressed the button to the fiftieth floor and announced, we've had to move your office.

"I knew it was too good to be true," Cathy half-jokingly groaned. Small offices had been her lot in life, she thought. It was nice to have a big one for a change, but getting back to a cramped ten-by-ten was like going home. So, she was surprised when Samantha walked her into her new office that not only was twice as large as the one she had just vacated, but also had windows on two perpendicular glass walls that faced Central Park. Dropping her attaché case on the floor, she couldn't speak. She could only hug Samantha and cry on her shoulder.

Patting her on the back, Samantha joked, "Hey, be careful you don't want to hurt that new nose of yours."

Overwhelmed by everything that her supervisor - and friend - had done for her, Cathy couldn't say, "Thank you," and "I can't believe how wonderful you've been to me," and "You're incredible," enough.

"Don't be so shocked by the office," Samantha suggested, handing Cathy her new business card. "It's the approved size for a Senior Vice President."

Cathy stared at her business card in disbelief. Isabel Circe, Senior Vice President and Chief Operating Officer, Business Affairs Department. Besides everything else, she couldn't believe that Samantha remembered that she had always wanted to go by the name Isabel instead of Cathy.

Delighted by all that she did for her friend, there was a smile on Samantha's face. "It'll take a little time after all these years, but people eventually will get used to calling you Isabel. We just won't tell your father."

This was too much for her, so she sat down on the $4,000 Italian leather chair, behind the $40,000 hand-carved, Brazilian and Turkish wood desk, which hovered over a $20,000 Persian wool carpet. Facing the desk were two matching guest chairs that cost $2,500 each, and off to one side was a coordinated couch, coffee table, and two more guest chairs. All tolled, the office furnishings were over $150,000. A far cry from the metal desk and used chair she lived with most of her working life.

She simply could not speak, so Samantha, broke the silence, "Enjoy your office and your new title. Let's have lunch today, and I'll bring you up to date on what has been happening while you were gone. We have a meeting scheduled in Athens next Friday with the Greek Department of Defense. They want to update their early warning system and we're going to bid on it. Can you make it?"

A trip to Athens, too! She couldn't believe all that had happened and it wasn't even 10 a.m. "Yes, yes, of course."

"Welcome back." Samantha kissed Isabel on the cheek, and she and Rod exited.

Sitting beside her desk was a box with all the materials from her home office that Samantha brought in after the move. Opening the lid, her eyes were immediately drawn to the cell phone that rested on top of everything else.

Running her fingers over the bloodstains that smeared the keys, she re-lived that night and began to cry.

Over the years, she'd had many cell phones, but none ever felt as important as this one. At first she thought she would frame it - blood stains and all - and hang it on the wall behind her desk. It would remind her of the days when she allowed herself to be a victim. But, she decided against that, since it might shock visitors to her office. Then, she thought she would use this as her cell phone for the rest of her life, but she decided against that too, because then this life-saving device would be just another electronic gizmo that had technical problems. Finally, she decided to keep it in her top drawer and whenever she felt that she was being taken advantage of or used by someone else, she would look at it and remember her days as a lamb and not a lion

Also in the carton, was her black leather attaché case. The thought crossed her mind that she should write a conclusion to "The Record of Physical and Mental Abuse Performed Against Catianna Isabel Circe at the Hands of Frederick Mardred," just so it would be written somewhere that people can change, that they're not trapped by destiny.

Reaching into the inner pocket of the attaché case, she retrieved the disk and popped it into the new computer on her desk. Burrowing down a few levels, she reached the file she had buried, Erin's Homework. But as soon as she had opened it, she closed it. She wasn't ready to face her past. Not today. It was still too painful. Maybe someday.

It occurred to her that on the office server, hidden in a password-protected file, were all the notes she had collected on the questionable, and possibly illegal, activities of Samantha and the rest of Senior Management. Secure server or not, it was dangerous to leave that information in a place where an astute hacker could access it, so she decided to delete it completely and protect Samantha, as she had been protected by her.

Sliding it into the trash can icon on her computer screen, she thought, maybe it would be a good idea to have a back-up of the information. It would be a shame to just delete all those hours of research. She copied it to the same memory stick as Erin's Homework and titled the file Erika's Book Reports.

Staring at the two folders on her computer screen was like staring at her life. One was her past and one was her future. One was about being the pathetic challenger and the other was about being the indisputable champion. One was about physical brutality, the other was about corporate power. One was about being Cathy, the other was about being Isabel.

The phone rang, and instantly, she knew she was back. Sick leave was over. Her secretary informed her that it was Stanley Klein. "Hello, Stanley, how are you?" Her voice was cold, because somewhere in her mind, Stanley was connected with Fred and the horror her life had been.

"Oh, thank God you finally came in," he exploded. "I can't tell you what a disaster this has all become. They've closed the South St. Paul office and scattered the sales force. I've been suspended pending an investigation and I can lose all my retirement benefits. The university is suing me. I've had to hire a lawyer, and I'm getting threats from Fred. It's costing me a fortune."

"I'm sorry to hear all that, Stanley." She said the words because it was an appropriate response, but clearly her voice was dispassionate. Still staring at the two folders on her computer screen, she added, "But why are you telling me all this?"

"Why am I telling you?" His voice cried with disbelief that she would even say those words. "It's all because of you and your boyfriend that I'm in this mess!"

In a casual and removed voice, she offered, "I'm reading the file now (which she wasn't). It looks like to me that you're in this mess because you promoted the wrong person to the job."

"I did this for you! You asked me to promote that deadbeat boyfriend of yours! You promised me a vice presidency if I promoted him!" His voice was filled with horror and desperation.

Isabel was distracted, she opened the folder labeled "Erika's Book Reports" and reviewing her notes about Samantha.

"I don't know what you're talking about, Stanley. We never had a deal." Marie Antoinette's voice was probably just as distant and uncaring when she suggested that the starving people of France eat cake if they couldn't get bread.

"We never had a deal? We never had a deal! Of course, we had a deal!" He was a drowning man, and the lifeguard that he had waited for kept moving the rescue pole out of his reach. "If you don't help me, I going to sue you, and sue the company, and I'm going to call the President and the Chairman of the Board, and I'm going to get you fired!"

While she felt no obligation to help him, she did acknowledge that he could cause some problems for her in her new position, and since he had nothing to lose by creating a ruckus, she thought it better to squelch him rather than have to defend herself against his accusations.

"Well, Stanley," she began, resenting the fact that he tried to bludgeon her with his threats, "here's the way I see it. Since I was the Vice Present of Human Resources over your office, I feel some corporate sense of responsibility for your separation from the company." The word "separation" rang loud and clear. He wasn't coming back.

"We can do one of two things," she continued as if deciding what to do with an over-ripe banana. "We can immediately terminate your employment for your attack on a client and all the legal problems that you've caused the company. You certainly are welcome to sue us and call anyone you like, but you don't have a lot of credibility with anyone here."

"I didn't attack anyone," he screamed. "It was your boyfriend! And you made me put him in that job! If I hadn't done you a favor none of this would have happened!"

She continued in the same dispassionate voice, "Not only will you lose all benefits, but we would probably counter sue you and we'd be in the courts for years. That would cost you thousands and thousands of dollars. Do you have that much money, Stanley, or would you have to get a second mortgage on your house."

She could hear him try to muffle his whimpering.

"Or," and she used a lighter, happier tone for this, "you can take advantage of the Early Retirement Plan that we're offering to executives at your level. Not only would you receive the full benefits of an employee who had completed his vesting, but you'd be entitled to health benefits until Medicare kicks in."

He didn't respond for a long time, but she knew she had beaten him down. "I really have to know right now, Stanley. It's my first day back and

I have a lot to do."

He still didn't respond.

"What is it going to be, Stanley? I have too many other things to do and I want to resolve this right now. Who am I sending an e-mail to? The legal department or the payroll department?"

In a weak, defeated voice, he said, "I'll take early retirement."

"Good decision, Stanley." Her voice was victorious. "I'll have payroll send you the paperwork." And, then she added, "I'll also be sending you a letter that you have to sign before you can receive your benefits that outlines your... obligations... under our settlement."

Being a mouse all his life, all he could say to the cat who had just eaten him was, "Thank you."

If he said anything else, she never heard it since she hung up the phone.

With her fingers still sore from when Fred stomped on them, she opened her e-mail in-box. As usual, there were hundreds, and as usual, she scanned the list to see if anything seemed to demand immediate attention. About halfway down, calling out like Broadway marquee, was an e-mail from Chris.

While she was in the hospital he left many messages, but she never returned them, and she instructed her secretary that if he called the office to just take a message and then throw it away. Knowing that she was out of the hospital (he called there every day), he decided to try to reach her by e-mail. Her first instinct was to ignore it. After all, what could he say to defend his actions (inactions)? But wondering about it became a distraction, so she finally opened it.

Cathy,

I'm so sorry I couldn't come to be with you.

I feel like I've spent the last 20 years apologizing to you for not coming to a hospital in Minneapolis to visit you, and here I am doing it again.

Can you ever forgive me? Can we get past this?

I love you. I always have and I always will.

Yours forever and ever,

Chris

Reading his e-mail brought a tear to her eyes, as so many memories of their years together flooded back to her and into her heart. She had placed so much hope, and so many dreams, in him, for so many years, she couldn't just leave him hanging in cyberspace, so she responded.

Chris,

When I was 16 years old, I met the man I would love my entire life. I think about him everyday.

I miss him quite a bit.

Good-bye.

Isabel

Chris wept when he read her e-mail. He was back in San Diego and had been touring the client's factory all day.

He sat for a moment in his hotel room, staring out the window at the sun setting behind the horizon, and at the sailboats racing to get home before dark. Just before he was supposed to go downstairs for dinner with the client, he rummaged through his attaché case and found the business card he had been saving. He called, and since no one answered, left a voice-mail in as happy a voice as he could muster.

"Hello, Abigail, this is Chris, the guy you knocked into the gutter a couple of weeks ago. I'll be back in L.A. next week and wanted to know if you're available for lunch."

The End

www.ingramcontent.com/pod-product-compliance
Lightning Source LLC
Chambersburg PA
CBHW020635020726
47494CB00001B/196